GW01159277

Coding Chemistry

Hazel Montgomery

Published by Hazel Montgomery, 2024.

CODING CHEMISTRY

First edition. October 9, 2024.

Copyright © 2024 Hazel Montgomery.

ISBN: 979-8227075802

Written by Hazel Montgomery.

Chapter 1: Awkward Encounters

My first day at ByteWave Solutions felt like stepping into a parallel universe where social cues were replaced by lines of code. I stood by the coffee machine, staring at the steam swirling above it, my heart racing as I tried to remember the advice my sister had given me: "Just be yourself, Nat!" As I turned to introduce myself to the team, my mouth betrayed me, and I accidentally referred to our product as "ByteMe." The office erupted in laughter, and I felt my face flush a deep crimson. Little did I know, that moment would spark an unexpected connection with Ethan Mercer, the effortlessly charming marketing executive who leaned against the doorway, amusement dancing in his bright blue eyes.

Ethan had that rare quality that made him seem simultaneously approachable and completely out of reach. With tousled dark hair that defied gravity and a casual wardrobe that still managed to look impeccable, he seemed like the kind of guy who belonged on a magazine cover. As I stumbled through my introduction, he stepped forward, his smirk growing wider, and offered a hand. "Don't worry, Nat. It's not the worst product name I've ever heard." The warmth of his palm against mine sent an unexpected thrill through me, a jolt that was both exciting and terrifying.

After my embarrassing start, I clung to the hope that I could navigate the rest of the day without further mishaps. My desk was tucked away in a corner of the expansive open-plan office, surrounded by vibrant green plants and walls adorned with quirky artwork—some abstract, some oddly relatable. Each piece seemed to whisper secrets of creativity and innovation, and I imagined they'd witnessed countless awkward introductions like my own. Settling in, I glanced around, taking in the kaleidoscope of personalities buzzing with purpose, laughter, and the clatter of keyboards.

As the day unfolded, I tried to immerse myself in the rhythm of the workspace, feigning confidence with every keystroke. Each email I sent felt like a small victory, yet I couldn't shake the lingering embarrassment from my initial blunder. During lunch, I found myself in the break room, sipping a lukewarm soda while trying to blend in with a group discussing their latest weekend adventures. The conversation flowed effortlessly around me—stories of mountain hikes, spontaneous road trips, and culinary exploits that would make any Instagram foodie jealous. I wished I could join in, but every time I opened my mouth, the words evaporated into nothingness.

Just as I thought I might retreat to my desk, Ethan sauntered in, his presence commanding the room like the spotlight at a concert. "Hey, Nat!" he called, his voice smooth as silk. "Are you a fan of cliffhangers or happy endings?" My heart raced, and I suddenly felt like I was being put on the spot in the most delightful way possible.

"Happy endings, of course!" I replied, trying to keep my tone light, hoping to convey a sense of confidence I didn't quite feel. "Cliffhangers are overrated. Life is unpredictable enough as it is." The moment I finished speaking, a flash of realization crossed Ethan's face, his eyebrows arching in genuine interest.

"Bold choice," he said, leaning against the counter, a teasing glint in his eyes. "So, you're telling me you prefer the fairy tale over the suspense? You might find this place to be a bit more... suspenseful than you expect."

His words hung in the air, thick with an undercurrent I couldn't quite decipher. The rest of the break room faded into the background as I locked eyes with him, the world narrowing down to just the two of us. There was a challenge in his gaze, a dare to dig deeper into the mysteries surrounding ByteWave.

"Are you saying this place is full of surprises?" I shot back, my pulse quickening. "I could use a few more plot twists in my life."

The laughter from the group faded into the background, and for a heartbeat, it felt like we were the only two people in the room.

Ethan leaned in, lowering his voice conspiratorially. "Trust me, you have no idea. This place is a mix of brilliance and chaos. I could take you on a tour—if you're up for it."

I could feel my cheeks warm at the implication. "A tour? So I can see all the places where I might embarrass myself next?"

He chuckled, the sound rich and inviting. "Only if you promise to be entertaining while doing it."

"Deal," I said, my heart fluttering with a mix of nerves and excitement. It was a bold step, a leap into the unknown, and for the first time that day, I felt a sense of belonging.

As we strolled through the labyrinth of desks, I found myself relaxing in his presence, his light-hearted banter drawing me in like a moth to a flame. He introduced me to various departments, each filled with eccentric characters who welcomed me with open arms and witty jibes that made me laugh. I quickly discovered that the office was more than just a workplace; it was a mosaic of personalities, each piece contributing to the vibrant tapestry of ByteWave.

Yet, as the laughter filled the air, a shadow lurked just beyond my perception. I couldn't shake the feeling that beneath the playful banter and camaraderie, there was something more profound at play. The office felt charged with a tension that was palpable, like the moment before a storm, and I wondered if Ethan knew more than he let on.

As our tour came to an end, Ethan turned to me, his expression softening. "You fit in here, Nat. Don't let anyone tell you otherwise."

I smiled, warmth spreading through me at his words. Perhaps this place wouldn't be so bad after all, and maybe, just maybe, I had stumbled into my own happy ending amid the chaos of ByteWave Solutions.

As the afternoon wore on, the buzz of the office settled into a comfortable rhythm, the clattering of keyboards and hushed conversations forming a backdrop to my newfound determination. I sank into my desk chair, determined to channel the spirit of productivity that Ethan seemed to exude effortlessly. My screen flickered to life, and I found myself staring at an avalanche of emails—each one a reminder of how very much I had to learn.

Just as I was about to drown in a sea of spreadsheets, a message pinged on my screen. It was from Ethan. "Want to grab a drink after work? I promise to help you decode the ByteWave lingo. Consider it a primer for survival." My heart skipped, not just at the invitation but at the playful challenge woven into his words.

I took a moment to compose myself, my fingers hovering over the keyboard. What if I said yes? What if I made a complete fool of myself again? But the promise of an evening spent with Ethan, laced with the intrigue of shared secrets, was far too tempting to resist. "Count me in. Just promise you won't call me 'ByteMe' again," I replied, my fingers flying across the keys as a grin crept onto my face.

The workday crawled by, each passing hour thick with anticipation. The sun began its descent, painting the sky with strokes of pink and orange, a beautiful contrast to the sterile office walls. When the clock finally struck five, I felt a rush of relief mingled with excitement. I gathered my things, my heart racing as I made my way to the exit, where Ethan leaned against the wall, a casual yet alluring figure.

"Ready for your crash course?" he asked, pushing off the wall and falling into step beside me. There was a lightness in his tone, a hint of mischief that set my nerves at ease.

"Only if you promise not to make fun of my learning curve," I shot back, a playful smile dancing on my lips.

"Promise," he said, raising his hands in mock surrender. "No jokes, just revelations."

The air outside was crisp, the kind of early evening chill that invigorated the senses. We walked to a nearby pub, the chatter from the street mingling with the faint sound of music wafting through the open windows. The dimly lit interior welcomed us like an old friend, its rustic charm adorned with vintage posters and warm wooden accents. As we settled into a corner booth, I couldn't shake the feeling that this evening might be the beginning of something more than just friendship.

Ethan ordered us drinks—a couple of craft beers with whimsical names that matched the quirky decor. "So, Nat, tell me about your journey to ByteWave. What's the story behind the girl who accidentally named our product 'ByteMe'?"

"Honestly?" I began, biting my lip, unsure of how much I wanted to share. "I've always been more comfortable behind a screen than in front of people. I mean, growing up, I was the shy kid who hid in the library with a book while everyone else was at parties. My sister practically had to drag me out to socialize."

Ethan leaned in, genuine curiosity in his bright blue eyes. "I find that hard to believe. You seem perfectly capable of holding your own."

"Right up until I tripped over my own words." I chuckled, recalling the mortifying moment. "But I'm trying to change that. I want to step out of my comfort zone, you know? Even if it means embarrassing myself occasionally."

"That's the spirit," he said, lifting his glass in a toast. "To brave new adventures and the courage to stumble along the way."

We clinked glasses, and I felt a warm rush of camaraderie swell between us, a connection that felt promising and undeniably electric. We dove into easy conversation, trading stories and laughing over shared experiences. I discovered that Ethan had a knack for finding the humor in even the most mundane situations, and before long, I found myself leaning into the conversation, opening up in a way I hadn't anticipated.

"Okay, but tell me," I pressed, "what's the wildest thing you've ever done at work? Any embarrassing moments?"

His eyes sparkled with mischief as he leaned back, arms crossed. "Oh, where do I begin? There was that time I accidentally sent a company-wide email with a meme about our competitor. It was supposed to be a private joke with my team, but I hit 'reply all' instead."

I gasped, laughter bubbling up uncontrollably. "What happened?"

"Let's just say, I became a meme myself," he said, his smile infectious. "For weeks, I was the face of 'ByteWave's Friendly Fire.'"

"Wow, I need to step up my game. My 'ByteMe' gaffe can't hold a candle to that."

As we continued to swap stories, the atmosphere around us faded into the background, leaving just the two of us in our little bubble. I reveled in the lightness of the moment, the initial nerves ebbing away like a receding tide.

Yet, amid the laughter and easy banter, an unexpected tension began to creep in, a flicker of uncertainty that made me question whether this connection was as simple as it seemed. Every time Ethan leaned closer, the air thickened with unspoken words and possibilities. He was charming, engaging, and genuinely interested, but what if I read the signs wrong? What if he saw me as nothing more than a quirky new colleague to entertain?

Just as I was about to voice my concerns, a loud crash erupted from the bar, snapping me from my reverie. I turned to see a group of rowdy patrons, their laughter and shouting cutting through the warmth we had created. I felt a momentary twinge of annoyance—couldn't they see we were having an important conversation? But Ethan's laughter mingled with theirs, and it broke the tension in my chest.

"Hey, it's a pub. It's bound to be chaotic," he said with a grin, eyes twinkling as he leaned closer. "Besides, chaos makes for the best stories."

"Right," I said, my heart racing at the proximity. "And it seems like you have plenty of those."

His gaze locked onto mine, and I felt the world around us blur as the music faded into the background. "What if we created our own story?" he asked, the sincerity in his voice sending a thrill through me.

Before I could respond, the energy shifted again. The door swung open, and a gust of wind swept through the bar, carrying with it an unexpected chill. I shivered involuntarily, and for a moment, I caught a glimpse of something dark in Ethan's eyes, a flicker of uncertainty that mirrored my own. But as quickly as it came, he smiled, pushing away the moment like a fleeting shadow.

"Let's order some food," he said, his voice lightening. "Nothing like carbs to fuel our creative endeavors."

As he gestured for the server, I couldn't shake the feeling that beneath the laughter and witty exchanges lay a deeper layer of complexity. The evening was unfolding beautifully, yet a sense of unpredictability lingered, hinting that the story we were beginning to write together might hold more surprises than either of us anticipated.

As we settled into a comfortable rhythm at the pub, the chatter around us morphed into a distant hum, allowing our conversation to take center stage. The drinks arrived, frosty mugs adorned with condensation, and I relished the bitter-sweet taste of the craft beer. It was refreshing, a perfect complement to the budding chemistry I felt with Ethan.

"I hope you're ready for the big leagues," he teased, leaning back in his seat, his confident demeanor somehow infectious. "ByteWave is a wild ride. The moment you think you've got it all figured out, you'll discover another layer of chaos. Kind of like this beer—full-bodied with an unexpected twist."

"Sounds just like my life," I replied with a playful smirk, swirling my drink. "Full-bodied chaos and the occasional twist."

"Let me guess," he said, raising an eyebrow, "your life story is a blend of awkward moments and plot twists that would make a soap opera proud?"

"Pretty much," I laughed, "my high school graduation speech could have been titled 'How to Trip Over Your Own Words and Still Look Graceful.'"

Ethan chuckled, leaning forward as if entranced by my story. "I'll bet you have some doozies. What's your favorite disaster?"

I took a sip, stalling as I contemplated the most embarrassing moment I could share without completely losing my dignity. "Okay, here goes. There was this one time during a school presentation, I had prepared meticulously—slides, notes, the works. I got up there, and instead of saying 'projector,' I called it a 'protractor.'"

His laughter rang through the air, loud and unfiltered, drawing a few curious glances from nearby tables. "A true classic! Did they even notice?"

"Oh, they noticed. My best friend still reminds me of it every chance she gets," I said, shaking my head. "I think I've become her unofficial comedy act."

"Sounds like you're a natural at captivating an audience," he remarked, his eyes sparkling. "And hey, if you ever need a partner for the act, I'm all in."

Our laughter faded into an easy silence, the kind that felt charged with unspoken possibilities. I couldn't help but wonder where this newfound connection might lead us. There was a spark, a chemistry that tingled just beneath the surface, and it made me feel bold.

"What about you?" I asked, breaking the quiet. "Any memorable blunders on your end?"

Ethan leaned back, a thoughtful expression crossing his face as he took a sip of his beer. "Let's see... I once spilled coffee all over the CEO during a crucial meeting. I was so nervous I couldn't stop fidgeting. The irony? I was pitching a new client engagement strategy."

"No way! What did you do?"

He shook his head, a grin tugging at the corners of his mouth. "I froze. Just stood there, paralyzed while everyone else burst into laughter. He took it like a champ, though—ended up turning it into a running joke about being 'brewed for success.'"

I was still chuckling when a sudden loud crash shattered the ambiance, drawing our attention to the bar. A patron had accidentally knocked over a stack of glasses, sending them tumbling to the ground. I winced at the sound, and Ethan's laughter faded.

"Looks like the chaos has arrived," he said, scanning the scene with amusement.

"Just when I thought we had a moment of peace," I replied, unable to shake the feeling that the night had shifted.

As the bartender rushed to clean up the mess, the mood in the pub darkened, and a ripple of discomfort swept through the crowd. I could see a couple at the far end of the bar exchanging hurried whispers, their faces pale and anxious. My instincts tingled, a sense that something was off.

"Hey, are you okay?" Ethan's voice broke through my thoughts, his gaze steady and concerned.

"Yeah, just... a strange vibe, you know? It feels like something is brewing beneath the surface." I gestured subtly toward the couple, who now sat hunched over their drinks.

Ethan followed my gaze, his brow furrowing slightly. "You have an uncanny ability to read people, don't you?"

"I guess I just pick up on things. My sister says it's my superpower, but sometimes I wish I could turn it off."

"Why's that?" he asked, his expression shifting into something more serious.

"It can be overwhelming. Everyone wears a mask, and it's hard to find genuine connections when you're constantly aware of their undercurrents." I sighed, feeling the weight of the conversation. "But then again, maybe it's what led me here. To this moment."

Ethan's gaze softened, the intensity between us palpable. "Maybe it's all part of the adventure," he mused, leaning in closer. "The chaos, the connections, the moments that make us feel alive."

Just as the words left his lips, the lights flickered above us, plunging the bar into a brief, eerie darkness. The laughter faded, replaced by murmurs of concern as patrons exchanged glances, unsure of what was happening. When the lights returned, I felt a chill dance down my spine.

The couple at the bar now stood, their faces set with determination. They locked eyes with Ethan and me, and for a fleeting second, I could see something—something urgent and desperate flickering in their expressions.

Then, without warning, the man stepped forward, his voice rising above the chatter. "We need to talk. It's about ByteWave."

The bar fell silent, all eyes turning toward our table. My heart raced as I exchanged a bewildered glance with Ethan. This wasn't the kind of twist I had expected for our evening.

"What do you mean?" Ethan asked, leaning forward, his voice steady but laced with curiosity.

"It's important. There are things happening behind the scenes—things you both need to know," the woman added, urgency tinging her tone.

I swallowed hard, my mind racing with possibilities. Suddenly, this night felt far more significant than just drinks and laughter. A dark cloud loomed over our playful conversation, and I sensed that whatever was coming could alter the course of everything we had just begun to explore.

"Let's step outside," Ethan suggested, his gaze sharp as he assessed the situation.

Before I could process his words, the man nodded, urgency etched into every feature. "We don't have much time."

And just like that, the vibrant world around us morphed into something darker, heavier, as if the very walls of the pub held secrets we were only beginning to unravel. I took a deep breath, clutching my drink tightly as we rose from the table, heart racing with trepidation and intrigue. Little did I know, stepping outside would lead us into a storm far beyond anything I could have imagined, where every choice would bear consequences and every revelation would be a catalyst for change.

Chapter 2: The Code Conundrum

The fluorescent lights of the office hummed incessantly, casting a sterile glow over the rows of desks scattered like islands in a sea of cubicles. I sat in the midst of it all, fingers poised over the keyboard, staring at lines of code that swirled before me like an indecipherable spell. The task seemed straightforward: optimize the customer feedback loop for our latest product. Simple, right? I chuckled to myself, realizing that I might as well have been trying to decipher an ancient script, considering how frequently my brain stuttered on the simplest of algorithms.

Just then, Kevin swooped in, his presence looming like an unwelcome storm cloud. He had that tendency—unlike the rest of us, who were merely trying to keep our heads above water, he was the self-proclaimed captain of this ship, convinced that his every critique was a life preserver. "You're not seriously going to leave that line in, are you?" he sneered, peering over my shoulder as if he could physically claw at my confidence.

I resisted the urge to roll my eyes, clenching my jaw instead. "It's a work in progress," I replied, attempting a breezy tone that did nothing to mask the irritation bubbling beneath. Kevin, with his meticulously styled hair and perfectly pressed shirt, seemed completely impervious to the fact that my confidence was steadily draining like the last drops of my lukewarm coffee.

"Work in progress or not, we need results. Our stakeholders won't tolerate mediocrity." With that, he sauntered away, leaving a trail of tension in his wake. I leaned back, letting out a slow breath, wishing I could code away my frustration just as easily as I debugged my lines. I turned back to the screen, my fingers hovering over the keys, grappling with a mixture of anxiety and determination. Who knew a few lines of code could feel like a battlefield?

It was one of those late nights when the office turned into a desolate landscape, the ticking clock morphing time into a relentless creature. I had fully surrendered to the chaos of caffeine and code, and as the minutes melded into hours, the world outside faded away, consumed by the thick veil of exhaustion that surrounded me. My mind churned like a blender set to high, mixing fragmented thoughts with snippets of brilliance, but no clear outcome emerged. In that haze, my phone buzzed beside me, a welcome distraction from the oppressive silence of the office.

Ethan's name glowed on the screen, a spark of warmth igniting in my chest. He had a knack for showing up when I needed it most, like a late-night pizza delivery but infinitely more comforting. I tapped my finger on the screen, and before I knew it, he was standing at the door, two steaming cups of coffee in hand, his playful smile brightening the dimness of the room. "I figured you could use a refill. You look like you've been wrestling with a particularly nasty bug."

"More like I'm the bug at this point," I replied, taking one of the cups gratefully, the rich aroma enveloping me like a warm blanket. "And I've got Kevin lurking around like a hawk, just waiting for me to slip up."

Ethan leaned against the doorframe, amusement dancing in his hazel eyes. "Kevin is like the human version of a software update—unnecessary and always popping up at the worst times." I laughed, appreciating his wit, which somehow made the unbearable hours melt away. In that moment, I felt the weight of Kevin's judgment lift, replaced by the easy banter we often shared.

"Is he always like this?" I asked, stirring my coffee absentmindedly, the steam curling upward like whispers of encouragement.

"Pretty much. Just remember, he's not the one coding your program. You are." His words were simple, yet they resonated like a gentle reminder that I was indeed capable, regardless of Kevin's oppressive shadow. "And if he keeps bothering you, I could always take him on in a coding duel. Winner gets to be the lead on the project."

"Now that's a tempting offer," I replied, grinning at the thought of Ethan facing off against Kevin in a digital showdown. "Though I'd probably lose my job in the process."

Ethan chuckled, and for a moment, the darkness of the office and the pressures of the project faded into the background. He slipped into the chair beside me, the tension that had gripped my shoulders loosening under the warmth of his presence. We fell into easy conversation, bouncing ideas off each other, and suddenly, the code that had felt so forbidding began to transform under the light of our collective creativity.

"I have to say, your knack for turning every project into a group therapy session is impressive," I teased, nudging him lightly. "Should I be paying you for this counseling service?"

"Only if I can charge you in caffeine. It's my preferred currency," he replied, taking a sip from his cup with a mock-seriousness that made me laugh again. The laughter came easily, like a gentle tide washing over the jagged rocks of my anxiety.

With each joke and shared smile, my spirits lifted, and suddenly, I saw the lines of code before me not as a tangled mess but as a canvas waiting for strokes of brilliance. "You know," I began, my fingers poised over the keyboard again, "if we just tweak this loop here—"

We dove into the code together, Ethan's excitement palpable as we navigated the intricacies of optimization. The room buzzed with creativity, the flicker of my laptop screen illuminating our faces as we lost ourselves in the logic. It was as if the world had faded into a background hum, leaving only us, two minds intertwining to solve the conundrum laid out before us.

Time slipped away unnoticed, and for the first time that night, I felt a surge of confidence flow through me, invigorated by the blend of caffeine and camaraderie. The chaotic rhythm of the office faded, replaced by the comforting melody of our laughter and the clatter of keys, and for the first time, I believed that maybe, just maybe, I could conquer this challenge—bugs, Kevin, and all.

Ethan's presence was a refreshing breeze, sweeping away the cobwebs of my self-doubt. As we collaborated on the project, the office transformed into a vibrant ecosystem where creativity blossomed amidst the sterile surroundings. Each keystroke felt like a pulse of energy, and our laughter rang out, breaking the monotony of corporate life. The walls, usually drab and indifferent, seemed to lean in closer, eager to hear our banter.

"Okay, what's our next move?" I asked, leaning closer to the screen, my focus sharpened by the comforting presence of my coffee companion. "We've streamlined the feedback algorithm, but I can't help but think there's more we can do."

Ethan leaned back, a contemplative look on his face. "How about we add a feature that not only captures the feedback but analyzes sentiment? If we can pinpoint how customers feel about the product, we can tailor our responses to hit the emotional sweet spot."

"Like a mood ring for customer opinions?" I quipped, my fingers flying across the keyboard as I envisioned the new direction. "Should we include a glittery option? You know, to really capture the sparkle of satisfaction?"

"Only if we can add an iridescent button that says 'Satisfaction Guaranteed,'" he shot back, grinning. The light banter felt good, like the warm embrace of sunshine breaking through a cloudy sky. I found myself smiling more than I had in days, buoyed by the camaraderie that made the seemingly insurmountable project feel like a playful challenge.

As the clock ticked on, our laughter grew louder, and the mundane office atmosphere transformed into a sanctuary of ideas. But just as I began to revel in the thrill of creation, the door creaked open, and there stood Kevin, arms crossed and eyebrows furrowed, like a storm cloud suddenly blocking out the sun.

"What's going on here?" His tone dripped with suspicion, a predator sensing vulnerability in its prey. "I hope you two aren't getting too distracted. Remember, we have deadlines to meet."

"Just discussing some ideas to make the feedback system even better," I replied, attempting a casual tone that belied the tension in my stomach. "You know, going above and beyond."

Kevin's eyes narrowed, assessing us like a hawk surveying its territory. "Well, make sure you focus on what's important. We need to impress the stakeholders, not entertain each other." He turned on his heel and strode out, leaving behind an echo of disapproval that hung in the air like a bad smell.

"Wow, talk about a buzzkill," Ethan muttered, rolling his eyes. "I swear he's got a sixth sense for killing enthusiasm."

"Maybe he's secretly a robot programmed to suppress creativity," I suggested, shaking off the oppressive weight of Kevin's presence. "He might just malfunction if we get too innovative."

Ethan laughed, the sound ringing out like music in the otherwise sterile office. "Let's make sure we push all the right buttons, then. You know, the ones that will make him explode in a shower of logic and spreadsheets."

"Sounds like a plan," I replied, my spirits lifted again. "Let's dive back in and make this feedback system sparkle."

We threw ourselves back into our work, ideas bouncing between us like popcorn kernels in a hot pan. With each passing minute, the code began to take shape, evolving into something we both felt proud of. Hours slipped by unnoticed as we hammered away at the keyboard, our dialogue interspersed with bursts of laughter and moments of silence as we focused intently on the screen.

Suddenly, my phone buzzed again, breaking the rhythm of our work. A message from my best friend, Clara, lit up the screen: "Did you get abducted by aliens? You've been MIA all week! Let's do dinner tonight!" I hesitated, the thought of stepping away from our project tugging at my conscience.

"Everything okay?" Ethan asked, glancing at my phone with curiosity.

"It's Clara. She wants to know if I'm still alive," I said, chuckling softly. "I might have to make an appearance or she'll assume I've been replaced by an AI version of myself."

"Definitely wouldn't want that," Ethan replied, his tone mock-serious. "You need to maintain your human connections. Plus, I hear dinner is a great source of inspiration. Just look at all the best ideas that come from late-night snacks."

His playful demeanor made it easy to contemplate stepping away, so I sent a quick reply: "Dinner sounds great! I'll be there."

As I tucked my phone away, the sense of accomplishment from our work washed over me again. "I should probably go. I can't keep hiding from the world forever," I said, the thought lingering in my mind like a bittersweet farewell.

"Take a break. Reconnect with reality, but don't forget to bring some of that inspiration back with you," Ethan encouraged, a hint of genuine warmth in his gaze.

With one last glance at the screen, I felt a pang of reluctance but also a surge of excitement. Leaving this cocoon of creativity was hard, but the thought of Clara's exuberance and the adventures that awaited outside the office walls was equally enticing.

"Promise me you won't turn into a pumpkin while I'm gone," I joked, pushing back my chair with determination. "Or worse, a poorly coded algorithm that can't compute."

"Only if you promise to bring me back something delicious," he countered, a teasing glint in his eyes.

As I made my way toward the exit, I couldn't shake the feeling that Ethan was becoming more than just a partner in coding; he was a spark in my life, igniting a flame that had dimmed under the relentless scrutiny of Kevin's leadership.

Stepping into the cool evening air, I inhaled deeply, feeling the weight of the day melt away like snow under the sun. Clara's laughter echoed in my mind, and the vibrant colors of the setting sun painted the sky with shades of gold and pink.

I hadn't realized how much I needed this escape until I was surrounded by the familiar sounds of the city: the distant chatter of people dining, the soft clinking of cutlery, and the faint strumming of a street musician's guitar. My heart swelled with anticipation, grateful for the chance to reconnect with the world beyond code and algorithms, knowing that inspiration was just around the corner, waiting for me to dive back into it.

The evening unfolded like a delicate tapestry, woven with the vibrant threads of laughter and the warmth of friendship. Clara's favorite Italian bistro buzzed with life, the smell of garlic and fresh basil enveloping me like a cozy embrace as I entered. The soft lighting and rustic decor set a perfect stage for our much-anticipated reunion, a welcome distraction from the relentless grind of the office.

Clara, already seated at our usual table, waved excitedly, her hands animated as she recounted the latest happenings in her life. "You will not believe what happened at the gallery opening last week," she exclaimed, her eyes sparkling with enthusiasm. "Someone spilled red wine all over that painting everyone was raving about! I swear, it was like a scene from a movie."

I settled into my seat, the familiar comfort of her presence washing over me. "Let me guess, the artist had a meltdown, right?" I leaned in, eager to soak up the details.

"Almost! But no, it was even better. The artist tried to play it cool and said it was an 'interactive installation' meant to provoke thoughts about chaos and beauty. Like, really?" Clara rolled her eyes dramatically, and I couldn't help but laugh. "Only in the art world can a red wine stain be rebranded as a deep philosophical statement."

Our conversation flowed effortlessly, each anecdote pulling me further away from the stress of the office and the looming shadow of Kevin's criticism. I relished Clara's quick wit and ability to spin everyday events into captivating tales, each punchline sharp enough to pierce through my lingering doubts.

"Speaking of chaos, how's work treating you?" she asked, her tone shifting slightly, eyes narrowing with genuine concern.

I hesitated, the weight of my recent struggles creeping back into my mind. "Oh, you know, just the usual. I'm working on a project that's more complicated than assembling IKEA furniture without the instructions."

"Kevin still breathing down your neck?" she queried, the concern deepening in her voice.

I nodded, swirling the wine in my glass absentmindedly. "Like a hawk. He's convinced that my entire existence hinges on his approval, which, let's be honest, is quite the pressure."

Clara leaned in, her expression turning serious for a moment. "You're brilliant, you know that, right? Don't let anyone—especially Kevin—make you doubt that. Just remember, even the best programmers have their off days."

Her words felt like a warm blanket wrapping around my shoulders, and I took a deep breath, grateful for her unwavering support. "Thanks, Clara. I really needed that."

As the evening wore on, we reminisced about old times, exchanging stories that felt like little treasures locked away in our shared history. The ambiance of the restaurant faded into a gentle background hum, and the chaos of my day became a distant memory. Laughter echoed off the walls, mingling with the clinking of glasses and the tantalizing aromas wafting from the kitchen.

Once dessert arrived—a decadent tiramisu that made my heart sing—I felt a sense of contentment settle in, a respite from the world of code and deadlines. Clara and I indulged, savoring each bite, and I felt the vibrant energy of our friendship flow freely, easing the tension that had gripped me for weeks.

"Okay, enough about me," I said, wiping the chocolate dust from my lips. "What about your love life? Still avoiding dating like the plague?"

Clara sighed dramatically, her expression one of mock defeat. "You know me too well. It's like I'm on a mission to become the ultimate cat lady, but I only have a goldfish."

I laughed, but the familiar pang of concern nestled in my chest. "You deserve someone who appreciates your quirky brilliance, not just someone to fill the void."

"Oh please, I'm saving myself for someone who can match my level of sarcasm," she shot back, a playful glint in her eye. "If they can't handle my witty comebacks, they're not worth my time."

As the night drew to a close, we finally stepped out into the cool air, the streets alive with the sounds of laughter and music filtering through open windows. Clara slipped her arm through mine, a gesture that felt both grounding and familiar.

"I'll walk you home. No arguments," she declared, her tone leaving no room for protest. "Plus, I need to tell you more about the wine fiasco. It gets better."

"Okay, okay, but only if you promise not to give away the punchline before we get to my door," I replied, chuckling as we strolled along the tree-lined street, the moonlight casting soft shadows around us.

As we walked, a sudden sense of unease settled over me, an inexplicable tension that crackled in the air like static. My thoughts drifted back to the office and the weight of unfinished projects, but Clara's laughter brought me back, grounding me in the moment.

We reached my apartment building, the comforting familiarity of home wrapping around me like a safety blanket. "Thank you for tonight," I said sincerely, my heart swelling with gratitude. "I really needed this."

"Anytime, my friend," she replied, pulling me in for a quick hug. "Just promise me you won't let Kevin get under your skin. He's not worth it."

I nodded, ready to embrace the new week with a renewed sense of confidence. Just as I turned to head inside, my phone buzzed in my pocket, the sudden noise cutting through the peaceful night like a sharp knife.

"Who is it? Your secret admirer?" Clara teased, eyes twinkling.

I fished the phone out, glancing at the screen. My heart dropped. The message was from Ethan: "We need to talk. It's about the project. Something's come up."

"Uh-oh," Clara said, noticing my sudden change in demeanor. "That sounds serious."

Before I could respond, the sound of footsteps echoed behind us, and I turned to see Kevin emerging from the shadows, his expression unreadable in the dim light. He took a few deliberate steps closer, his features sharpening against the night. "I thought I might find you here," he said, voice laced with an unsettling calmness that sent a shiver down my spine.

"What do you want?" I shot back, feeling the adrenaline spike in my veins.

"I just wanted to discuss your work on the feedback project. There are... some developments you should be aware of." His eyes glinted with a mix of intent and something darker, an unsettling promise of what was to come.

As the weight of his words hung in the air, the world around us shifted. I glanced at Clara, confusion etched on her face, before turning back to Kevin. A chill crept up my spine, and suddenly, the night didn't feel so safe anymore. My heart raced, and the weight of uncertainty settled heavily in my chest. What had he discovered? What did he mean by "developments"? The questions loomed, and I could feel the ground beneath me start to tremble as I braced for what lay ahead.

Chapter 3: Misfired Signals

Coding had become my lifeline, a digital tapestry woven with late-night sessions and the comforting glow of my laptop screen. Each keystroke felt like a heartbeat, pulsing with the thrill of creativity and the dread of impending deadlines. My desk, a chaotic landscape of energy drink cans, snack wrappers, and scattered notes, became a sacred space where ideas blossomed, and late-night musings turned into real projects. On those quiet evenings, when the world outside faded into shadows and my apartment turned into a realm of code and caffeine, I found a companion in Ethan.

He entered my life like a soft breeze on a stifling day, effortlessly bringing warmth and laughter. His presence turned my solitary rituals into something almost festive. The air buzzed with electricity whenever we were together, a constant hum of friendly competition and playful banter. He had an uncanny ability to turn mundane coding problems into grand quests, infusing our late-night debugging sessions with humor. One evening, as we sat cross-legged on the floor, surrounded by open laptops and tangled charging cables, I found myself straining to decode a particularly stubborn algorithm.

"I swear this code is out to get me," I muttered, staring at the screen with narrowed eyes. "It's like trying to teach a cat to fetch."

Ethan leaned back, his trademark grin dancing on his lips. "Maybe it just prefers laser pointers and a cozy sunbeam instead of fetch," he shot back, his voice teasingly light. "Have you tried asking it nicely?"

I couldn't help but laugh. The way he could weave levity into even the most frustrating moments made the tension dissolve like sugar in warm tea. But that night, something shifted in the atmosphere, an invisible thread pulling tighter between us. While I was busy ranting about the injustices of an algorithm, I let slip a confession that had haunted me for years, "You know, I'm terrified of public speaking. Like, if I had to present in front of our entire team, I'd rather face a bear."

The words tumbled out before I could stop them, and for a heartbeat, silence fell. Ethan's gaze softened, his expression transforming from playful to contemplative. "Public speaking, huh? I can't even look over a balcony without feeling like I might plummet into oblivion," he admitted, his voice surprisingly earnest.

It was a startling revelation, knowing that beneath his confident exterior lay the same insecurities I wrestled with daily. We exchanged stories, sharing fears like secrets tucked away in the corners of our hearts. His admission drew me in further, weaving an intricate tapestry of trust that felt both exhilarating and terrifying. In those moments of vulnerability, I glimpsed the man behind the charming facade, and it made me want to understand him even more.

Yet, as our friendship deepened, I couldn't shake the lingering awkwardness that clung to me like a second skin. Ethan's laughter often rang in my ears long after he left, a melody I adored but also feared. The lines between friendship and something more began to blur, and I often caught myself questioning what exactly he felt. It wasn't just his contagious laughter that drew me in; it was the way he seemed to see right through me, unraveling my carefully constructed barriers with a single glance.

The company decided to host a team outing to celebrate our latest project launch—a casual affair, they assured us. I dressed carefully, opting for a flowy blue dress that made me feel both comfortable and confident. I was ready to let loose, to embrace the fun, and perhaps even flirt a little. As the evening progressed, laughter echoed through the air, blending with the upbeat music and the clinking of glasses.

Amid the festivities, Ethan's playful banter drew me in, sparking that familiar electric feeling in my stomach. His teasing remarks felt like an invitation, and I misread the warmth of his laughter as something more than mere camaraderie. It was in this haze of joy and lightheartedness that I decided to take a leap, a leap that would send me tumbling into an abyss of embarrassment.

With a confidence that felt entirely misplaced, I grabbed his hand, feeling the warmth radiate from his skin. "Ethan, I just want to say—"

But the world spun out of control before I could finish. A burst of laughter from the group nearby drowned out my words, and suddenly, I blurted out my feelings in a reckless declaration, "I like you! Like, really like you!"

The room fell silent, every gaze turning toward me, wide-eyed and expectant. Time froze, and a hot flush crept up my cheeks. I wanted to disappear, to shrink into the floor like a deflated balloon. Laughter erupted, a mixture of surprise and delight echoing around us. My heart raced, a cacophony of mortification and disbelief pounding in my ears.

But then I caught Ethan's eye, and to my astonishment, he wasn't laughing at me; instead, his warm smile radiated genuine affection. The embarrassment that threatened to consume me shifted, morphing into a flutter of hope. Despite the cacophony of laughter surrounding us, in that moment, it felt as if we were the only two people in the room. The sound faded into the background, replaced by an unspoken connection that hung in the air between us.

As the laughter subsided, I held my breath, waiting for his response. He stepped closer, that familiar playful glint dancing in his eyes. "Well, you certainly know how to make a grand declaration," he teased, his voice light and teasing. "Can I get a redo on the 'I like you' part? Maybe in a less crowded setting?"

My heart raced, a mix of embarrassment and exhilaration swirling within me. "Only if you promise to return the favor," I shot back, a playful smirk gracing my lips.

The tension shifted again, no longer filled with the weight of awkwardness but rather buoyed by the thrill of possibility. Laughter transformed into a sweet melody, one that suggested that perhaps I hadn't misread his intentions after all. In that moment, surrounded by friends and a haze of uncertainty, I felt a flicker of hope ignite within me. Maybe, just maybe, my blunders were not the end of my story, but rather the beginning of something beautiful and unexpected.

The aftermath of my unintended proclamation hovered in the air like the last notes of a favorite song, a sweet tension that sparked every nerve in my body. Ethan's playful banter turned into a playful game of glances, and I felt as if the world around us was pulsing to the rhythm of my racing heart. My cheeks still burned with embarrassment, but the laughter from my coworkers transformed from a sharp sting to a soft hum that mingled with the giddy possibility of what might come next.

As the night wore on, we found ourselves gravitating toward one another, a magnetic pull that defied the crowd around us. I tried to maintain my composure, laughing at jokes and participating in conversations, but my mind kept circling back to Ethan's smile. It was the kind of smile that suggested he had a secret—a delightful little whisper that he, too, might have felt something stir in that chaotic moment.

"Can I offer you a drink?" he asked, leaning in close enough that I could catch a whiff of his cologne, a blend of cedarwood and something citrusy that was refreshingly unexpected. It seemed to linger in the air like a promise, teasing my senses and making the tiny hairs on my arms stand on end.

"Sure, but only if you promise to spill the secret of your mysterious charm," I replied, trying to keep my tone light despite the whirlwind in my chest.

He chuckled, the sound deep and warm, wrapping around me like a cozy blanket. "Only if you share yours first. That declaration was pretty spectacular, you know."

"Right? Who knew that public speaking could lead to such... attention?" I rolled my eyes playfully, my heart fluttering at the thought of how easily I'd spilled my feelings. "Honestly, I thought I was going to faint when I realized what I said. I mean, if there's a prize for embarrassment, I'm pretty sure I'd win it."

Ethan leaned against the bar, crossing his arms and regarding me with an amused expression. "If it helps, you've earned yourself a fan club. I've never seen someone turn beet red and still manage to look charming."

I smirked, shaking my head. "Charming? More like a walking cautionary tale." But there was something intoxicating about his gaze, a glimmer that made me feel seen in a way I'd never experienced before.

The drinks arrived, a vibrant swirl of colors that mirrored the exuberance of the evening. I took a sip of my mojito, the minty freshness igniting my senses, while Ethan opted for something dark and mysterious—a whiskey on the rocks that matched the enigmatic aura he seemed to radiate. We clinked glasses, a silent toast to this unpredictable night that had taken an unexpected turn.

"So, what's next for us?" I asked, my curiosity getting the better of me. "Should we brace ourselves for more team outings where I might accidentally declare my undying love for you in front of the entire office?"

Ethan laughed, the sound rich and genuine. "If you do, I'll make sure to have a camera ready. Think of it as an opportunity for some viral content."

I chuckled, but a flutter of uncertainty twisted in my stomach. What if my accidental confession had somehow changed the dynamic of our relationship? What if he didn't feel the same way I did? "But seriously, Ethan, I didn't mean to..."

"Make a scene?" he interrupted, his eyes sparkling. "You didn't. You made my night." His sincerity wrapped around my worries, soothing the tension that threatened to resurface.

Before I could respond, a sudden loud cheer erupted from the group of coworkers nearby, followed by the unmistakable sound of someone proposing a round of shots. A sense of adventure rippled through the room as people began to move closer, the laughter and chatter swelling into a joyful cacophony. I caught a glimpse of several colleagues leaning toward the makeshift dance floor, where a lively crowd had begun to gather.

"Come on, let's join them!" Ethan said, grabbing my hand and leading me toward the thrumming heart of the party. I stumbled slightly, the sudden movement catching me off guard, but he tightened his grip, his fingers warm against my skin.

We danced and laughed, losing ourselves in the rhythm of the night. The world outside faded, and for those few moments, it felt like nothing existed but the pulsing beat and the electric connection sparking between us. I couldn't help but glance at him, marveling at the way his hair fell slightly over his forehead, his carefree laughter echoing in my mind like a song I didn't want to end.

As the night wore on, the rhythm shifted, the crowd becoming a blur of swaying bodies and bright lights. At one point, I found myself breathlessly laughing, leaning against a wall to catch my breath when a wave of giddiness hit me, making me feel dizzy and alive. Ethan stood beside me, a bemused smile on his lips, as if he enjoyed every moment of my spontaneous revelry.

"I didn't know you had such moves," he teased, his eyes glinting with amusement.

"Just you wait until I unleash my signature move—the 'Awkward Penguin,'" I shot back, attempting to imitate a flailing bird while giggling uncontrollably.

His laughter echoed, filling the air with warmth. "I think I need to see that in action. Perhaps we can turn it into a team-building exercise?"

Before I could respond, a familiar face approached us, her expression painted with a mischievous grin. Jenna, our marketing lead, had clearly had a few drinks. "What are you two lovebirds plotting over here?" she teased, her tone laced with playful sarcasm.

"Just discussing dance moves," I replied quickly, trying to deflect the attention. "Ethan is particularly fond of the 'Awkward Penguin.'"

"Oh, trust me, it's a classic," she laughed, leaning in conspiratorially. "But don't let him fool you. He's the one who danced like a swan last week at karaoke night. Pure elegance."

"Hey, now," Ethan interjected, a mock-seriousness taking over his features. "I'm a graceful gazelle on the dance floor. The swan was a deliberate choice—a metaphor for my hidden charm."

Jenna burst into laughter, shaking her head. "Right, because nothing says charm like a flailing bird."

As the three of us bantered back and forth, I couldn't help but feel a sense of belonging. It was a lighthearted moment that felt like the calm before a storm, an invitation to explore the uncharted waters of my feelings for Ethan. Just as I began to relax into the night, a sudden thought pierced through the revelry. Was I really prepared to navigate this newfound complexity of emotions? The prospect of potential heartbreak loomed, casting shadows over my playful banter.

But the night held an undeniable magic, and I was determined to savor every minute of it. With a mixture of anticipation and trepidation swirling in my gut, I smiled at Ethan, ready to embrace whatever unpredictable turn our story would take next.

The afterglow of the night lingered like the scent of freshly brewed coffee, warm and inviting, as I awoke to sunlight filtering through the curtains. I could hear distant chatter from the street below, the world waking up to a new day while I lay wrapped in a cocoon of blankets, still processing the whirlwind of emotions from the previous evening. My mind flickered back to Ethan's laughter, the way his eyes sparkled with mischief and warmth, and the unexpected comfort that came from our shared moments.

I rolled out of bed and padded to the kitchen, still clad in my pajamas, my hair a wild halo of curls. The aroma of coffee beckoned, and I brewed a fresh pot, hoping to find clarity in the caffeine. As I leaned against the counter, I couldn't shake the feeling that my life was on the precipice of something thrilling yet terrifying. What had begun as simple coding sessions had transformed into something so much more complex, so intricate, weaving together our vulnerabilities and playful exchanges into a tapestry I wasn't sure I was ready to explore.

After a hurried breakfast and a quick shower, I dressed in my usual attire—a comfortable pair of jeans and a soft sweater that draped over my shoulders. I grabbed my laptop, the device that had become both a lifeline and a source of anxiety, and headed to the office. With every step I took, the anticipation grew, and my stomach twisted in knots. Would Ethan act differently after my bold declaration? Would things feel strained or shift into something new?

When I walked into the office, the familiar buzz of activity enveloped me, but my gaze instinctively searched for Ethan. There he was, across the room, laughing with Jenna and a couple of other coworkers. His head was thrown back in genuine amusement, and for a moment, I felt a pang of longing. Would our camaraderie transform into something more, or had I thrown a wrench into our delicate friendship?

"Hey, look who it is! The queen of grand declarations!" Jenna's voice cut through my thoughts like a knife. She bounced over with that trademark mischievous grin plastered across her face. "I hope you're ready to take the office by storm today."

"Please don't," I replied, attempting to stifle the embarrassment that threatened to bubble back up. "I already feel like a walking meme."

"Why would you feel that way? You're practically the star of the show!" She nudged me with her elbow. "Everyone is talking about your 'courageous' confession."

"Courageous? More like foolhardy," I muttered under my breath. But despite my words, a small smile tugged at my lips. There was a part of me that reveled in the attention, even if it was tinged with embarrassment.

As the morning progressed, I tried to focus on my tasks, diving into lines of code that swirled like an elaborate puzzle waiting to be solved. Yet, every few moments, my gaze drifted toward Ethan, who seemed oblivious to my internal struggle. He was engrossed in conversation, laughter spilling from his lips like sunshine. It struck me that he might not have given my confession much thought after all.

Just when I thought the day would stretch on forever, Ethan wandered over, his expression relaxed and open. "Hey, can we talk?"

My heart did a little flip as I nodded, fighting the instinct to flee the scene. We slipped into the break room, the door shutting behind us with a soft click that felt momentous. The chatter of our coworkers faded, replaced by the hum of the fridge and the faint scent of leftover takeout lingering in the air.

"I wanted to check in after last night," he said, leaning against the counter, arms crossed casually. His demeanor was inviting, but my nerves danced like fireflies in the dim light.

"Yeah, I—"

"You know, you shouldn't be embarrassed about what you said," he interrupted, the sincerity in his voice cutting through my rambling thoughts. "I think it was really brave of you."

"Brave?" I echoed, the word rolling off my tongue like it didn't quite fit. "More like impulsive. And now I'm stuck navigating the aftermath."

"Why do you think it's such a disaster?" Ethan asked, tilting his head slightly, a playful glint in his eye. "Are you regretting it?"

I opened my mouth to respond but hesitated. Regret wasn't exactly the right word. "Not regretting, just... confused. I don't want to make things weird between us."

His expression softened, and for a moment, we were suspended in silence, a shared understanding passing between us. "We can figure it out together, you know," he said gently. "Friendship is built on misfires, and maybe that's just part of our story."

"Part of our story?" I echoed, my heart racing as the implication sank in. Was he suggesting that there was a potential for more? The idea felt like a heady cocktail, intoxicating yet dangerous. "What if I misread everything?"

"Then we misread it together," he replied, his smile widening. "But I don't think you misread anything. There's something real here, isn't there?"

The air crackled with electricity, and I felt a rush of adrenaline flood my veins. There was something undeniably magnetic about him that pulled at my heartstrings, urging me to lean closer. But just as I contemplated taking that leap, the break room door swung open, and in strode Maxwell, our project manager, with his usual authoritative demeanor.

"Ethan! We need to discuss the latest deliverables," he announced, his voice cutting through the moment like a cold wind. "I want everyone on the same page before the client meeting tomorrow."

"Of course," Ethan replied, pulling away from our intimate bubble. "Just a moment."

I watched, a mixture of relief and frustration swirling within me. Just when we were about to address the elephant in the room, reality crashed back in. I forced a smile, trying to hide the disappointment creeping in.

As Ethan and Maxwell dove into a work discussion, I felt the weight of uncertainty settle heavily on my shoulders. There was so much left unsaid, and the moment I had hoped would clarify things instead felt like a teasing glimpse into a future I yearned for but couldn't yet grasp.

The day dragged on, a parade of tasks punctuated by brief conversations with coworkers and the ever-present background hum of my swirling thoughts. I stole glances at Ethan, who seemed fully immersed in work, and I couldn't help but wonder if I had imagined the connection we shared or if it had all been a figment of my overactive imagination.

As evening approached, the office began to empty out, the sounds of chatter fading to whispers. I gathered my things, feeling a tug of disappointment that I hadn't been able to address my feelings properly. Just as I turned to leave, I caught sight of Ethan standing near the entrance, his expression intent.

"Hey," he said, catching my gaze. "Are you free later? I thought we could grab a coffee and talk?"

"Coffee sounds great," I replied, unable to hide my eagerness.

"Perfect. I'll meet you at our usual spot in an hour?"

"See you then," I called back as I stepped outside, the cool evening air brushing against my skin, sending a thrill of anticipation racing through me.

Time seemed to stretch, each passing minute a tantalizing reminder of the conversation that awaited us. As I arrived at the café, my heart raced with anticipation, a mix of hope and uncertainty swirling within me. Would we finally unravel the tangled threads of our relationship?

The aroma of freshly brewed coffee filled the air, wrapping around me like a warm hug. I settled into a corner table, watching the world pass by through the window, the evening glow casting a golden hue over the bustling street. My mind raced with possibilities—each scenario flickering like a candle in the wind.

When Ethan arrived, the moment felt charged, the air thick with unspoken words. He slid into the seat across from me, his expression thoughtful. "Thanks for meeting me," he said, his voice steady yet warm. "I've been thinking a lot about what you said."

"Me too," I admitted, my heart pounding. "I just—"

But before I could finish my thought, the café door swung open with a sharp clang, and in walked a figure that froze me in place. A woman, tall and striking, with long hair cascading over her shoulders, walked straight to our table, her eyes locking onto Ethan with a familiarity that sent a shiver of unease through me.

"Ethan," she said, her voice smooth as silk. "I was hoping to find you here. We need to talk."

My breath hitched in my throat as the weight of the moment settled heavily upon us, casting shadows over everything we had begun to build. A silent storm brewed between us, the uncharted territory of our feelings suddenly eclipsed by the presence of someone who could change everything.

Chapter 4: The Great Office Bake-Off

The morning light poured through the floor-to-ceiling windows of the office, bathing the open-plan workspace in a soft, golden glow. It was a Monday, which already put me in a grumpy mood, but today was different. Today, we were having a bake-off, orchestrated by none other than our well-meaning, overly enthusiastic manager, Susan. While some employees buzzed with excitement, I felt a sinking pit in my stomach as I contemplated the impending chaos. Baking, in my mind, was an art form reserved for the culinary elite—not for someone like me, whose most recent attempt at cooking had resulted in a pan of charred, unrecognizable substance that might have doubled as a doorstop.

As the day wore on, my colleagues buzzed about ideas, recipe swaps, and flour brands like they were discussing last weekend's football game. Meanwhile, I hovered near the coffee machine, cradling my mug of lukewarm coffee as if it were a life raft in a sea of flour and sugar. My best friend, Sarah, flitted by, her hair a wild halo of curls and her eyes sparkling with mischief. She grabbed my arm and tugged me along, her enthusiasm infectious.

"Come on, Emily! This is your chance to shine! You'll totally win with your...unique take on baking!" she exclaimed, a knowing smile playing on her lips.

"Unique? You mean disastrous. My last cake could have been a weapon," I muttered, half-heartedly trying to pull away from her grip.

"Oh, please! If anything, it was an avant-garde piece of modern art. Just think of it as performance baking," she quipped, rolling her eyes playfully.

"Performance baking," I echoed, the term wrapping around me like a warm blanket, bringing a fleeting sense of courage. Maybe, just maybe, I could channel my inner artist.

After much deliberation and a few frantic calls to my mother for guidance, I decided on making chocolate chip cookies. How could one possibly go wrong with such a classic? But of course, life has a way of throwing curveballs. I envisioned a serene afternoon filled with the enticing aroma of melting chocolate and gooey dough. Instead, I found myself in a whirlwind of flour, sugar, and sheer panic as my ancient mixer sputtered and died, leaving me to blend the ingredients by hand.

Let's just say that my hands weren't quite up to the task. Flour clouded the air like a dense fog as I wrestled with the stubborn mixture, my heart racing faster than the blades of the broken mixer. And just when I thought I was in the clear, I realized I had forgotten to add the eggs. The mixture, which had stubbornly clung together like a failed relationship, now resembled something more akin to a sad pile of sludge.

By the time I finished, my cookies looked like they had been subjected to a volcanic eruption. I placed them on a plate that had seen better days, wiped my brow, and considered the absurdity of my culinary endeavor. I could either face my colleagues and their inevitable teasing or opt for a dramatic exit, slipping out the door like a baker in the night.

"Dramatic exits are overrated," I mumbled to myself as I walked into the brightly lit office kitchen. Laughter and chatter filled the air, creating an atmosphere thicker than the smoke that had enveloped my last cooking attempt. As I approached the table laden with cookies, cakes, and pies that looked like they belonged in a gourmet bakery, a wave of self-doubt washed over me.

"Look! It's our very own baking disaster!" someone called, and laughter erupted. My cheeks flushed a shade of crimson that could rival a ripe tomato.

"Thanks, guys, really," I managed, feigning a smile as I set my plate down.

To my surprise, Ethan, the charming and annoyingly perfect guy from accounting, swooped in like a knight in shining armor. He grinned, his blue eyes sparkling with mischief, and picked up one of my cookies.

"Ah, Emily's gourmet delights! The best part of the bake-off!" he proclaimed dramatically, inspecting the cookie with exaggerated reverence. "Such a bold choice, going with the 'charred' aesthetic. Very avant-garde!"

I laughed despite myself, my heart racing. There was something magnetic about Ethan, something that made my palms sweaty and my knees weak in a way I hadn't expected.

"Thanks, I guess," I replied, trying to hide my flustered state behind a layer of sarcasm. "You should really try one. They're deliciously burnt."

He took a big bite, chewing thoughtfully, and nodded with a seriousness that made me giggle. "Mmm, the flavors really come alive! A little smoky, a touch of despair... a true culinary journey."

Our playful banter caught the attention of others nearby, and soon, we found ourselves the center of a small crowd. Laughter bubbled around us, and I felt an unfamiliar warmth blooming in my chest. Perhaps this bake-off wasn't going to be the catastrophe I had envisioned.

As the judging began, Ethan and I naturally teamed up, and the kitchen transformed into our own chaotic arena. We worked side by side, the heat of the oven mingling with the chemistry that crackled in the air between us. Mixing, baking, and bantering, our playful competition felt charged, and every joke felt laced with an unspoken tension. I caught myself stealing glances at him, how his brow furrowed in concentration and how he effortlessly charmed the judges with his banter.

"Is it just me, or are you trying to distract the judges with your rugged good looks?" I teased, nudging him playfully as I dusted flour from my hands.

He laughed, the sound rich and warm. "Maybe a little bit of both. But, in my defense, the cookies have to taste good too!"

Our playful exchange made my heart race in ways I wasn't ready to fully comprehend. As he leaned closer, I could smell the faint hint of his cologne mingling with the scent of freshly baked goods—a mix that made my head spin. It was absurd how easy it was to lose myself in his laughter, how the world around us faded into a blur.

The bake-off unfolded like a romantic comedy, complete with flour fights and laughter echoing off the walls, but amidst the chaos, I realized that this moment was more than just a competition. With every passing second, the playful banter turned into something deeper, something that felt achingly sweet. I could almost taste it, the realization that perhaps, in this bizarre world of burnt cookies and charming smiles, I had stumbled upon something truly delicious.

The bake-off transformed our typically mundane office into a vibrant carnival of scents and colors, a veritable paradise of flour-dusted chaos. The kitchen buzzed with excitement as colleagues showcased their creations: a towering lemon meringue pie glistened under the fluorescent lights, while cupcakes adorned with meticulous frosting art seemed almost too pretty to eat. I, on the other hand, stood by my slightly scorched chocolate chip cookies, feeling like the unwelcome guest at a lavish banquet.

Ethan flitted between tables, his presence magnetic as he offered compliments and playful jabs in equal measure. The judges—a mix of our office's upper management—had gathered like hawks circling their prey, armed with forks and an insatiable appetite for critique. As they sampled each dish, I found myself watching Ethan more than the judges, captivated by his effortless charm. His laughter echoed through the kitchen, wrapping around me like a warm embrace.

"Let's get this over with," I muttered to Sarah, who stood beside me, glancing nervously at the growing line of judges. "I'm convinced they're going to need a new panel after tasting mine."

"Stop it! Just look at Ethan. If he can flirt with the judges while juggling five cupcakes, you can do this!" she encouraged, nudging me playfully. "Channel your inner baking goddess or something!"

"Baking goddess? I'm more like the baking troll who lurks under the bridge, ready to scare away any unsuspecting passersby," I replied, earning a snort of laughter from her.

"Your cookies are not that bad. Besides, the judges love a good story. Just tell them you were aiming for a new trend in gourmet charcoal cookies."

Before I could retort, Ethan approached, his gaze bright and teasing. "So, are we ready to dazzle the judges with our... unique offerings?" He held up one of my cookies, inspecting it with exaggerated seriousness. "I must say, Emily, these look incredibly... rustic."

"Rustic is code for 'what on earth happened here,'" I said with mock seriousness.

"Exactly! It's a culinary statement. They won't know what hit them," he grinned, his blue eyes sparkling with mischief.

With a dramatic flourish, Ethan laid out our cookie platter in front of the judges, who eyed it with an air of skepticism. Their expressions shifted from intrigue to bewilderment as they sampled the burnt offerings, and I held my breath, half-expecting a dramatic fallout of criticism.

"This is quite bold!" one of the judges remarked, chewing slowly. "What do you call these?"

"Charcoal Chic," Ethan announced, and I nearly choked on my laughter. "A sustainable choice, perhaps for the eco-conscious eater."

The judges exchanged glances, clearly unsure if they were being pranked or if Ethan was serious. I watched in disbelief as they scribbled notes, their faces a mixture of confusion and delight. It was pure madness, yet I couldn't help but feel a rush of warmth at the absurdity of it all.

"Bold indeed!" another judge chimed in, taking another bite. "There's a certain... texture to it."

"Not unlike the floors of my first apartment," I whispered to Ethan, and he chuckled, nodding in agreement.

As the judging continued, the playful atmosphere swirled around us, and I realized I had never felt more at ease in such chaos. Each playful jab from Ethan felt like a dance, and before I knew it, we had become the comedic duo of the bake-off.

Finally, as the last of the judges savored our creation, I caught a glimmer of surprise in their eyes. They hadn't outright condemned our cookies; instead, they seemed bemused, intrigued by our audacity. I shot Ethan a look, silently sharing my disbelief.

"See? We're the stars of the show," he said, leaning close enough that I could smell the faintest hint of cinnamon lingering on his shirt. "What's next? A dance-off?"

"I'd probably trip and take down half the office with me," I laughed, imagining the calamity. "But it would make a great story!"

As the day progressed, the bake-off continued to unfold like a whimsical play. Colleagues mingled, sharing their baked creations and trading stories, while Ethan and I fell into a rhythm that felt both familiar and exhilarating. The warmth between us began to simmer, underscored by a tension I hadn't expected to feel. It was more than just a friendly rivalry—it was as if we were two halves of a whole, navigating the unpredictable waters of both baking and budding attraction.

When the judges finally announced the winners, I felt my heart leap into my throat. The excitement in the air was palpable as they revealed the best creation. To my utter shock, Ethan and I placed third—an impressive feat for our "gourmet charcoal" cookies.

"Third place!" I squealed, unable to contain my excitement. "We did it! How did we manage to impress them with this?" I gestured dramatically to our slightly deformed cookies.

Ethan beamed, his face lit with triumph. "It's all about confidence, Emily! If you strut like you own the runway, even the burnt cookies will look appealing."

"I'll take that advice for my next culinary disaster," I quipped, the laughter bubbling up again.

In the jubilant chaos of the aftermath, Ethan pulled me aside, away from the crowd. The kitchen felt suddenly intimate, like a hidden nook amidst the loud festivities. "Hey, I just wanted to say..." he started, his expression shifting to something more serious, yet still playful.

"Please don't tell me you've decided to quit your day job to become a professional cookie critic," I interrupted, unable to resist the urge to tease him.

He chuckled, shaking his head. "No, I'm serious. I had a lot of fun today. You were brilliant, and your cookies... well, they were definitely memorable."

"Memorable like a traffic accident?" I teased, though my heart raced at his compliment.

"Memorable in the best possible way," he replied, stepping closer. The warmth radiating from him was palpable, and I suddenly felt hyperaware of the space between us. "You've got a spark, Emily, and I'm not just talking about the flour explosion earlier."

My breath caught in my throat. The tension crackled between us, palpable and electric, as we stood there, the world around us fading into a gentle hum. I couldn't help but notice the way his gaze held mine, earnest and inviting, as if we were sharing a secret in a crowded room.

"Are you suggesting I should open a bakery?" I asked, trying to keep the tone light, though a part of me wondered if there was something more brewing beneath our playful banter.

"Only if you promise to call it 'Emily's Gourmet Disasters'—I'd visit every day," he shot back, his grin disarming.

"Ha! Sounds like a plan. Just make sure to bring a fire extinguisher," I replied, laughter bubbling up again, but there was something in his gaze that made my heart flutter, a hint of vulnerability beneath the teasing.

"Actually, how about we take our baking skills to the next level?" he suggested, his tone shifting ever so slightly. "We could team up for a real cooking class—an adventure outside of the office. What do you say?"

The invitation hung in the air, filled with possibility and a hint of something deeper. My heart raced, and the idea of stepping beyond our playful rivalry into something more tangible sent a thrill of excitement coursing through me. This could be the start of something delightful, messy, and utterly unpredictable—a recipe for an adventure I never saw coming.

The day unfolded like a well-orchestrated dance, and as I stood with Ethan in the kitchen, the warmth of his presence sent a delightful shiver through me. The air was thick with the mingling scents of burnt sugar and frosting, creating an odd but enticing aroma that seemed to wrap around us. As he leaned closer, the world around us faded away, and I couldn't help but notice the way his smile brightened his whole face, making it impossible to think about anything but the moment we were sharing.

"Are you sure you're ready for this?" I teased, a hint of challenge in my voice. "I mean, one false move and we could end up with another round of 'gourmet disasters.'"

Ethan chuckled, an infectious sound that made my heart flutter. "Bring it on. If we burn down the kitchen, we'll just blame it on the charcoal chic trend you started."

"Perfect! I can already hear the headlines: 'Local Office Team Bakes Up a Storm—Literally!'" I shot back, reveling in the lighthearted banter that felt as natural as breathing.

As we navigated the last details of our baking endeavor, I caught sight of Sarah, who was leaning against the counter with a knowing smirk. She raised an eyebrow at us, clearly enjoying the spectacle of our flirtation. I felt a mix of embarrassment and thrill; we were in our own bubble, but I couldn't shake the feeling that she was ready to burst it with a well-placed quip.

"Just make sure you don't drop the eggs this time, Emily!" she called out, laughter lacing her words.

"Noted! I'll avoid any egg-related catastrophes," I replied, grinning. But as soon as I turned back to Ethan, I felt the comfortable warmth of our earlier moments begin to shift. There was a spark in his eyes, a playful challenge hanging in the air.

With the judges now seated at the makeshift tasting table, Ethan leaned in closer, our arms brushing together as we stirred our batter. "Alright, here's the plan," he whispered conspiratorially. "We charm the judges with our personalities first, and then we'll dazzle them with our culinary genius."

"And if that fails?" I asked, biting my lip, the thrill of the moment sending my heart racing.

"Then we serve them our cookies and hope they have a sense of humor."

With a shared look of mischief, we placed our cookie sheets in the oven, timing our banter perfectly with the tick-tock of the clock as we waited for our fate to bake. "While we're waiting, what's your favorite dessert?" he asked, curiosity lighting his features.

"Hmm, that's a tough one," I pondered, leaning against the counter. "It has to be tiramisu. It's elegant, layered, and a little caffeinated, just like me."

Ethan smirked, a twinkle in his eye. "And just as likely to keep you awake all night?"

"Precisely! What about you?"

"Chocolate lava cake," he declared, as if the answer was obvious. "It's warm, gooey, and kind of messy, just like my personality."

"Confident and charming, I see," I teased, feeling emboldened by his playful spirit. "I can appreciate a guy who knows how to embrace his messy side."

"Oh, I can show you just how messy I can get," he said, leaning in closer.

The teasing atmosphere morphed into something electric, a palpable tension humming between us. My breath caught in my throat as I realized how much I wanted to step closer, to bridge the gap that felt both thrilling and terrifying. But just as I contemplated taking that leap, the timer dinged, jolting us back to the present.

"Showtime!" Ethan exclaimed, his excitement contagious. Together, we opened the oven, revealing a tray of cookies that looked surprisingly decent, their edges just the right shade of golden brown.

"I think we did it!" I gasped, momentarily forgetting my earlier doubts.

"More than just did it, I'd say. We nailed it," he replied, flashing a triumphant smile that made my heart skip.

With the cookies cooled and our hearts racing, we plated our creations with an artistic flair that belied the earlier chaos. As we approached the judges, I felt a swell of nerves, my stomach flipping in anticipation. This was it—the moment of truth.

"Ladies and gentlemen, prepare yourselves for a culinary experience unlike any other," Ethan declared, his voice booming with playful seriousness. "We present to you, the bold and adventurous: Charcoal Chic cookies!"

Laughter erupted, easing my nerves, and I felt a rush of gratitude for Ethan's ability to light up the room. The judges sampled our cookies, their faces a mix of amusement and confusion. As they chewed, I held my breath, convinced this could either be a triumphant moment or a comically disastrous ending.

"Wow," one judge finally said, her eyebrows raised in surprise. "These are... surprisingly good!"

Ethan shot me a triumphant grin, and I couldn't help but laugh.

As the judging continued, a palpable buzz of excitement filled the air. I felt lighter, buoyed by the energy swirling around us. Perhaps this bake-off was about more than just cookies; it was about connection, laughter, and something I couldn't quite place yet but felt brewing between Ethan and me.

As the results drew nearer, Sarah nudged me, her eyes twinkling with mischief. "I've got a bet going that you two are going to end up as the bake-off power couple," she whispered.

I rolled my eyes but felt a blush creeping up my cheeks. "Please, we're just having fun."

"Fun that looks a lot like chemistry to me," she winked before wandering off to chat with someone else.

Just then, Ethan caught my gaze, his expression shifting to something more serious. "So, about that cooking class..."

I met his eyes, a rush of emotions swirling within me. "I'd love that," I replied, the sincerity of my words washing over me.

But before he could respond, the head judge cleared her throat, drawing our attention back to the crowd. "And now, for the moment you've all been waiting for: the winners of the Great Office Bake-Off!"

The room fell silent, anticipation hanging thick in the air. As the judge began announcing the top three teams, my heart raced. "In third place, for their adventurous spirit and unique presentation..."

"Here it comes!" Ethan whispered, barely able to contain his excitement.

"Emily and Ethan with their Charcoal Chic cookies!"

The room erupted into cheers and laughter, and Ethan threw his arms around me, pulling me into a celebratory hug that sent a delightful shock through me. I wrapped my arms around his neck, feeling the warmth of his body against mine as we reveled in our victory.

But just as I was about to pull away, I felt an unmistakable tension in the air, a shift that made the back of my neck prickle. I turned slightly, my gaze darting around the room, and there, standing at the entrance, was someone I hadn't expected to see.

Jack—my ex, arms crossed and a smirk plastered across his face, watching me with an intensity that sent my heart plummeting.

"Looks like you're doing well, Emily," he called out, his voice dripping with sarcasm.

Ethan's grip on me tightened, and I felt the sudden weight of tension pull me down, a stark contrast to the buoyant joy we'd just shared. I opened my mouth to respond, but no words came, a whirlwind of emotions swirling within me.

"Everything alright?" Ethan asked, his voice low, concern etching his features.

I glanced back at Jack, whose expression was a mix of smugness and something darker. "Just peachy," I managed to say, though my heart raced with uncertainty.

As I tried to steady myself, the laughter and applause from the bake-off faded into the background, and the world around us felt charged with an unsettling energy, as if the air had thickened, and the moment stretched into an eternity.

"Good luck with your baking career, Emily," Jack taunted, stepping further into the room, his presence casting a shadow over my newfound joy.

And just like that, the playful atmosphere shifted, leaving me suspended between a past I thought I had moved on from and the thrilling new connection I was forging with Ethan, who stood beside me, clearly sensing the storm brewing.

Chapter 5: The Unexpected Confession

The sun hung low in the sky, casting a warm, golden hue across the city as I settled into the worn wicker chair on the roof terrace. The clinking of dishes and the hum of conversation below blended with the soft whispers of the bay breeze. Each breath I took was infused with the salty tang of the ocean, mingling with the tantalizing scent of the artisanal sandwich I had just unwrapped. I let my gaze wander over the vibrant cityscape, but my mind was a restless sea of thoughts, waves crashing relentlessly against the shore of my insecurities.

Ethan sat across from me, a steady presence amidst the chaos that brewed within. His tousled dark hair caught the light, giving him an almost ethereal glow, and his piercing blue eyes seemed to see right through me, cutting past the layers of pretense I often wore like armor. It was just a casual lunch, a break from the monotony of work, yet the air felt electric, charged with unspoken words and what-ifs. As I nibbled on my sandwich, I felt a knot tightening in my stomach, the familiar weight of self-doubt anchoring me in place.

"I can't keep doing this," I blurted out, my voice barely above a whisper, yet it felt like a declaration to the universe. Ethan raised an eyebrow, his expression shifting from casual curiosity to genuine concern. I took a deep breath, the heaviness of my thoughts spilling out like a long-held secret. "Every day at work, it's like Kevin is determined to tear me down. I can't shake this feeling that I'm not good enough, that I'm just... floating along."

Ethan leaned forward, resting his elbows on the table, his intensity making me feel both vulnerable and safe. "Kevin? That guy's a tool. Seriously, who does he think he is?" His voice was laced with indignation, the kind of protectiveness that made my heart skip. I couldn't help but laugh softly, despite the turmoil inside me.

"Tool is putting it lightly," I replied, a hint of a smile breaking through. "He has a PhD in belittling people. It's like he's on a mission to make me doubt every decision I make."

With each word, I could feel the weight of my frustrations lifting, the sunlight pooling around us like a warm embrace. Ethan's expression shifted, a mix of determination and empathy that tugged at my heartstrings. "You're brilliant, Natalie. Don't ever let him make you feel otherwise." His hand reached across the table, his fingers curling around mine in a gentle squeeze. The contact sent a jolt through me, a spark igniting something that had been smoldering beneath the surface.

I blinked, momentarily speechless. "You think I'm brilliant?" The question hung between us, disbelieving yet hopeful.

"Absolutely. You've got ideas that would make anyone else's head spin," he said, his voice steady and sincere. I could feel the heat radiating from his palm, and for a moment, the world around us faded—the distant sounds of the city and the blinding sun melted away, leaving only Ethan's gaze locked onto mine.

"Just look at you, sitting here, defying gravity while you juggle a full-time job and still manage to be a decent human being," he continued, a teasing smile tugging at the corners of his lips. "You could write a book about surviving office politics. I'd read it."

His playful banter was a balm to my fraying nerves, and I couldn't help but return the smile, my heart fluttering wildly. "Maybe I should. I could call it How to Survive a Shark Tank Without Losing Your Mind."

"That sounds like a bestseller," Ethan grinned, and for a heartbeat, I allowed myself to believe that maybe, just maybe, I could rise above Kevin's incessant critiques.

"Thanks for being here, Ethan. It means a lot." I said, squeezing his hand back, a rush of gratitude swelling in my chest.

"Anytime. But seriously, if he gets too much, I'll put a whoopee cushion on his chair," he joked, his eyes sparkling with mischief.

"Ah, the classic whoopee cushion strategy. What a bold move," I teased back, my laughter ringing out like a melody against the backdrop of the setting sun. Yet beneath the levity, a deeper connection was weaving itself between us, one that made my heart race and my cheeks warm.

We fell into a comfortable silence, the air thick with unspoken words and the kind of anticipation that leaves one breathless. I watched the sun sink lower, casting a fiery glow across the Golden Gate Bridge, the horizon painted in shades of orange and pink that felt almost surreal. In that moment, the world seemed to shimmer with possibility, and I couldn't shake the feeling that something significant was about to unfold.

Then, without warning, the air shifted, the tension palpable. Ethan's fingers lingered over mine, his gaze intensifying as if he were wrestling with thoughts too profound to voice. I could feel my heart pounding, each beat echoing the uncharted territory we were tiptoeing into. "Natalie," he began, his voice low and steady, "there's something I've been wanting to tell you."

Time slowed as the weight of his words hung in the air, thick and charged. I held my breath, anticipation prickling my skin. The warmth of the sun faded, replaced by the chill of the uncertainty looming before us. Whatever he had to say could change everything, and as the world around us dimmed, I realized I was ready to hear it, even if my heart trembled at the thought of what it might mean for us both.

Ethan's gaze held mine, a silent challenge lingering in the air between us as he prepared to share whatever it was that weighed on his mind. I felt a tremor of anticipation ripple through me, mingled with the remnants of our earlier banter. The golden light filtering through the leaves above us painted dappled patterns on the table, creating a moment so picturesque it felt almost scripted. But the palpable tension told me we were about to step off the scripted path, veering into uncharted territory.

"Before I say anything," he began, his voice low, drawing me in, "you have to promise you won't laugh." A lopsided grin tugged at his lips, but his seriousness grounded me.

"Ethan, I've seen you turn into a panther without a moment's notice. I'm pretty sure I can handle whatever you're about to throw at me," I replied, attempting to mask my nerves with humor.

He chuckled, the sound warm and genuine, but it faded quickly as he shifted in his chair, the weight of his next words pressing down on us both. "Okay, but really, this is important. I haven't told anyone, and I trust you."

My stomach fluttered, a rush of adrenaline fueling my curiosity. "You know you can trust me," I said, squeezing his hand again, the warmth radiating between us intensifying.

Ethan took a deep breath, his fingers lacing with mine, anchoring me in this moment. "I've been thinking about this for a while now," he started, his gaze flicking down to our hands before meeting my eyes again. "I'm not the only one who's had a rough go at it lately. I've been battling my own demons, and I think I'm finally ready to confront them."

My heart raced as I leaned in, the world around us fading once more. "What kind of demons?"

He hesitated, his expression shifting to one of vulnerability. "Remember when I told you about my dad? The reason I don't talk to him anymore?"

I nodded, the memory of his words washing over me. Ethan had mentioned a fractured relationship, something that seemed to hang like a storm cloud over him, but he hadn't gone into detail.

"Things weren't great," he continued, his voice thick with emotion. "He was... well, let's just say he had his priorities all wrong.

He always pushed me to be someone I wasn't, to fit into a mold that just wasn't me. When I finally broke away, it was like shedding a skin, but the scars lingered."

I felt a pang of sympathy for him, the depth of his pain touching a part of my own that I often kept hidden. "Ethan, I had no idea. That sounds... really hard."

"Yeah," he sighed, rubbing the back of his neck as if trying to erase the memory. "But the thing is, after I cut ties with him, I had this moment of clarity. I realized I've been holding onto the anger, and it's been eating away at me."

"That makes sense," I said gently. "Sometimes, letting go is harder than it seems."

"Right? And it's easier to blame someone else for your problems than to look inward." He paused, his brow furrowing in thought. "But I don't want to do that anymore. I want to be better, for myself and for the people I care about."

I felt the air crackle between us, the intimacy of the moment growing heavier. "You're already doing that, you know," I said softly. "Just by acknowledging it."

He smiled, a small, genuine lift of his lips that melted some of the tension. "Thanks. But here's the thing—I think I might need to confront him, to find closure, you know? I've been holding back, afraid of what it might do to me."

My heart thudded in my chest. "You're thinking of reaching out to him?"

"Yeah, I am." His voice was steady, but I could see the flicker of uncertainty in his eyes. "But I'm scared, Natalie. What if it goes wrong? What if it just opens old wounds?"

"That's a valid fear," I replied, my fingers tightening around his. "But it might also be the step you need to truly move forward. You're strong enough to handle whatever comes next."

He nodded, and for a moment, we sat in comfortable silence, the sun inching lower in the sky, painting everything in warm hues. It was a moment suspended in time, a brief escape from the chaos of life, yet the gravity of our conversation held us in place.

"Ethan," I started, my voice barely above a whisper, "I don't want to lose you."

He looked at me, surprise etched across his features. "Lose me? Where is this coming from?"

"I mean, if you're diving into all of this, I just... I worry. It's a lot. And what if you need space?"

His expression softened, and he leaned closer, his warmth wrapping around me like a safety net. "I appreciate that, truly. But you're not going to lose me. You're the one person who's made me feel like I'm more than my past. If anything, I want you by my side when I face it."

My heart soared at his words, an unfamiliar feeling blooming within me. It was both exhilarating and terrifying, an invitation to step further into the unknown.

"Okay," I said, my voice steadier than I felt. "I'll be there for you. But just so you know, I'll expect a dramatic retelling of how it goes down. Like, Pulitzer Prize material."

He laughed, the sound brightening the atmosphere. "I'll make sure it's worthy of your attention, don't worry."

As we sat there, the sun dipped below the horizon, the world around us transitioning from vibrant colors to muted shades of twilight. But it was more than just a sunset; it felt like the closing of one chapter and the beginning of another, the lines between our lives blurring in the most beautiful way.

"Let's make a deal," he proposed, his tone shifting slightly. "For every step I take toward confronting my past, you share a victory from your work, no matter how small. It'll remind us that we're both on this journey."

I smiled, feeling the warmth of camaraderie wash over me. "Deal. But I expect updates on your epic showdown."

"Oh, it'll be a saga, complete with dramatic music and possibly slow-motion," he grinned, and I couldn't help but laugh.

The air was lighter now, filled with the promise of what lay ahead. Together, we would face our challenges, our laughter mingling with the gentle breeze, weaving a tapestry of shared experiences. And as we basked in the fading light, I couldn't shake the feeling that something profound was unfolding between us—a connection that, for better or worse, was about to change everything.

The fading sunlight bathed the roof terrace in hues of gold and rose, casting elongated shadows that danced against the backdrop of the Golden Gate Bridge. As Ethan and I sat there, laughter still lingering in the air, I felt the weight of unspoken thoughts shift between us, a tangible energy that was both exciting and terrifying. My mind was racing, processing the implications of his words and the sincerity in his gaze. He had peeled back layers I didn't even know I had, exposing my vulnerabilities while offering warmth and understanding.

"So, what's next on the Ethan road to emotional enlightenment?" I teased, hoping to lighten the moment even as my heart raced at the thought of the depth of his honesty.

He chuckled, shaking his head as if to dismiss the gravity of our conversation. "Well, after the grand showdown with my dad, I'm thinking about therapy."

I nodded, genuinely impressed. "That sounds like a solid plan. Maybe you can even get a discount for bringing emotional baggage."

Ethan smirked, leaning back in his chair. "I'll be sure to negotiate the best deal for my mental chaos. You can bet on it."

We exchanged a playful banter that wrapped around us like a cozy blanket, but beneath it all, my heart thudded with anticipation. His openness had ignited something in me, a kind of shared vulnerability that deepened our connection. It was unsettling in the best possible way.

"Okay, my turn," I said, hesitating for just a moment before continuing. "You've shared your struggle, and I want to share mine. I feel like I'm on this tightrope at work, constantly worrying that I'll fall."

Ethan's expression shifted to one of understanding. "What do you mean?"

"The pressure to prove myself, to not just keep my head above water but to thrive, is overwhelming," I confessed, the words pouring out before I could hold them back. "Kevin's critiques feel like poison. He doesn't just want to keep me in my place; he seems to relish it."

Ethan's eyes darkened with a flicker of anger. "That's messed up. Why does he get off on making you feel small?"

"Because some people derive power from belittling others. It's a control thing," I replied, a mixture of resignation and defiance in my tone. "I've spent so long trying to appease him, to show I'm capable, that I'm starting to lose sight of who I am."

"Don't let him take that from you," Ethan said firmly, his grip on my hand tightening. "You deserve to feel confident in your abilities. You are capable, and anyone who can't see that needs their vision checked."

"Especially since I've been known to single-handedly handle a three-month-old spreadsheet," I quipped, attempting to inject humor into the somber conversation.

"Three months? Impressive," he replied, the corner of his mouth quirking up. "But in all seriousness, maybe it's time to start pushing back. Speak up, or even report him. You've got to protect your own space."

"Reporting Kevin feels like trying to swim upstream. It's exhausting just thinking about it."

"I get it. But if you don't speak up for yourself, who will?"

I considered his words, feeling a swell of determination mingled with doubt. "You're right, I know you are. But it's one thing to acknowledge my worth and another to fight for it."

"Sometimes, a single act of bravery is all it takes to set off a chain reaction," he encouraged, his voice soothing yet firm. "I believe in you."

The intensity of his belief swept over me, a tide that pulled me along. "Thank you, Ethan. Really. It's just... I've spent so much time playing it safe, it feels foreign to consider anything else."

"That's exactly why you need to take that leap," he urged, his eyes bright with encouragement. "What's the worst that could happen? You find your voice and discover it's louder than you ever thought possible."

Just as the weight of his words began to settle in, a cacophony of laughter erupted from below, drawing my attention momentarily. I glanced down to see a group of colleagues from work gathered around a table, their carefree spirits a stark contrast to the seriousness of our conversation. Among them, I caught a glimpse of Kevin's unmistakable posture, his bravado radiating even from a distance.

"Look," I said, gesturing toward the crowd. "There's Kevin, probably plotting his next condescending remark."

Ethan followed my gaze, and his expression darkened momentarily. "That guy seriously needs to be knocked down a peg. I could take him, you know."

I laughed, the image of Ethan throwing punches at my boss eliciting a chuckle I hadn't expected. "I appreciate the sentiment, but I think we should keep you out of the HR report."

"Fair enough. But I won't hesitate if you ever need me to step in," he replied, his eyes sparkling with mischief.

I grinned, feeling lighter in his presence. "You might just be the best emotional support I've ever had."

Just then, a text pinged from my phone, cutting through the warmth of our conversation like a sudden chill. I fished it out of my bag, glancing at the screen. It was a message from Jess, my best friend.

Hey, just wanted to check in. Are you okay? I heard Kevin was in a mood today. Don't let him get to you!

I felt a rush of gratitude for her thoughtfulness, a reminder that I had people who cared about me. I quickly typed back a reassuring response, but before I could hit send, Ethan leaned closer, his expression suddenly serious.

"Hey, can I ask you something?"

"Of course," I replied, my heart quickening as I sensed the shift in the air.

"What if we take our little 'journeys' together? Like a pact of sorts."

I blinked, caught off guard by the suggestion. "You mean like a 'find our inner strength' support group?"

"Exactly! A weekly meeting of the self-improvement club, where we share progress, strategies, and, yes, snacks."

I couldn't help but laugh, the image of us sitting in a circle with a plate of cookies suddenly amusing. "I like the sound of that. But can we include coffee and maybe a good playlist?"

"Only the best for our healing," he said, his voice taking on a mock-serious tone.

As we chuckled, I felt a warmth growing between us, the shared vulnerability evolving into something more profound. Then, just as the laughter faded and the moment shifted back to something more serious, I caught sight of movement from the corner of my eye.

A figure was approaching from the staircase leading up to the terrace, and my heart dropped as recognition hit me. It was Kevin, striding toward us with an air of confidence that made my skin crawl. The easy banter that had just wrapped us in warmth dissolved, replaced by a tightening knot in my stomach.

Ethan's expression hardened, sensing the shift in my demeanor. "You okay?"

"Yeah, just—"

"Hey, look who's here!" Kevin's voice boomed as he reached the top of the stairs, his smile dripping with insincerity. "I didn't expect to find you two lovebirds up here, all alone. How romantic."

Ethan's jaw clenched, and I could see the protective instinct flicker in his eyes. "We're just enjoying the view, Kevin. Something you wouldn't understand," he shot back, the sharpness of his tone startling even me.

Kevin's smile faltered for just a second, his facade cracking. "Is that so? I hope you're not trying to hide from work. You know how I feel about slacking off."

"Funny, I thought we were supposed to be supporting each other, not tearing each other down," I retorted, surprising myself with the strength in my voice.

"Support? That's rich coming from you. You're the one who hides behind your excuses," he sneered, clearly reveling in the confrontation.

Ethan's hand tightened around mine, a silent affirmation that I wasn't alone in this. I felt a surge of determination flood through me, the vulnerability we had shared transforming into a fierce resolve. "Maybe it's time someone called you out on your behavior."

Kevin's eyes narrowed, and the tension crackled in the air, thick and oppressive. "You think you can challenge me? You've got a long way to go."

As I met his gaze, a rush of adrenaline surged through me. This was it—the moment where I could either let him intimidate me or stand my ground. I opened my mouth to respond, but before I could utter a single word, my phone buzzed again.

The screen lit up with an unexpected notification: a message from an unknown number. My heart raced as I swiped it open. The words sent a chill down my spine:

You should really watch your back. Things are about to get messy.

I glanced at Ethan, the worry etched on his face reflecting my own. The air around us shifted again, the playful banter evaporating into an atmosphere thick with uncertainty. Just as Kevin leaned closer, ready to unleash another round of insults, the world around me blurred into a haze. I had a feeling that this was only the beginning of a far more complicated struggle—one that would demand everything I had.

Chapter 6: The Interference

As I settled into my usual corner of the bustling café, the air was thick with the rich aroma of freshly brewed coffee mingling with the sweet scent of cinnamon rolls that danced tantalizingly beneath my nose. The cozy interior, with its mismatched furniture and splashes of color on the walls, felt like a sanctuary—a comforting escape from the outside world where ambitions collided and egos clashed. I loved this place. It was where I had first discovered my passion for creativity, hidden between the pages of my notebook, where the characters of my life breathed life into my ideas.

But today, I wasn't here for inspiration; I was here for solace. I took a sip of my caramel latte, its warmth spreading through me like a hug, while I watched the world move at its usual frenetic pace. Outside, people dashed by in a blur, umbrellas bobbing like colorful mushrooms, their heads down against the rain that had decided to grace us with its presence. It was a contrast to the storm brewing in my own life, one that seemed to revolve around Kevin—a name that had begun to feel like a curse on my tongue.

The lines of our friendship had blurred, and my once-comfortable existence felt more like walking a tightrope strung high above a pit of snapping jaws. Kevin had once been a supportive colleague, but as our collaborative projects transitioned into something more intimate, his demeanor had shifted. Gone was the playful banter that had originally drawn me to him; now, it was as if I was navigating a minefield, each misstep threatened by his barbed comments.

"Did you really think that was a good idea?" His voice sliced through my thoughts like a knife, bringing me back to the present and reminding me I was far from alone. I glanced up to find him leaning against the doorframe of my workspace, arms crossed, his smirk as infuriating as ever.

"I did," I shot back, trying to keep my voice steady despite the flicker of insecurity he ignited within me. I gestured towards my laptop, where the outlines of our latest project loomed like unwritten chapters of a story waiting to be told. "The feedback from the team was positive."

He rolled his eyes dramatically, a gesture so over-the-top I half-expected him to start a soap opera about the struggles of the office. "Positive? Or are you just trying to convince yourself? Maybe next time, you could think a little more critically before you waste everyone's time."

With every word, I felt my confidence erode like the tides pulling at the shore. Yet, it was in moments like these that I could hear Ethan's voice echoing in my mind—reminding me of my worth and the creativity that sparked like fireworks when I believed in myself.

"I think I'll take the team's opinion over yours," I retorted, my voice a shade firmer. "You know, the team that's actually working on this project instead of trying to undermine it?"

Kevin's face darkened, his expression morphing into something I couldn't quite place—resentment or perhaps envy? But I had learned to recognize the ugly underbelly of jealousy creeping into his words, and for the first time, I didn't flinch.

The tension in the room thickened, charged with the unsaid and the unwanted. I could see the gears in his head turning, plotting my next misstep, and I refused to give him the satisfaction. It was easier now, knowing I had Ethan as my ally. His steadfast belief in my abilities acted like armor against Kevin's snide remarks, bolstering my resolve.

Yet, the battle was far from over, and the escalating tension weighed heavily on my shoulders as days turned into weeks. Each team meeting felt like a stage where Kevin performed his act of destruction, nitpicking my ideas and laughing off my contributions.

Despite the heartache, I remained steadfast, my determination ignited by Ethan's unwavering support.

But then came that fateful day. I had ventured into the cramped break room, hoping for a moment of peace as I sipped on a too-sweet chai latte. The rhythmic sound of coffee brewing was my only company, a gentle hum that soothed my frayed nerves. That's when I overheard Kevin's voice, low and conspiratorial, just outside the door. My heart sank as I leaned closer, straining to catch the words that slipped through the cracks.

"...it'll be easy," he said, his tone dripping with malicious intent. "We'll take their project idea, tweak it just enough to make it ours. No one will know it's a copy. And with our connections, we can present it as a fresh concept. They'll never see it coming."

Panic clawed at my chest, a cold grip that threatened to suffocate me. I felt as if the walls of the break room were closing in, my sanctuary transformed into a prison of deceit. The realization hit me like a punch to the gut—this wasn't just a personal vendetta; it was a calculated move to sabotage everything I had poured my heart into. My project, our project, was at risk, and Kevin's ambition was a whirlwind threatening to uproot everything.

With a newfound determination surging through my veins, I stepped back from the door, my mind racing. I had a chance to expose him, to unravel the web of lies he had spun around our team. I could no longer be the passive observer in this theater of manipulation. No, I would take center stage, and I would shine. My heart raced, fueled by a blend of fear and righteous anger. I was ready to confront him, to call him out, and protect the hard work that had become a part of me.

As I marched back to my desk, the din of the café faded, replaced by the pounding of my heart, each beat a reminder of the fight ahead. I would not let Kevin's ambition destroy what we had built. I would reclaim my voice, and in doing so, I would protect not only my project but also my place within the team. I had allies, I had Ethan, and together, we would turn the tides. The game was changing, and this time, I would be the one to write the ending.

The tension in the office was palpable, like a tightrope stretched thin between a summer storm and the calm before it. I could feel it crackling in the air, a charged energy that urged me to take action. My resolve crystallized with each passing day, buoyed by Ethan's support. We would meet for lunch, our conversations effortlessly flowing between laughter and the serious discussions about my project, his laughter acting as a soothing balm against the sharp edges of Kevin's comments.

Ethan had a way of making even the most mundane things feel special. Whether it was a shared sandwich or a simple stroll through the sunlit park nearby, he infused those moments with a warmth that chased the shadows away. Today, however, that warmth was accompanied by a fire burning within me—a fierce determination to confront Kevin and protect my work.

I arrived at the office earlier than usual, the stillness of the early morning hours allowing me to gather my thoughts. The fluorescent lights buzzed overhead, illuminating the sea of empty desks, each a testament to the potential chaos of the day to come. I settled into my seat, fingers dancing across the keyboard as I prepared my notes for the meeting. With each stroke, I envisioned Kevin's incredulous expression when I presented the evidence of his betrayal.

When the team gathered, the atmosphere shifted. Kevin sauntered in, his confidence a sharp contrast to the way I felt, like an imposter cloaked in determination. His usual smirk was present, a small twitch at the corner of his lips, but today, it did little to quell the growing tension in my chest. The meeting unfolded like a scripted play, the usual banter dulled by the weight of what I planned to reveal.

"Let's get right to it, shall we?" Kevin's voice rang out, and I couldn't help but roll my eyes internally. His bravado was exhausting, and I could feel the others' unease echoing my own. As we dove into discussions, he continued to interject with pointed comments aimed directly at me, each one a reminder of the undercurrent swirling beneath our professional surface.

"Are you sure you want to take the lead on this part? I thought we were prioritizing quality over enthusiasm," he quipped, his eyes glinting with a mischief that only fueled my resolve.

"Funny, coming from someone whose idea of quality is spouting off someone else's work," I shot back, the words slipping out before I could second-guess myself. A hushed silence fell over the room, my colleagues shifting uncomfortably in their seats as they caught the tension in the air.

Kevin's expression faltered for a fraction of a second, but then he quickly masked it with a faux chuckle. "I see someone's feeling feisty today. But let's keep our focus on the project."

The meeting trudged on, but I could feel my pulse quickening, adrenaline coursing through my veins as I mentally prepared for what came next. I waited, my thoughts racing as the conversation swirled around us, and finally, the moment presented itself. The discussion shifted to my project proposal, a perfect segue for me to expose Kevin's betrayal.

"Before we proceed," I began, my voice steady despite the storm of emotions swirling inside me. "I think it's important that we address something I overheard." The room fell silent, the weight of my words hanging heavily in the air.

Kevin's smirk faltered as he leaned forward, curiosity piqued. "Oh? And what would that be?"

I took a deep breath, drawing strength from the knowledge that I was standing on solid ground. "I overheard you planning with someone from—" I paused for dramatic effect, "—a competing firm, discussing how to steal our project idea."

Gasps echoed around the table, the shock evident on every face. Kevin's expression darkened, his façade slipping as he tried to regain control of the room. "That's a serious accusation," he snapped, though I could see the unease creeping into his voice.

"I wouldn't say it if I didn't have proof." My heart raced as I glanced at my laptop, knowing I had the emails saved, along with timestamps and details of their plans. The atmosphere was electric, a palpable tension that had everyone on edge.

"Why don't you enlighten us then? Or are you just throwing out accusations to distract from your own shortcomings?" Kevin's words dripped with condescension, but my determination didn't waver.

"Let's not deflect here, Kevin," I replied, leaning in closer, locking eyes with him. "The truth is, I've worked too hard to let someone like you undermine everything I've accomplished. You may think you can play these games, but I'm not backing down."

Ethan's hand brushed against mine, a silent promise of support, grounding me amidst the chaos. I took another steadying breath, the courage swirling within me bolstered by his unwavering presence.

The tension escalated, voices rising as my colleagues exchanged incredulous glances. I could see them weighing the options, contemplating whether to side with the person who had consistently belittled my contributions or the one who had taken a stand.

"Enough!" The shout came from a corner of the table. It was our supervisor, an imposing figure who commanded respect with her no-nonsense attitude. "We will not have this kind of behavior in my office. If you have evidence, present it, or we will move on to the next agenda item."

The room fell silent, eyes darting between me and Kevin, the air thick with anticipation. This was it. I opened my laptop and began to pull up the evidence, each click echoing like a countdown, the stakes rising with each passing second. I felt the heat of the spotlight on me, and with every detail I revealed, I could sense the shift in the room. The tide was turning.

"Here," I said, my voice rising in confidence as I displayed the incriminating emails, the plans for the project laid bare before my colleagues. "Kevin was in discussions with a competitor, trying to share our ideas for their own gain."

The collective gasp echoed around the table, the disbelief palpable. I watched as Kevin's expression shifted from smug confidence to a cold fury, his facade crumbling like a house of cards. My colleagues shifted uncomfortably, their loyalties visibly teetering.

"This is absurd! You can't just accuse me of—" Kevin spluttered, but the evidence was laid out before him, the truth hanging like a guillotine.

Ethan's grip tightened around my hand, a silent acknowledgment that I had stepped into a territory where I would not back down. I could feel the adrenaline coursing through me, fueling my resolve as I faced down the very person who had tried to sabotage my work. In that moment, surrounded by a storm of tension, I realized I was no longer that timid girl hiding in the background; I was a force to be reckoned with, ready to claim my space and demand the respect I deserved.

The silence that followed my revelation stretched across the room, thick enough to slice with a knife. The flickering fluorescent lights overhead seemed to blink in slow motion, each heartbeat resonating in my ears like a drum signaling a battle. Kevin's face turned a shade of crimson that could only be matched by the hot flush creeping up my own neck, but I stood firm, the tremor in my voice long gone. I had crossed a line, but it felt exhilarating to be on the offensive.

"Really? You think those emails prove anything?" he sneered, his bravado a thin veil over his mounting panic. "This is nothing but a desperate ploy to distract from your shortcomings. Maybe you should focus on doing your job instead of whining."

"I've never heard whining that sounded so much like the truth," I shot back, my sarcasm sharper than ever. "But what would you know about honesty, Kevin? Your ego's already taken up all the space for that."

Around the table, my colleagues exchanged glances, their expressions a mixture of disbelief and intrigue. A murmur of agreement rippled through the group, and I could see the tide shifting in my favor. The tension in the air crackled like static, a palpable shift that signaled something more than just the end of a meeting.

"Let's take a look, shall we?" Our supervisor's voice cut through the charged atmosphere, authoritative yet curious. She leaned in closer to the screen, her brow furrowed as she read the contents of the emails displayed before us. "If what you're saying is true, this is a serious breach of trust. We can't tolerate this kind of behavior in our team."

Kevin's composure unraveled further, and I could see the wheels turning in his mind as he scrambled for a counterattack. "This is absurd! You're all taking her side based on flimsy accusations and a little bit of email digging?" His tone grew desperate, the bravado evaporating into thin air. "What about the hard work I've done? What about the contributions I've made to this project?"

"Contributions that, might I remind you, have been undermined by your own actions," I countered, my voice steady. "If you spent less time trying to sabotage me and more time collaborating with the team, we wouldn't be in this situation."

"Are you sure it's sabotage, or are you just not as good at your job as you thought?" Kevin snapped, his frustration morphing into aggression, but I could see the glimmers of doubt in the eyes of our colleagues.

Before I could respond, Ethan stood up, his tall frame casting a shadow over Kevin. "You're not just undermining her work; you're undermining the integrity of our entire team. What you're doing isn't just unprofessional—it's unethical."

The words hung in the air, and for a brief moment, Kevin faltered, the walls closing in around him. The gravity of what he had done was finally dawning on him.

As the meeting wrapped up, my heart raced, the adrenaline pumping through my veins like wildfire. I could feel the eyes of my colleagues on me, some glinting with admiration, others with lingering doubt. I hadn't just defended myself; I had taken a stand for the entire team, pushing back against the toxicity that Kevin had tried to cultivate. I stepped outside the conference room, hoping to catch my breath, but the hallway felt suffocating, as if the very walls were closing in.

"Hey, that was incredible," Ethan said, his voice breaking through the whirlwind of my thoughts. I turned to see him leaning against the wall, arms crossed, a grin spreading across his face that made my heart flutter. "You were like a lioness defending her territory."

I laughed, the tension melting away slightly as I soaked in his praise. "I guess it's nice to know my roaring is louder than Kevin's barking," I replied, still riding the high of adrenaline.

"But you know this isn't over," Ethan cautioned, his expression turning serious. "Kevin won't take this lying down. He'll retaliate, and we need to be prepared for whatever he might throw at us."

"Then let him try," I said defiantly, my spirit igniting again. "I'm not backing down. He may think he can scare me, but I've fought too hard to let someone like him dictate my worth. I'm ready to defend what I've built."

Just as I was feeling on top of the world, the ground beneath me shifted once more. Kevin stormed out of the conference room, fury etched across his features, followed closely by our supervisor. "You better watch your back!" he shouted, his voice echoing through the hallway. "This isn't over, and I will make sure everyone knows just how incompetent you are. You think you're safe? You're mistaken."

I could feel the blood rush to my head, a mix of anger and fear swirling within me. "What's he planning?" I whispered to Ethan, but his eyes narrowed, a shadow of worry crossing his face.

"I don't know, but I don't trust him. We need to be vigilant. He's cornered now, and cornered animals are the most dangerous," he replied, his voice low and urgent.

Suddenly, the sound of shuffling footsteps caught my attention, and I turned to see our supervisor walking back toward us, a grave look on her face. "We need to talk," she said, her tone serious. "There's something you both need to know."

I exchanged a glance with Ethan, confusion rippling between us. My heart raced as we followed her to her office, dread pooling in my stomach. Whatever was coming next, I could sense it would shake the very foundation of what we had built.

"Sit," she instructed, closing the door behind us with a definitive click. The atmosphere shifted, and my pulse quickened as the weight of her words loomed like a dark cloud overhead. "I've received some concerning information about Kevin. It seems he's been in discussions not just with our competitor but with other parties who have a vested interest in sabotaging our project."

"What?!" I gasped, the gravity of her statement crashing down on me like a tidal wave.

"Yes," she continued, her gaze steady and unyielding. "We need to prepare for the fallout. This could escalate quickly, and I want you both to be aware of the possible implications."

Ethan and I exchanged worried glances, the implications of her words spiraling into a vortex of uncertainty. What did Kevin have planned, and how far was he willing to go to destroy what we had worked for?

Before we could gather our thoughts, the door swung open again, and the intern from the next department rushed in, breathless. "You need to see this! Kevin's put out an urgent memo," she panted, her face pale and strained.

My heart dropped as she handed over a printout, the bold letters screaming of betrayal and upheaval. I glanced down, dread pooling in my stomach as I read the words: "Project Rebranding: A New Vision, A New Direction."

The memo outlined a complete overhaul of our project, crediting Kevin as the mastermind behind the shift, completely undermining everything I had contributed. The world around me blurred, and I felt as if the ground had fallen out from beneath my feet.

"Kevin's going to try and take the whole thing for himself," I murmured, disbelief washing over me.

Ethan's jaw clenched as he took the memo from my hands, scanning it with narrowed eyes. "He's going to try to steal everything we've worked for. We need to act fast before this gets out of hand."

But as I looked back at our supervisor, her face grim and contemplative, I couldn't shake the feeling that this was just the beginning of a far more dangerous game. The stakes were rising, and I knew we were in for a fight that would test everything we believed in. I had stood up against Kevin once, but now, with the threat of everything I cared about hanging in the balance, it felt like the real battle had just begun.

Chapter 7: Code Red

Fueled by adrenaline, I moved through the dimly lit office like a phantom, my heart racing as I sifted through a mountain of documents scattered across my desk. The fluorescent lights flickered intermittently, casting shadows that danced ominously on the walls. Kevin's emails glared back at me from the screen, a tapestry of arrogance and entitlement woven into every word. Each click of the mouse felt like a countdown to a confrontation I both craved and dreaded. I was poised on the edge of a precipice, ready to leap but reluctant to look down.

As I scanned the messages, my fingers trembled slightly. They held the evidence I needed: inappropriate remarks, manipulation of figures, and a blatant disregard for company policy. The realization that I had proof against someone who had belittled me for far too long sent a rush of exhilaration through me. I could finally take control of my narrative, strip away the power Kevin had wielded like a sword over my head. But as the initial thrill began to fade, a heavy blanket of uncertainty settled over my shoulders. Was I really prepared to destroy him? A career could be shattered in an instant, and despite his arrogance, I hesitated.

In the stillness of the office, I replayed the countless times Kevin had dismissed my ideas in meetings, his condescending smirk echoing in my mind. It was if I could still feel the sting of his words, sharp and cutting like the edge of a finely honed blade. The internal conflict was almost unbearable, and I could feel my stomach knotting with unease. How could I hold this man accountable for his actions without losing a piece of my own soul in the process?

"Hey, are you alright?" Ethan's voice broke through my thoughts, gentle yet steady, as he leaned against the doorway. His casual demeanor contrasted sharply with the turmoil swirling inside me. He was my anchor, always there when the waves of doubt threatened to drag me under. I sighed, running a hand through my hair in a futile attempt to push back the mounting anxiety.

"I'm just... working on something," I said, my voice coming out far weaker than I intended. "It's about Kevin."

Ethan's brow furrowed, and he stepped inside, shutting the door behind him. "I know he's been difficult. But you're not going to do something rash, are you?"

I shook my head, frustration bubbling beneath the surface. "No, I just... I have evidence. I could report him, Ethan. I could bring him down."

The room felt charged, and the air thickened with unspoken tension. Ethan crossed his arms, studying me with a look that made me feel both seen and vulnerable. "And what will that accomplish? Will it make you feel better?"

"I want to make him pay for how he's treated me. For how he treats everyone!" My voice raised slightly, fueled by the memories of his dismissive laughter, the way he'd roll his eyes at me as if I were a child throwing a tantrum.

"I get that. But you have to ask yourself if that's the right thing to do. Are you sure you want to be the one to pull the trigger?"

His words were a cold splash of reality, forcing me to take a breath and really think. What did I want? Justice? Closure? Or was it revenge dressed up as righteousness? I turned back to my screen, the emails glowing ominously, and the answer seemed to loom larger than life.

"Maybe I just want to show him that I'm not afraid of him anymore," I murmured, almost to myself. "I want him to know that I'm not the scared little girl he thinks I am."

Ethan moved closer, a thoughtful expression softening his features. "You're not. But remember, strength isn't just about confrontation. It's about choosing your battles wisely. You're better than him, and you know it. But there's a fine line between standing up for yourself and becoming the very thing you despise."

I met his gaze, the intensity of his blue eyes grounding me in the moment. "You're right. I don't want to become a monster to defeat one."

The corners of his mouth quirked up, a hint of pride in his smile. "Good. So what's the plan?"

As we discussed my options, clarity emerged from the fog. I needed to bring the evidence forward, but I wouldn't be the lone warrior. I would present it to our manager, with Ethan by my side. Together, we could ensure that our concerns were heard without me stepping too far into the shadowy realm of vengeance.

The next day, we scheduled a meeting with our manager, each minute crawling by as we prepared ourselves. I could feel the weight of the evidence in my hands, heavy and tangible, a paradox of power and fear.

When the moment finally arrived, I stepped into the conference room with Ethan beside me, his presence a steady reassurance against the storm brewing in my chest. I took a deep breath, filling my lungs with the scent of polished wood and fresh coffee, and faced the manager.

"Thank you for meeting with us," I began, my voice steady but soft. "We have something important to discuss."

The air grew thick with tension, and I felt every heartbeat as I laid out the details of Kevin's misconduct. My words flowed, supported by Ethan's silent strength, and I could almost see the weight of the truth settle around us like an invisible cloak. Kevin would be held accountable, and I would stand tall in the aftermath, not as a vengeful spirit but as a woman reclaiming her power.

As the discussion unfolded, I noticed Kevin lurking just outside the glass doors, his expression darkening as he caught sight of us. There was a fire in my chest, ignited by the knowledge that I was no longer afraid. I turned my back to him, focusing on the conversation, allowing Ethan's quiet confidence to anchor me through the storm.

The conference room hummed with an uneasy energy as I faced my manager, the air thick with anticipation. The fluorescent lights overhead flickered, casting a harsh glare on the polished table where my trembling hands rested. Ethan sat next to me, his presence a steady reminder that I wasn't alone. He had this way of keeping the chaos at bay, as if the world outside those glass walls could not reach us.

"I appreciate you both taking the time to meet today," my manager began, his voice smooth but firm. I could tell he sensed the weight of what we were about to disclose. I took a deep breath, the scent of freshly brewed coffee mingling with the tension in the air. It was now or never.

"Thank you for seeing us, Dave," I said, channeling every ounce of confidence I could muster. "We have some serious concerns regarding Kevin's conduct."

Ethan's gaze flicked to mine, a subtle nod of encouragement. I plunged forward, recounting the details of my findings with a clarity that surprised me. Each word felt like a carefully constructed brick in a wall of integrity I was building. I laid out the evidence meticulously, detailing the manipulation of figures and the inappropriate remarks, ensuring that every piece of information was clear and concise.

As I spoke, I could see the shift in Dave's demeanor. His brows furrowed, and the lightness in the room dissipated. I could almost feel the weight of Kevin's impending reaction lurking just beyond the door. "This is serious," he finally said, his voice lowered. "We can't have this kind of behavior affecting the team."

The air felt electric as I continued to lay everything bare. It was cathartic, an exhilarating release of all the pent-up frustration I had held for so long. I had imagined this moment countless times—my chance to stand up, to be seen, and to demand accountability. Yet, as I concluded my presentation, a creeping doubt gnawed at me. Was I truly prepared for the consequences that would follow?

A sudden knock interrupted my thoughts, and Kevin strode into the room, his confidence palpable. "What's going on in here?" His tone was casual, but the glint in his eyes betrayed a sense of danger. The shift in atmosphere was instantaneous; he sensed the storm brewing, and I could practically hear the gears in his mind turning.

I glanced at Ethan, who remained stoic beside me, but I could feel the tension radiating off him in waves. "Kevin," I began, my voice steadier than I felt. "We were just discussing some feedback about your recent conduct."

"Feedback?" He laughed, the sound sharp and mocking. "You think you're going to talk to me about feedback?" His gaze moved from me to Ethan, a calculated assessment. "Did you put her up to this, Ethan? We both know she's not capable of handling anything without your support."

The jab struck deep, and for a brief moment, I felt the wind knocked out of me. But then I remembered Ethan's words, the quiet strength he had provided. "I don't need anyone to handle this, Kevin. I'm more than capable of standing up for myself."

His smile faltered, replaced by a scowl that could curdle milk. "You should know your place, and it's certainly not here in this meeting."

"Actually, my place is right here," I countered, feeling a surge of adrenaline. "And I'm not going anywhere until I've made my point clear."

Ethan shifted slightly, the intensity of the situation wrapping around us like a live wire. "Kevin, we have serious evidence against your behavior," he stated calmly, his voice a grounding force. "You can't intimidate us into silence."

Kevin's demeanor changed, the playful arrogance replaced by a cold, calculating demeanor. "You think you can take me down? Do you have any idea who I am?"

"Someone who is about to learn that actions have consequences," I shot back, my heart racing.

Dave intervened, his tone firm. "This isn't a game, Kevin. We have a responsibility to this team, and your actions have jeopardized that."

For a moment, silence enveloped the room. Kevin's face flushed with anger, and I could almost see the wheels turning in his head, formulating a retaliation. "You're making a huge mistake," he warned, his voice low and menacing.

"Or maybe you're the one making the mistake by not understanding that your time is up," I replied, my voice steady despite the tremors of fear coursing through me.

The confrontation hung in the air, thick and suffocating. It was as if time had paused, each heartbeat echoing louder than the last. I braced myself for the fallout, knowing that no matter what came next, I had crossed a line that couldn't be uncrossed.

Kevin's eyes narrowed, and I could see the flicker of a threat in their depths. "You'll regret this," he said slowly, each word dripping with venom. "You think you're safe here? You think anyone will believe you over me?"

"I guess we'll find out, won't we?" I replied, adrenaline coursing through my veins like wildfire. I felt a sense of power wash over me, eclipsing the fear.

With a dismissive wave of his hand, Kevin turned and stalked out of the room, his footsteps echoing down the hallway like a warning.

The moment he left, a wave of relief washed over me, quickly followed by a realization of what lay ahead. I had stepped into uncharted territory, and the stakes were higher than I could have imagined. I exchanged glances with Ethan, who offered a slight smile—a mixture of pride and concern. "You handled that well."

"I can't believe I just did that," I whispered, feeling the adrenaline ebbing away, leaving behind a mix of exhaustion and exhilaration.

"Sometimes, the hardest part is just showing up and being yourself," Ethan replied, his gaze steady. "You took a stand today, and that's what matters."

Just then, Dave cleared his throat, regaining our attention. "I'll need to conduct an official investigation into this matter, which means we'll need your full cooperation moving forward."

I nodded, still processing the whirlwind of events. "Of course. I'll provide everything I have."

"Good. I appreciate your courage," he said, a hint of respect shining in his eyes. "This company needs employees who are willing to stand up for what's right."

As we left the conference room, I could feel the heaviness of the moment settle around me. I had taken a leap into the unknown, and while I felt proud, I was acutely aware that a storm was brewing. Kevin's fury wouldn't go unchecked, and I braced myself for the repercussions that were sure to follow.

"Whatever happens next, we face it together," Ethan said quietly, placing a reassuring hand on my shoulder.

His warmth was a beacon amid the uncertainty, grounding me in the chaos that lay ahead. Together, we would navigate the aftermath of this confrontation, and I felt a surge of determination rise within me. This was only the beginning, and I was ready to fight.

The atmosphere shifted as we stepped back into the main office, the buzz of conversations and the click of keyboards starkly contrasting the weight of our previous encounter. I felt like a ship navigating turbulent waters, the adrenaline still thrumming through my veins. Colleagues glanced up, some whispering, their eyes flickering between Ethan and me, the tension palpable. I knew Kevin wouldn't take our confrontation lying down; he was far too proud for that.

"Hey, you two! Did I just see Kevin storming out?" Jess, a bubbly co-worker with a knack for dramatic flair, approached, her curiosity evident in her wide eyes. "What happened?"

Ethan stepped in smoothly. "Just a little team meeting about improving communication. You know how it is." His smile was easy, but I could feel the unspoken truth hanging in the air, heavy and ominous. Jess frowned, unconvinced, but thankfully didn't press further.

"Let me know if you need backup," she chirped, her usual lightness not quite breaking through the tension.

"Thanks, Jess," I replied, forcing a smile that felt like it might crack. I wanted to believe that we could shrug this off, but the shadows of doubt loomed large. I walked toward my desk, and Ethan followed, his presence a comforting weight beside me.

"Do you think we did the right thing?" I asked, my voice barely above a whisper. I could feel my heart rate picking up again, a relentless drumbeat reminding me of everything that was at stake.

"Absolutely," he replied, his tone firm. "But it's going to get bumpy, especially if Kevin decides to retaliate. Just keep your guard up."

I nodded, grateful for his reassurance yet acutely aware of the unease gnawing at my insides. The office was alive with the sounds of ringing phones and quiet chatter, yet I felt oddly isolated in the midst of it all. I resumed my work, but the words blurred together on the screen, a muddled mess of data that felt increasingly insignificant compared to the storm brewing around us.

The afternoon dragged on, each minute stretching into what felt like an eternity. I couldn't shake the sensation that Kevin was lurking, waiting to strike back. Just as I settled into a rhythm, a notification pinged on my phone. A message from Ethan appeared on the screen: Meet me in the break room. Now.

My stomach flipped, and I quickly stood, making my way through the maze of desks. The break room, usually a haven for casual banter and coffee breaks, felt charged with urgency as I entered. Ethan was leaning against the counter, arms crossed, his expression serious.

"I just talked to Dave," he said, his voice low. "Kevin's already spinning a story. He claims we're misinterpreting his actions, painting it as a misunderstanding."

My pulse quickened. "He wouldn't dare! Everyone knows what he's like."

Ethan shook his head. "That's the problem. He's been here longer than both of us combined. He knows how to work this place. If he can convince Dave that we're overreacting..."

I felt a wave of frustration wash over me. "But we have the evidence! How can he possibly turn this around?"

Ethan's gaze softened as he met my eyes. "We just need to be prepared for what's coming. Kevin's got a reputation, but he's not invincible. We're not alone in this. I've got your back, and you know others will, too."

"Yeah, but it still feels like we're standing on the edge of a cliff," I replied, anxiety threading through my words. "What if he drags us down with him?"

Before he could answer, a loud voice echoed from the hallway. "Where are you two hiding?" It was Kevin, his tone dripping with feigned cheerfulness. My heart raced as I exchanged a glance with Ethan, the unspoken understanding between us palpable.

"We should probably—" I started, but the door swung open before I could finish. Kevin sauntered in, a façade of confidence plastered on his face, but I could sense the tension crackling in the air.

"Just wanted to check in on my favorite pair of whistleblowers!" he said, the words laced with sarcasm. "I hope you're not plotting anything sinister in here."

Ethan straightened, his posture shifting into something more confrontational. "Just discussing the company's direction, Kevin. You know how it is."

"Sure, of course," he replied, his smile unfaltering. "But I think it's time you both remember where your loyalties should lie. I've done a lot for this team, and I won't let a couple of ungrateful upstarts tarnish my reputation."

My throat tightened as Kevin's gaze fixed on me, the threat lurking beneath his words unmistakable. "Just remember, the truth is subjective, and perception can be a very powerful tool."

With that, he turned on his heel and left, the door slamming shut behind him. The air was thick with tension, and I could feel my heart pounding in my chest.

"What was that about?" I whispered, my voice barely above a breath.

Ethan ran a hand through his hair, clearly agitated. "He's trying to intimidate us. We can't let him. This is our moment to stand firm."

Before I could respond, the office intercom crackled to life, cutting through the silence. "Attention, everyone. We have an urgent all-hands meeting in the conference room. Please gather immediately."

A sense of dread washed over me. "What do you think this is about?"

Ethan shrugged, but I could see the worry etched on his face. "Whatever it is, we need to stick together."

We moved quickly to the conference room, the murmurs of our colleagues echoing in the hallway. The atmosphere was tense, anticipation hanging like a heavy fog as we filed into the room. Dave stood at the front, his expression grave.

"Thank you for gathering so quickly," he began, scanning the room with a serious look. "I regret to inform you that there have been some serious allegations regarding workplace conduct. We are conducting an investigation into these claims, and I expect full cooperation from everyone involved."

The room erupted in murmurs, shock rippling through the crowd. My stomach sank as I realized the implications of his words. Kevin had wasted no time in launching a preemptive strike. I glanced at Ethan, who was now tense beside me, his jaw set in determination.

"This isn't just about us anymore," I whispered, fear creeping into my voice. "He's trying to drag the whole team into this."

"Stay calm," Ethan replied, his voice steady, but I could see the concern mirrored in his eyes. "We'll face this together. Just stick to the truth."

As Dave continued to outline the procedures for the investigation, I felt a growing sense of dread. The walls seemed to close in around me, and I couldn't shake the feeling that Kevin was orchestrating something far more sinister than we had anticipated.

Then, just as Dave finished his remarks, the conference room door burst open. Kevin strode in, his expression triumphant, an unexpected smirk plastered on his face.

"Sorry to interrupt," he said, his tone dripping with condescension. "But I believe I have some information that might change the course of this little meeting."

The room fell silent, all eyes on him, the tension rising to an unbearable peak. My heart raced as the implications of his presence settled heavily in the air. I could feel the ground shifting beneath me, and in that moment, I understood that this was far from over. Kevin was ready to fight back, and I braced myself for the storm that was about to unfold.

Chapter 8: The Fall-Out

The air in the office was thick with a tension that buzzed like a swarm of agitated bees. After I had unmasked Kevin's deceit, the atmosphere shifted dramatically. Conversations that had once flickered with mundane pleasantries now crackled with excited murmurs. My colleagues, their eyes wide with disbelief, darted glances my way, whispers trailing like shadows in their wake. It was exhilarating and disorienting all at once, the feeling of being at the center of a tempest I had unwittingly unleashed.

Kevin, once the undisputed king of the cubicle jungle, was now a furious tempest himself. His face, normally a mask of confidence, was twisted with rage and humiliation. I had never seen someone unravel so quickly, his bravado stripped away like peeling paint on a long-abandoned building. He shouted, hurling accusations that ricocheted off the walls, the echoes of his anger bouncing around the office like a pinball, leaving everyone breathless.

"Who do you think you are?" he spat at me, his voice dripping with venom. "You think this is a game? You'll regret this."

I stood my ground, heart hammering in my chest, a curious blend of fear and defiance coursing through my veins. I wasn't the timid girl who had stumbled into this corporate world; I had taken a stand, and though guilt gnawed at the edges of my mind, I couldn't help but feel a flicker of pride amidst the chaos. It was like standing on the precipice of a high cliff, feeling the wind whip around me, daring me to jump.

Ethan, my steadfast ally, had slipped into the background, observing the fallout with a mixture of concern and admiration. His dark eyes, filled with a blend of sympathy and pride, met mine across the room, and in that moment, I felt a connection stronger than the turbulent atmosphere surrounding us. He had always seen me as more than the awkward girl lost in a sea of polished professionals, but now I was thrust into the spotlight, and I wasn't quite sure how to handle it.

The day stretched on, an endless series of conversations buzzing around me like a hive of honeybees. I could hear snippets of gossip floating through the air, each phrase punctuated with disbelief and awe. "Did you see her? She actually stood up to him!" "I can't believe she did that—who knew she had it in her?" Each comment wrapped around me, and for a moment, it felt as if I had stepped into a different version of myself, one who was brave and unyielding.

But as the excitement faded, a heavy weight settled on my shoulders. Was I really brave, or merely impulsive? Was my defiance a sign of growth, or an act of desperation? I couldn't shake the image of Kevin's enraged face, the way his demeanor had crumbled under the weight of truth. As I watched my colleagues celebrate my small victory, the hollow feeling in my chest deepened.

The relentless ping of the email notifications on my computer screen brought me back to reality. My promotion had come through, a shiny reward dangling before me like a carrot on a stick. But I couldn't relish it. Instead, it felt like a bitter reminder of the cost at which it had come. The walls of the office seemed to close in, and for the first time, I questioned the authenticity of the applause surrounding me. Did they truly celebrate my bravery, or was it simply the thrill of the drama that captivated them?

As the sun dipped lower in the sky, casting a warm glow through the office windows, I found a moment of solitude in the break room. The hum of the coffee machine was a comforting backdrop as I poured myself a cup, my hands trembling slightly. My reflection stared back at me from the stainless steel surface, and I barely recognized the woman I saw there. There was a resilience in her eyes that hadn't been there before, but beneath it lay the uncertainty that twisted in my gut.

"Hey," Ethan's voice broke through the haze, warm and inviting. He stepped into the break room, leaning casually against the doorframe. "You okay?"

I managed a smile that didn't quite reach my eyes. "Just contemplating the meaning of life and whether I'll need a new wardrobe now that I'm a big shot." The sarcasm tumbled out, a shield to mask my inner turmoil.

He chuckled softly, stepping closer, his presence a comforting anchor. "You did something incredible today. You stood up to him. That's not just big; it's monumental."

I took a sip of the bitter brew, feeling the heat seep through me. "Or it's just a moment of impulsive bravado. I can't help but feel a bit guilty, you know? What if I've ruined his life?"

"His life was already on a downward spiral long before you entered the picture," Ethan replied, his tone turning serious. "You did what needed to be done. You're not responsible for his choices."

"But what about us?" I blurted, my voice barely above a whisper. "Is what we have just a reaction to all this? Or is it something real?"

Ethan paused, the intensity of his gaze holding mine captive. "I want to believe it's real. You've always been more than just the awkward girl at the office. You've got strength and heart, and that's drawn me to you."

The weight of his words settled around us, a shared understanding threading the air. Just as I was about to speak, the sharp ring of the office phone shattered the moment, pulling us back into the chaos that awaited us.

And just like that, the world resumed its relentless pace, leaving me grappling with questions that spun through my mind like leaves caught in a whirlwind. I had fought for myself, but at what cost? My heart raced, caught between the thrilling realization of my newfound strength and the uncertain depths of my evolving relationship with

Ethan. Would I find my footing in this tumultuous world, or would I be swept away by the currents I had set in motion?

The following days at the office unfolded like a surreal dream, where the ordinary had been swept away, replaced by a whirlwind of fervent chatter and clandestine glances. Each morning, as I navigated the maze of cubicles, the air buzzed with energy, charged like a live wire. My promotion had been the spark, igniting an inferno of curiosity and envy that crackled through the atmosphere, transforming my previously mundane existence into something akin to a soap opera.

My colleagues, who once treated me like a piece of furniture barely worth noticing, now approached me with a mix of reverence and caution. They'd gather in huddled clusters, their voices dipping to conspiratorial whispers when I passed by. I could almost hear the unspoken thoughts swirling around me: "How could she? What's next?" It was as if I had been painted into the center of an elaborate tableau, my previous anonymity stripped away, leaving me feeling simultaneously powerful and exposed.

Ethan continued to be my anchor amid this chaos. Each day, he sought me out for lunch, drawing me away from the gossip mill and into a world where I could breathe without the weight of expectation pressing down. Our conversations flowed easily, punctuated by laughter that danced lightly above the unease that had settled in my chest. But even in those moments of levity, I sensed an undercurrent of tension that gnawed at me. Was he truly as supportive as he seemed, or was there a deeper question lurking just beneath the surface?

"Another day, another wave of 'congratulations,'" I said, rolling my eyes as we settled into our usual corner of the café, the smell of fresh coffee mingling with the aroma of baked goods. "I half expect someone to give me a crown and start a parade."

Ethan chuckled, the sound warm and genuine. "You know, I think you'd pull off a crown quite well. Maybe a tiara? I can see it now: Queen of the Office."

"Only if you're my royal jester," I shot back, a smile breaking through my doubt. "Just promise not to trip while doing your silly dance."

He leaned back, feigning a deep thought. "I'd never trip—my dignity is on the line. But I can juggle if that would help."

The banter was a sweet respite from the turmoil that churned in my mind. Yet, as we shared our meal, I couldn't shake the feeling that this new dynamic between us had shifted from light-hearted to something heavier. With each laugh, I wondered if the laughter was a distraction from the reality of our situation.

Later that afternoon, I returned to my desk, only to be met by a scene that made my heart sink. A group of employees had gathered around Kevin's workstation, their expressions a mixture of disbelief and pity. I stood frozen for a moment, the tightness in my chest expanding as I remembered the fury and humiliation that had erupted just days earlier. My stomach twisted as I walked closer, curiosity and guilt warring within me.

"What's going on?" I asked, forcing my voice to remain steady despite the clenching of my insides.

Jessica, one of the more outspoken members of our team, glanced back at me, her eyes wide. "He's been called into HR. They said it's a 'serious matter.'"

A wave of sympathy washed over me, though I knew I should feel otherwise. Kevin's anger had been misplaced and wild, but there was a part of me that still regretted how far things had gone. It felt cruel, almost predatory, to stand by and watch his unraveling. The office was buzzing with speculation, the whispers turning sharper with each passing moment.

"Do you think they'll fire him?" another colleague asked, her voice barely masking the excitement behind her words.

"Good riddance if they do," Jessica replied, her tone slicing through the tension like a knife. "He was a tyrant. I always knew he'd get what was coming to him."

A knot tightened in my throat. "Isn't that a bit harsh?" I ventured, feeling like an outsider in a cruel game. "He's still a person."

"Yeah, but he treated people like dirt," she shot back, her expression hardening. "What goes around comes around."

As I stepped back from the crowd, feeling more isolated than ever, I heard a familiar voice behind me. "Hey, you okay?" Ethan's concern was palpable, grounding me once more.

"Just witnessing the aftermath of my actions," I said, a bitter taste creeping into my words. "It feels surreal."

His expression softened, and he gestured for us to step away from the chaos. We found a quiet corner, away from prying eyes and hushed voices. "You're not responsible for his choices. You did the right thing by exposing the truth."

"Maybe," I replied, biting my lip. "But I didn't anticipate this fallout. Watching him fall apart...it doesn't sit right with me. Was I supposed to feel like a hero?"

Ethan studied me for a moment, the weight of his gaze digging deeper than I expected. "You're not a hero, and you're not a villain. You're just someone who stood up for what's right. That's worth something."

"Is it, though?" I felt raw and vulnerable, the truth of my emotions spilling out like a broken dam. "What if it turns out this is all I'm capable of? Just making a mess of things?"

"Stop." His voice was firm, cutting through my spiral of self-doubt. "You're not making a mess. You're learning, just like the rest of us. And if you're worried about being just the 'awkward girl,' let me remind you that 'awkward' can be pretty damn brave when it needs to be."

His words hung in the air, a lifeline thrown amidst my stormy thoughts. I appreciated his kindness, but there was an unsettling truth in my heart. The more I unraveled this new chapter of my life, the more I feared that my identity was built on the remnants of others' failures rather than my own merit. What if Ethan's affection for me was rooted in pity or a sense of shared struggle? The notion twisted within me, and I felt a sudden surge of frustration.

"Why do you even care?" I asked, the words escaping before I could reel them back. "You could have anyone in this office, but you're here with me, trapped in my melodrama."

Ethan's expression shifted, an edge of determination flashing in his eyes. "Because I want to be here. I see you for who you really are, not just a 'victim' or 'hero.' I want to know the real you, flaws and all."

"Flaws and all, huh?" I replied, a teasing lilt creeping back into my voice. "That's a bold offer. You might end up regretting it."

"I'm counting on it," he said with a wink, and for a moment, the heaviness that hung in the air felt a little lighter.

As I stood there, caught between the whirlwind of gossip and the comforting presence of Ethan, I began to realize that perhaps I was more than just the awkward girl. I was someone willing to confront the chaos of my life, to navigate the uncertainty ahead. And with that thought, a small spark of hope ignited within me.

The weeks rolled on, and with each passing day, the echoes of that chaotic confrontation with Kevin faded into the background noise of office life. Yet, the residue of that moment clung to me like a stubborn stain, resistant to the efforts of everyday routine. I tried to shake off the guilt that sometimes curled around my thoughts like a cold fog, wrapping tighter when the laughter in the break room turned to murmurs about Kevin's imminent fate.

Ethan remained steadfast at my side, his easy smile a reassuring constant amid the shifting dynamics. He had a way of making the ordinary feel extraordinary, transforming even the most mundane lunch breaks into moments worth savoring. As we settled into our routine, our conversations danced from light-hearted banter to deeper musings about life, dreams, and the uncertainties that loomed ahead like shadows just beyond our reach.

"Have you thought about what you want to do next?" he asked one afternoon, leaning back in his chair, his gaze steady and curious.

I stirred my salad, the crisp lettuce mingling with a tangy vinaigrette, and contemplated his question. "Honestly? I'm not sure. I thought I'd finally found my footing, but now everything feels... unstable."

Ethan nodded, understanding glimmering in his eyes. "Change can be disorienting. It's like standing on shifting sand. One minute you're secure, and the next, you're scrambling to find solid ground."

"Exactly! And I don't want to be that person who needs a crisis to define herself," I admitted, a hint of frustration seeping into my voice. "What if I'm just the awkward girl who got lucky for a moment?"

"You're more than that," he insisted, his tone earnest. "You stood up to Kevin when no one else would. That's not luck; that's courage."

"Or stupidity," I replied, rolling my eyes. "You know I didn't even think before I acted."

"Sometimes, that's the best way to be." His eyes sparkled with mischief. "You can't overanalyze every decision. Life's too short for that, and I can tell you, it's exhausting."

I couldn't help but chuckle at the picture of Ethan as a philosophical life coach. "So, what's the secret then? Don't think at all?"

"Exactly," he grinned. "Just follow your instincts. Like I do when I order dessert before the main course."

"That's a life philosophy I can get behind," I said, raising my glass in a mock toast.

As laughter faded, a moment of comfortable silence enveloped us, the camaraderie palpable. But the quiet didn't last long. The door to the café swung open, and a commotion spilled in. Jessica rushed in, her face flushed, her eyes wide with urgency.

"You guys won't believe this!" she exclaimed, nearly breathless. "Kevin just got fired!"

The words hung in the air, electrifying the space around us. I felt the weight of that news settle heavily in my chest. "What happened?"

"He flipped out in HR," Jessica said, her excitement barely contained. "They showed him the evidence, and he just lost it. It was wild! He's been escorted out of the building."

I exchanged a glance with Ethan, the initial shock of the news morphing into something deeper. "I didn't think it would come to this," I murmured, the guilt surging back like a tide.

"Hey, this is good news," Ethan encouraged, his expression firm. "You did the right thing. You can't let his consequences weigh you down."

"Right," I agreed half-heartedly, feeling the tangle of emotions knotting in my stomach. As the café buzzed with the latest gossip about Kevin's downfall, I felt more like a spectator than a participant in my own life.

The day dragged on, the usual rhythm of work punctuated by whispers about Kevin's fiery exit. The office had transformed into a stage where everyone played a role in the unfolding drama, and I was uncomfortably aware of my place in it. Each time I entered the break room, conversations halted momentarily, heads turning to me with expressions that ranged from admiration to pity. I tried to ignore the prickling sensation of eyes on me, but it clung like a shadow.

Later that week, as I sat at my desk, buried under a pile of reports, I received an unexpected email from HR. The subject line was ominous: "Important Meeting." My stomach churned at the thought of what they might want. Did they plan to discuss the ramifications of my actions? Had they decided to blame me for Kevin's chaos?

I glanced at Ethan, who was engrossed in his own work. "I got an email from HR," I said, my voice wavering slightly. "I'm not sure what it's about, but it can't be good."

"Don't sweat it," he replied, offering a reassuring smile. "You did what needed to be done. Just be yourself in there."

"Right, the awkward girl who's now under scrutiny," I said, a hint of sarcasm creeping into my voice. "Perfect."

The meeting loomed over me like a dark cloud, and when the time finally arrived, I felt my heart pounding as I walked into the HR office. The room was stark and sterile, all muted colors and uncomfortable chairs that seemed to swallow me whole.

"Thank you for coming," the HR manager said, her tone polite but businesslike. "We wanted to discuss the recent developments and your role in them."

I nodded, trying to appear composed, though my insides felt like a blender set to high speed. "Sure."

"We appreciate your honesty and courage in bringing Kevin's behavior to light," she continued, her gaze steady. "However, we also want to ensure that this office remains a safe and welcoming environment for everyone. There will be changes in management structure moving forward."

"Changes?" I repeated, a sinking feeling taking hold. "What does that mean for my position?"

"There will be an evaluation of all staff roles, including yours," she stated matter-of-factly. "We want to ensure that you are supported in your new responsibilities and given the tools necessary to succeed."

"Tools? Like a toolbox?" I couldn't help but inject some levity into the grim situation, hoping to ease the tension.

Her lips twitched, almost a smile. "Exactly, but not quite in the literal sense. We want to offer mentorship opportunities and resources to help you navigate your promotion effectively."

Relief washed over me, but it was soon swept away by the undercurrents of uncertainty. "So, I'm safe?"

"For now," she said, her tone shifting slightly. "But you will need to navigate a delicate landscape. Kevin's departure has stirred quite the reaction, and you may find some colleagues less than supportive. Not everyone is pleased with the change."

I felt the weight of her words settle like lead in my stomach. I had stepped into the light, but shadows lingered, and not everyone was ready to embrace the new reality.

As I exited the HR office, I caught Ethan's eye across the room. He offered a small, encouraging nod, and I felt the connection between us tighten, an invisible thread woven from shared struggle and newfound strength. But the tension in the air was palpable, and I couldn't shake the feeling that the fallout from Kevin's actions was far from over.

Later that evening, I walked home, the crisp autumn air wrapping around me like a blanket. The leaves crunched underfoot, their colors vibrant against the darkening sky. The beauty of the moment felt almost surreal, a stark contrast to the turmoil swirling in my mind.

Just as I reached my apartment, I noticed something unusual—a dark figure loitering near my door. My heart raced, a chill creeping up my spine. As I approached cautiously, the figure turned, revealing a familiar face. Kevin stood there, his expression a mix of fury and desperation.

"What are you doing here?" I gasped, the realization hitting me like a slap in the face.

"I need to talk," he said, his voice low and urgent. "You have no idea what you've started."

Panic flared within me, and as the evening sky darkened above, I felt the ground beneath me shift once more, plunging me into a world where the rules had changed, and the stakes were higher than ever.

Chapter 9: Love in Unexpected Places

The gala buzzed with the kind of energy that only a room full of bright minds and ambitious dreams could conjure. As I stepped into the softly lit hall, the gentle hum of conversation surrounded me like a warm embrace. Glittering chandeliers cast a golden glow over the sea of elegantly dressed attendees, their laughter and clinking glasses creating a symphony of celebration that tugged at my heart. It was hard to believe that just a few months ago, I had felt like a ghost wandering through my own life, invisible to the world around me. Yet here I was, nestled amidst the crème de la crème of the tech world, ready to watch Ethan unveil a campaign that had consumed his every waking hour.

Draped in a simple yet elegant black dress that hugged my curves just right, I felt like a character pulled from the pages of a romance novel. My hair tumbled down my shoulders in soft waves, a stark contrast to the crisp, minimalist aesthetic of the venue. The dress swished around my legs as I navigated through the crowd, but my heart raced for a different reason: Ethan. Just thinking about him made my cheeks warm. There was something magnetic about his presence, a gravity that pulled me closer with each passing second. He was at the center of the room, effortlessly commanding attention as he mingled with colleagues and potential investors, his eyes sparkling with enthusiasm.

I watched him, captivated by the way he spoke, hands animatedly gesturing as he shared the vision behind our marketing campaign. There was a natural elegance to how he moved through the crowd, his laughter ringing out like music. And then he caught my eye. Our gazes locked, and in that moment, the world around us faded into a soft blur. Time seemed to stretch, allowing me to savor the raw connection we shared. I saw the flicker of recognition in his expression—an acknowledgment of something deeper than just professional admiration.

As the evening unfolded, I meandered through the gala, my heart swelling with pride for Ethan and the remarkable work we had created together. Our campaign wasn't merely a business venture; it was a testament to our late-night brainstorming sessions, the cups of cold coffee left abandoned on our desks, and the laughter that echoed through the office whenever an idea went awry. I felt my cheeks flush as I recalled how many times Ethan had pushed me to voice my opinions, coaxing me from my shell, igniting my confidence in ways I had never thought possible.

Eventually, I found myself at the edge of the room, standing by a large window overlooking the city skyline. The lights twinkled like stars strewn across an indigo canvas, the skyline a silhouette of ambition and hope. It was then that Ethan approached me, a glass of sparkling water in hand. He leaned against the window frame beside me, his presence radiating warmth, effortlessly bringing a smile to my lips.

"Beautiful night, isn't it?" he remarked, glancing out at the shimmering lights. His voice was smooth, like honey sliding over a warm biscuit, making my heart skip a beat.

I turned to him, catching a glimpse of the earnest look in his eyes. "Almost as beautiful as the view," I replied, letting my words hang in the air, feeling bold and flirty all at once.

He chuckled, a low, rich sound that sent pleasant shivers down my spine. "You're too kind. But honestly, I've never felt more alive than I do right now, standing here with you."

The atmosphere between us thickened, electrified by the unsaid words hanging in the air. It was an unexpected kind of tension, the kind that hinted at deeper emotions simmering just beneath the surface. Ethan's gaze shifted from the cityscape to my face, studying me with an intensity that made my heart race. I wondered if he could see through the layers of uncertainty and fear I had cloaked myself in for so long.

"You've always been the brightest star, Natalie," he whispered, his breath warm against the cool night air. The sincerity in his tone melted any remaining barriers I had built around my heart. My breath caught in my throat, and I felt a flutter of hope intertwining with the fear of vulnerability.

Before I could process my emotions, he reached out, brushing a stray hair behind my ear. The simple touch sent a jolt of electricity coursing through me, igniting a warmth that spread from my fingertips to my toes. It was a moment so tender, so intimate, that it felt as though the rest of the world had evaporated, leaving only the two of us suspended in our own universe.

"What if we took a leap together?" I suggested, my voice a soft murmur. The suggestion hung in the air, heavy with potential. I was terrified at the thought of what could happen if we crossed that line, but the yearning inside me demanded that I at least voice the possibility.

Ethan's eyes sparkled with surprise, and then an understanding that sent my heart into a dizzying spin. "Are you sure? Because once we jump, there's no turning back," he replied, a mix of excitement and caution threading through his words.

"I'm ready," I affirmed, surprising myself with the conviction in my tone. "I want to embrace everything—this moment, this life, and whatever it means for us."

With that, the wall I had carefully constructed around my heart began to crumble, brick by fragile brick. The future loomed ahead, wild and unpredictable, but standing there with Ethan, I felt a thrilling sense of possibility unfurling within me. It was a strange dance of hope and fear, yet I realized that the greatest adventures often began with a single step into the unknown.

As the crowd swelled and the music swirled around us, we stood side by side, our hearts beating in rhythm to a melody only we could hear. In that magical moment beneath the glow of the city lights, I felt an exhilarating rush of love blossoming between us, and I knew that I was ready to embrace the unexpected journey ahead.

The evening unfurled like a finely woven tapestry, each thread shimmering with promise and intrigue. As Ethan and I stepped back into the thrumming heart of the gala, the atmosphere crackled with energy. Laughter bubbled around us, interspersed with the sharp clinks of champagne glasses and the hum of animated conversations. Yet, despite the crowd, there was a cocoon of intimacy surrounding us, woven from shared glances and unspoken understanding.

Ethan's earlier words lingered in the air like an intoxicating perfume, pulling me closer to him. I watched as he moved seamlessly through the crowd, engaging with industry leaders and potential clients, his confidence like a magnet drawing everyone in. But it was in those rare moments when our eyes met that I felt the world shrink down to just the two of us—two souls orbiting in a universe of possibility.

"Have you thought about what you want to do next?" Ethan asked, his brow slightly furrowed as he poured another glass of sparkling water. We found a quiet corner, away from the flurry of excitement. I could see the flickering lights reflecting in his deep blue eyes, making them twinkle like the stars above us.

"I mean, aside from making our product the next big thing?" I replied, leaning against the railing, the cool metal grounding me as my heart raced. "I've been thinking about branching out into more creative marketing strategies. Something that makes people feel rather than just see."

Ethan leaned closer, his voice dropping to a conspiratorial whisper. "What about a series of immersive experiences? Something that engages the senses—smell, sound, touch. Imagine a campaign that brings our product to life in ways that people can't just scroll past on their feeds."

"Now you're speaking my language," I grinned, feeling a surge of excitement at the thought. "It's like turning marketing into a sensory art form."

He nodded, clearly enjoying the banter. "You could even incorporate local artists to create unique installations. It would not only promote the product but also support the community."

I laughed softly. "So now I'm an art curator too? I might need a raise for that."

"Consider it a career advancement," he shot back, his smile wide and genuine, illuminating the space around us. "With all your talents, you deserve it. You have a way of making everything sound more enchanting."

In that moment, I felt a rush of affection. The easy way we bounced ideas off one another, the seamless blend of professional respect and personal connection, sent my heart fluttering. This wasn't just a colleague; Ethan was becoming a vital part of my life, weaving himself into the fabric of my everyday thoughts.

Just as I was about to respond, the gala's host took the stage, drawing everyone's attention. The spotlight washed over him, casting dramatic shadows on the walls as he began to unveil the night's highlights. I felt the energy shift in the room, the anticipation palpable as the host introduced our campaign.

I held my breath as Ethan stepped forward, adjusting his tie in a manner that was both endearing and slightly ridiculous. The audience quieted, eager eyes trained on him, and I couldn't help but swell with pride as he began his presentation. The way he spoke, with a perfect mix of enthusiasm and expertise, had the crowd hanging on his every word. It was as if he transformed from a colleague into a commanding figure, owning the stage with ease.

"Tonight," he said, his voice booming across the room, "we're not just unveiling a campaign; we're inviting you into an experience—a journey that captures the essence of our product and how it can transform lives."

I listened, entranced, as he detailed every facet of the campaign with vivid imagery. He spoke of innovation and creativity, infusing every sentence with a passion that was contagious. I could see how the crowd leaned forward, their interest piqued, nodding along with every point he made.

When he finished, the applause erupted like fireworks, a chorus of clapping and cheers that echoed in my heart. Ethan smiled, that boyish grin lighting up his face as he soaked in the well-deserved accolades. I couldn't help but feel a rush of admiration, not just for his talent, but for the way he ignited inspiration in those around him.

As he descended from the stage, he sought me out among the throng of admirers. Our eyes locked, and in that moment, a thousand unspoken words passed between us. I was both proud and envious, wishing I could harness the same kind of energy he exuded so effortlessly.

"You were amazing!" I exclaimed, throwing my arms around him in a spontaneous hug, forgetting the formalities of the evening. "You absolutely lit that stage up."

He laughed, the sound rich and warm, his arms wrapping around me in return. "Thanks, but I had a secret weapon," he said, his voice low as he leaned closer, almost conspiratorial. "I knew you were watching."

Flustered, I pulled back, a teasing smile playing on my lips. "You're laying it on thick now, Ethan. Trying to charm me into giving you a raise?"

He shrugged, that playful glimmer in his eyes. "Can you blame me? I like to reward hard work, and you've been my biggest motivator."

As the night wore on, I found myself pulled into conversations with various attendees, but my heart always returned to Ethan. We exchanged glances and secret smiles across the room, a silent acknowledgment that something special was blossoming between us. But the night took an unexpected turn when a woman approached Ethan. She was impeccably dressed in a sleek red gown, her dark hair cascading over one shoulder. I felt an inexplicable flutter of insecurity as she began chatting with him, leaning in closer, her laughter ringing out like bells.

I told myself it was silly to feel threatened—Ethan was clearly a man of charisma and charm, drawing people in like moths to a flame. Yet, watching them from a distance, I couldn't shake the unease creeping into my thoughts. What if this was just a fleeting moment for him, a distraction before he moved on to something—or someone—better?

But just as my insecurities threatened to take over, Ethan turned away from the woman and walked toward me, his expression thoughtful yet determined. "You ready to get out of here?" he asked, his gaze steady and reassuring.

"Is it that bad?" I replied, trying to sound lighthearted but knowing I had let jealousy seep into my voice.

"Not at all," he chuckled. "But I'd rather be somewhere we can talk without the noise and the distractions."

I nodded, feeling the tension inside me dissolve with his words. His presence was like a balm to my insecurities, a reminder that whatever fleeting moment had just passed, our connection was genuine and real. As we stepped out into the cool night air, I felt a surge of hope, ready to embrace the unpredictability of what was to come.

The cool night air enveloped us as we stepped out of the bustling venue, and for a moment, the chaotic energy of the gala melted away, leaving only the distant sounds of laughter and music behind.

I took a deep breath, savoring the crispness of the evening while feeling the lingering warmth of Ethan's presence beside me. The city skyline twinkled like a million stars scattered across the horizon, and I couldn't help but marvel at how the world seemed to mirror the whirlwind of emotions brewing within me.

"Where to now?" Ethan asked, his voice light, yet a hint of sincerity tugged at his words. He glanced at me, his eyes reflecting a curiosity that made my heart flutter.

"Anywhere but back in there," I replied, unable to hide the playful smirk creeping onto my face. "I don't want to see another champagne flute or hear another corporate buzzword for at least a week."

"Agreed. But what do you suggest? A midnight stroll? An ice cream run? Or perhaps you'd like to scale a building?" He grinned, his brow raised in mock contemplation.

"Building scaling sounds fun," I shot back with a laugh. "But I think I'll need a harness for that. How about ice cream? It's much less likely to land us in jail."

"Ice cream it is, then!" He turned on his heel, leading me down the vibrant street filled with the hum of late-night revelers and the soft glow of street lamps. The atmosphere felt electric, and as we walked side by side, I could sense an unspoken connection deepening between us, drawing us closer with each step.

As we approached the quaint little ice cream parlor, the smell of freshly baked waffle cones wafted through the air, igniting my senses. The tiny bell above the door jingled as we entered, and I felt a rush of nostalgia wash over me. This was the kind of place I had frequented with my friends during lazy summer evenings, giggling and sharing secrets over melting scoops of ice cream.

Ethan held the door open for me, and I slipped inside, my heart racing at the thought of sharing this familiar space with him.

"What's your favorite flavor?" he asked, scanning the colorful array of choices.

"Definitely mint chocolate chip," I declared, a fond smile creeping onto my face. "The more chocolate chips, the better. It's the only way to eat mint ice cream, in my opinion."

He chuckled, shaking his head. "I'm more of a cookie dough kind of guy. Always go for the classic."

"Classic, huh? Bold choice," I teased, nudging him playfully. "What's next, wearing socks with sandals?"

He pretended to gasp, placing a hand dramatically over his heart. "I'd never commit such a fashion crime! I leave that to the rebels of the ice cream world."

We shared a laugh, and as I placed my order, I stole glances at him, relishing the way his smile lit up the room. With our cones in hand, we stepped back outside, the cool night air mixing with the warmth of the sweet treats. We leaned against the building, licking our ice cream as the sounds of the city enveloped us.

"Tell me something," Ethan said, a thoughtful expression crossing his face. "What's the most ridiculous thing you've ever done in the name of love?"

I tilted my head, considering the question. "Well, there was that time I tried to impress a guy in high school by singing a karaoke duet. I was so nervous I completely forgot the lyrics and just stood there, frozen like a deer in headlights while he took the mic and finished the song solo."

Ethan chuckled, a deep, rich sound that made my heart flutter. "That sounds mortifying."

"It was!" I admitted, laughing at the memory. "But at least I got a free meal out of it—he felt so sorry for me that he treated me to dinner afterward."

"Very strategic move, I must say," he replied, his eyes dancing with amusement. "I think my most ridiculous moment involved a flower delivery gone wrong. I wanted to surprise my girlfriend at the time, but I accidentally sent them to my mom instead. She was thrilled, but it didn't quite have the romantic effect I was going for."

"Oh no!" I exclaimed, nearly snorting ice cream through my nose. "Did you at least get brownie points with your mom?"

"Absolutely," he said, grinning. "But it cost me a weekend of chores to make up for it."

We continued exchanging embarrassing stories, our laughter blending with the sounds of the city, and I felt as if the weight of the world was lifting off my shoulders. In this moment, everything else faded into the background; it was just us, enjoying the simple pleasure of each other's company.

As we finished our ice cream, Ethan's gaze grew serious, and he looked at me with an intensity that sent a shiver down my spine. "Natalie," he began, his voice low, "I need to be honest. These past few months have changed everything for me."

My heart raced, caught in a whirlpool of anticipation and anxiety. "What do you mean?" I asked, holding my breath as I waited for his words.

He took a step closer, the warm glow from the streetlights casting shadows across his face. "You're not just a colleague to me anymore. I care about you—like, really care. And I've been trying to figure out how to say it without complicating things."

The world around us blurred, the bustling streets fading into a gentle hum. My stomach flipped at his admission, a mix of excitement and fear swirling within me. "I care about you too, Ethan," I confessed, my voice barely above a whisper.

Just as we were about to lean in closer, the shrill sound of a siren pierced the air, breaking the moment like a bubble. We turned to see a police car pull up to the curb, its lights flashing ominously. My heart sank as the officers began to exit the vehicle, their expressions serious and focused.

"Natalie!" a voice called out from behind us, cutting through the tension. I turned to see a familiar face rushing toward us. It was Jake, my boss, his face flushed with urgency. "We need you back at the office—now."

Ethan looked between us, confusion flickering across his features. "What's going on?"

"I don't know," I admitted, anxiety pooling in my stomach. "But it doesn't look good."

As I turned to follow Jake, my heart raced not just with the uncertainty of what awaited us at the office, but with the realization that I was caught in the middle of something far more complicated than I had anticipated.

"Wait!" Ethan called after me, his voice filled with concern. "What about us?"

I hesitated, torn between the urge to run back to him and the pressing need to understand what had just interrupted our moment. "I don't know! I'll call you as soon as I can!"

The gravity of the situation pulled me away, but as I rushed down the street with Jake, I couldn't shake the feeling that everything had just shifted. The vibrant night, once filled with laughter and possibility, now hung heavy with uncertainty, leaving me teetering on the brink of something I could neither control nor fully understand.

Chapter 10: New Challenges

The gentle lapping of waves against the shore provided a soothing rhythm as I stood on the sun-kissed deck of Ethan's family beach house, soaking in the salty air that felt like a balm to my frazzled nerves. The late afternoon sun draped everything in a golden hue, casting long shadows and turning the world into a dreamy painting. I inhaled deeply, the scent of ocean breeze mingling with the faint aroma of pine from the nearby trees. Each breath felt revitalizing, an antidote to the mounting pressures of my new role as lead developer.

I had imagined this retreat as a break from the relentless pace of work—a space where creativity could flow as freely as the ocean tide. Yet, as I gazed out at the horizon, where the sky kissed the water in a breathtaking blend of oranges and purples, I felt the familiar tightening in my chest. The project looming over me—an intricate revamp of our customer feedback system—was an ambitious endeavor, and I was acutely aware that my success hinged not only on my skills but also on the trust others had placed in me.

Ethan stepped out from the kitchen, a wide grin illuminating his face as he approached with two mugs of steaming coffee. "I thought a little caffeine might help spark some inspiration," he said, his voice warm and inviting, as he handed me a mug. The touch of our fingers sent a spark of electricity through me, a reminder that beneath our professional camaraderie lay something deeper, something thrillingly uncertain.

"Thank you. I'll need all the inspiration I can get," I replied, taking a sip of the rich brew. The warmth seeped through me, battling the cold tendrils of anxiety that wrapped around my thoughts.

Ethan leaned against the railing, his gaze sweeping over the ocean. "You know, I have a feeling this coding retreat is going to be legendary," he said, his tone light but with an undercurrent of sincerity that made my heart flutter. "Just you, me, and a whole lot of code to conquer."

"Legendary, huh? Let's hope it doesn't turn into a debugging nightmare instead," I teased, unable to suppress the smile that tugged at my lips.

"We'll make it work," he replied confidently, a sparkle of mischief in his eyes. "Besides, I brought my secret weapon."

"Your secret weapon?" I raised an eyebrow, intrigued.

Ethan reached into his pocket and pulled out a small, brightly colored fidget spinner. "Guaranteed to clear the mind and enhance creativity," he declared, holding it up triumphantly.

"Very impressive," I laughed, shaking my head at his antics. "I didn't realize I'd be coding alongside a professional fidget spinner aficionado."

As he spun the device with a flourish, I couldn't help but admire how effortlessly he lightened the atmosphere. The anxiety I had been carrying began to ebb, replaced by an eagerness to dive into the work ahead. "Alright then, let's get to it," I said, setting my coffee down and leading the way into the cozy living room that served as our makeshift office.

Inside, the room was filled with a mix of modern comfort and beachy charm—soft, oversized couches, colorful throw pillows, and a massive window that framed the stunning ocean view. A large wooden table was scattered with our laptops and notebooks, a testament to our impending creative storm.

We settled in, the buzz of the world outside fading as we immersed ourselves in lines of code, ideas bouncing between us like a vibrant game of catch. I could feel the tension of the past few weeks slowly dissolving, replaced by a camaraderie that was both invigorating and comforting. Ethan had a knack for breaking down complex problems into manageable pieces, and his insights often guided me to solutions I hadn't considered.

As the sun dipped lower in the sky, painting the room in hues of amber and rose, I glanced up from my screen to find Ethan studying me intently. "You alright?" he asked, his brow slightly furrowed.

I hesitated, weighing my words. "It's just... this project is bigger than I anticipated. I want to impress everyone, but the stakes feel higher now."

Ethan leaned forward, resting his elbows on the table. "You're going to knock it out of the park. Remember, you were chosen for this role because you're brilliant. They see your potential, even if you don't yet."

His encouragement felt like a lifeline, pulling me back from the brink of self-doubt. "Thanks. I really needed to hear that," I admitted, my heart swelling with gratitude.

He smiled, a genuine warmth radiating from him that made my insides flutter. "I'm here for you, you know. We'll figure it out together."

As the evening deepened, we traded stories and laughter, the hours slipping away unnoticed. Our banter flowed effortlessly, each quip sparking laughter that rang through the otherwise quiet house. The more time I spent with Ethan, the more I realized how much I cherished his presence—his support, his humor, and the way he made me feel seen in a world where I often felt like a mere cog in the machine.

But just as I began to feel a sense of ease settling over me, a nagging thought crept in—what if this retreat was just a temporary reprieve? What if, back in the corporate chaos, I wouldn't be able to maintain this sense of empowerment? The vulnerability of those thoughts unsettled me, casting a shadow over the otherwise bright evening.

"Earth to Ella!" Ethan's playful voice pulled me from my spiral. "You've been staring at your screen like it holds the meaning of life."

"Sorry! I was just—" I started, but he interrupted with a laugh.

"Lost in thought, huh? Well, come back to reality; I have a wild idea."

I raised an eyebrow, curiosity piqued. "And that would be?"

"Let's take a break and go for a walk on the beach. The stars are starting to come out, and I hear the ocean does wonders for clarity."

His suggestion sparked a flicker of excitement within me. Maybe a walk under the stars would bring some clarity to my swirling thoughts, and the notion of sharing that moment with Ethan felt exhilarating.

"Alright, lead the way," I said, my heart quickening as I stood and brushed off my jeans, ready to step into the evening's embrace.

The cool sand felt pleasantly gritty beneath my bare feet as we walked along the shoreline, the waves rhythmically crashing against the shore like a soothing heartbeat. Each step brought a refreshing splash of saltwater, sending little shivers up my spine and igniting a sense of adventure within me. The air was thick with the scent of the ocean, mingling with the sweet, lingering traces of sunscreen. Ethan walked beside me, his hands casually tucked into the pockets of his shorts, a relaxed demeanor that only deepened my appreciation for this moment.

"You know," he said, glancing at the stars beginning to twinkle above, "I used to think that the ocean was like a giant, endless canvas. Every wave is a brushstroke, every sunset a new masterpiece."

"Is that your artistic way of saying I should be inspired by nature?" I teased, nudging him playfully. "I mean, I'm just trying to debug a system here, not paint the Mona Lisa."

He laughed, the sound rich and inviting, and I felt the warmth of our camaraderie wrap around me like a cozy blanket. "Touché. But sometimes a little inspiration can go a long way in coding. Think of it as a different kind of art."

"Okay, Picasso," I shot back, shaking my head. "But I have to admit, you make a compelling argument. Nature does have a way of sparking creativity."

As we strolled, the moonlight reflected off the ocean, casting a silvery path that seemed to beckon us further along the beach. A sense of liberation enveloped me; the constraints of my corporate responsibilities and the weight of expectations drifted away with each crashing wave. I felt like I could breathe again, like I could finally find my rhythm in the chaos.

"Do you ever feel overwhelmed by all the expectations? I mean, with the project, with work, with everything?" Ethan's voice cut through my musings, his expression suddenly serious.

My heart quickened. "All the time," I admitted, glancing sideways at him. "I think I'm still getting used to this whole 'lead developer' thing. It's like wearing a new pair of shoes—great at first, but then you realize they're not broken in yet, and you're just waiting for the blisters to show up."

He chuckled, but there was a depth to his eyes that made my stomach flutter. "I think you're handling it better than you give yourself credit for. I've seen how passionate you are about your work. It's inspiring."

"Thanks, but it's easy to look good on paper," I said, waving my hand dismissively. "The reality is, I'm terrified of failing. What if I screw everything up?"

Ethan stopped, his gaze locking onto mine with a weight that felt both intimidating and comforting. "What if you don't? What if you rise to the occasion and blow everyone away? You're talented, Ella. Don't let self-doubt rob you of the chance to prove it."

His words wrapped around me like a warm hug, melting away some of my apprehension. I felt lighter, as if he had plucked the heavy weight of fear right off my shoulders. "You really know how to say the right thing at the right time, don't you?"

"Years of practice," he replied with a playful wink, before breaking into a run toward the water. "Race you to the waves!"

Before I could react, he was off, laughter spilling from his lips like a melody. I was momentarily caught off guard, but the playful spirit ignited within me, and I sprinted after him, my laughter mingling with his as we splashed into the cool embrace of the ocean. The water was shockingly refreshing, enveloping us in its brisk embrace as we tried to dodge the crashing waves.

"Too slow!" Ethan called over his shoulder, splashing water back at me. I retaliated with a wave of my own, sending him sputtering, which only sent us both into fits of laughter.

As we splashed and raced along the shoreline, my earlier anxieties seemed to dissolve with every crashing wave. It was just us, two friends caught up in the simplicity of the moment, unburdened by deadlines or expectations. For that fleeting evening, I was just Ella—the girl who loved coding, who adored the ocean, who enjoyed Ethan's presence more than she cared to admit.

Eventually, we collapsed onto the warm sand, breathless and exhilarated, the ocean stretching out before us like an endless promise. The stars twinkled above, seemingly nodding in agreement with the beauty of this spontaneous adventure.

"Okay, I officially declare this coding retreat a success," Ethan announced, flopping onto his back, arms splayed wide. "Who knew debugging could be so... refreshing?"

"Best brainstorming session I've ever had," I replied, still catching my breath as I lay beside him, our shoulders brushing in the comforting silence. "Maybe the ocean really is a good muse."

As we lay there, the sound of the waves providing a tranquil backdrop, I couldn't shake the feeling that this moment was more than just a break from reality. There was a connection simmering beneath the surface—an electric energy that buzzed between us, something that felt both exhilarating and terrifying.

"Ella," he said suddenly, breaking the silence, his tone shifting to something more serious. "Can I ask you something?"

"Of course," I replied, turning to face him.

"What's your biggest fear when it comes to the project?"

I took a breath, the weight of his question settling heavily between us. "Honestly? That I'll fail to deliver. That I'll let everyone down—my team, my boss... myself. It's like standing at the edge of a cliff, and the ground below is constantly shifting."

Ethan turned on his side to face me, his expression earnest. "You're not standing at the edge; you're flying, Ella. You just have to trust your wings."

I opened my mouth to respond, but the sincerity in his eyes caught me off guard. He wasn't just saying words to comfort me; he genuinely believed them. There was a moment—one heart-stopping moment—where I felt the pull of something deeper, something that surged between us like the tide itself.

"Thanks, Ethan. You have a way of making me feel like I can do anything," I said softly, feeling the warmth of his gaze wrap around me.

"Just telling it like it is," he replied, the corners of his mouth turning up in that boyish smile that sent my heart racing.

But before I could respond, a sudden shriek shattered the tranquility of the moment, echoing from the direction of the house. We both sat up, the serenity of our conversation swept away in an instant.

"What was that?" I asked, the lightness in my chest replaced by a surge of adrenaline.

"Let's check it out," Ethan said, rising to his feet and running toward the sound, urgency in his stride. I followed closely, my heart pounding not just from the sprint but from the tension that had erupted so suddenly.

As we reached the house, I could see a group of people gathered near the entrance, their voices a mix of confusion and concern. My mind raced with possibilities. Had someone gotten hurt? Was there an emergency?

Ethan pushed through the small crowd, and I stayed close behind him, my curiosity piqued. When we reached the front, I was met with a sight I never expected. A small dog, soaking wet and shivering, stood in the doorway, looking thoroughly dejected as it quaked in the cool night air.

"Oh, poor little guy," I gasped, my heart melting at the sight. "Is he okay?"

A girl in the crowd knelt down, holding out a hand. "He just wandered onto the property. I think he fell into the water!"

"Someone must have lost him," Ethan said, kneeling beside the girl and reaching out to the shivering pup. "Hey, buddy, it's okay. You're safe now."

As Ethan coaxed the dog closer, I felt a warmth spread through me, not just for the puppy, but for the way Ethan instinctively took charge, his gentle nature shining through. The tension from earlier melted away as the little dog, sensing kindness, slowly approached him, nuzzling his face against Ethan's hand.

"He's adorable," I breathed, squatting beside Ethan to get a better look. "What should we do?"

"I think we should bring him inside, dry him off, and figure out if he has a collar," Ethan suggested, glancing at me with that same spark of determination that had drawn me to him from the start.

I nodded, excitement bubbling within me. "I'll grab a towel!"

The unexpected shift in the evening's mood added a layer of unpredictability that I hadn't anticipated, but as I dashed into the house, I couldn't shake the feeling that this little adventure was exactly what we needed. Together, we were not just problem-solvers;

we were caretakers, and maybe—just maybe—this small moment of joy would ripple into something even larger.

The towel felt plush and warm in my hands as I rushed back to the living room, the laughter of the small gathering now a backdrop to my focused mission. I could still hear Ethan's soothing voice coaxing the shivering dog, and a surge of determination washed over me. The puppy had no idea how this night was about to unfold, and neither did we.

As I returned, I spotted Ethan still crouched on the floor, gently rubbing the dog's fur, his fingers delicately gliding over the damp coat. "There you go, little buddy," he murmured, his tone low and reassuring. The puppy seemed to relax, finally realizing that he was safe.

"Here!" I said, tossing the towel to Ethan, who caught it with a grin. "It's not a fancy spa treatment, but it'll do."

"Hey, I can make anything feel like a spa day," he replied, his playful energy infectious. "Watch and learn." He began drying the puppy with exaggerated motions, raising his eyebrows and pretending to have an imaginary audience. "And now we have a rare sighting of the elusive 'Ethan, the Dog Whisperer.'"

The laughter bubbled up inside me, and I found myself grinning at his antics. The dog, clearly unfazed by Ethan's performance, wriggled under the towel, looking both confused and grateful. "Okay, I admit it," I chuckled. "I might have underestimated your grooming skills."

Ethan shot me a mock-indignant look. "Underestimating the Dog Whisperer? I'll remember that for the next time we're debugging. I'll make sure to let my skills go to waste!"

The atmosphere felt alive, charged with the spontaneity of the night. The laughter and warmth seemed to thaw away the remnants of my earlier anxieties, and for the first time in days, I felt light-hearted and carefree.

"Have you thought about what we'll do with him once he's dry?" I asked, watching as Ethan wrangled the puppy, who was now fully enjoying his towel bath, wagging his tail furiously and shaking droplets everywhere.

"First things first: name the poor guy. We can't just keep calling him 'the puppy' forever," he replied, the corners of his mouth turning up in a grin.

"Fair point. How about something beachy? Like 'Salty'?" I suggested, my eyes sparkling with mirth.

"Salty it is!" Ethan declared dramatically, holding the puppy aloft as if he were presenting a trophy. "Meet Salty, our new coding companion!"

As the rest of the group cooed over Salty, I took a moment to breathe it all in—this unplanned evening had turned into something magical, and it filled me with an overwhelming sense of belonging.

A young woman in the gathering, her hair tousled and sandy, leaned down to scratch behind Salty's ears. "Is anyone going to check for a collar? We should see if he has an owner," she suggested, looking around with concern.

Ethan nodded, still holding Salty. "Good idea. Let's check him over."

While we all gathered closer, Ethan carefully turned the puppy to check for identification. My heart raced, anticipation swirling with a hint of unease. What if Salty had been lost for days? What if he had been abandoned? A sharp pang of sympathy settled in my chest.

Ethan's fingers gently probed through the damp fur, revealing a small, faded collar. "Aha!" he exclaimed, the excitement palpable. "We have a collar!"

He carefully unclasped it, revealing a name tag that glinted in the dim light. "His name is Rusty!" he announced, eliciting a collective "aww" from our impromptu gathering.

"Rusty? Sounds like a dog with character," I remarked, feeling a warmth spread through me. "I hope we can find his family."

"Me too," Ethan replied, his eyes flickering to mine, the weight of the moment hanging between us. "But first, let's get him warm and comfortable."

As we set up a little bed for Rusty in a corner of the living room using towels and blankets, I felt the sense of camaraderie grow stronger. We were no longer just a group of friends; we were a team united by a common goal—a mixture of empathy and fun that felt almost familial.

The evening progressed with laughter and storytelling as we took turns cradling Rusty, who had become the star of the night. He rolled around, playfully nipping at our fingers and stealing our hearts with his antics. I marveled at how this unexpected twist had transformed our coding retreat into a lively gathering, and as I caught Ethan's eye, I couldn't help but smile.

Then, just as we settled down to resume our coding discussions, a sudden knock echoed through the house, sending a ripple of surprise through the group. The sound reverberated, sharp and demanding, as if it were a portent of something significant.

"Did anyone order an unexpected visitor?" I joked, attempting to dispel the tension that hung thick in the air.

Ethan glanced at me, a flicker of uncertainty crossing his features. "Not that I know of. Stay here; I'll check it out."

Before I could object, he was already moving toward the door, his silhouette framed by the soft light spilling from the living room. I followed, a sense of foreboding creeping in as he turned the handle. The atmosphere had shifted, and the carefree laughter from moments before felt like a distant memory.

As Ethan swung the door open, my heart raced, pounding in my ears. The night was still, but there was a tension in the air that felt almost electric. Standing on the porch was a figure cloaked in shadows, the moonlight barely illuminating their face.

"Excuse me," the stranger said, their voice a low, gravelly tone. "I'm looking for my dog."

I held my breath, the significance of the moment crashing over me like a wave. Rusty's ears perked up, sensing the tension, and he made a small whimpering sound, glancing back at me with those big, expressive eyes.

"Is... is your dog named Rusty?" Ethan asked, his tone cautious but edged with hope.

The stranger stepped forward, and for a heartbeat, I could feel the pulse of the night quicken.

"Yes," the figure replied, their voice barely a whisper now, laden with emotion. "That's my Rusty."

A silence fell, heavy and thick, wrapping around us like a dark shroud. In that moment, I understood that this night had taken a turn I never saw coming, and as the stranger's gaze locked onto Rusty, I felt a wave of uncertainty wash over me. This was just the beginning of a twist I couldn't have prepared for, and whatever lay ahead felt both thrilling and daunting, a promise of challenges yet to come.

Chapter 11: The Beach House Escape

The moment we arrived at the beach house, the salty breeze and crashing waves washed away my stress like footprints erased by the tide. The vibrant blue of the sky seemed to blend seamlessly with the ocean, creating a picturesque canvas that felt almost unreal. Ethan's family welcomed me with open arms, their warmth wrapping around me like a cozy blanket on a chilly evening. As we settled into the quaint, sun-kissed home, it felt as if I had stepped into a postcard of summer bliss, the kind that made you believe everything would turn out okay.

The house, a charming structure with weathered wooden beams and cheerful yellow shutters, exuded a sense of history. Each creak of the floorboards whispered stories of laughter and love, and I could almost hear the echoes of summers long past. The living room, adorned with seashells and nautical knickknacks, was the heart of the home. Large windows opened up to a panoramic view of the ocean, letting in the refreshing scent of salt and sand. I felt a sense of belonging here, as if the waves had called me back to a place I didn't know I'd missed.

Days melted into a delightful routine. We spent our mornings hiking along the rugged cliffs, the sun kissing our skin while the ocean roared below. With every step, I felt more alive, the crisp air filling my lungs and awakening something within me that had been dormant for far too long. Ethan walked beside me, his laughter mixing with the sound of the waves, creating a symphony of joy that made my heart dance. His presence was intoxicating, and I found myself stealing glances at him, my cheeks warming as I caught him watching me in return.

At night, we gathered on the deck, the sky transitioning from a vibrant blue to a velvety canvas speckled with stars. The distant sound of laughter and splashing waves formed a backdrop to our late-night coding sessions. We were both passionate about tech, often exchanging ideas and debating the best ways to tackle our projects. But beneath the playful banter, an unspoken connection simmered, electric and tinged with a hint of danger.

One evening, as we settled around a crackling fire, the smell of roasting marshmallows filling the air, I couldn't help but marvel at the way the flames danced, casting flickering shadows across Ethan's face. His eyes sparkled with mischief, and for a moment, I felt as if the universe had conspired to create this perfect moment just for us.

"Alright, marshmallow expert," he teased, holding out a perfectly toasted s'more. "Tell me your secret. How do you get them to be so perfectly golden?" His playful challenge made me grin.

"Oh, it's all in the wrist, Ethan," I replied, mimicking an exaggerated flick of my wrist as I reached for the gooey treat. "You have to rotate it just the right amount, and don't be afraid to get a little closer to the flame. It's all about balance."

He raised an eyebrow, feigning disbelief. "A master of marshmallow alchemy, are we? I must admit, I'm impressed."

"Don't be too impressed," I said with a smirk, "I've burned my fair share of marshmallows, and let's just say they tasted like a campfire disaster."

His laughter rang out, a melodic sound that sent shivers of excitement down my spine. The warmth of the fire paled in comparison to the warmth blossoming in my chest. I found myself leaning in, captivated by the way his eyes twinkled like the stars above, and for a heartbeat, the world melted away, leaving just the two of us suspended in this perfect moment.

"Do you think we'll ever just... escape?" I asked suddenly, the question escaping my lips before I could censor myself. "I mean, from everything? Just run away to a place where no one knows us, and we can be whoever we want?"

His gaze turned serious, and the playful light in his eyes dimmed. "Sometimes, I think about it," he admitted, his voice low and thoughtful. "It'd be nice to leave behind the pressures, the expectations. Just be free, you know?"

I nodded, feeling a flicker of understanding. The weight of our lives felt heavier than the summer air around us, and in that shared vulnerability, I sensed a bond forming—a connection deeper than mere friendship. The fire crackled, and the shadows danced, casting our silhouettes against the wooden deck, a backdrop to our unspoken dreams.

Just then, a sudden wave crashed against the cliffs, startling me from my thoughts. I glanced at Ethan, and in that fleeting moment, I saw something shift in his expression—an intensity that made my heart race. It was as if he could see straight through to my soul, peeling back the layers of my guarded heart. But just as quickly, he masked it, and the moment was gone, replaced by his easy smile.

"Let's not think about escaping right now," he said, his tone lightening again. "We have s'mores to conquer."

And just like that, the moment was deflected, but the spark lingered, crackling like the fire between us. I felt alive in ways I had never anticipated, the joy of being with him outshining the complexity of our situation. As we continued to roast marshmallows, laughter mingling with the sound of waves, I knew this summer would change everything.

But the sands of time shift unpredictably, and as the sun dipped below the horizon, casting a golden glow across the sky, I couldn't shake the feeling that the escape we longed for might not come as easily as we hoped.

The days slipped by like grains of sand between my fingers, each one more perfect than the last, filled with adventures that seemed ripped from the pages of a novel. The beach house became our sanctuary, a place where laughter echoed off the walls and the salty air infused everything with a sense of freedom. Mornings were spent in a rhythm of lazy brunches, the sun streaming through the windows as we feasted on pancakes and fruit, our conversations spilling over with easy camaraderie. I reveled in the way Ethan's laughter made my heart flutter, each sound sending ripples of warmth through me.

One afternoon, we decided to explore a hidden cove that Ethan had mentioned, a place where the rocks jutted out dramatically over the water, offering a stunning view of the horizon. We packed a small picnic—sandwiches, chips, and a few of those ridiculously sweet lemonade drinks that came in brightly colored cans—and set off down a narrow, winding path. The sun hung high in the sky, casting a golden glow over everything, and I felt buoyant, as if the weight of my usual worries had been left behind with each step.

As we reached the cove, the sight took my breath away. The water sparkled under the sun like a million tiny diamonds scattered across the surface. The cliffs rose majestically, their rugged beauty a perfect backdrop to our little adventure. I spread out a blanket on the warm sand, feeling the sun seep into my skin. Ethan flopped down beside me, a grin splitting his face, and for a moment, everything felt perfect.

"This place is incredible," I breathed, gazing out at the waves crashing against the rocks. "How did you find it?"

Ethan shrugged, his gaze fixed on the horizon. "Just stumbled upon it one day. I guess I was lucky. But it's even better with company."

A flutter of warmth spread through me at his words. I tore open the can of lemonade, taking a sip that was far too sugary for my taste but refreshing nonetheless. "You know, you really should come with a warning label. 'May cause excessive smiling and heart palpitations.'"

He chuckled, leaning back on his elbows. "Well, I'll try to tone it down. Wouldn't want to endanger your health."

I rolled my eyes, suppressing a smile. "I can handle it. Just don't blame me if I suddenly need a defibrillator."

Ethan grinned wider, the corners of his eyes crinkling in that way I had grown to adore. The moment was interrupted by a sudden splashing sound. Turning, I saw a group of teenagers nearby, their laughter ringing out as they jumped into the water, splashing each other like a scene from a summer movie. I envied their carefree spirit, but as I watched Ethan, I realized I wouldn't trade our quiet moments for anything.

"Wanna go for a swim?" he asked, glancing at the water. The invitation hung between us, charged with the excitement of youthful spontaneity.

I hesitated, a spark of nervousness flickering in my chest. "Uh, I didn't exactly pack a swimsuit."

Ethan smirked, a twinkle in his eyes that suggested mischief. "You could always go in your clothes. That's the beauty of summer. You dry off in no time."

"Are you serious?" I laughed, half-tempted by the idea. "What if I end up looking like a drowned rat?"

"Consider it a character-building experience," he shot back, his tone playful. "Plus, I promise not to take any pictures."

He was so disarmingly charming that I found myself nodding, the thrill of adventure pushing me beyond my usual caution. "Alright, you convinced me."

With that, I leaped to my feet, running toward the water while Ethan laughed behind me. The cool ocean embraced me like a breath of fresh air as I plunged into the waves. The initial shock of the chill made me squeal, but I quickly adjusted, surfacing with a whoop of exhilaration.

Ethan joined me moments later, the water splashing around us as he swam closer. Our laughter mingled with the crashing waves, a joyous cacophony that echoed against the cliffs. I couldn't remember the last time I felt so free, so utterly and unapologetically alive.

We splashed each other, the playful competition escalating into a full-fledged water fight. In those moments, nothing else mattered—no past, no worries about the future, just the two of us lost in the present, surrounded by the beauty of the world. When I finally tackled him with a wave of water, he retaliated with a laugh, pulling me closer until our bodies collided, both of us sputtering with laughter.

"Okay, truce?" he panted, a teasing light in his eyes as he wiped water from his face.

"Truce," I agreed, though the mischief still danced in the air between us.

As we floated in the shallow waves, the sun began to dip lower, painting the sky in hues of orange and pink. "This is what summer is all about," I said, sighing contentedly as I let the water cradle me.

"Yeah, it's nice," Ethan said, his voice softer now. "But it's even better when you share it with someone."

The sincerity in his tone made my heart skip a beat, a mix of exhilaration and uncertainty swirling within me. I glanced at him, trying to decipher the meaning behind his words, but his gaze was fixed on the horizon, the light casting a soft glow on his features. The moment felt heavy with unspoken possibilities, a tension that left me breathless.

Suddenly, a loud shout from the shore jolted us both out of our thoughts. The group of teenagers was calling for a game of beach volleyball, their energy infectious. "Hey, join us!" one of them hollered, waving us over.

Ethan's face lit up, and he turned to me, an eager smile spreading across his face. "What do you say? Up for a little competition?"

I hesitated, the thrill of the game pulling at me, but the uncertainty still lingered. "I'm not exactly a volleyball pro."

He laughed, splashing water in my direction. "Neither am I! That's the point. It'll be fun, I promise."

And just like that, with the sun dipping below the horizon, I found myself swept into a world of laughter, competition, and camaraderie, the connection between Ethan and me shimmering like the water around us, alive and pulsing with untold stories waiting to unfold.

As we joined the group for beach volleyball, the evening sun cast long shadows over the sand, creating a golden glow that felt almost magical. Laughter erupted around us as the teenagers called out, their excitement contagious. I found myself swept along in their enthusiasm, the previous tension between Ethan and me dissolving with every playful dig and spike.

The game quickly turned chaotic, and I discovered that my athletic skills were more suited for dodging flying balls than actually hitting them. "Nice try!" Ethan called, dodging a rogue serve that sailed just over my head. His laughter rang out, a bright sound that echoed against the backdrop of crashing waves.

"Thanks for the vote of confidence!" I shot back, my hands on my hips in mock indignation. "I'll have you know that my primary talent lies in being a professional bystander."

Ethan winked at me, his eyes dancing with mischief. "You're doing a great job! That was some impressive dodging."

As the game progressed, I became more comfortable, diving into the sand with reckless abandon. Each time I managed to hit the ball—even if it was purely accidental—cheers erupted from the group, lifting my spirits higher. I felt a growing camaraderie with the teenagers, my initial hesitation melting away like ice cream on a hot day.

After an intense rally, Ethan and I found ourselves at the back of the makeshift court, panting and giggling. "Okay, I admit it," I said, brushing sand from my arms. "This is way more fun than I expected."

He shot me a teasing grin. "Told you! Sometimes you just have to throw yourself into it."

"Let's not get carried away," I replied, feigning seriousness. "I draw the line at synchronized swimming."

The laughter continued, a symphony of carefree joy, but as the sun dipped lower, casting shades of pink and purple across the sky, a ripple of tension passed through the group. One of the teenagers, a girl with striking red hair and a quick smile, pointed toward the horizon. "Look at that!" she exclaimed, her voice laced with a mix of wonder and concern.

Following her gaze, I squinted into the distance. Dark clouds were gathering ominously on the horizon, the once bright sky transforming into a foreboding gray. The atmosphere shifted abruptly, the warm breeze turning sharp and cool as a chill swept through the air.

"Uh-oh," Ethan said, his expression mirroring my growing unease. "Looks like a storm is brewing."

The mood of the group shifted as the clouds churned, the impending storm casting a shadow over our carefree afternoon. The laughter faded, replaced by murmurs of concern. "We should head back," someone suggested, glancing nervously at the sky.

"Yeah, let's pack up," Ethan said, his voice steady. "We don't want to get caught out here."

As we hurried to gather our things, I couldn't shake the feeling that the storm was more than just a meteorological phenomenon. The air was thick with anticipation, an electricity that set my senses on edge. I stole a glance at Ethan, who was rolling up the picnic blanket, his brow furrowed with thought.

We made our way back to the beach house, the sand shifting beneath our feet as the wind picked up, howling like an angry beast. "Do you think it'll be a bad storm?" I asked, my voice barely audible over the roar of the wind.

Ethan looked at me, concern etched on his face. "Probably just a summer squall. They can be intense but usually pass quickly."

His reassurances were meant to calm me, but as the first drops of rain began to fall, a knot of anxiety twisted in my stomach. We reached the beach house just as the storm unleashed its fury, rain pouring down in heavy sheets, the sound like a thousand drums beating against the roof. We hurried inside, shaking off the sand and water, and I felt a sense of relief wash over me as I closed the door against the tempest outside.

Inside, the house felt cozy and safe, but the atmosphere had changed. Ethan's family busied themselves with preparations, securing windows and checking supplies. I could sense the tension in the air, and I tried to shake it off as I helped them gather flashlights and candles.

"Is this really necessary?" I asked, glancing at Ethan, who had settled at the kitchen table, deep in thought. "It's just a storm, right?"

"It's best to be prepared," he replied, his tone clipped. "We've had power outages before during storms like this."

His seriousness made my heart race. "Okay, but you're not planning on making me huddle in a corner with a flashlight and a horror movie, are you?"

A smile tugged at his lips, and for a moment, the tension broke. "Only if you promise to scream really loudly at the scary parts."

"Deal," I said, unable to suppress a grin.

As the wind howled outside and rain lashed against the windows, we settled in for what felt like a long night. Candles flickered in the dim light, casting dancing shadows on the walls, and Ethan and I exchanged playful banter while the rest of his family prepared for the worst.

Just as I began to relax, a loud crash echoed from the beach outside, followed by a deafening silence. My heart dropped, the air thick with anticipation as everyone froze, eyes darting toward the windows.

"What was that?" I whispered, my throat dry.

Ethan's expression turned grave. "I don't know. But I think we should check it out."

The sudden seriousness of the moment sent a thrill of fear through me. "Check it out? In the middle of a storm? Are you crazy?"

"It might be nothing," he said, but I could see the uncertainty in his eyes. "But we should make sure everyone's okay."

The hesitation hung between us, and I could feel the weight of the decision pressing down. I wanted to protest, to suggest we stay inside where it was safe, but something in me stirred—a mixture of curiosity and concern.

Before I could change my mind, Ethan stood, and I followed him as he led the way to the door. As we stepped outside, the storm roared around us, rain soaking us instantly. We moved cautiously toward the sound, hearts pounding in our chests, the darkness thickening as the wind howled.

Then, just as we rounded the corner of the house, I froze. The crashing sound had come from the beach, and there, illuminated by flashes of lightning, stood a figure.

"What is that?" I gasped, my voice lost in the wind.

Ethan squinted into the darkness, his eyes widening in disbelief. "I have no idea, but we should go back!"

But it was too late. The figure turned, and in that moment, our eyes locked. A jolt of recognition shot through me, followed by a chilling realization. I took a step back, panic rising as the figure took a step forward, rain drenching them, revealing a face I had never expected to see again.

"Lily?" the voice called out, and my heart raced.

What was she doing here? And why did she look like she'd just walked out of a nightmare?

Chapter 12: Confessions at Sunset

The air was thick with the scent of salt and sea, mingling with the faint whiff of the sun-kissed earth, as I stood beside Ethan, the golden sand warm beneath my bare feet. The horizon was ablaze with colors, a magnificent canvas of oranges, pinks, and purples that seemed to set the very world around us aflame. Each wave lapped at the shore with a gentle insistence, echoing the tumult of emotions churning within me, a symphony of desire and fear harmonizing beautifully with the rhythmic crash of the ocean.

Ethan stood close, his presence a steady anchor against the vastness of the twilight sky. His tousled hair caught the dying light, giving him an almost ethereal glow, while the soft contours of his face held a depth I longed to explore. I could see in his eyes a flicker of uncertainty, mirrored by the knots twisting in my stomach. It was in this moment, with the world falling away around us, that I felt an overwhelming urge to speak the truths I had kept buried beneath layers of apprehension. My heart raced as I turned toward him, my voice trembling with the weight of my confession.

"I've admired you for so long, Ethan," I began, the words spilling forth like the tide reaching for the shore. "It's not just your talent in marketing, though that's incredible, but the way you always seem to see the best in everyone—even me. You have this way of making people feel like they matter, and it's something I've struggled with for a long time." The vulnerability in my words hung between us, a delicate thread woven into the tapestry of the moment.

His expression softened, and I could see the surprise blooming in his eyes, as if I had just unlocked a door to a hidden room in his heart. "You think so?" he asked, his voice low, a hint of incredulity lacing his tone. "I've often felt like I'm just... pretending. Like I'm not quite enough. Your belief in me has made me realize that vulnerability is strength, not a weakness." There was a raw honesty in his admission, a glimpse into the insecurities that lay beneath the surface, and it struck a chord within me. We were two imperfect souls, fumbling through the complexities of our lives, and in that shared vulnerability, I felt an unbreakable bond forming between us.

The sun continued its descent, casting long shadows that danced across the sand. The moment felt suspended in time, as if the universe had conspired to bring us here, together, just as the stars began to twinkle shyly in the evening sky. As the last rays of sunlight dipped below the horizon, leaving only a soft glow in their wake, I took a step closer to him. The air was charged, electric, as if the world around us held its breath, waiting for something to happen.

"What if we stopped pretending?" I suggested, my voice barely above a whisper, daring to tread where I had always feared to go. "What if we embraced the messiness of who we really are?" My heart pounded fiercely against my ribs, the anticipation swirling in the air like the ocean mist that kissed my cheeks.

Ethan's gaze bore into mine, searching for something, perhaps reassurance or a signal of my sincerity. "I'd like that," he replied, the corners of his mouth lifting into a tentative smile that lit up his features. It was a smile that held promise, the kind that made my insides flutter.

As I stood there, caught in the depths of his gaze, an invisible thread pulled me closer. Without thinking, I reached out, my fingers brushing against his. A spark ignited at the point of contact, and I could see in his eyes the flicker of desire that mirrored my own.

"Can I?" I asked, the question heavy with unspoken implications. The moment stretched, the world around us fading into the background, as he nodded slowly, a silent invitation that sent a shiver down my spine.

And then it happened—our lips met, softly at first, a gentle collision that sent shockwaves through my entire being. The kiss was tentative, exploring, as if we were both testing the waters of this new territory. His lips were warm and inviting, a balm to the insecurities that had plagued me for far too long. It felt like coming home, a sanctuary amidst the chaos of the world.

As the kiss deepened, I could feel the weight of the moment—a surge of emotions I had never dared to entertain before. Passion intertwined with tenderness, and the kiss unfolded into something more profound, more meaningful than either of us could have anticipated. I melted into him, my heart racing as if it were trying to keep up with the whirlwind of feelings that threatened to sweep me off my feet.

The sound of the waves crashing against the shore faded into a gentle lullaby, wrapping us in an intimate cocoon. In that suspended moment, I let go of my fears, my doubts, and all the reasons that had kept me from embracing what was right in front of me. I was no longer just a girl standing on the beach; I was a part of something beautiful and transformative, and the realization washed over me like the tide, surging with a promise of hope and love.

But as we pulled away, breathless and wide-eyed, the lingering tension hung thick in the air, reminding us that this moment, while magical, was only the beginning of a much larger journey. Unspoken questions loomed, casting shadows over the sun-drenched warmth that had enveloped us. Would this moment of connection withstand the storm brewing on the horizon? Would we be brave enough to face whatever came next, together?

As the last vestiges of sunlight slipped away, leaving a curtain of indigo behind, the air turned cooler, wrapping around us like a soft blanket. I could hear the whispers of the ocean, the gentle lapping of waves against the shore echoing the rhythm of my heartbeat. The kiss had left me breathless, a heady mix of exhilaration and uncertainty swirling inside me. We stood in that charged silence, our hands still lingering near each other, each fingertip tingling with possibility.

"What now?" Ethan asked, breaking the stillness, his voice low and slightly hesitant, as if he were afraid to disturb the fragile magic we had just created. He was so close I could see the way his lashes cast shadows across his cheeks, the way the corners of his mouth still held that flicker of joy. It was a question that carried weight, a question that made my heart race anew as it drew me deeper into the moment.

"Now?" I echoed, trying to gather my thoughts, feeling both excited and terrified at the prospect of what this could mean. "Now we figure out how to navigate this... whatever this is." I gestured between us, my voice light, attempting to temper the seriousness of the moment with a playful air. But beneath the surface, my heart thudded with uncertainty. I had been so careful to keep my emotions at bay, and now I was standing at the edge of something vast and unknown.

He chuckled softly, a warm sound that wrapped around me like a comforting embrace. "I'm all for navigating uncharted waters, but I have to admit, I might need a life jacket."

"Who said anything about a life jacket? We can just go with the flow." I laughed, and the sound felt like a release, a relief that we could still find humor amid the serious implications of our kiss. But as I watched his expression shift from playful to contemplative, I sensed a deeper layer of anxiety lurking beneath his easygoing demeanor.

"I just want to make sure I don't mess this up," he said, running a hand through his hair, a gesture I found endearing in its vulnerability. "You mean a lot to me, and I don't want to be the reason you regret this."

"Regret?" I scoffed lightly, but there was a tremor of sincerity in my voice. "Ethan, I think we both know there's no going back now. I mean, unless we get hit by a tidal wave or something."

He raised an eyebrow, his lips twitching into a teasing smile. "Well, I'm not exactly equipped for tidal waves. Maybe we should just stay on the beach and avoid any disasters."

"Sounds like a plan." I nudged him with my shoulder playfully, but the conversation had taken a turn that I hadn't expected. His concern hung heavy in the air, and I could feel the weight of my own insecurities creeping back in, mingling with the uncertainty of what this new dynamic meant for us.

"Seriously, though," he continued, his tone sobering, "I want to know you, all of you. The good, the bad, and everything in between. I don't want to gloss over things like we're painting a fence."

"Is that your marketing wisdom talking?" I teased, but the underlying seriousness of his words struck a chord.

"Maybe. Or maybe it's just me wanting to be real with you." He paused, searching my eyes. "You've shown me how to embrace being myself. I want to do the same for you."

The sincerity in his gaze sent a warmth coursing through me. I had spent so long wearing masks, afraid to let anyone see the parts of me that felt too broken, too flawed. The idea of being real, of peeling back the layers of my insecurities, felt daunting yet exhilarating.

"Okay, so here's the thing," I said, taking a deep breath, my pulse quickening. "I've always been scared to let anyone in. It's easier to keep people at arm's length, you know? But with you, it's different. You make me want to take that leap."

"Then let's leap together," Ethan replied, his voice a steady anchor amidst my swirling thoughts.

In that moment, as the stars began to blink awake in the twilight sky, I felt a shift within myself. The vulnerability I had long feared was no longer a weight I had to bear alone. The horizon glimmered with possibilities, and I found myself wishing that the world could remain suspended in this perfect, delicate balance of uncertainty and hope.

As if sensing the change in atmosphere, a distant storm began to brew, the winds picking up and sending ripples across the ocean's surface. The clouds rolled in, dark and ominous, threatening to obscure the beauty we had just shared.

"Looks like a storm is coming," I said, trying to maintain the lightness in my tone even as a shiver of unease raced down my spine. "Should we worry about getting drenched?"

Ethan grinned, a flash of mischief dancing in his eyes. "Only if you want to add a splash of adventure to this evening. How about a little run to the car?"

Before I could respond, he took off, laughter bubbling from him like an infectious melody, pulling me into the chaos of the moment. I ran after him, our footsteps echoing in the sand, the storm overhead echoing the wildness of our laughter. As we sprinted towards his car, I felt a thrill coursing through me, the kind that came from letting go of inhibitions and simply embracing the moment.

We barely reached the vehicle before the first drops of rain began to fall, each one a cool reminder of the tempest brewing above us. I was breathless, both from the sprint and from the exhilaration of what had just transpired. As I fumbled with the car door, Ethan caught my arm, pulling me close, the warmth of his body a stark contrast to the chill in the air.

"Maybe we should start keeping an eye on the weather," he said, his voice low and teasing, the humor a comfortable thread woven into the tension that still lingered between us.

"Or maybe we just embrace the storms together," I replied, my heart racing in my chest.

With a smirk, he opened the door for me, and I slipped inside, the warmth of the car cocooning me in safety as the rain began to pour down in earnest. The world outside blurred into a wash of grey, but inside, the air was charged with unspoken promises and a connection that felt undeniable.

The rain drummed against the roof like a thousand tiny hands, urging us forward into uncharted territory, and I realized that perhaps the storm outside wasn't something to fear. Instead, it was a new beginning, a chance to explore what lay ahead with the person who had already become so integral to my journey.

Rain hammered against the car, each drop splattering with the insistence of a thousand heartbeats, and I could feel the tension that had sparked between Ethan and me settle into something warmer, more profound. The inside of the car felt small, intimate, and just a bit thrilling, the kind of thrill that made the mundane suddenly feel like an adventure. Ethan's hand lingered on the door handle, his eyes darting between mine and the storm outside as if weighing the moment against the tempest brewing in the skies.

"I guess this is the part where we decide if we're the kind of people who watch the rain or the kind who run into it," he said, his lips curling into a playful smirk. The gleam in his eyes promised mischief, and I felt my pulse quicken with the prospect of what that might mean.

"Isn't it a bit cliché to run in the rain?" I teased back, crossing my arms with mock seriousness. "I mean, we could just sit here and discuss the philosophical implications of our choices while getting drenched. Isn't that the grown-up thing to do?"

Ethan chuckled, the sound rich and warm, a perfect counterpoint to the storm's fury. "What's the fun in that? Clichés exist for a reason. They're the heart of all great stories." He opened the door, rain cascading in like a curtain, and for a heartbeat, I hesitated. My heart thrummed in my chest as I weighed the risk of embracing this wild, reckless side of myself against the comfort of predictability.

But predictability felt so boring, and the warmth of Ethan's playful spirit beckoned like a siren's call. I threw caution to the wind, lunging forward and leaping into the rain. "Alright, cliché it is!" I yelled, laughter bubbling up as the cool water soaked through my clothes. The sensation was electrifying, liberating, and for that moment, I felt like I was flying.

Ethan followed suit, his laughter mingling with the rain as he caught up to me, spinning me around in a whirlwind of joy. "Look at us! A pair of soggy romantics!" he exclaimed, and I couldn't help but laugh even harder, the sound echoing across the deserted beach.

The world around us blurred into a wash of grey and color, a beautiful mess of raindrops and laughter. Each step through the sand sent splashes of water up our legs, and the exhilaration of the storm felt like a promise—one that whispered of daring moments and uncharted territory.

"I can't believe I'm doing this," I shouted over the downpour, unable to contain my grin as I danced under the open sky.

"Me neither!" Ethan replied, eyes sparkling with the thrill of spontaneity. He caught my hand, and together we spun in circles, letting the rain drench us completely. For the first time in what felt like ages, I was utterly free, unshackled from my fears, my doubts, and everything that had kept me from truly living.

As the rain intensified, a clap of thunder rumbled overhead, a deep sound that reverberated in my bones. I glanced at Ethan, whose expression had shifted from playful to pensive. "We should probably find some shelter," he said, glancing at the horizon where dark clouds rolled ominously. But just as I nodded in agreement, a flash of lightning split the sky, illuminating the world around us in stark brilliance.

Before I could even process the moment, Ethan suddenly pulled me close, shielding me from the torrential downpour. The warmth of his body enveloped me, and for an instant, the outside world faded, leaving just the two of us and the electricity crackling in the air between us.

"You're crazy, you know that?" he murmured, his breath warm against my ear, his voice low and urgent, sending a shiver of excitement through me.

"Maybe I like it that way," I replied, my voice a playful challenge. "What's life without a little chaos?"

But even as the words left my lips, I couldn't shake the feeling that this chaos might lead to something deeper, something we were both unprepared for. I stepped back slightly, my heart racing not just from the thrill of the rain, but from the sudden realization of how close we had become—physically and emotionally.

"Let's get inside," I suggested, my voice steadier now, as I searched for clarity amid the whirlwind of feelings that threatened to overwhelm me.

"Right. The café down the street might still be open," he agreed, and together we darted back toward the car, laughing as the rain continued to pelt down, our footsteps a chaotic rhythm in the storm.

We hopped into the car, breathless and laughing, but the moment we closed the doors, an uneasy silence fell between us. The storm outside raged on, but inside the car, the atmosphere shifted, becoming heavy with the weight of unspoken words. I could see Ethan's brow furrow as he glanced at me, the lightheartedness of our earlier banter replaced by something deeper, something that made my heart race and my stomach twist in knots.

"What are we doing?" he finally asked, his voice breaking through the tension.

"What do you mean?" I replied, playing innocent even as I felt the truth curling in my gut.

"You know what I mean," he said, exhaling sharply. "This—whatever this is between us. It's not just a passing moment, is it?"

"No, it's not," I admitted, my heart pounding as I faced the reality that had been looming ever since our kiss. "But it's complicated, Ethan. I'm... I'm not sure I know how to do this. I've never really—"

He reached for my hand, his fingers brushing against mine, sending an electric jolt through me. "Neither have I. But what if we tried? What if we just... leaned into it?"

Before I could respond, another flash of lightning illuminated the car, momentarily blinding me. As I blinked to regain my vision, a strange shape caught my eye in the distance, moving just beyond the edge of the beach, half-hidden in the shadows of the palm trees swaying in the storm.

"Did you see that?" I gasped, my voice a mix of disbelief and fear.

"What?" Ethan turned sharply, his expression shifting from curiosity to concern.

"There's something out there," I said, my heart racing anew, the previous intimacy forgotten as adrenaline surged through my veins.

He squinted into the darkness, tension flooding the space between us. "What do you mean? It's just the storm, right?"

But even as he spoke, I knew it was more than that. A figure emerged from the shadows, its form shrouded in the rain, moving with a grace that felt unnatural. My breath hitched, a cold dread settling deep in my stomach as the reality of the unknown approached, cutting through the warmth of our earlier connection like a knife.

"It's not just the storm, Ethan. It's—"

Before I could finish, the figure stepped fully into view, the headlights of the car illuminating a face that sent chills down my spine, a face I recognized all too well. The rain poured down, mingling with my rising panic as I whispered the name that had haunted my thoughts, a name that now echoed in the storm's fury.

"Lily."

Ethan's voice dropped to a whisper as the figure moved closer, its expression unreadable, but the glint in its eyes revealed a truth that sent my heart racing. This was no mere coincidence. The storm had brought us here for a reason, and as the darkness closed in, I realized that we were about to face something far more dangerous than either of us had anticipated.

Chapter 13: The Ripple Effect

The moment I stepped back into the office, the sharp scent of coffee mingled with the low hum of fluorescent lights, jolting me back to reality. It was as if the vibrant sun-soaked days at the beach had been nothing but a mirage, and now I was plunged into the stark, sterile world of cubicles and corporate chatter. The excitement of my recent promotion was like a double-edged sword, glittering with the promise of opportunity but dulled by the razor-sharp edges of jealousy and suspicion that surrounded me.

"Look who finally decided to grace us with her presence!" Karen's voice sliced through the morning drone. She leaned back in her chair, arms crossed, a smirk playing on her lips. Karen had never been shy about her opinions, especially when it came to me. Her brow arched, and a flicker of amusement danced in her eyes. "What's it like being the golden girl now?"

"Enlightening," I replied, my voice steady but my heart racing beneath the surface. "Thanks for asking." I pushed past her desk, trying to shake off the unease that tightened like a vise around my chest. But the quiet whispers began as I made my way to my own cubicle, threading through the maze of desks and fluorescent lights. I could feel their eyes on me, and every hushed conversation felt like a silent indictment.

"Did you hear she got promoted? Must be nice to have friends in high places," someone murmured just loud enough for me to catch. I paused, allowing the words to sink in like poison, dulling my senses. The insinuation that I had somehow weaseled my way to the top stung more than I wanted to admit.

Ethan's desk was a small sanctuary amidst the chaos, and I made my way toward it, seeking solace in the warm, inviting smile that greeted me. He stood, holding a steaming cup of coffee in his hand,

and the tension on my shoulders eased slightly as I caught a whiff of the rich aroma.

"Congratulations, boss lady," he said, his voice low and genuine, cutting through the noise like a ray of sunlight. He handed me the coffee, his fingers brushing against mine, a simple gesture that sent a spark of comfort through me. "I'm proud of you, really."

"Thanks," I replied, forcing a smile that felt more like a mask. "But I think I might need your help. It seems some people think I didn't earn it."

Ethan's expression shifted from supportive to defensive in an instant. "Forget them. You worked your ass off for this. Let them talk. They're just jealous."

"I know, but it's not just chatter anymore. It's getting to me." I took a sip of the coffee, savoring the rich taste as I tried to quell the unease brewing in my stomach. "And it's making things... complicated between us."

"Complicated how?" He leaned closer, concern etching lines on his forehead, and for a moment, I was lost in the depths of his hazel eyes, the world around us fading.

"I feel like I'm being pulled in two directions. Between the job and... well, us," I said, gesturing vaguely. "I want to succeed here, but I don't want to jeopardize what we have."

"You're not going to lose me over some office politics," he assured me, his voice firm yet gentle. "I'm in this for the long haul, remember?"

"Easier said than done," I muttered, glancing back at the bustling office. "With Kevin lurking around like a vulture, it's hard to feel secure."

At the mention of Kevin, the warmth of the moment faded like sunlight behind a cloud. Kevin, my former mentor turned adversary, was not one to be underestimated. His eyes were sharp, and his smile was often a prelude to something sinister. Since my promotion, he had taken to undermining me at every turn, casting shadows of doubt over my achievements. His presence was like a dark cloud, threatening to rain on my parade at any moment.

"Just focus on your work, and let me handle him," Ethan said, determination lacing his words. "I'll have a chat with him if it comes to that."

"No, don't. I don't want to make it worse," I replied quickly, panic rising at the thought of Ethan confronting Kevin. "I can handle it. I just need to prove that I deserve to be here."

"Okay, but you don't have to do it alone," he pressed, reaching out to squeeze my hand, a reassuring gesture that grounded me amidst the turmoil. "You have me, and I'll stand by you, no matter what. We'll get through this together."

His unwavering support sent a wave of warmth through me, but the lingering tension between my personal and professional life felt like a tightrope walk over an abyss. I wanted to lean into him, to bask in the comfort he offered, yet the weight of the office dynamics loomed large.

As the day wore on, my resolve was put to the test. Kevin cornered me in the break room, a charming smile plastered on his face that didn't quite reach his eyes. "Congratulations, Sarah. I see you've made quite a splash," he said, his tone dripping with sarcasm. "Funny how those who know how to charm the right people tend to get ahead, isn't it?"

I clenched my jaw, fighting the urge to snap back. "I earned my promotion, Kevin. I worked hard, and I won't apologize for it."

"Hard work? Or just a friendly relationship with your superiors?" His words were a blade, slicing through my confidence.

I stood my ground, refusing to let him see how much his words affected me. "I believe in merit over connections. You should try it sometime."

The tension between us crackled like static electricity, but Kevin merely chuckled, the sound devoid of humor. "We'll see how long that perspective holds up in this cutthroat environment."

As I turned to leave, I felt a shadow trailing behind me, an insidious whisper of doubt curling around my heart. The ripple effect of my promotion had begun to shape my reality, and I couldn't shake the feeling that I was just one misstep away from tumbling into a whirlpool of resentment and betrayal. But I wasn't about to let Kevin win. I was determined to hold onto my dreams, even as the storm clouds gathered on the horizon.

The following days unfurled with an unsettling rhythm, a cacophony of office gossip serving as an unwelcome soundtrack to my life. The hum of the fluorescent lights overhead seemed to buzz louder, each flicker punctuating the silent judgments lurking in the corners of the open office space. I threw myself into work, hoping that my performance would silence the naysayers. With each completed project, I envisioned my confidence growing, but it felt more like bandaging a wound that had only begun to bleed.

I kept my head down, drowning out the whispers and the prying eyes. Karen's taunts echoed in my mind like an annoying pop song I couldn't escape. It wasn't just the rivalry that kept me awake at night; it was the realization that my success had turned me into a target. Even the printer seemed to smirk at me, jamming at the most inopportune moments as if it too wanted to join the chorus of my self-doubt.

Ethan's presence was a welcome balm. His unwavering support was like a lifeline, steadying me even as I felt myself teetering on the brink of doubt. One afternoon, as I stared blankly at a spreadsheet that had begun to blur, he slid a cup of tea onto my desk, breaking my concentration.

"You know," he said, leaning against the cubicle wall, his casual posture a stark contrast to my tense frame, "it's scientifically proven that tea improves brain function. You need all the help you can get."

I chuckled softly, grateful for his attempts to lighten the mood. "You'd think they'd have given me a lifetime supply when I got the promotion."

"Maybe it's a conspiracy. They're trying to keep the competition at bay," he joked, winking at me as he pulled up a chair beside mine. "In all seriousness, you're doing great. Don't let anyone shake your confidence."

His gaze held a mix of sincerity and warmth that made my heart race. But just as I began to relax, the office door swung open, and in walked Kevin, his presence akin to a storm cloud rolling in on a bright day. I could feel the tension shift in the room, like a coiled spring ready to snap.

"Ah, the new favorite!" Kevin exclaimed, his voice dripping with sarcasm as he made his way toward us. "Are we sharing tea now? Or is that just a privilege for those who've earned it?"

I gritted my teeth, unwilling to give him the satisfaction of my anger. "It's just tea, Kevin. But it's nice to see you've found your way back to the office."

"Very clever, Sarah. But we both know clever doesn't cut it around here," he shot back, his eyes glinting with malicious amusement. "You might want to keep an eye on your 'team,' they seem a bit... restless."

Ethan's grip on my hand tightened under the table, and I could feel the heat radiating off him as he prepared to retaliate. "Why don't you mind your own business, Kevin? Sarah's doing just fine."

"Oh, I'm sure she is," Kevin said, turning his gaze back to me, the smirk plastered on his face more condescending than ever. "Just remember, those who climb too quickly often have a nasty fall."

With that, he sauntered away, leaving a trail of tension so thick you could cut it with a knife. I took a deep breath, feeling the weight of his words. "I don't know how you handle him," I said, shaking my head.

"He's all bark," Ethan replied, but the slight crease in his brow told me he wasn't as confident as he wanted to appear. "And if he tries to come after you again, he'll have to deal with me."

His protective nature warmed my heart, but the thought of dragging him into my battles made my stomach churn. "I can't keep relying on you for backup. This is my fight."

"Yeah, well, it's one I'd rather help you with. I mean, who wants to see you get hurt? You've worked too hard for this."

I looked into his eyes, a flicker of gratitude swelling within me, but just as quickly, doubt crept back in. "I appreciate it, but I also need to prove that I deserve this. I can't let anyone think I'm just playing the sympathy card."

The evening passed in a blur of deadlines and distracted glances. Each time I glanced at the clock, it seemed to mock me, the seconds ticking away with a slow, painful insistence. As night fell and the office began to empty, I took a moment to gather my thoughts, knowing that my resolve was wearing thin.

The familiar sound of a chair scraping across the floor broke my concentration, and I turned to see Ethan lingering by the door, his expression unreadable. "Hey, you heading out?"

I sighed, pinching the bridge of my nose in frustration. "I was going to stay a little longer. There's still so much to catch up on."

"Come on, you've been at it for hours," he said, moving closer. "Let me take you to dinner. You need a break from this madness."

A soft smile tugged at my lips, but the knot in my stomach tightened. "You don't have to babysit me, you know."

"I'm not babysitting. I'm rescuing you. There's a difference." His lighthearted tone made it hard to resist, and I found myself chuckling despite the tension still clinging to me.

"Fine. But only if you promise to pick the place and not just the closest taco stand."

"Deal," he grinned, and in that moment, it felt like the walls of the office melted away, leaving only us in a world of our own.

As we stepped outside, the fresh evening air enveloped us, carrying the scent of blooming flowers and the distant sounds of laughter from a nearby café. I inhaled deeply, grateful to escape the confines of my workspace, if only for a moment.

Dinner turned into a delightful reprieve from the chaos. We settled into a cozy booth, the low light casting a warm glow around us. As we ordered, I couldn't help but admire how effortlessly Ethan navigated our conversation, the way his eyes sparkled when he spoke about his latest project, or how he made me laugh with his dry humor.

"Do you ever think about what we'll be like in ten years?" I asked, my curiosity piqued as I watched him lean back in his seat, a thoughtful expression crossing his face.

"Ten years?" he echoed, eyebrows raised. "If I had a dime for every time someone asked me that, I'd probably be running my own startup by now."

"Okay, fine. What about five years?" I pressed, leaning forward, intrigued by his perspective.

"I'd like to think we'll be here, sitting in this same booth," he replied, his gaze steady and sincere. "Maybe I'll have a couple of restaurants by then, and you'll be head of your department, fending off jealous colleagues left and right."

I laughed, but as the sound faded, a strange unease washed over me. "What if things change?"

Ethan reached across the table, his fingers brushing against mine, grounding me. "Change is inevitable, but that doesn't mean it has to be bad. We're in control of our own stories."

His words resonated with me, igniting a flicker of hope in my chest. Yet, as we finished dinner and stepped back into the night, I couldn't shake the feeling that Kevin's words were still lurking in the shadows, waiting for the perfect moment to strike. Life was a dance, and I was determined to lead, even as the music threatened to falter.

The next few days were a blur of late nights and early mornings, the rhythm of my life becoming a frenetic dance between deadlines and self-doubt. Each morning, I donned my professional armor: a sharp blazer, the perfect heels, and a smile that, if I was lucky, would not waver as I stepped into the office battlefield. Yet, no matter how well I masked my anxiety, the stares from my colleagues weighed heavily on my shoulders.

It wasn't just Kevin's voice echoing in my mind; it was the collective murmur of discontent that filled the office like a thick fog. I often found myself retreating to the break room, clinging to the comforting rituals of coffee and snacks, but even those moments of solace were tinged with tension.

"Looks like someone's on a power trip," Karen quipped one afternoon, her gaze pointedly flicking to my desk, where I was buried in reports. "Hope you don't forget us little people when you're up there in the clouds."

I straightened my back, fighting the urge to respond with a biting retort. "You know, Karen, they say the view is best from up high, but the air is pretty thin. You should try it sometime."

Her eyes narrowed, but before she could muster a reply, Ethan appeared at my side, his expression a blend of amusement and concern. "Don't engage, Sarah. They're not worth the effort."

"Right. Because I'd hate to see you lose your position of power in the office hierarchy," I shot back, trying to keep the banter light even as I felt my heart racing.

Ethan chuckled, easing some of the tension that clung to my skin like a second layer. "Well, I'm not above a little friendly rivalry. Just remember, the best way to prove them wrong is to keep doing what you're doing."

"Yeah, I guess. But it's hard to ignore the whispers," I admitted, my smile faltering. "It feels like everyone is waiting for me to stumble."

"Well, if they're waiting, they'll be waiting a long time." His eyes sparkled with determination, igniting a flicker of hope within me. "And I'll be right here to catch you if you do."

His support felt like a lifeline in the storm, and I clung to it as I dove back into my work, determined to drown out the noise around me. But just as I thought I was gaining ground, a wave of unexpected chaos hit.

One afternoon, I was knee-deep in a presentation when Kevin sauntered over, a self-satisfied grin plastered across his face. "Got a moment?" he asked, his voice honeyed with false politeness.

"Depends on what you want," I replied, trying to project an air of nonchalance.

"Oh, just wanted to let you know I'm taking over the client meeting next week," he announced casually, as if discussing the weather. "Management felt I would be a better fit for the role."

The words hung in the air like a sudden chill. "You're taking my meeting? But I—"

"Don't take it personally. They just think your expertise is... best utilized elsewhere," he said, his tone dripping with insincerity. "After all, it's a big world out there, and we need to keep our best people in the right places."

I clenched my fists, fighting the wave of frustration bubbling to the surface. "You think I'll let you waltz in and take credit for my hard work? Not a chance, Kevin."

He shrugged, a predator reveling in the thrill of the chase. "Just doing what's best for the team, right? Let's not forget, it's all about appearances."

With that, he turned on his heel, leaving me simmering in disbelief. I felt like a jack-in-the-box, ready to spring into action but momentarily immobilized by his audacity.

Ethan, who had witnessed the whole exchange from a distance, came up beside me, his face set in a frown. "What did he want?"

I sighed, running a hand through my hair. "He just claimed my client meeting. Apparently, I'm not a good fit."

Ethan's expression darkened. "That's ridiculous. You've been prepping for that meeting for weeks! We need to talk to HR."

"No," I interjected quickly, shaking my head. "I don't want to escalate things. It'll only make it worse."

"Not fighting back feels like letting him win," Ethan insisted, his voice tense. "You have to stand up for yourself, Sarah."

I looked at him, caught between my desire to protect my position and the fear of making things worse. "And what if it backfires? What if they side with him? I can't risk losing everything I've worked for."

Ethan stepped closer, his tone softening. "I get it. But you can't let fear dictate your choices. You deserve that meeting, and you have every right to defend your work."

His conviction stirred something deep within me, and for the first time, I began to feel the faintest flicker of rebellion ignite against Kevin's relentless undermining. Maybe it was time to take a stand.

That evening, as I sat at my desk preparing for the upcoming meeting, the realization struck me that this was more than just a fight for professional respect; it was about reclaiming my identity.

The line between work and personal life had begun to blur, and I could feel the weight of expectations pressing down on me. I wanted to be the woman who fought for her dreams, not just a pawn in someone else's game.

Ethan stopped by, bringing dinner and the kind of warmth that melted the stress of the day. "I thought we could work through some strategies together," he said, setting the food on my desk. "Nothing like a little fuel to fire up the brain."

As we settled into the evening, sharing ideas and laughter, I felt the boundaries of my anxiety begin to dissolve. "You really believe I can turn this around?" I asked, the question hanging in the air like a tightrope waiting for me to take the first step.

"Absolutely. You just need to trust yourself. You've got this," he encouraged, his eyes gleaming with faith in me.

That faith became a lifeline, and I began to strategize. I would gather my notes, prepare a strong defense for my position, and request a meeting with management. But just as I felt the excitement of empowerment swell within me, my phone buzzed, pulling me back to reality.

A text from Karen lit up the screen: "You need to see this. Kevin's up to something. Meet me in the lobby."

A shiver ran down my spine, the words twisting my stomach. I shot a glance at Ethan, whose brow furrowed with concern. "What is it?"

"I don't know, but I have a feeling it's not good," I said, my pulse quickening as I gathered my things, the taste of anxiety souring the air between us.

"Let's go together," he insisted, matching my pace as we moved toward the lobby, the excitement of my newfound resolve dimming under a blanket of dread.

Karen was waiting, her expression serious as she gestured for us to follow her outside. The chill in the air mirrored the growing apprehension in my gut. "I overheard something—Kevin's planning to sabotage your next client meeting. He's telling everyone you're incompetent and that he should take the lead."

My heart raced, fury and disbelief colliding within me. "What? How can he even—"

Before I could finish my thought, a familiar figure emerged from the shadows, his face twisted into a triumphant smirk. Kevin stood there, flanked by a couple of colleagues who appeared far too eager to join his cause.

"Looks like the new management darling has some competition," he taunted, his tone laced with malice. "Let's see how far you really climb, Sarah. I hope you're ready for the fall."

The air crackled with tension, and I felt the world shift beneath me as Kevin's words settled like a heavy fog. I glanced at Ethan, who was visibly tense, and in that moment, I understood that this was the beginning of a battle I hadn't anticipated—a fight for my reputation, my position, and my very identity.

"Game on, Kevin," I said, my voice steady despite the whirlwind of emotions inside me. "Let's see who falls first."

But as I stepped forward, ready to confront the storm, a sudden realization gripped me. Was this merely a prelude to a much larger game?

Chapter 14: Turning Point

The conference room hummed with the low buzz of anticipation as I sat in the back, my palms slick against the polished wood of the table. The flickering overhead lights cast a sterile glow on the whiteboard where I had meticulously sketched out my ideas in vibrant colors just days earlier. The scent of fresh coffee lingered in the air, mixing with the faint smell of cleaning supplies, a reminder of the countless hours I had spent here, pouring over data and crafting the presentation that was supposed to launch my career. The stakes had never felt higher, and yet, a storm brewed within me, an unsettling mix of excitement and dread.

Kevin strode to the front, his sharp suit a striking contrast to my more casual attire. He had always held a certain charisma, the kind that commanded attention, but I knew better than to trust the glint in his eye. He flashed a confident smile as he tapped the microphone, preparing to deliver what should have been my moment—the culmination of my hard work and late nights spent battling fatigue and self-doubt. I could practically hear the clock ticking down to my defeat.

He started strong, outlining the project's goals, throwing in jargon-heavy phrases that danced around my concepts. I felt my heart sink as I realized what was happening. Kevin wasn't just presenting; he was stealing. With each word, he twisted my carefully constructed arguments into a narrative that glorified himself and downplayed my contributions. The room, full of colleagues and superiors I respected, hung on his every word. My stomach churned as a hot wave of anger surged through me, threatening to engulf my composure.

As he transitioned into my core findings, the ones I had poured my soul into, I could feel my breath hitch. The taste of betrayal soured my coffee as it bubbled up, a visceral reminder of the friendship I thought we had forged. With every slide he clicked through, my resolve began to harden like steel. The weight of his deceit pressed down on me, but rather than crush me, it ignited a spark.

"Excuse me," I interrupted, my voice slicing through the chatter like a hot knife through butter. The room fell silent, all eyes darting between Kevin and me. His brow furrowed slightly, surprise flickering across his face, but I wasn't done.

I rose from my seat, my heart pounding with each step toward the front of the room. "What Kevin is presenting here are my findings, and I can't stand by and let that happen." The words flowed out with a steadiness I didn't know I possessed. "If we could go back to slide three..." I gestured toward the screen, feeling a rush of adrenaline course through me as I took control of the narrative.

A murmur rippled through the audience, the tension palpable as I began to unpack my data, the colors on the screen shifting from sterile white to the vivid hues I had chosen. The graphs displayed the intricate dance of numbers and insights I had unearthed during my research. I shared the nuances of my methodology, the rationale behind every decision, each piece of information feeding into a bigger picture that I had painstakingly crafted.

Ethan, seated at the back, leaned forward, a look of disbelief and pride mingling on his face. His smile, warm and supportive, wrapped around me like a lifeline, and suddenly, I wasn't just fighting for my work—I was fighting for the belief in myself that I had almost lost.

Kevin stood frozen, his confidence fading as I continued to reclaim my narrative, piece by piece. The flush of red creeping up his neck betrayed his inner turmoil, a stark contrast to the cool façade he had maintained up until this moment. I could see his mind racing, trying to find a way to regain control, but I pressed on, buoyed by the unexpected support from my colleagues. I could feel their shifting energy, sensing their alignment with me, as whispers of my name floated through the room.

The atmosphere crackled with electricity, and with every passing second, I felt a weight lifting from my shoulders. The room shifted from a sea of uncertainty to one of solidarity, and I couldn't help but bask in the newfound support. The fear that had gripped me earlier melted away, replaced by an undeniable sense of empowerment.

Finally, I reached the conclusion of my presentation, my voice steady and confident. "In conclusion, it's imperative that we acknowledge the collaborative effort that has gone into this project. My findings are not just numbers—they're the result of teamwork, dedication, and a genuine desire to innovate."

A thunderous applause erupted, drowning out the remnants of Kevin's presentation. It was a chorus of affirmation, of shared triumph, and in that moment, I knew I had taken a pivotal step not just in my career, but in my life. As I stepped down, the applause still ringing in my ears, I caught Ethan's eye. His expression was a mixture of pride and admiration, and I felt an overwhelming rush of gratitude.

In the aftermath of the presentation, as colleagues congratulated me and the weight of the day began to settle, I found myself standing in the corner of the room, a bright smile plastered across my face. I had faced down betrayal and emerged stronger. As I reflected on the experience, I realized that this moment wasn't just about my career; it was about reclaiming my identity and believing in my worth.

The hum of chatter in the conference room faded as I navigated my way through the clusters of colleagues, the remnants of applause still echoing in my ears. The scent of fresh coffee hung in the air, a comforting reminder of the fuel that had carried me through long nights of preparation. Yet, beneath that comfort lay a simmering tension, an undercurrent of uncertainty about what the fallout from my bold confrontation might be.

As I made my way toward Ethan, I could feel the eyes of the room on me, a mixture of admiration and curiosity swirling in their gaze. I could sense their collective whisperings, the buzz of speculation about Kevin's audacious attempt to steal my thunder and my unexpected defiance. In that moment, the adrenaline that had spurred me on began to ebb, leaving behind a cocktail of exhilaration and trepidation.

"Nice save there, warrior princess," Ethan said, a playful glint in his eyes as he leaned against the wall, arms crossed. His casual posture was deceiving, hiding the intensity of the moment we had just shared. "I thought for a second you were going to hurl a stapler at his head."

"Tempting," I replied, my heart still racing. "But I figured I'd keep it classy. Besides, a well-placed verbal jab is far more effective."

He chuckled, his laughter warm and genuine, wrapping around me like a cozy blanket on a winter's day. "You definitely delivered one of the best jabs I've ever seen. I can't believe he thought he could pull that off."

My stomach fluttered as I caught his eye, the admiration sparkling within them. I hadn't realized how much I craved that look of approval until it washed over me, filling the empty spaces that Kevin's betrayal had left behind. "I just couldn't let him walk all over my work," I admitted, glancing back toward Kevin, who stood at the front, looking deflated and defeated, as if he had just realized the depths of his own hubris.

"Can you blame him?" Ethan shrugged, an easy grin breaking across his face. "He's always been the type to steal the spotlight, but it takes guts to shine the light back on yourself."

Just then, our manager, Lisa, approached, her expression a blend of disbelief and admiration. "You were incredible in there! I've never seen anyone turn the tide so quickly. It was like watching a gladiator in the arena. Kevin won't be trying that again anytime soon, I promise you."

"Let's hope not," I replied, the pride swelling in my chest. "I'm not looking to be his next victim."

As the crowd began to disperse, the buzz of excitement dissipating into the air, Ethan leaned in closer, his voice lowering conspiratorially. "So, what's next? Are you going to throw a party? Maybe a small celebration for the brave warrior who fought the dragon?"

I couldn't help but laugh at the imagery. "Maybe I should. But for now, I just want to find a quiet corner and breathe for a moment. This was way more exhausting than I anticipated."

"Then let's escape. I know a perfect little café around the corner that serves the best chocolate croissants. It'll be our victory feast." His smile was infectious, and I found myself swept up in his enthusiasm.

Before I could second-guess myself, I nodded. "Sure, why not? A sweet treat sounds like the perfect way to celebrate."

We left the conference room, the chatter and laughter of colleagues trailing behind us as we stepped into the brisk air outside. The sunlight was a sharp contrast to the fluorescent glow of the office, invigorating and alive. I took a deep breath, letting the fresh air fill my lungs, the weight of the presentation slowly lifting from my shoulders.

As we walked side by side, our conversation flowed effortlessly, each word weaving a bond that felt familiar and easy. Ethan had a way of making everything seem lighter, his laughter punctuating our discussions about work, life, and everything in between. It was refreshing to have someone who saw me as more than just a colleague, who recognized my potential and genuinely cared about my success.

The café came into view, a cozy little spot nestled between towering buildings, its windows adorned with flower boxes bursting with color. The inviting aroma of freshly baked pastries wafted through the air, pulling me inside like a moth to a flame. As we settled at a small table near the window, I felt a wave of contentment wash over me.

"Okay, so tell me," Ethan said, leaning in with that playful spark in his eyes, "do you think Kevin will come back with a vengeance? Maybe a revenge plot involving staplers and glitter?"

I snorted, nearly spilling my water. "Glitter? I think that might be too ambitious for him. Besides, I'm ready for any glitter bombs he might launch. I'll just set up a glitter shield."

"Brilliant strategy," he laughed, and as he took a sip of his coffee, I caught the hint of mischief in his smile. "But seriously, how do you feel about what just happened? I mean, standing up to him like that—it takes a lot of courage."

I paused, considering his question. "Honestly, I feel liberated. It was like breaking free from this invisible barrier I had been stuck behind. For so long, I let my insecurities dictate my choices. But in that moment, I found my voice."

He nodded, his expression softening. "You deserve to be heard, and I think today was a turning point for you. You've got what it takes to go far in this industry. Just remember, sometimes you have to fight for your place at the table."

The warmth in his words wrapped around me, and for a brief moment, I allowed myself to bask in that support. It felt exhilarating to be seen, to have someone recognize the hard work I had poured into my career. But beneath that exhilaration lurked a flicker of uncertainty, whispering that this victory was merely a prelude to greater challenges ahead.

As we chatted and laughed over our pastries, my mind wandered to the looming deadlines and projects awaiting my attention back at the office. The sense of impending responsibility tugged at me, a reminder that the journey I was on was just beginning. But amidst those thoughts, I also felt a surge of optimism. The strength I had unearthed today was a catalyst, a promise of what I could achieve if I continued to believe in myself.

"Cheers to new beginnings, then," Ethan said, raising his coffee cup in a toast.

I clinked my cup against his, laughter bubbling up once more. "And to glitter shields and courageous warriors."

"Always," he replied, the warmth of his smile igniting something bright within me.

The atmosphere of the café buzzed with the sounds of clinking cups and hushed conversations, creating a warm cocoon that felt worlds away from the tension of the conference room. With every sip of my rich, chocolatey coffee, I felt a little more anchored, a little more in control. The world outside was a blur of movement—people rushing past, their lives unfolding in hurried steps—while I was here, caught in a moment that felt almost suspended in time.

Ethan leaned back in his chair, his arms crossed, the sunlight catching the playful curls of his hair. "So, what's the plan now? Ride this wave of momentum straight to the top, or are you going to take some time to plot your revenge? Maybe a clandestine operation involving cupcakes and glitter?"

I chuckled, imagining a covert mission involving sticky frosting and sparkles. "As tempting as that sounds, I think I'll focus on the climb. Revenge sounds exhausting."

"True," he agreed, nodding sagely. "And cupcakes can be distracting. Though I could definitely use a distraction from the pile of work awaiting me."

I could relate; the afterglow of my presentation felt bittersweet with the knowledge that reality was waiting just around the corner.

"Do you think Kevin will retaliate?" I asked, my brow furrowing at the thought.

Ethan shrugged, a playful smile dancing on his lips. "If he's smart, he'll lay low for a while. After all, you just pulled a power move that could rival any superhero's cape flip. But then again, people like him rarely act in their own best interest."

"Isn't that the truth?" I sighed, the initial thrill of my victory dimming slightly. "I just wish I could shake this nagging feeling that I haven't seen the last of him."

"You'll handle it," he said confidently. "You showed everyone today that you're not just a pretty face in the office. You've got grit." His words wrapped around me like a reassuring hug, and I couldn't help but smile.

Just then, my phone buzzed, pulling me from our easy banter. The screen lit up with a message from Lisa: We need to talk. ASAP. My stomach sank, the joy of the moment slipping away like sand through my fingers.

"Everything okay?" Ethan noticed the change in my demeanor, the concern etched on his face.

"Lisa wants to meet," I replied, my voice steadier than I felt. "I can't shake the feeling it's about Kevin."

He leaned forward, concern etched across his features. "Do you want me to come with you? I can be your backup. Or your emotional support human."

I appreciated the offer, but I couldn't help but shake my head. "No, I need to do this on my own. If Kevin's plotting something, I need to face it without anyone else's influence clouding my judgment. But I promise to fill you in after."

"Fair enough," he said, though his expression didn't quite match his words. "Just remember, I'm a phone call away if you need backup. Even if it means showing up with glitter."

A laugh bubbled up at the thought, and I felt a little lighter. "I'll keep that in mind."

As I stepped out of the café and into the bustling streets, the world around me felt sharper, more vibrant, the colors more pronounced. Yet, beneath that vibrancy lay an undercurrent of tension, an unsettling feeling that something was brewing just out of sight. My heart raced as I made my way back to the office, the familiar route feeling alien as anxiety coiled around my thoughts.

Lisa's office door was ajar when I arrived, the faint sound of her voice rising and falling, punctuated by the click of her keyboard. I knocked gently before stepping inside, the cool air of the room hitting me like a wave of calm. She looked up, her expression unreadable.

"Thanks for coming in," she said, gesturing for me to take a seat. Her voice was steady, but there was an edge to it that made me sit a little straighter.

"What's up?" I asked, trying to keep my tone light, though I could feel the tension coiling in my stomach.

"I want to talk about Kevin," she began, her gaze locking onto mine with an intensity that made my heart race. "And about the fallout from today's presentation. You made quite an impression, but it's drawn attention—not all of it positive."

"What do you mean?" My pulse quickened, each word echoing ominously in my mind.

"Some of the higher-ups are concerned about how Kevin might respond. He's been known to retaliate in unexpected ways, and they want to ensure that you're protected. They're contemplating a possible reassignment for you, just to be safe."

The words landed like a lead weight in my stomach. "A reassignment? For standing up for myself?" The injustice twisted like a knife, and I struggled to keep my composure.

"It's not a punishment," she rushed to clarify. "They just want to make sure you're not in a position where Kevin could undermine you again. It's not personal. It's... strategic."

"Strategic?" I echoed, incredulous. "It feels personal to me. I didn't back down today just to be shuffled around like a pawn."

Lisa sighed, running a hand through her hair. "I know it feels that way, but sometimes these decisions are made to protect the company's interests. They see your potential and want to ensure it's not stifled by internal politics."

I swallowed hard, the frustration boiling within me. "And what if I don't want to go? What if I want to stay and confront Kevin head-on?"

Her eyes softened, the understanding reflecting in her gaze. "I admire that spirit. But sometimes, stepping back can be the strongest move you make. You have to think about your career, about the bigger picture."

As she spoke, a flicker of something caught my eye. I turned toward the window, my breath catching in my throat. Outside, the street was alive with motion, but my focus sharpened on one figure. Kevin was standing on the corner, his eyes scanning the crowd, a predatory look on his face as he searched for something—or someone.

"Can you excuse me for a moment?" I asked, my heart racing as I leaned closer to the glass.

"Of course," Lisa said, her voice a muted echo as I stood, my eyes locked on Kevin. Just as he turned to disappear down the alley, a shiver ran down my spine. Something felt off—something darker was unfolding.

As I stepped back, ready to voice my concerns, the world tilted. My phone buzzed again, vibrating violently in my pocket. I fished it out, the screen lighting up with a new message that made my blood run cold: I know what you did. And I won't let this go.

My heart raced as I glanced at Lisa, who was now watching me closely. I opened my mouth to speak, but before I could say anything, the door burst open behind me, and Ethan stepped in, his face pale.

"Listen," he said, his voice low and urgent. "I just heard something you need to know. It's about Kevin—"

But before he could finish, the lights flickered overhead, plunging the room into semi-darkness. The hum of the building died down, leaving an unsettling silence in its wake. I could feel my pulse quickening, the weight of uncertainty pressing down as Ethan's eyes widened in alarm.

And then, from somewhere deep within the building, I heard a loud crash, a sound that shattered the stillness and echoed ominously through the air, leaving us all on edge, frozen in the moment before chaos erupted.

Chapter 15: Love Under Pressure

The air in the office hummed with the rhythm of productivity, the clatter of keyboards punctuating the silence as I buried myself in my work. Outside, rain drummed against the glass windows, creating a symphony of nature that should have felt soothing. Instead, it felt oppressive, a reminder of the storm brewing not just outside, but within the tangled web of my relationship with Ethan. The aftermath of our presentation had turned into a whirlwind of success, but beneath the surface lay the churning currents of stress and fatigue. It was as if our joy was a fragile balloon, dangerously close to being pricked by the sharpness of reality.

We had once shared easy laughter over mugs of coffee, our fingers brushing against each other as we reached for the sugar. Now, every minor setback felt like a crack in the foundation we had built. Late-night coding sessions that used to be our escape became battlegrounds where every miscommunication and misstep felt magnified. I could still remember the vibrant spark of our initial connection—the way his eyes lit up with excitement when he solved a particularly tricky problem, how his laugh could draw me in like a moth to a flame. But now, it felt as if the pressure of deadlines and expectations had stripped away those moments of joy, leaving us floundering in the murky waters of frustration.

The night I deleted the line of code, everything came to a head. I had been staring at the screen for so long that the numbers and letters began to blur into an indecipherable mass. My mind raced with the thousand thoughts of what needed to be done, yet all I could do was watch helplessly as my fingers executed a command that would erase hours of work. The moment it dawned on me what I'd done, a cold wave of panic surged through me, tightening my chest. Ethan's reaction was instantaneous. His face went pale, eyes wide with disbelief.

"Did you just delete that entire function?" he asked, his voice barely above a whisper, the tension in the air crackling like static electricity.

"I didn't mean to! It was an accident!" I pleaded, my voice rising in pitch as the reality of the situation set in.

"An accident? That was a critical part of the project! We can't just—" he cut off, running a hand through his hair in frustration. The gesture made my stomach drop, a stark reminder of how easily things could spiral out of control.

"You think I wanted this to happen?" I snapped, the heat of the moment igniting a fire in my belly that I couldn't contain. "I've been under so much pressure lately! You think I don't care about this project? About us?"

As our words collided, the air thickened with unspoken fears and pent-up frustrations, each accusation and rebuttal pulling us further apart instead of bringing us together. I could see the frustration etched on his features, the way his jaw clenched as if trying to hold back a tide of emotion. It was a fight born from exhaustion, the culmination of late nights and endless revisions, and a growing sense that we were losing the intimacy that once defined us.

Finally, silence enveloped the room, heavy and suffocating, as we both realized we had crossed an invisible line. It was an eerie moment, the calm after the storm, where the echoes of our argument lingered like the last notes of a haunting melody. I looked at Ethan, and his gaze fell to the floor, disappointment shadowing his handsome features. In that instant, I felt the sharp pang of regret, as if I had shattered not just our project, but a fragile piece of our relationship.

"I'm sorry," I said, the words barely a whisper, as if I was afraid to break the spell of silence that had settled between us. "I didn't mean to make this about us. I just... I need a break."

His eyes met mine, and the fire of anger had dimmed, replaced by something softer and more vulnerable. "We both do," he replied, his voice weary yet tender. "But I don't want to lose what we have. I don't want this project to ruin us."

As the rain drizzled down the windows, I felt the weight of his words wrap around me like a warm blanket. It became evident that we needed to step away from the chaos, to reconnect on a level that didn't involve code or deadlines. We needed to remember the spark that had brought us together in the first place.

That night, we decided to take a detour from our usual routine. Instead of diving into more lines of code, we stepped out into the rain, letting the droplets wash away our frustrations. We walked hand in hand, the world around us blurred by the downpour, our laughter rising above the storm. Each step felt like a deliberate choice, an acknowledgment that amidst the chaos, we could find our way back to each other.

We wandered to our favorite café, the one that smelled of roasted coffee and freshly baked pastries. The warmth enveloped us as we settled into a booth, our fingers entwined across the table. It was in that moment, surrounded by the comforting hum of conversation and the rich aroma of our drinks, that I realized how much I had missed this—just being with him, without the weight of expectations looming over us.

"You know," I began, a playful smile tugging at my lips, "for someone who usually has all the answers, you've been quite the mess lately."

Ethan raised an eyebrow, a grin breaking through the remnants of our earlier tension. "Hey, I can only handle so much pressure before I crack. Just like that line of code."

I laughed, the sound bubbling up like a release valve, letting go of the heaviness that had built up inside. "Let's promise to never let work come between us again. Or at least, to find a better way to handle it."

He nodded, his expression earnest. "Deal. No more late-night coding sessions unless they come with a side of dessert."

The playful banter ignited the warmth that had been smothered by stress, the connection between us reigniting with each shared smile. And as we left the café, hand in hand under the rain-soaked sky, I felt a renewed sense of hope. Perhaps the pressures of life would always loom, but together, we could weather any storm.

The rain had settled into a soft drizzle by the time we made our way back to the office, a light mist that clung to the air and swirled around us like a playful ghost. I felt lighter, almost buoyant, as if the weight of our earlier argument had evaporated along with the storm clouds. Our fingers entwined, we slipped through the glass doors, the familiar hum of the office buzzing around us. The glow of the screens created a comforting backdrop, but as we sat down, I realized the atmosphere had shifted. The usual chaos of deadlines and endless meetings loomed ahead, threatening to overshadow our newfound resolve.

"Let's try to keep our coding sessions to a minimum this week," Ethan suggested, his voice low but firm, as if speaking too loudly might summon the specter of stress back into our midst. "How about we set specific hours for work, then leave it behind?"

I nodded, appreciating his practicality. "Agreed. We can use the mornings to tackle the big stuff and keep the evenings for... well, anything but coding." My smirk matched his, a shared understanding passing between us. The unspoken truth was clear: we needed to reclaim the joy of simply being together.

As the week unfolded, we embraced our new strategy. Mornings became our sacred time, filled with caffeine-fueled focus and the clacking of keys that felt productive rather than pressured. The afternoons were a different story; they morphed into playful banter and spontaneous outings. One sunny Tuesday, we found ourselves at a local farmer's market, our arms laden with fresh produce and baked goods. The atmosphere was vibrant, a kaleidoscope of colors and sounds that enveloped us. I caught Ethan's eye, and he shot me a smile that melted my heart like butter on a warm biscuit.

"Do you think we can make something edible with these?" he asked, holding up a particularly lumpy squash. The ridiculousness of the vegetable made it hard to stifle my laughter.

"I think we can make a very interesting—if not entirely edible—dish," I replied, shaking my head. "I mean, who knew squash could look so... defiant?"

He grinned, pulling me closer as we weaved through the bustling crowd. The laughter and chatter of families surrounded us, their joy spilling over like the vibrant produce. We sampled strawberries that burst with sweetness, the juice running down our fingers, and enjoyed a piece of freshly baked pie that felt like a stolen moment of bliss.

In the midst of the joviality, however, a nagging thought crept into my mind. Our days were filled with laughter, but I couldn't ignore the ticking clock of deadlines waiting at the office. I had learned that avoidance could only go so far, and I sensed the inevitable return of the tension that had haunted us. Ethan, ever the perceptive one, caught my fleeting glance towards the bakery where we had just indulged.

"What's on your mind?" His question cut through the joyful atmosphere, grounding me.

"Just thinking about how we'll juggle all this work with everything else," I admitted, biting my lip. "I want this to last, Ethan, but I don't want us to lose sight of why we're doing it."

He paused, considering my words. "It's about balance, right? We can't let the work become our entire lives. If we do, we might just end up in another late-night argument over deleted code."

I nodded, grateful for his understanding. "Then we make a pact. If we feel overwhelmed, we call it out. No more bottling it up until it explodes."

"Deal," he replied, sealing our promise with a soft squeeze of my hand. We walked through the market, surrounded by laughter and light, feeling more like partners than colleagues, each moment shared a brick in the foundation of something precious.

The weeks passed with a delicate dance of productivity and play, but just as the rhythm settled, an unexpected twist struck. One afternoon, while I was deep in a project, an email notification pinged on my screen. The subject line read: "Urgent: Meeting Request." The sender was our boss, a name that usually conjured thoughts of conference rooms and corporate jargon. My stomach dropped as I opened it, the message within a stark reminder of the pressure lurking just beneath our newfound joy.

"We need to discuss the project's progress. I expect everyone to be present tomorrow at 9 AM," the email read, cold and commanding. I could practically hear the clock ticking down the hours until that meeting, each second like a metronome counting down to an impending storm.

I sighed, rubbing my temples as I glanced over at Ethan, who was typing furiously. "Looks like our lighthearted moments might have to be put on hold," I murmured, a mix of anxiety and frustration bubbling up.

"What's going on?" he asked, lifting his gaze from the screen.

I relayed the email, and his brow furrowed, the carefree atmosphere between us rapidly dimming. "Great. Just what we need," he said, sarcasm lacing his tone. "A meeting that feels like a ticking time bomb."

"Let's not freak out just yet. We can prepare tonight. We'll tackle this together," I replied, trying to infuse a sense of calmness into the brewing storm.

We spent the evening poring over our work, the atmosphere charged with tension as we dissected every detail of our project. Ideas flowed, but so did our anxiety, weaving through our dialogue like a shadow. Each time I glanced at the clock, I felt the pressure mounting, weighing heavy on my chest.

"Remember what we promised?" Ethan asked, breaking the tension with a chuckle as I absentmindedly crumpled yet another piece of paper. "No bottling it up, right?"

"You're right. I just—" I hesitated, searching for the right words. "I don't want to disappoint anyone. Not after all the hard work we've put in."

His gaze softened. "You won't. No matter what happens, we've come this far together. We'll figure it out."

His words, meant to comfort, sent a jolt of determination through me. This was our moment to show what we could achieve, to prove that love and ambition could coexist. As we prepared for the meeting, I realized this was our chance to reclaim our power, to turn the external pressure into a force that strengthened us rather than tore us apart.

The night stretched on, but it felt different now—less like an impending doom and more like a shared challenge. With each passing hour, I found myself leaning into the moment, remembering why we had embarked on this journey together in the first place. Love, like code, thrived on collaboration, and I was ready to tackle whatever came next with Ethan by my side.

The day of the meeting arrived, the morning sun breaking through the clouds like a spotlight illuminating our little corner of chaos. I sat across from Ethan at our usual table in the café, the scent of freshly brewed coffee mingling with the sweet aroma of pastries. The atmosphere was charged with a nervous energy, each sip of coffee a reminder of the high stakes awaiting us. I could see the determination in Ethan's eyes, his jaw set and brow slightly furrowed as he methodically reviewed our notes.

"Ready to wow them?" he asked, a playful grin tugging at the corners of his mouth despite the tension.

"Only if you promise to wear your most impressive 'we totally have our act together' face," I shot back, nudging him playfully. His laugh broke through the seriousness, and for a moment, the weight of the impending meeting slipped away, replaced by our shared camaraderie.

As we packed up and headed to the office, I felt a strange mix of excitement and dread bubbling in my stomach. The office hummed with activity, a flurry of coworkers rushing to and fro, all unaware of the storm brewing beneath the surface of our project. The conference room loomed ahead like a stage, each step echoing our growing apprehension.

Inside, our team gathered around the long, polished table. The room was lined with glass walls, the city skyline creating a breathtaking backdrop that felt almost surreal given the gravity of the situation. Our boss, a tall figure with an air of authority, stood at the front, arms crossed as he surveyed the room. The moment felt suspended in time, a perfect freeze-frame of anxiety and anticipation.

"Let's get started," he announced, cutting through the chatter. My heart raced as I took a seat beside Ethan, the proximity grounding me as I prepared for the storm ahead.

We presented our work with a blend of enthusiasm and determination, but as the discussion unfolded, I could sense a shift in the air. Questions began to fly like arrows, targeting our every misstep. My confidence wavered under the weight of scrutiny. The earlier banter faded into the background, replaced by a cacophony of doubts and concerns.

"Can you explain why this feature is lagging?" our boss asked, his eyes narrowing as he leaned forward. I felt Ethan tense beside me, and I quickly exchanged a glance with him, silently communicating our shared resolve.

"Of course," I replied, pulling myself up. "We had a few unforeseen challenges, but we're addressing them. We've made significant progress, and we're committed to delivering the final product on time."

"Significant progress, or just a few patches?" he retorted, and I could feel the heat rising in my cheeks. My pulse quickened as I mentally scrambled for reassurance.

Before I could respond, Ethan stepped in, his voice calm and steady. "We've identified the bottlenecks, and we're implementing solutions that will enhance our workflow. I'm confident we'll turn this around."

His confidence radiated through the room, and for a fleeting moment, I found solace in his unwavering presence. But the relief was short-lived, as our boss shifted the focus back onto the problems, dissecting our progress with a critical eye. Each critique felt like a blow, and I could see Ethan's frustration simmering just beneath the surface.

As the meeting dragged on, the atmosphere thickened with tension. I could sense Ethan's mounting irritation as he held back from interrupting, but the frustration bubbled beneath his composed exterior. "You know, sometimes the best solutions aren't found by dissecting every detail," he finally said, his tone sharp, cutting through the relentless critique.

Our boss's gaze snapped to him, surprise mingling with annoyance. "And sometimes, when you don't dig into the details, you end up with half-baked results. We need answers, not deflections."

Ethan opened his mouth, ready to respond, but I reached over, squeezing his hand under the table. "Let's focus on the way forward,"

I said, my voice steady but firm. "We've learned from this process, and we're committed to improving. We'll address the concerns and ensure that we meet our deadlines."

As the meeting concluded, the tension hung in the air like a thick fog. We filed out of the conference room, silence enveloping us as we walked side by side.

"You did great," I reassured Ethan, though I could see the turmoil swirling in his eyes.

"I could have said more," he replied, frustration lacing his tone. "I hate feeling like we're constantly on the defensive."

"I know. But sometimes it's about playing the long game," I said, trying to keep my voice light. "Besides, it's not over yet. We've got this."

His gaze softened, but I could see the storm clouds brewing just beneath the surface. We returned to our desks, the noise of the office a dull hum in the background. But the moment we sat down, an email notification popped up on my screen, the subject line bold and foreboding: "Immediate Action Required: Project Status Review."

"Ethan, look at this," I said, my heart sinking as I read the message aloud. "We have to submit a full status report by the end of the day."

Ethan's expression shifted from concern to irritation. "Are they serious? After that meeting? They're just piling on more stress."

"We need to show them that we can handle this," I replied, my determination solidifying. "Let's put everything we've got into this report and prove them wrong."

As we dove into the work, the hours flew by, filled with a mix of adrenaline and anxiety. We collaborated seamlessly, our earlier connection resurfacing as we navigated through the data. It felt invigorating, almost intoxicating, the way our minds clicked together, solving problems like a well-oiled machine.

But as we neared the final touches of our report, an unexpected twist sent shockwaves through our focus. My phone buzzed, the notification lighting up the screen with an alarming message. "Your project has been flagged for potential delay."

"Wait, what?" I exclaimed, my heart racing as I read the message again, trying to make sense of it. "They can't just flag us like this! We've been working our tails off!"

Ethan leaned over to read the screen, his expression darkening. "This isn't good. If they think we're falling behind... It could jeopardize everything."

Panic surged through me as I tried to process the implications. "We can't let them think we're struggling. We need to find out who flagged us and why."

"Agreed. But first, let's finish this report and then deal with the fallout," he said, determination fueling his words.

As we hit send on the report, a weight lifted momentarily, but the undercurrent of anxiety remained, gnawing at the edges of my focus. Together, we made our way to our boss's office, the stakes higher than ever.

"Knock, knock," Ethan said, his voice light, though I could see the tension coiling within him.

Our boss looked up, eyebrow raised, but there was a flicker of curiosity in his expression. "What can I do for you?"

"About the flagged project," I began, my voice steady despite the uncertainty coursing through me. "We'd like to discuss the reasoning behind that."

"Ah, yes. It's important you understand the implications of your current progress. There are standards we must uphold," he replied, leaning back in his chair, a faint smile on his lips.

My heart raced as I prepared for whatever came next, but before I could respond, a loud crash echoed through the office, causing us all to turn abruptly. Papers flew off desks, and the lights flickered ominously. A sense of unease washed over me, like a sudden chill cutting through the heat of the moment.

"What the hell was that?" Ethan shouted, gripping the edge of the desk.

I glanced at our boss, who looked genuinely startled for the first time. "Everyone stay calm!" he ordered, but the urgency in his voice only heightened my anxiety.

As the lights dimmed further, a sinking feeling settled in my stomach. Something was wrong—far more wrong than just our project being flagged. I could feel it in the air, like the stillness before a storm, and in that moment, I realized that the pressures we faced at work were the least of our concerns.

Before I could voice my thoughts, the building shuddered again, and the power flickered off completely, plunging us into darkness. Panic rippled through the office as people scrambled for their phones, the atmosphere thick with uncertainty.

And just as quickly as it had begun, everything went silent, leaving us teetering on the edge of an impending disaster.

Chapter 16: The Reconnection

Sunlight filtered through the delicate leaves of the San Francisco Botanical Garden, creating a dappled pattern on the ground that danced like playful fairies. I had envisioned this day as a gentle reminder of our past, a chance to rekindle the warmth that had begun to fade between us. As I carefully spread the picnic blanket over a patch of emerald grass, I could hardly contain my excitement. The sweet scent of blooming jasmine wrapped around me, its fragrance mingling with the faintest hint of damp earth, igniting memories of carefree summer days.

Ethan arrived just moments later, his face lighting up with a mixture of surprise and delight. The warmth of the sun highlighted the soft angles of his jaw, and his smile—oh, that smile—could melt the most stubborn of hearts. I could feel the tension that had settled like a heavy fog between us begin to lift. I had missed this, the effortless connection that used to flow between us, like the rhythmic ebb and flow of the tide.

"Is this a date?" he teased, dropping onto the blanket beside me with a casual grace that was both endearing and infuriating. "Because if it is, I demand gourmet food and a serenade."

I chuckled, opening the wicker basket to reveal our picnic spread. "Well, I can't guarantee gourmet, but I did whip up my famous turkey and avocado sandwiches. And if you're lucky, I might even share my secret cookie stash."

"Turkey and avocado? You really know how to treat a guy right," he said with a playful smirk, reaching for a sandwich. As he took a bite, a look of sheer bliss washed over his face. "Mmm, this is good. You really should consider opening a food truck."

I leaned back on my elbows, watching him relish the flavors. "And what would I call it? 'Emily's Edibles'? How original."

"Let's keep brainstorming; we'll come up with something catchy. How about 'Ethan's Envy'?" He raised an eyebrow, leaning closer as if he were about to reveal a great secret. "That way, everyone will wonder why they can't have your cooking, and I can live in my own little bubble of pride."

I laughed, the sound ringing through the air like a melody. It felt so refreshing, so alive. "You'd be the jealous boyfriend who can't share his girlfriend's cookies. It has a nice ring to it."

As we settled into a comfortable rhythm, I couldn't help but notice how the vibrant flowers around us seemed to echo the rekindling of our connection. Poppies swayed in the breeze, their fiery hues a stark contrast to the tranquil greens, mirroring the spark that flickered between us. I thought of all the times we had walked these paths, carefree and filled with laughter, before life had thrown us off course.

"I was thinking about that weekend at the beach," I said, taking a deep breath. The salt air, even now, tinged my memory with warmth. "You remember that day we got lost trying to find that hidden cove?"

Ethan grinned, his eyes sparkling with nostalgia. "Of course! We ended up at that little shack selling the worst fish tacos ever, and you insisted we give them a chance. I still think you were trying to torture me with those."

"Hey, I stand by my choice! It was an adventure, right? Plus, we did find that stunning sunset afterward," I replied, letting the memory wash over me. "It was worth it, even if we both felt like we'd been poisoned."

"I think I still have the fish taco seasoning in my clothes. They should have warned us about their spices," he said, shaking his head in mock horror. "But the sunset was beautiful, especially with you beside me."

There it was—the warmth that ignited my heart. As I looked into his eyes, I realized that all the laughter in the world couldn't mask the distance we had let grow between us. I needed to confront it, to peel back the layers of confusion and doubt that had crept in like unwelcome shadows.

"Ethan," I began, my voice trembling slightly. "Can we talk about everything that happened? About us?"

His expression shifted, a flicker of concern passing over his features. "Yeah, of course. I've been waiting for the right moment." He took my hand in his, the warmth of his touch grounding me. "I want to hear everything."

Taking a moment to gather my thoughts, I gazed at the soft petals of a nearby flower, its beauty a reminder of resilience. "I guess I just got scared. I've always struggled with opening up about my feelings. When things started to feel heavy between us, I panicked. Instead of leaning into it, I pushed away."

"I get that," Ethan said softly, his thumb caressing the back of my hand. "But you have to know, I felt it too. I was scared, too. I thought maybe I was the one pushing you away."

"No, it was me," I insisted, my heart racing as I opened the floodgates of my emotions. "I felt like I was drowning in my own insecurities. I didn't want to bring you down with me."

"Em, you could never bring me down. I care about you too much," he replied earnestly, his eyes boring into mine. "But you need to trust me. We can weather the storms together. You don't have to shoulder this alone."

The honesty in his voice wrapped around me like a comforting blanket, warming my heart. "I don't want to lose you, Ethan. I've realized that now. I miss you—your laughter, your silly jokes, just... everything."

"I miss you too," he admitted, a hint of vulnerability creeping into his voice. "And I promise to do better. We can rebuild this, I swear it."

As he squeezed my hand tighter, I felt the last of my fears dissolve into the breeze, swept away by the power of his promise. Here, surrounded by the beauty of the garden, I could see the path ahead—a path filled with growth, connection, and the kind of love that could withstand even the harshest storms.

The sun hung high in the sky, its golden rays filtering through the trees, casting a warm glow over the garden. Ethan's gaze lingered on the vibrant flora, his eyes reflecting the wonder of the world around us. I watched him as he pointed out an unusually large daisy, its petals fanning out like a sunburst.

"Did you know that daisies can symbolize innocence and new beginnings?" he said, a playful grin spreading across his face. "So, essentially, this flower is like our relationship. It has potential, just waiting to bloom."

I rolled my eyes, but a smile tugged at my lips. "Are you saying we're like a flower? I don't think I have the patience for a gardening metaphor right now."

"Hey, I'm just saying there's room for growth here. You know, you can't rush art," he quipped, a twinkle in his eye that hinted at deeper truths lying beneath the surface.

"Is that why you keep rearranging the furniture at your apartment? Are you creating an artistic masterpiece?" I shot back, relishing the lightness that had returned to our banter.

"Guilty as charged," he admitted, feigning seriousness as he dramatically glanced at the sky. "My living room is a canvas, and every piece of furniture is a brushstroke. I call it 'Chaotic Youth.'"

As laughter bubbled between us, I felt a surge of gratitude. We were carving out a space where vulnerability mingled effortlessly with humor, creating a safety net that felt all too familiar. Yet the underlying tension still whispered in the corners of my mind, threatening to intrude on our moment.

The peaceful atmosphere shifted as I considered what lay ahead. "Ethan," I began, hesitating. "I want to talk about where we're going from here."

He turned to me, his playful demeanor softening into something more serious. "Yeah, I think we need to. It's like we've been dancing around the issue, and I'm not exactly the best dancer."

"Tell me about it," I teased lightly, but I could feel the weight of my words linger in the air. "We've been avoiding the real conversations. I don't want to slip back into old patterns. It's not good for either of us."

"You're right," he said, his tone earnest. "I can't keep pretending everything is fine when it's not. I want us to be better than just fine; I want us to be great."

The honesty in his voice struck a chord within me. "Great requires effort, Ethan. It requires us to be open, even when it's uncomfortable."

"Are you saying we need to have a 'state of the relationship' talk?" He grimaced, but there was a spark of humor in his eyes. "I didn't sign up for the relationship counseling part of this."

"Unfortunately, it's part of the package. If I'd known you were this resistant, I would've brought a therapist along for moral support," I said, teasingly nudging him with my shoulder.

We both chuckled, but the laughter faded as the reality of our situation settled back into the space between us. I knew we couldn't ignore the cracks in our foundation. "I'm scared of losing you again," I admitted, my voice barely above a whisper.

Ethan squeezed my hand tighter, his expression softening. "You're not going to lose me. Not now, not ever. We've come too far for that. But I need you to trust me, even when things get rough."

"I do trust you," I assured him, my heart swelling at the sincerity in his eyes. "But I can't shake this feeling that something's lurking in the shadows, waiting for us to slip up again."

"Maybe that something is just us being human," he said thoughtfully, his thumb brushing over the back of my hand. "We're not perfect, and we don't have to be. We just need to communicate, even when it's difficult."

The truth of his words hung in the air, and for the first time, I felt a flicker of hope. I nodded, the gesture igniting a sense of resolve within me. "Let's promise to talk, even when we're scared. No more bottling up feelings, no more avoidance. Deal?"

"Deal," he said, his voice steady. "And if you ever think about running off to the hills without me, just know I'll be right behind you, chasing you down."

I laughed again, and it felt like a balm to my weary soul. "Just try not to catch me too quickly. I like to think of myself as a graceful gazelle. You know, elusive and all that."

"More like a baby deer learning to walk," he replied, a smirk creeping onto his lips. "But I can handle that challenge."

As the sun dipped lower in the sky, the golden hues shifted to warm oranges and pinks, wrapping around us like a comforting blanket. We fell into a comfortable silence, our fingers entwined as we watched the colors dance across the horizon. I was acutely aware of how this moment, simple yet profound, felt like the first step toward healing.

Yet, just as I started to relax into the beauty of it all, a sudden gust of wind sent a flurry of petals swirling around us, casting a magical spell over our picnic. It was enchanting, but then, amidst the petals, I noticed a figure in the distance, moving with urgency toward us. My heart sank as I recognized a familiar silhouette.

"Not now," I muttered under my breath. "Of all times..."

"Do I detect a hint of trouble?" Ethan asked, his voice laced with curiosity.

I sighed, releasing his hand reluctantly. "Just a bit of a distraction. I think we might need to put our heart-to-heart on hold."

As the figure drew closer, my pulse quickened, a knot forming in my stomach. I could tell by the way Ethan shifted his weight that he sensed my unease too. We were on the brink of something beautiful, and now it felt like the ground beneath us was about to shift again.

"Hey, can you two lovebirds spare a moment?" the newcomer called out, a teasing lilt in his voice.

My brother, Jason, sauntered toward us, his carefree attitude sharply contrasting the tension that had just begun to dissipate. He had a knack for interrupting at the worst possible times.

"Of course, you'd pick this moment," I groaned, knowing he meant well but also wishing he'd realized that some conversations deserved privacy.

"Am I interrupting something profound?" Jason teased, plopping down on the blanket without an invitation.

Ethan shot me a look, and I could see the flicker of frustration in his eyes. "Well, we were in the middle of a very intimate discussion, but by all means, feel free to jump right in."

Jason raised an eyebrow, undeterred. "Intimate? Wow, what did I walk into? Should I get some popcorn for this?"

As my brother launched into his usual banter, I felt the tension twist and curl in my stomach again, but I was determined not to let it ruin the moment we had fought so hard to reclaim. Ethan and I exchanged glances, the unspoken agreement lingering between us that we would finish our conversation later.

Sometimes, life had a way of presenting distractions that challenged our focus. But even in that moment, surrounded by laughter and the glow of an evening sun, I couldn't shake the feeling that our story was just beginning to unfold. With Ethan by my side, I felt ready to face whatever twists life had in store for us, even if it meant battling through interruptions and surprises together.

The laughter from my brother was like a sudden splash of cold water, jolting me from the warm bubble of connection Ethan and I had just begun to rebuild. Jason sprawled on the blanket, stretching like a cat that had just woken from a long nap. "You know, I thought I was interrupting a moment, but it looks like I've crashed a comedy show instead," he remarked, snickering as he snagged one of my homemade cookies.

"Believe me, if you had any sense of timing, you would've stayed away," I shot back playfully, but the slight annoyance simmering beneath my voice betrayed my true feelings. The mood had shifted dramatically, and I felt Ethan's body tense beside me.

"Hey, I was just doing my part to ensure the romantic atmosphere doesn't get too sappy," Jason replied, wiping crumbs from his lips with mock seriousness. "Don't tell me you two were about to start discussing your feelings or something equally horrifying."

Ethan smirked, leaning back on his hands, his gaze darting between me and my brother. "Oh, you have no idea how horrifying our conversations can get. We were just discussing the merits of chaotic living room arrangements and whether flowers could symbolize our relationship."

"Now that sounds riveting," Jason said with exaggerated enthusiasm, "But really, you two need to lighten up. Life is too short to waste on deep conversations all the time. I mean, look at me—master of the impromptu fun." He threw a wink my way, clearly reveling in his role as the comic relief.

I tried to suppress a smile. "You do have a talent for making things ridiculous, that much is true. But maybe there's a reason why deep conversations matter."

"Fine, you're right. But I bring the fun!" Jason declared, throwing his arms wide as if he were the host of some outrageous game show. "Let's play a game. I'll ask you both questions, and you have to answer truthfully. No holding back."

"Are we still talking about flowers, or have we moved on to relationship confessions?" Ethan asked, a glimmer of mischief lighting up his eyes.

"Anything goes! The world is our oyster," Jason proclaimed, barely containing his laughter. "Okay, first question: What is your biggest fear about dating?"

The playful banter made me squirm. A part of me wanted to confide everything—my deepest fears, the insecurities that had kept me up at night—but the easy camaraderie felt fragile, as if the honesty we had just begun to cultivate could shatter under pressure.

"Let's see, my biggest fear? It's pretty simple," I said, stealing a glance at Ethan. "I'm terrified of losing myself in someone else. You know how relationships can sometimes swallow you whole."

Ethan nodded, his expression serious. "That's valid. But I think it's also important to find someone who helps you grow rather than stifles your individuality."

"Wow, so philosophical," Jason teased. "But it's true. You guys have to keep each other grounded. Okay, next question! What's the most embarrassing moment you've had together?"

I could feel my cheeks heat up at the memories that rushed to the forefront. "Oh, that one time we went to that karaoke bar and I forgot the lyrics to our favorite song. I just stood there, mouth open, while Ethan took the mic and saved my dignity. Totally embarrassing."

Ethan chuckled, clearly amused by the memory. "You were in such shock that you just stared at me. It was like watching someone turn to stone mid-performance."

"And you handled it like a champ! Everyone loved your rendition of 'I Will Survive,'" I shot back, a sense of nostalgia warming my heart.

Jason feigned a swoon. "I'm telling you, I should've been there! You two were meant for the stage. A true Broadway moment."

"Enough about our glorious stage debut," I said, eager to steer the conversation away from anything too intimate again. "What about you, Mr. Master of Fun? What's your most embarrassing moment?"

"Oh, come on, that's a low blow!" Jason protested, laughing. "You know I'm far too cool for embarrassment. But there was that time I tripped and fell into the fountain at the park while trying to impress that girl. I was wet, miserable, and my dignity was floating in the water. A classic Jason moment."

"Ah yes, the moment when you went from charming to drenched," I grinned. "I'm pretty sure that's how you ended up in the friend zone."

The lightness in our banter began to fill the space, and I felt the tension of earlier dissipate, but an undercurrent of uncertainty lingered. Jason continued to pose questions, each one more ridiculous than the last, and we all laughed until our sides hurt. I could see the warmth returning to Ethan's expression, but something inside me still felt unresolved.

The playful game eventually began to lose steam, and as Jason took a moment to sip his drink, I glanced at Ethan. "Can we pick up where we left off?" I asked, my heart racing slightly as I braced for whatever honesty lay ahead.

Before he could respond, Jason's phone buzzed, and he leaned over to check it, his face quickly shifting from jovial to serious. "Uh-oh," he muttered, his brows furrowing. "I think I just got some news that might change things up a bit."

"What do you mean?" I asked, my heart sinking at the unexpected shift in energy.

"There's been an incident downtown," Jason replied, his voice low. "Some sort of disturbance. I think they're evacuating the area."

My stomach dropped. "What kind of disturbance?"

"I don't know! It's all over social media," he said, scrolling through his phone with frantic fingers. "It looks serious, like people are getting hurt."

Ethan shot up, the playful atmosphere evaporating in an instant. "We should go. If there's any danger, we can't just sit here."

"Wait—what are you talking about?" I asked, panic creeping into my voice. "We can't just leave!"

"We need to check on things," Ethan said firmly, glancing between Jason and me. "It might be safer to be with a crowd."

I opened my mouth to protest, but Jason's phone buzzed again, his expression growing more troubled. "They're saying it's near the park where we had that barbecue last week. I think we should move. Now."

Every instinct in me screamed to stay put, to cling to the safety of our picnic and the beautiful moment we had just shared, but the urgency in their voices left no room for argument.

As we stood up, gathering our things in a rush, my heart raced with the prospect of what we were about to face. The sun, once a comforting presence, now seemed to cast long shadows that danced ominously around us.

"Stay close, okay?" Ethan said, his voice low but steady as he guided me by the arm.

With Jason leading the way, we rushed out of the garden, the bright colors and laughter fading into a distant memory. The closer we got to downtown, the heavier the atmosphere felt, a thick veil of anxiety hanging in the air.

As we rounded the corner, the sounds of chaos began to fill our ears—shouts, sirens, the unmistakable thud of something heavy hitting the ground. I felt a chill race down my spine, an unsettling sense that whatever was unfolding was only the beginning.

And just as we stepped onto the main street, a figure appeared from the chaos—a silhouette standing defiantly against the backdrop of swirling smoke. My heart stopped as recognition washed over me, disbelief mingling with fear.

"Ethan!" I shouted, panic tightening my chest. "Do you see that? Who is that?"

But before he could answer, the figure turned, and with a flash, I caught a glimpse of eyes that burned with an intensity I had never seen before. My breath caught, and the world around me shifted, reality blurring into something unrecognizable.

This was no ordinary disturbance; this felt like a storm brewing, and I was standing right at the eye of it.

Chapter 17: The Curveball

The sun hung low in the sky, casting long shadows across the bustling office of Greene & Associates. I shuffled through the maze of cubicles, a steaming cup of coffee in one hand and a stack of reports in the other. The air was thick with the scent of freshly brewed java mingling with the sharp tang of copier toner, a heady mix that usually fueled my morning hustle. But today, my heart raced with an uneasy rhythm, echoing the whispers that danced around the office like specters of unease.

Kevin's promotion loomed over us like a storm cloud, dark and ominous. The news had spread through the corridors with the speed of wildfire, igniting a flurry of speculation and suspicion. Had he charmed his way into the upper echelons with more than just his questionable ethics? I could almost hear the office gossip sharpening its teeth, hungry for juicy details about his ascent. It was as if the entire team had shifted their focus from deadlines to drama, a reality show unfolding in our little corner of the corporate world.

As I navigated the labyrinth of workstations, I could feel eyes darting my way, some filled with sympathy, others with barely concealed amusement. My pulse quickened; each heartbeat was a reminder of my own insecurities. Kevin had been a thorn in my side since day one, a constant reminder of my struggle to find my footing in this cutthroat environment. How could he be rewarded for his deceitful tactics while I had to grind endlessly just to be noticed?

"Hey, are you okay?" Ethan's voice broke through my turbulent thoughts like a lifebuoy in a stormy sea. He leaned casually against the wall, arms crossed, his tousled hair catching the light as he tilted his head in concern. The mere sight of him brought a flicker of warmth to my anxious heart.

"I will be once this day is over," I replied, attempting a wry smile that felt more like a grimace. "But with Kevin's promotion, I doubt today will be smooth sailing."

Ethan pushed himself off the wall, his posture shifting to one of guarded strength. "You've faced worse. Remember that time you nailed that client presentation while juggling a broken printer and a surprise fire drill?"

"Those were mere hiccups," I quipped, rolling my eyes. "This is Kevin. He's the human equivalent of a black hole—no light escapes him, and he's incredibly good at sucking the life out of the room."

Ethan chuckled, and the sound was a balm to my fraying nerves. "True, but he can't take your talent away. You deserve to be here just as much as he does. Don't let his promotion intimidate you. You're capable, and you've worked hard to get here."

With those words swirling in my mind, I headed to my desk, the small clutter of papers a comforting sight. I arranged my reports with deliberate care, grounding myself in the familiar. Every report was a reminder of late nights spent poring over data, of projects I had poured my heart into. As I sorted through the chaos, I felt a spark of determination ignite within me. I wasn't about to let Kevin's underhanded tactics steal my shine.

"Hey, boss lady!" Jess chirped as she approached, her bright smile a beacon amidst the office's gloom. She waved her arms dramatically, her long, dark curls bouncing with her movements. "Heard about the big promotion. Want me to throw a 'Congratulations on Selling Your Soul' party?"

"Only if you promise to bring the cake," I said, laughing despite the tension that knotted my stomach. "I might need a sugar high to face him."

"Deal," she winked, her enthusiasm infectious. But as she walked away, the laughter faded, leaving a lingering sense of dread in its wake.

The clock ticked on, the minutes stretching into a long, agonizing wait. I fidgeted with the corner of a document, my mind racing with strategies on how to approach the inevitable confrontation. How could I navigate this treacherous terrain? The thought of facing Kevin, now elevated to a position of power, sent shivers down my spine. I could almost hear the sharp, cutting tone he would adopt, the condescension dripping from his words as he tore into my accomplishments.

Just as I had settled into a rhythm of anxious anticipation, the office door swung open. Kevin strode in, confidence radiating from him like heat from a fire. He wore his tailored suit as if it were armor, a smug smile plastered on his face that sent the whispers swirling anew.

I took a deep breath, reminding myself of Ethan's words. This was my moment to stand my ground, to reclaim my narrative. "Time to put Kevin in his place," I whispered under my breath, the words invigorating me with a surge of defiance.

As he walked past my desk, our eyes met, and for a brief second, I could see a flicker of surprise cross his face. "Still here, I see," he remarked, his voice smooth, laced with that familiar condescension.

"Last I checked, this was still my job," I shot back, surprising myself with the sharpness of my tone. The small victory electrified my resolve, fueling my determination to confront him head-on.

Kevin chuckled, his arrogance palpable. "Good luck with that. You might need it."

With a newfound sense of purpose, I stood, straightening my shoulders and leveling my gaze at him. "Oh, I plan to. Just remember, you didn't claw your way up alone. You might want to keep an eye on who's watching."

The tension in the room crackled, a silent acknowledgment that this was just the beginning. With every heartbeat, I felt the power shift in my favor. The winds of change were stirring, and I was ready to embrace whatever storm awaited me.

The day dragged on like molasses in winter, each tick of the clock amplifying the tension that gripped the office. I sat at my desk, the cacophony of ringing phones and frantic keyboard tapping providing an oddly comforting backdrop. With every passing moment, I steeled myself for the confrontation that awaited me, mentally rehearsing the perfect retorts and clever comebacks. Kevin was a master manipulator, a puppeteer who reveled in controlling the strings of office politics, and I was determined not to be his marionette any longer.

"Ready for round two?" Jess peeked around my cubicle wall, her expression a mix of concern and mischief. Her vibrant floral dress was a sharp contrast to the gray cubicle landscape, and her presence was like a splash of paint on a monochrome canvas. "I'm thinking we should arm you with a battle strategy. Maybe some witty comebacks? Or a paper airplane launcher?"

"Paper airplane launcher?" I raised an eyebrow, amused despite my nerves. "What do you think I'll do, launch them at his head when he inevitably tries to undermine me?"

"Hey, it could work," she replied, a grin splitting her face. "The element of surprise! But really, I could help you craft some clever comebacks. Something along the lines of, 'I'm sorry, Kevin, did you mean to say that out loud?' Or perhaps, 'Your ego called; it wants a bigger office.'"

I laughed, the tension in my shoulders easing ever so slightly. "If only witty repartees could take the place of a good old-fashioned confrontation. But who knows? Maybe I'll surprise him with a well-timed retort."

As the clock crept toward lunchtime, I found myself lost in thoughts of the past. Memories of Kevin's condescending smirks and backhanded compliments danced through my mind like unwelcome guests. I had worked hard to carve my niche in this company, navigating through the treacherous waters of office politics while keeping my head above water. The idea of Kevin now wielding more power felt like a betrayal, not just to me but to the entire team who had believed in merit over manipulation.

"Lunchtime!" Jess declared, snapping me back to the present. "Join me? I need a break from this circus, and I can't eat alone while you sit here, plotting your glorious comeback."

"Why not?" I shrugged, gathering my things. "A change of scenery might do me good."

The cafeteria buzzed with chatter, the clatter of trays and laughter mixing into a warm, inviting hum. I slid into a seat at our usual table, where the sunlight streamed through the windows, creating a soft glow around Jess. As we chatted about everything from the latest office gossip to our weekend plans, I felt the tight knot in my stomach begin to loosen, if only for a moment.

Then, as if on cue, Kevin entered the cafeteria, his presence demanding attention. Heads turned, and conversations hushed as he strode to the buffet line, an aura of confidence surrounding him. I watched him with a mixture of disdain and disbelief, wondering how someone so adept at playing the game could be rewarded.

"Looks like the king has arrived," Jess muttered, rolling her eyes. "What do you think he'll do next? Hold court over his subjects?"

I chuckled, grateful for her ability to lighten the mood. "Maybe he'll demand that we all bow down or risk being banished from the kingdom of Greene & Associates."

Just as I was about to take a sip of my drink, Kevin caught my eye from across the room. His smile was smug, the kind that could light up a room—if that room happened to be filled with sycophants. I met his gaze with a steely resolve, refusing to let him intimidate me.

"Keep your chin up," Jess whispered, nudging me gently. "You've got this. And remember, you're not in this alone."

After lunch, the afternoon stretched before me like a blank canvas, anticipation simmering in the air. I returned to my desk, each step heavy with the weight of what was to come. I flipped through reports, attempting to distract myself, but the words blurred together. My mind was racing, filled with scenarios that ranged from victorious comebacks to catastrophic failures.

Then, just when I thought I could manage the chaos in my mind, Kevin appeared at my desk, a predator closing in on its prey.

"Got a minute?" he asked, feigning nonchalance. His voice dripped with insincerity, and I resisted the urge to roll my eyes.

"Sure, what's up?" I replied, injecting as much casualness into my tone as I could muster.

"Thought we should chat about the upcoming project," he began, leaning against the edge of my desk with an air of authority that made my skin crawl. "I want to make sure you're clear on your responsibilities since, well, you know how these things can get... complicated."

I took a steadying breath, reminding myself of Ethan's encouragement. "I'm clear on my responsibilities, Kevin. I've been doing this for a while now."

His smile tightened, and I could see the gears turning in his head, searching for a way to undermine my confidence. "I just think it's crucial that we're on the same page. After all, the last thing we want is for things to go sideways, right?"

"Right," I replied, my voice steady, even as my heart raced. "But I assure you, I've managed to keep projects on track without your guidance. I'm confident I can handle this."

He blinked, a flash of irritation crossing his face, quickly masked by a charming grin. "That's what I like to hear. But let's be honest, you know how easy it is for things to fall through the cracks around here. Just keep me in the loop, and we'll both look good."

The subtle condescension gnawed at me, and I couldn't help but push back. "I appreciate your concern, but I think I can manage my workload without constant supervision."

The tension hung thick between us, a charged silence that crackled like static electricity. For a heartbeat, we stared each other down, two gladiators in the corporate arena.

"Just remember, this is a team effort," he finally said, his voice dropping to a conspiratorial whisper. "Don't let pride get in the way of collaboration."

"Believe me, I know all about collaboration," I shot back, feeling emboldened. "I just prefer working with teammates who don't view it as a competition."

Kevin's smile faltered, and for a moment, I reveled in the surprise etched on his face. It was liberating to finally voice what had been bubbling beneath the surface for far too long. As he stepped back, the tension eased, but a new layer of uncertainty settled in. What would be his next move? Would he retaliate, or had I finally given him pause?

With my heart pounding, I watched him walk away, a mix of exhilaration and apprehension coursing through me. I had faced him, but the battle was far from over. The war of words had only just begun, and I was ready to stand my ground.

The afternoon dragged on, the fluorescent lights buzzing overhead like angry hornets as I sat at my desk, fighting off a tidal wave of anxiety. I tapped my pen rhythmically against the polished surface, trying to distract myself from the parade of thoughts that lined up like contestants in a beauty pageant. Each one vying for my attention, each one more troubling than the last. The office was alive with a sense of anticipation, as if everyone could feel the palpable tension in the air. Kevin was now not just a thorn in my side; he was a looming shadow, a dark figure ready to cast doubt over everything I had worked for.

Jess had returned to her desk, and the muted chatter around us had picked up again, but my mind was a whirlpool of unease. I glanced over at Kevin's cubicle. He was on a call, his voice smooth and persuasive, the very picture of corporate charisma. I wondered how many people he'd had to step on to get to where he was now. That thought curled like smoke around my heart, stinging and bitter.

"Looks like he's already at it," I murmured to Jess, who had resumed her typing.

"Ugh, don't even," she replied, shooting me a sympathetic glance. "He's going to play this like he's some kind of corporate messiah. Just be careful. You know he's not above using your hard work against you."

"Trust me, I know. But I won't let him do that again." My voice was steadier than I felt. I had faced difficult clients and even tougher deadlines, but dealing with Kevin was a whole different game.

The clock ticked slowly, mocking my impatience. I was waiting for my chance to confront him directly, to set the record straight once and for all. My thoughts drifted to Ethan, who had been my rock through this storm. He always knew just what to say to make me feel like I could conquer anything, even a ruthless colleague like Kevin.

Just then, the sound of the office door swinging open snapped me back to reality. My heart raced as Kevin stepped in, a triumphant gleam in his eyes, his energy infectious. I could feel the tension shift in the room as he strode confidently toward the conference room at the far end, his presence demanding attention.

"Looks like someone's ready to charm the socks off the executives," Jess whispered, her voice barely concealing her disdain.

I smirked, leaning back in my chair. "Let's see how well that charm holds up when the truth starts to unravel."

The next hour felt like waiting for the kettle to boil, each minute stretching into eternity. I watched Kevin through the glass partition, his animated gestures and exaggerated expressions aimed at impressing the higher-ups. The team's chatter faded into the background, and my focus sharpened. I needed to prepare, to gather my thoughts and craft a counter-strategy that would highlight my contributions without sounding defensive.

Finally, the conference room door swung open, and Kevin emerged, a satisfied smile plastered on his face. He caught my eye and shot me a smug look that could curdle milk. "Hope everyone's ready for the changes coming our way. Big things are happening!"

As he moved past my desk, I could feel my pulse quickening again. "Can't wait to hear your plans," I replied, my voice carrying a teasing lilt that surprised even me.

He stopped in his tracks, a flicker of irritation flashing across his face before he recovered. "Oh, you'll hear all about it, don't you worry. I'll make sure you're informed—especially since you'll be working closely with me."

"Working closely? Is that your way of saying I'm going to be your scapegoat?"

"Touché." He smirked, then turned away, dismissing me like I was an insignificant fly buzzing around his head.

Determined to get the last word, I called after him. "Just remember, I'm not afraid to stand up for what's right, Kevin. Don't underestimate me."

He paused, a glimmer of something dangerous in his eyes. "Oh, I never underestimate anyone, especially not my competitors."

With that, he walked away, leaving a wake of tension and uncertainty in his path. I felt the eyes of my coworkers on me, a mix of surprise and admiration. Had I really just stood up to him?

"Bravo!" Jess cheered quietly, leaning over to offer a fist bump. "I think you might've just thrown down the gauntlet."

"I hope I didn't just sign my own death warrant," I admitted, half-joking.

The rest of the afternoon passed in a blur, filled with half-hearted attempts to focus on work while my mind kept circling back to Kevin's threat. I knew he would strike back, and I couldn't shake the feeling that he was capable of something far more sinister than mere office politics.

As the day began to wind down, a familiar voice broke through my thoughts. "You still in one piece?" Ethan appeared at my desk, a warm smile illuminating his face.

"Barely," I replied, managing a grin. "I had a showdown with Kevin. It didn't end in a fireball, so I consider it a win."

"Good! You're getting stronger, I see," he said, leaning against the edge of my desk. "But we need a plan for whatever he throws next. You know he won't take it lying down."

"True, and that's what worries me. He's dangerous, Ethan. I can feel it in my bones."

Just then, the office phone rang, shattering the moment. I picked it up, ready to redirect my attention to work. "Greene & Associates, this is Mia."

"Mia, it's Kevin," came the cool voice on the other end.

I felt my stomach drop. "What can I do for you?"

"Can you come to my office for a moment? I think we need to discuss your role in the upcoming project."

"Sure, I'll be right there."

As I hung up, the weight of foreboding settled heavily on my chest. "Looks like I'm being summoned," I said, forcing a lightness into my tone.

"Be careful," Ethan warned, his expression turning serious. "He might try to pull something."

I nodded, pushing my chair back and standing tall, despite the trepidation creeping into my heart. "I'll be fine. I'm not letting him intimidate me again."

I walked toward Kevin's office, each step echoing with uncertainty. The corridor felt like a long tunnel leading me toward something inevitable, the air thick with anticipation. I knocked lightly and pushed the door open, stepping into the lion's den.

Kevin sat behind his desk, a smirk playing on his lips as he gestured for me to take a seat. "Thanks for coming. I thought it was time we cleared the air. You and I are going to be working closely, after all."

"I'm listening," I said, crossing my arms defensively as I settled into the chair opposite him.

He leaned back, an air of confidence radiating from him. "I've been thinking about how to maximize our potential as a team. You've got a lot of talent, Mia, and I wouldn't want to see it wasted."

"Flattery won't save you, Kevin," I countered, my voice steady.

"Oh, I know. But what if I told you that you could be part of something bigger? An initiative that could really propel your career forward?"

"What's the catch?"

He smiled, a smile that sent a chill down my spine. "Let's just say I need someone who can keep secrets."

My heart raced. "What kind of secrets?"

Before he could answer, the intercom buzzed, cutting through the tension like a knife. "Kevin, we have a situation in the conference room."

He sighed, his expression darkening. "Excuse me for a moment."

As he rose, I felt a strange sense of urgency in the air, something shifting just beneath the surface. I sat there, waiting for him to return, my mind racing with questions and possibilities. What was going on? And what did he mean by keeping secrets?

Just then, the door burst open, and a breathless intern rushed in, panic etched on her face. "Kevin, we need you right now. It's bad."

Kevin turned, his demeanor shifting instantly from relaxed to urgent. "What happened?"

The intern's eyes darted to me before she replied, "It's about the project. You need to see this."

Panic flickered in the pit of my stomach as Kevin shot me a look filled with uncertainty. "I'll be right back," he said, rushing out.

Alone in the office, the walls felt like they were closing in. Something was definitely amiss, and I had the unsettling feeling that I was at the center of it all. What secrets were lurking in the shadows, and was I about to find out more than I bargained for?

I rose from my seat, compelled by an inexplicable urge to uncover the truth. Taking a step toward the door, I felt a chill ripple through the air. Just as I reached for the handle, the lights flickered, plunging the room into darkness. My breath caught in my throat.

Then, a loud crash echoed from the conference room. My heart raced as I froze, unsure of what lay beyond the door. The silence that followed was deafening, punctuated only by the distant murmurs of confusion from the office outside. I hesitated for just a moment, weighing my options, before pushing the door open.

What I discovered on the other side would change everything

Chapter 18: Face to Face

The air was thick with a cocktail of anxiety and anticipation as I stood backstage, peering through the curtain at the crowd gathered in the dimly lit auditorium. A kaleidoscope of faces, each wearing expressions that danced between excitement and trepidation, flickered under the warm glow of the stage lights. This was Kevin's moment—the grand send-off he'd been orchestrating for weeks. He strode onto the stage like a peacock, ruffling his feathers for an audience that had once worshipped at the altar of his so-called brilliance.

Clad in a tailored suit that screamed "success" louder than his hollow words, Kevin began his speech, his voice dripping with a condescending charm that grated on my nerves. Each phrase was a carefully crafted note in his symphony of self-promotion, woven with half-truths and audacious claims about his 'legendary' contributions to the company. The way he recounted his triumphs made my skin crawl, particularly as he deftly interspersed veiled barbs aimed at my own achievements, minimizing my efforts as mere footnotes in his grand narrative.

I could feel my blood boiling, each boast inflating my resolve to confront him. He had always played the role of the untouchable, the reigning king of our corporate jungle, and today, he was determined to remind everyone of his sovereignty. But as the sound of his condescending laughter rang through the hall, I felt something shift within me—a fierce determination that sparked like a match igniting dry kindling. The moment was ripe for defiance.

I pushed through the curtain and stepped into the spotlight, the warmth of the stage lights washing over me, a stark contrast to the cold sweat on my brow. Silence fell like a curtain, a collective gasp rippling through the audience as they turned their attention from the self-appointed ruler to me. I could feel Kevin's eyes narrow, his confident smirk faltering just a fraction, but that was all the encouragement I needed.

"Kevin," I began, my voice steady but resolute, "I appreciate the tales you weave. They're almost as entertaining as the reality I've lived." The audience shifted, a murmur of surprise rippling through the crowd, but I pressed on, emboldened by the electric energy of the room. "While you've been busy spinning your version of success, I've been busy working, learning, and growing in ways you might not even recognize."

The tension thickened, palpable as I recounted my journey—my struggles, the late nights, the hurdles I'd leaped to carve my own niche in this world that so often favored the loudest voice. "When I started here, I was the underdog, but I learned to stand my ground. I didn't let the naysayers or your dismissive remarks define me." Each word struck like a hammer, resonating within the audience as I pointedly glanced at Kevin, whose façade was now cracking, the fear in his eyes growing more apparent.

"I've built a reputation not by standing on the shoulders of giants but by clawing my way up from the ground. So, if you want to call this send-off a celebration, let's celebrate the real work—no, the real people—who made this company thrive." The applause erupted like fireworks, vibrant and loud, a celebration of not just my words but the spirit of resilience I had come to embody. In that moment, I was no longer just a footnote in Kevin's story; I was the protagonist in my own.

As the clapping died down, Kevin's expression morphed from irritation to something darker, a flicker of vulnerability crossing his features. It was a moment of reckoning, one I had long awaited. "You think you've won? That this changes anything?" His tone was a mix of disbelief and anger, but I could see the cracks beneath his bravado. It was intoxicating, the way the power had shifted. I leaned closer, driven by a mixture of adrenaline and defiance.

"Maybe not everything," I replied with a wry smile, "but it certainly changes my story. You see, Kevin, the difference between you and me is that I don't need to tear others down to feel strong. I can lift myself and others up. Maybe that's something you'll never understand."

His eyes darkened, and for a fleeting moment, the room felt charged with an unsaid challenge. Would he retaliate? Would he try to silence me as he had countless times before? But I had crossed a threshold, and there was no going back. The air crackled with tension as he processed my words, the realization settling in that I was no longer his prey but a force to be reckoned with.

The applause began to swell again, the crowd echoing my sentiments, and with each clap, I felt more anchored in my truth. The warmth of their support wrapped around me, shielding me from Kevin's withering gaze. I was more than a mere participant in this game; I was a player ready to change the rules.

In that triumphant moment, I understood the profound power of my voice. It was not just an instrument for speech but a weapon against silence, against oppression, and against those who wielded power without merit. I vowed never to let anyone—especially not Kevin—muffle my spirit again. This was my stage now, and I would make sure my voice echoed long after the lights faded.

The echoes of my journey reverberated in the auditorium, the realization dawning that this was not just a moment of triumph over Kevin but a testament to every struggle I had endured. As I stepped back, the applause a rising tide, I felt lighter, as if the weight of his belittling shadows had finally been lifted. This was not merely my victory; it was the dawn of a new era—one where I would stand tall, unapologetically me, ready to embrace whatever came next.

The applause resonated in my ears, a symphony of support that drowned out Kevin's simmering rage. I relished the moment, basking in the warmth of the crowd's energy, each clap a reminder that I had taken back my narrative. As I stepped down from the stage, adrenaline coursing through my veins, I caught sight of Kevin's face—a blend of disbelief and fury. He was no longer the untouchable figurehead, and I couldn't help but feel a thrill at having knocked him off his pedestal, even just for a moment.

"Nice speech," a voice chirped from beside me. It was Jenna, my closest friend and staunchest ally, her smile radiant. "You really showed him!"

I grinned back, buoyed by her enthusiasm. "Thanks! I didn't think I had it in me, honestly. But standing up there, I felt... powerful." The realization was intoxicating. For so long, I had been the wallflower, the one who shrank into the background whenever Kevin played his self-important games. Today, I had shed that skin, and it felt good.

Jenna's eyes sparkled with mischief. "Well, now that you're the heroine of the hour, what's next? Going to give him a run for his money in the boardroom?"

I laughed, the sound bubbling up from a place of genuine joy. "Maybe I'll throw a few water balloons at him next time he tries to undermine me." The thought of it, absurd and playful, sent a rush of exhilaration through me.

The post-speech mingling began, and the crowd slowly shifted away from the stage, conversations buzzing like bees in a blooming garden. But Kevin stood frozen, his hands clenching and unclenching by his sides, an unsettled storm brewing behind his icy blue eyes. As people filed past him, I felt a pull, a magnetic urge to confront him one last time. Perhaps it was foolishness, or maybe the residue of adrenaline still coursing through my veins. Whatever it was, I took a step toward him.

"Hey, Kevin," I said, my voice smooth, almost playful, despite the way my heart raced. "Congratulations on your 'success.' I hope the new job pays well for all those years you spent polishing your ego."

His gaze snapped to me, sharp and accusing, as if I had just slapped him. "You think this changes anything? You think this little stunt makes you a player?" His words dripped with condescension, but I stood firm, refusing to let his toxicity penetrate my newfound resolve.

"Maybe not everything, but it certainly changes my perspective on you," I replied, crossing my arms, my stance unyielding. "I've spent too long hiding in your shadow, and I'm done with that."

"Good luck with that," he shot back, a sneer twisting his lips. "But remember, the spotlight can be blinding. You'll regret stepping into it."

"Blinding? Please." I waved my hand dismissively, an amused smile playing on my lips. "If it's blinding, it's because I'm finally shining. You should try it sometime. It might help you realize just how small you really are."

He scoffed, his face turning a shade of crimson that hinted at more than mere embarrassment. "You'll be begging for forgiveness before long. They'll turn on you like they always do."

A part of me wanted to sink into that familiar pit of fear, the one Kevin had cultivated in me for far too long. But instead, I met his gaze with unwavering confidence. "If they do, I'll handle it. I won't let a bully dictate my worth anymore."

With that, I turned on my heel, leaving him to simmer in his own contempt. The crowd around me felt different now, invigorating and welcoming, and I inhaled the scent of fresh coffee and pastries wafting from a nearby table. I gravitated toward the buffet, filling my plate with an array of treats, as Jenna flanked me with excitement bubbling over.

"You were incredible!" she exclaimed, her enthusiasm infectious. "The way you called him out! I could practically feel the tension crackling between you two. It was like watching a gladiator match!"

I chuckled, taking a bite of a blueberry scone. "Thanks! It felt like a release, to finally voice everything I'd been holding back."

"Speaking of releases, did you see how his face dropped when you mentioned your accomplishments? Priceless!"

"Honestly, it was like watching a balloon deflate," I replied, my grin widening. "I should have brought a camera for that Kodak moment."

As we laughed and munched on snacks, a shadow crossed my path. I looked up to see Ethan, Kevin's right-hand man and a guy who had always been friendly to me—almost too friendly. He had that disarming smile, the kind that could charm the scales off a snake, but today, his expression was grave.

"Hey, can we talk?" he asked, his voice low and serious.

"Now?" I raised an eyebrow, the lightness of the moment shifting into something more weighty. Jenna stepped back, sensing the change in atmosphere.

"Yeah, it's important."

I hesitated, glancing back at Jenna, who gave me an encouraging nod. "Sure," I said, following Ethan to a quieter corner of the room.

"What's going on?" I asked, crossing my arms defensively as I leaned against the wall.

Ethan glanced around, his eyes darting, as if the very walls had ears. "It's about Kevin. I don't think you should underestimate him."

I scoffed lightly, half-tempted to laugh at the absurdity of it. "Are you kidding? Did you see the way he was sweating bullets up there? He's all bluster and no bite."

"No, really." Ethan's tone was grave, his brows knitted together. "Kevin has a way of twisting situations. He's not just going to let you walk away from this. You might think he's a joke, but he'll retaliate. He has connections, and he knows how to play dirty."

A chill danced down my spine at his words. "What do you mean? What's he going to do? Hire a hitman?"

Ethan shook his head, his expression serious. "No, but he'll sabotage you. He has people in high places, and he'll use them to undermine you—trust me."

I swallowed hard, the weight of his words sinking in. "You're saying he's going to play dirty?"

"He'll make your life miserable if he can," he warned, his tone urgent. "He's not going to let you take the reins without a fight."

My mind raced, panic clawing at the edges of my resolve. But I couldn't show weakness—not now. "Let him try. I've dealt with bullies before, and he's just another one on my list."

Ethan stepped closer, his intensity almost palpable. "Just be careful. I don't want to see you get hurt because of him. You're stronger than you think, but he's cunning."

"Thank you for the warning, Ethan, but I can handle myself," I said, my voice steady despite the storm brewing within me.

As he studied me, I caught a flicker of admiration in his eyes, but it was quickly replaced by concern. "Just don't underestimate the lengths he'll go to. This is a chess game, and you need to stay three moves ahead."

His words lingered in the air as he walked away, leaving me alone with my thoughts. The festive atmosphere faded slightly as the reality of the situation loomed over me. Could Kevin really pull something like that? The idea of his retaliation set my mind racing, but I couldn't let fear seep into my bones. I had fought too hard for my place to let anyone dictate my worth.

Resolute, I turned back toward Jenna, determination igniting within me. If Kevin thought he could intimidate me into submission, he was about to find out just how wrong he was. With each step I took, I felt the thrill of the fight rising within me, eager to reclaim not just my narrative but to rewrite the rules of this game.

The energy in the room pulsated like a live wire, buzzing with a sense of victory and anticipation. I felt an electric thrill coursing through me as I rejoined Jenna, her eyes wide with excitement. "You were on fire! I mean, did you see his face? He looked like he'd bitten into a lemon!" Her laughter was infectious, and I found myself chuckling despite the turmoil that lay ahead.

The crowd gradually dissipated, but the echo of my words lingered, wrapping around me like a warm blanket. My mind, however, remained on high alert, acutely aware of Kevin lurking in the periphery, his simmering anger a palpable force. As the last of the attendees filed out, I caught a glimpse of him huddled with a group of his loyal followers, the tension in their voices rising like steam from a kettle. I didn't want to let their whispers—or Kevin's wrath—distract me from celebrating my moment.

"I need a drink," I announced, eager to wash away the adrenaline still coursing through my veins. "Something strong, preferably spiked with a sense of triumph." Jenna laughed again, her eyes sparkling with mischief.

"I'll drink to that. But first, let's check in with the battlefield." She gestured toward Kevin and his entourage, where a thick tension hung like fog, wrapping around them.

"Maybe we should just let them stew for a bit," I suggested, raising my glass to toast to our little victory instead.

"Or we could throw some verbal fireballs their way," she quipped, an eyebrow raised.

As we approached, I felt the air shift, thick with Kevin's simmering anger. His cohorts, a mix of sycophants and yes-men, were quick to glance my way, their expressions morphing from admiration to disdain as they noticed my presence.

"Ah, the champion of the underdogs graces us with her presence," Kevin drawled, his tone dripping with sarcasm. "What's it like up there on your high horse?"

"Wonderful, thanks," I shot back, grinning as Jenna snorted in laughter beside me. "But it's hard to see you from up here. You might want to invest in a taller stool next time."

The air crackled as Kevin's eyes narrowed, a mix of rage and disbelief flashing across his features. "You think you can just waltz in here and take over? This isn't a fairy tale; this is business."

"Then you should know better than to underestimate your competition," I retorted, feeling the swell of confidence rise within me. "I've learned from the best, after all—being a bully must come with its own set of lessons."

His face twisted in anger, but before he could respond, Jenna chimed in, her voice light and teasing. "Oh, come on, Kevin. You've had your moment to shine. It's our turn to take the stage now."

I shot her a grateful smile, thankful for her unwavering support. "Exactly. Perhaps you should consider a career change, Kevin. You could be a motivational speaker—if only your audience was filled with masochists."

Laughter erupted around us, and Kevin's temper flared. "You think this is over?" he growled, venom lacing his words. "You're in over your head, and you'll see that soon enough."

I held his gaze, unwavering. "Bring it on, Kevin. I'm not afraid of a little competition."

His smirk faded into a scowl as he stepped closer, invading my space. "I hope you can swim because you're about to get tossed into the deep end. Enjoy your moment in the sun while it lasts."

With that, he turned on his heel, marching away, his entourage following like obedient ducklings. I felt a rush of adrenaline mixed with unease as I realized the weight of his words.

"What was that about?" Jenna asked, her voice suddenly serious, the teasing tone dissipating.

I shrugged, trying to mask the flutter of uncertainty in my stomach. "Just another round in our ongoing game of corporate chess. He thinks he can intimidate me, but I'm not backing down."

"Just be careful. You know he can play dirty."

"Let him try," I replied, forcing a smile to ease the tension. But inside, the truth of Jenna's words clawed at me. Kevin was nothing if not cunning, and I had just thrown a match into a powder keg.

As we made our way to the bar, the din of chatter faded into a low hum, the haze of victory beginning to dim. I picked up my drink, the coolness of the glass a welcome reprieve from the warmth of the room. With a quick glance around, I took in the faces of my colleagues, some still buzzing from my confrontation with Kevin. Others looked concerned, their whispers weaving through the crowd like an unsettling current.

"Hey, you alright?" Jenna asked, her brow furrowed with concern.

"I will be," I replied, forcing down the gnawing feeling of unease. "This is just another hurdle. I can handle it."

"Just remember, you're not alone in this," she reminded me, her voice steady. "We're all rooting for you. You have a team."

I nodded, grateful for her reassurance. But as I took a sip of my drink, I couldn't shake the nagging feeling that Kevin's parting words were more than just bluster. The uncertainty of what he might do next loomed in the air like an impending storm.

As the evening wore on, I tried to shake off the shadows that clung to my thoughts, allowing myself to enjoy the camaraderie surrounding me. Laughter erupted from every corner, stories were shared, and plans for the future floated like confetti through the air. For a moment, I allowed myself to believe that I had truly conquered my fears, that I had stepped into the light and claimed my space.

But just as I felt a sense of normalcy return, my phone buzzed in my pocket, jolting me back to reality. I fished it out, the screen illuminating my face with an urgent glow.

"Unknown Caller," it read, and my heart sank. The feeling of dread settled back into my stomach as I answered.

"Hello?" I said, my voice steady despite the unease creeping back in.

A moment of silence hung in the air, heavy and foreboding, before a low voice broke through the static. "You've made a mistake, and now you're going to pay for it."

My heart raced as the reality of the threat settled over me like a dark cloud. "Who is this?" I demanded, trying to keep the tremor from my voice.

"You'll find out soon enough. Just remember, Kevin isn't the only one who can play dirty."

The call ended abruptly, leaving me staring at my phone in shock, the world around me fading into a blur. The laughter and chatter became distant echoes as the chilling words replayed in my mind.

Jenna noticed my expression and rushed to my side. "What happened? Are you okay?"

I opened my mouth to speak, but no words came out. All I could do was stare at the phone, the weight of the warning settling heavily in the air. In that moment, it was clear: the game was far from over, and the stakes had just been raised.

"Something's coming, isn't it?" she whispered, sensing my unease.

"Yes," I finally managed to say, my heart racing. "And it's not going to be pretty."

As I stood there, the full gravity of Kevin's threat hung over me, and for the first time, I felt a chill in the air, a promise of the storm that was about to break.

Chapter 19: Love and Ambitions

The café was a refuge tucked away from the bustling streets of Greenhaven, a charming little spot with deep mahogany wood and golden fairy lights that twinkled like distant stars. As the aroma of freshly brewed coffee enveloped us, I absently toyed with the delicate porcelain cup in my hands, letting the warmth seep into my palms. Ethan sat across from me, his eyes reflecting the gentle flicker of the candlelight that danced between us, illuminating the conflicted emotions etched on his face.

"Can you believe it?" he asked, a hint of excitement mingling with uncertainty in his voice. "This is everything I've ever wanted."

The words hung in the air, thick and tangible. New York—a city pulsing with opportunity, ambition, and an intensity that was both intoxicating and terrifying. I had envisioned it so many times for him, picturing Ethan, with his vibrant energy and magnetic charm, thriving in an environment that matched his talent. Yet now, sitting here, I couldn't shake the feeling that each syllable of his enthusiasm was a dagger piercing my heart.

"I know it's your dream, Ethan," I replied, forcing a smile that felt brittle on my lips. "But what about us?" The question trembled on the edge of my tongue, a hesitant whisper that felt too heavy to articulate. I couldn't be selfish; I wanted him to succeed. But how could I support him while feeling my own dreams start to fray around the edges?

"Us," he echoed, his brow furrowing slightly. "What do you mean?"

My heart raced as I struggled to find the right words. "You're talking about moving to a city that never sleeps, and I'm here... I mean, what if—"

"What if I don't come back?" His voice was steady, but the fear beneath it was unmistakable. I could see it in the way he fidgeted with the napkin, twisting it in his fingers until it looked like a wrinkled origami of frustration. "That's not what I want."

"Isn't it?" I leaned in, the question a careful thread woven into the tension between us. "You're about to embark on a career that could change everything. How can we compete with that?"

Ethan's eyes, which had danced with the thrill of ambition just moments before, now darkened with an emotion I couldn't decipher. "I'm not just going to New York to find success; I'm going for us. I want a future. I want stability. I want..." He paused, searching for the right words, his gaze dropping to the table. "I want to build something."

I swallowed hard, feeling as if the ground beneath us had shifted. The idea of a future—our future—had always seemed so tangible, like a summer breeze promising warmth and laughter. But now it felt distant, precarious, like trying to catch smoke with bare hands. "But what does that mean for now? How do we manage this?"

His silence hung between us, an invisible barrier that grew thicker with every heartbeat. The café bustled around us, laughter and clinking cups creating a soundtrack that felt disjointed, as if the world outside had no idea of the storm brewing in our little corner.

"I want to make it work," he finally said, his voice low but determined. "But I can't pretend this isn't a big deal. I want you with me, but I also don't want to hold you back. What do you want, Lily?"

What did I want? I had spent so long wanting Ethan, wanting to be part of his world. But in that moment, my own desires seemed to crumble under the weight of his ambition. I wanted to chase my dreams, too, but could I do that while loving him? I took a deep breath, steadying myself against the tempest of my feelings. "I want us to be happy," I replied, the truth flooding out before I could second-guess it. "But I also don't want to be the reason you miss out on something incredible."

"Then why does it feel like a choice?" he pressed, his gaze piercing mine. "Why does it feel like we have to pick?"

"Because that's how life works, right? We have to make sacrifices." The words tumbled from my lips, but I could feel the heaviness of them, the truth that lingered just beneath the surface. "I thought we could have it all, but maybe that's just a fantasy."

His expression shifted, the flicker of anger and sadness melding into something softer. "It's not a fantasy if we're both willing to fight for it," he said, the conviction in his voice igniting a spark of hope within me.

I wanted to believe him. I wanted to believe that love could conquer distance, ambition, and fear. But as I looked into his eyes, I saw the weight of his dreams resting heavily on his shoulders, the burden of making a choice that felt all too real.

"What if we tried?" I ventured, my heart pounding with the suggestion. "What if we took it one day at a time? You go to New York, and we see how it feels. If it's too much, we figure something else out. We're good at solving problems, right?"

Ethan's lips curled into a half-smile, tinged with uncertainty. "One day at a time, huh?"

"Exactly. I mean, we've survived a lot together. We can survive this, too." The conviction in my voice surprised me, even as a tiny voice in the back of my mind whispered its doubts.

"Okay," he agreed, albeit cautiously. "One day at a time." The relief that washed over me was palpable, yet beneath it lay an undercurrent of anxiety. Would we truly be able to navigate this uncharted territory?

As we finished our coffees, the café around us began to blur, the world outside fading into the background as we focused on the fragile promise we had just made. The sweet taste of hope lingered, even as uncertainty wrapped itself around our hearts like ivy, both beautiful and suffocating. I took his hand, the warmth of his touch grounding me, and together we stepped into the unknown, ready to face whatever awaited us.

The days that followed our café conversation felt like a delicate dance, a waltz on a tightrope strung high above the ground. Each moment was imbued with an electric tension, the kind that crackles in the air before a storm. Ethan and I navigated our routines with a carefulness that felt almost foreign, as if we were suddenly aware of every word, every glance, every brush of our fingers. Our connection, once effortless, now bore the weight of unspoken questions that lingered between us like shadows.

Every evening, I would return to my small apartment, the walls lined with memories of us—photos from spontaneous road trips, ticket stubs from our favorite concerts, and little notes he'd slipped into my bag, reminders of his affection. The cozy clutter felt like a sanctuary, yet the more I looked at it, the more I sensed the impending changes. The idea of him packing up and leaving for New York was a gaping hole in my chest, an ache that refused to fade.

One Friday night, in an attempt to reclaim a fragment of normalcy, I invited Ethan over for dinner. I spent the afternoon preparing his favorite—creamy pesto pasta, with a side of garlic bread that crackled delightfully when touched. As I stirred the pot, the fragrant aroma enveloped me, wrapping me in the warmth of anticipation. I wanted the evening to be special, a little pocket of happiness in the face of the unknown.

When he arrived, a hesitant smile played on his lips, but I could see the weight behind his eyes. I greeted him with a kiss that lingered, hoping to bridge the growing distance. "You're just in time. Dinner is almost ready."

"Smells amazing," he replied, his voice slightly strained as he glanced around, taking in the familiar sights that suddenly felt charged with meaning. "Did you bake that bread yourself?"

"Of course! I wouldn't dream of serving store-bought." I feigned indignation, rolling my eyes. "Unless it was an emergency, in which case I'd still take credit."

He laughed, the sound a soothing balm against the tension, and helped me set the table. As we settled down to eat, I couldn't shake the sense of impending change. The pasta twirled on my fork like a tangled knot of our lives, and as we shared bites, I felt the bittersweet joy that mingled with anxiety.

"I want to hear everything about your first day in New York," I said, attempting to steer the conversation toward lighter territory. "You'll have to keep me updated on all the skyscrapers and coffee shops."

"Deal." He smiled, but there was a flicker of something else—an uncertainty I couldn't quite place. "But you know, it's not just about the city. It's a whole new life. It's... daunting."

"Change is always daunting." I leaned forward, resting my chin on my hand. "But it's also an adventure, right? Just think of all the stories you'll have."

"Or all the ways I might screw it up," he countered, a wry grin tugging at his lips. "What if I trip on the subway steps and end up face-to-face with a rat the size of a dog?"

"Then I expect you to take a selfie for the 'gram," I replied, unable to help myself. "It'll go viral. You'll be an influencer overnight."

As we laughed, I felt the heaviness shift slightly, if only for a moment. But even amid the laughter, a sliver of unease threaded through our words, lurking just beneath the surface. We continued to share memories, weaving in and out of conversation, but I couldn't shake the thought that every shared smile was tinged with the knowledge that our time together was limited.

As dinner drew to a close, Ethan reached for my hand, his thumb tracing circles on my palm. "I've been thinking," he began, his expression turning serious. "About what you said—about taking it one day at a time. I really want that to be our focus."

"That sounds like a plan," I replied, my heart quickening with a mixture of hope and dread. "But... what if one day feels too hard?"

His eyes searched mine, darkening with sincerity. "Then we tackle it together. I don't want this to be a goodbye. I want it to be a new chapter. A really, really long-distance chapter."

The air felt charged with possibilities, yet the weight of reality bore down on me. "And what happens if one of us gets tired of that distance?" I ventured, a tremor in my voice that betrayed my anxiety.

"Then we make a plan. I'll come back. You can visit. We'll figure it out." He squeezed my hand gently, as if trying to ground us both amidst the swirling uncertainty. "You mean too much to me for this to be the end."

"Promise me something," I said, pulling my hand away to set my resolve. "Promise me we won't become strangers. No late-night texts that go unanswered or weeks without calls."

"I promise." His gaze was unwavering, steady like the mountains. "We'll be each other's first thought in the morning and last thought at night."

"I like the sound of that." A warm sensation spread through my chest, the spark of hope rekindled, even as my mind raced with questions. How would we hold on to the essence of us when we were so far apart?

After dinner, we moved to the living room, the glow of the soft lamp casting a cozy light over the space. I slipped into the comfortable rhythm of our evening routine, curling up beside him on the couch as a movie flickered to life on the screen. The film was a rom-com we'd both seen a dozen times, but it served as a perfect backdrop, a comforting cocoon against the reality we were facing.

But as the credits began to roll, the laughter faded, leaving behind the weight of our situation. I felt the surge of emotions welling up inside, each one fighting for its moment. "Ethan," I started, hesitating as the words caught in my throat. "What if... what if this is all just a beautiful distraction from what's really happening?"

He turned to me, his brow furrowed in concern. "What do you mean?"

"What if we're so focused on this 'us' that we forget to consider what it might mean to actually live our lives? What if we're just trying to convince ourselves that we can handle the distance when deep down, we're both scared?"

His expression shifted, the playful spark dimming as he considered my words. "I don't want to lose you, Lily. But I also don't want to put my dreams on hold. I thought you understood that."

"I do! I just... I just wish there was a way for us to thrive together, not just survive," I admitted, frustration bubbling to the surface. "Can't we have both?"

His silence felt like an answer, and I turned away, staring at the flickering screen, a rush of emotions swirling within me. Maybe love was meant to be this complicated, a mix of passion and uncertainty, each twist of fate pulling us closer while simultaneously threatening to tear us apart.

The silence between us stretched like a taut string, vibrating with unspoken fears and untold desires. I turned back to Ethan, whose expression was a mixture of frustration and confusion, a mirror of my own emotions. "You really think we can have it all?" I asked, my voice a whisper, afraid to disturb the fragile bubble that seemed to surround us.

"I want to believe it," he replied, his tone earnest, but the weight of the words hung heavy. "But it's not just about us anymore, is it? There are so many things to consider."

"Like what? Like how many coffee shops you can visit in New York?" I shot back, unable to contain the bite in my voice. "You've spent your whole life preparing for this moment. You can't just put your dreams on hold because of a little distance." The last phrase came out sharper than intended, but the words echoed my own internal struggle—the battle between wanting him to succeed and fearing the cost.

He sighed, leaning back against the couch, running a hand through his hair in a gesture I recognized well. "It's not a 'little' distance, Lily. It's New York! This is a huge opportunity. It means starting from scratch. Networking, building a reputation... and let's be honest, a few hundred miles."

I bristled at the mention of "starting from scratch." I had just found my footing in my career and in our relationship; it felt like a betrayal to even consider the idea of losing him to another city, another life. "You're making it sound like I'd just be some forgotten chapter in your story," I said, the sting of betrayal sharp in my voice. "Is that what I am to you? Just a 'once upon a time'?"

"Don't twist my words," he shot back, a hint of desperation creeping into his voice. "You know that's not how I see you. I just... I need to focus on this opportunity. If I mess it up, it's not just my career that's at stake; it's my future."

I stood abruptly, my heart pounding against my ribcage. "And what about my future? Don't I get a say in that? You act like it's all on you, but we're in this together, aren't we?"

The words hung in the air, heavy and potent. Ethan opened his mouth to respond, but instead, he fell silent, his brow furrowed as if he were trying to solve an impossible equation. I paced the room, my thoughts racing, piecing together the puzzle of our future, and it felt impossibly broken.

"I don't want to lose you," he finally said, his voice softer now, as if he were afraid of shattering the moment entirely. "But I also don't want to hold you back. You have your own dreams, too, right?"

"Of course I do! But this is about more than just dreams." I pivoted to face him, my hands clenched at my sides. "What happens when one of us gets busy? When life gets in the way? Do we just—what, start counting the days until we forget what it feels like to be together?"

Ethan's gaze dropped to the floor, and in that moment, I saw the flicker of fear in his eyes, the recognition that we were standing on a precipice, staring into an uncertain abyss. "I can't promise we won't face challenges," he said quietly. "But I want to try. I want us to try."

"Trying isn't enough if we're not both in it," I insisted, my voice rising again as frustration bubbled within me. "And right now, it feels like you're already packing your bags in your mind, leaving me behind. You're not even here with me. You're somewhere else, thinking about skyscrapers and bright lights, and I'm... I'm here in Greenhaven, wondering how we can survive."

With that, I turned and walked away, the tension thick enough to slice through. I didn't want to hear any more of his dreams if they came at the cost of our reality. I could feel my heart racing as I stepped out onto the small balcony, the cool night air a sharp contrast to the heated atmosphere inside.

The stars twinkled above, indifferent to the turmoil swirling in my chest. I took a deep breath, letting the crispness clear my mind. But the quiet wasn't enough to drown out the echoes of our argument. It was all too much—the possibility of losing Ethan to a city that pulsed with life while I was left behind, suffocating in a small town that suddenly felt too familiar, too stagnant.

Moments later, I heard the creak of the door behind me, and I turned to find Ethan standing there, a shadow against the glow of the living room light. "Lily," he began, stepping out into the night, the cool air swirling around us, charged with unspoken tension. "I didn't mean to make you feel like you're second place."

"Then don't," I replied sharply, crossing my arms over my chest. "This isn't just about you chasing a dream, Ethan. It's about what it means for us. I need to know that you're not just running away from here to start anew without thinking of what you're leaving behind."

"I'm not running away! I want to create something together, and it scares me that you might not see it that way." His voice trembled slightly, revealing the rawness of his feelings. "You're everything I want, Lily. But I also want this job. It's a chance for us to build a future, to be together in a way that isn't limited by the same old routines."

"Except you'd be building that future alone, Ethan!" I cried out, frustration boiling over. "We'd be hundreds of miles apart, and that's not a future. It's a fantasy."

Silence descended again, wrapping us in its heavy embrace. The air between us felt electric, charged with the unsaid, and I could see the conflict playing out across his face.

"We can make it work," he finally said, his voice low but resolute. "I know it's going to be tough. But love is about fighting for what you want, right?"

"Fighting isn't just about words," I said, my heart aching as I wrestled with the reality that loomed before us. "It's about action. It's about making decisions that consider both of us."

He stepped closer, the warmth of his presence almost disarming. "So what do you want?" His question was heavy, laced with uncertainty.

The world around us felt charged with possibilities and potential heartbreak, and as I stood there, wrestling with my emotions, I sensed the gravity of our situation. I took a deep breath, knowing that whatever I said next could change everything.

"I want us to be together," I whispered, feeling the truth resonate deep within me. "But I can't pretend that this isn't terrifying."

Before he could respond, the sudden ringing of my phone sliced through the air, startling both of us. I glanced down at the screen, my heart dropping as I recognized the name flashing in bold letters.

It was Kevin.

"What does he want?" Ethan's voice was taut, concern knitting his brows together.

I hesitated, the weight of uncertainty pulling me in two directions. "I don't know," I admitted, my fingers hovering over the screen. "But I don't think it's good."

"Maybe we should just ignore it," Ethan suggested, his expression shifting from worry to protectiveness.

I stared at the phone, caught between the past that had finally started to fade and the uncertain future we were trying to build. "What if he has something important to say?"

Ethan's gaze bore into mine, a silent question hanging between us. "Then you have to choose," he said, his voice steady, yet there was an underlying tremor that betrayed his own fears. "Choose whether to listen or to let him go once and for all."

The ringing persisted, each chime echoing the unresolved tension between us, the clock ticking down the moments that could define the rest of our lives. The decision felt monumental, and as I reached for the phone, I realized that whatever happened next could unravel everything we had fought to build.

Chapter 20: Decisions in the Dark

The rooftop bar was alive with a symphony of laughter and clinking glasses, the warm glow of string lights above us casting a gentle halo around Ethan and me. It felt like the world was celebrating, and yet, here I was, teetering on the edge of heartbreak. I sipped my whiskey sour, the tangy sweetness struggling to mask the bitterness rising in my throat. Below us, the city pulsed like a heartbeat, its vibrant energy electrifying the air, but my heart felt heavy, tethered to the moment we both knew was slipping away.

Ethan leaned against the railing, his gaze sweeping over the twinkling lights of the bay. The soft breeze tousled his dark hair, and for a moment, he looked like a painting—a silhouette against the sprawling cityscape, poised between the past and an uncertain future. I wanted to freeze this moment, to etch it into my memory before reality crashed in like a wave. "You know," I said, attempting to keep my voice light, "if you find a coffee shop in New York that makes better lattes than the ones at Fog City, I might just have to come after you with a spoon."

He chuckled, but the smile didn't reach his eyes. "You know I'd never betray our coffee shop, even for the bright lights of New York." There was a playful lilt in his tone, but underneath, I sensed a current of unease.

We fell into an easy rhythm of banter, each joke a flimsy shield against the heavy thoughts lurking beneath. Yet, as the sun sank below the horizon, the laughter dwindled, leaving silence thick with unspoken words. I turned to him, my heart racing, as if I were about to dive into the deep end without knowing how to swim. "What if..." I hesitated, the words dangling in the air, "what if this distance changes everything?"

He met my gaze, his blue eyes steady and resolute. "We'll make it work. People do it all the time." His confidence was a lifeline, yet the pang of doubt gnawed at me. How many couples had I seen slip through the cracks of long-distance relationships? Was love truly enough to bridge the miles?

"I just..." I started, but the words fizzled out like a deflated balloon. How could I voice my fears without sounding petty? What did it mean to support his dreams if it meant losing my own?

"Hey," he said softly, reaching out to tuck a stray strand of hair behind my ear. His touch sent a shiver down my spine, igniting the warmth that always enveloped me in his presence. "We'll figure it out, right? We'll schedule video dates, plan visits. And who knows, maybe I'll find a way to come back more often than you think."

"But what if you fall in love with someone else?" The question slipped from my lips before I could catch it, a quiet whisper tinged with the fear I couldn't contain. "What if you meet someone amazing, someone who's there?"

Ethan's expression shifted, his brows furrowing as if I'd just tossed a bucket of cold water over him. "What are you saying?"

"I don't know!" I exclaimed, the frustration bubbling over. "It's just—everything is changing. You're leaving, and I feel like I'm being left behind, like I'm just another piece of your past."

His jaw tightened, and I could see the internal battle play out behind his eyes. "You're not just a piece of my past. You're my present. You're—" He hesitated, and in that moment, I felt the weight of his uncertainty pressing down on us like a dense fog. "You're everything."

The sincerity in his voice wrapped around me, pulling me closer. But that closeness felt like a double-edged sword, both a comfort and a threat. "Ethan, you have your whole life ahead of you. And what if I can't keep up? What if I'm not enough?"

"Enough?" His laugh was incredulous, laced with disbelief. "You're more than enough. You're the one thing in this crazy world that makes sense to me." He paused, his fingers interlacing with mine, grounding me in that moment. "Don't you see? I want you to be part of my life, no matter where that takes me."

I wanted to believe him, to take those words and hold them close like a talisman against the uncertainties ahead. "What if we end up resenting each other?" I couldn't help but voice the fear that curled in my stomach like a coiled snake. "What if the distance turns us into strangers?"

His expression softened, and he tilted his head as if searching for the right words. "Then we fight. We fight to make it work. Because, honestly, I don't want to imagine my life without you in it."

His admission struck me with a force that took my breath away. The connection between us felt palpable, thrumming like the string of a well-tuned guitar. But as the neon lights of the bar flickered above, a shadow loomed in the recesses of my mind, a nagging reminder that love, no matter how fierce, couldn't always conquer the distance.

"I guess we'll just have to see how it goes," I said, forcing a smile that felt like a fragile façade. The truth was, I was terrified. Terrified of being left behind while he chased his dreams and terrified of chasing mine without him. As the last remnants of daylight melted into the horizon, I clung to the hope that our love could withstand the tests of time and distance.

But that hope felt like a flickering candle in a howling storm, fragile and easily extinguished. And beneath the laughter and the warm glow of the bar, the reality of our decisions lingered in the air, thick and suffocating.

The lights twinkled below us like fallen stars, each one a reminder of the countless moments we had shared in this city. Ethan leaned back against the railing, his profile illuminated by the soft glow of the bar's lights. I couldn't help but admire the way the city reflected in his eyes—a world full of promise and adventure. Yet, as I studied him, I felt an unexpected pang of regret. What if this was the last time I saw that spark in his eyes, the last time he laughed at my ridiculous puns?

"Okay, one more round?" I asked, attempting to lighten the mood, but even I could hear the tremor in my voice.

"Sure, but only if you promise to stop trying to bribe me with whiskey." He raised an eyebrow, a playful grin dancing on his lips. "It's not going to work. I'm not falling for your clever schemes."

I feigned shock, placing a hand dramatically over my heart. "How dare you question my motives! I thought we had an unspoken agreement—drinks are on me if you promise not to move to New York."

He laughed, and the sound filled the air between us, momentarily drowning out the noise of the bar. "Ah, yes, the classic 'one more drink for a lifetime of commitment' scheme. A timeless strategy, but I think I'll have to pass."

The banter felt good, like a balm to my anxious heart. But underneath the laughter, I could feel the cracks forming in my resolve. With each passing moment, reality crept closer, reminding me that soon he would be on a plane, leaving San Francisco behind like a dream fading in the light of dawn.

"So, tell me again why you're leaving this perfect paradise for the chaos of New York City?" I asked, trying to inject some levity into the conversation.

"Because," he replied, leaning closer, his voice low and conspiratorial, "it's the city where dreams go to become reality. Plus, they have excellent bagels." He waggled his eyebrows as if that alone was enough to seal the deal.

I rolled my eyes, but a smile crept onto my lips. "Ah, yes, the great bagel chase of twenty twenty-four. It makes perfect sense." I took a sip of my drink, letting the cool liquid ease the tension knotting in my stomach. "But seriously, you've got to give me more than that. What about the warmth of the West Coast? The ocean breeze? Me?"

"Please," he teased, waving a dismissive hand. "I can't survive on sunshine and ocean waves forever. A man's got to chase his dreams, and right now, mine are waiting for me on the other side of the country."

"Maybe we should just pack up and move to New York together, then," I suggested, half-joking. "We can become the world's greatest coffee shop duo, brewing lattes and solving mysteries."

"Or you could become the world's greatest barista who drinks too much coffee and writes about her miserable existence in a cramped apartment," he shot back, laughter bubbling between us. "Trust me, you're better off here."

The way he said it—the confidence in his voice, the ease in his smile—made it seem so simple. But the weight of his upcoming departure settled on my shoulders like a leaden cloak.

As the evening wore on, I couldn't shake the feeling that we were both trying to pretend the inevitable wasn't looming over us like a thunderstorm. The city buzzed around us, oblivious to the storm brewing in my heart. "You're really going to do it, aren't you?" I asked quietly, a shadow passing over my face.

He met my gaze, the laughter slipping away, replaced by a solemnity that sent shivers down my spine. "I have to. It's what I've always wanted, you know that. But that doesn't make this easy."

I could see the truth in his eyes—his resolve, his excitement—but also a hint of fear. It mirrored my own. "What if it changes everything between us?" I whispered, feeling vulnerable.

"Then we'll adapt," he said firmly, his grip tightening around his glass. "We'll make time for each other. We have to believe it can work."

"I want to believe that, but it feels so... uncertain. What if I'm not strong enough to handle it?"

"You're stronger than you think." He leaned closer, the warmth radiating off him filling the space between us. "We're a team, right?

Whatever happens, we'll face it together. Distance means nothing if we keep the connection alive."

I wanted to scream that distance meant everything. I wanted to tell him about my doubts, about the nights I would spend staring at my phone, waiting for a text that might not come. Instead, I swallowed hard and forced a smile. "Yeah, a team. Like Batman and Robin, except with fewer capes and more coffee."

"Exactly! And don't forget the bagels." His attempt to lighten the mood was admirable, and yet, the weight of our reality lingered like a heavy fog.

Just then, my phone buzzed on the table, a jarring intrusion into our delicate moment. I glanced at the screen, recognizing Hailey's name. I hesitated for a moment, the tension palpable. "Should I?"

Ethan nodded. "You better. I don't want you to miss any last-minute adventures."

As I swiped to answer, Hailey's voice crackled through the speaker, filled with excitement and a hint of mischief. "Hey! You'll never believe who just showed up at my door!"

"Who?" I asked, my curiosity piqued.

"Ryan! He just returned from his road trip, and he's in town for a few days. We're thinking of heading to that new arcade on Pier 39. Want to join?"

"Ryan's back?" I felt a rush of warmth at the thought of my friends rallying around me. "Absolutely! Just give me a second."

I looked at Ethan, who was watching me with an intensity that made my heart flutter. "Hailey and Ryan want me to join them at the arcade. It's a last hurrah before you leave."

"Go. Have fun." His smile was genuine, but there was something in his eyes that hinted at sadness, a flicker of loss I could feel in the air.

"Are you sure? I mean…" I trailed off, feeling torn.

"Of course. You should spend time with them while you can. I'll be fine. I promise to keep myself occupied by plotting my escape to New York," he said with a wink, trying to lift the somber mood.

I smiled back, but the ache in my heart deepened. "I'll text you later?"

"Definitely. I expect an update on all the shenanigans. And maybe a few snapshots of you wreaking havoc with Hailey and Ryan."

"Right, because that's all we ever do." I grabbed my bag and stood, reluctant to leave the sanctuary we had created for ourselves on that rooftop.

As I walked away, a part of me wanted to look back, to see the city in the golden glow of our shared moment, but I pushed those thoughts aside. I had to move forward, to embrace the night with my friends. The anticipation of laughter, of fun, mingled with the reality that this would be one of the last nights we spent together before our worlds diverged.

The arcade pulsed with energy, a riot of neon lights and exuberant laughter that enveloped me as I stepped inside. It was a stark contrast to the bittersweet evening I had just left behind on the rooftop. I was greeted by the cacophony of arcade games beeping and whirring, punctuated by the occasional cheer of triumph from someone hitting a jackpot. The atmosphere was intoxicating, a whirlwind of sounds and colors that should have swept me away, but the weight of Ethan's impending departure clung to my heart like a stubborn shadow.

"Welcome to the land of 8-bit dreams and overpriced snacks!" Hailey exclaimed, her eyes sparkling with excitement as she bounded toward me. "You ready to crush some high scores?"

"Absolutely, as long as I don't embarrass myself in front of Ryan," I teased, glancing around for my other friend. Ryan was standing by a racing game, his focus so intense that he looked ready to take on the world—or at least the next lap.

"Hey! Don't sell yourself short. Remember the last time we were here? You almost broke the machine!" Hailey laughed, nudging me playfully. "Ryan, get over here! We need you to witness a repeat performance!"

Ryan turned, his face lighting up when he saw me. "There you are! I was about to take on this game all by myself. Didn't want you to miss my inevitable victory," he said, a smirk plastered across his face.

"Right, because you definitely needed to win all by yourself, Mr. Showoff." I rolled my eyes, but the warmth of their presence washed over me like a welcome balm.

We settled into a booth near the back, surrounded by a kaleidoscope of flashing lights and the smell of buttery popcorn wafting through the air. It felt like a slice of carefree childhood, the kind I thought I had left behind when adulthood hit me like a freight train. But as we bantered back and forth, a part of me still ached for the rooftop and the promise of what was slipping away.

Hailey slid a plate of nachos between us, and I grabbed a chip, using it to gesture animatedly as I recounted my last conversation with Ethan. "He was so confident, but I just can't shake this feeling that we're heading for a disaster. Long-distance relationships are like trying to balance a spoon on your nose while riding a unicycle—possible but highly impractical."

"True, but you can't ignore the fact that Ethan has his whole future ahead of him," Ryan replied, his voice steady. "You should support him. Besides, it might be fun to see how far apart you can be before the universe intervenes."

"Universe, or just my questionable decision-making skills?" I shot back, my heart racing at the thought of it. "I mean, it's not like

I have a stellar track record with relationships. Maybe the universe is just trying to save me from myself."

Hailey waved her hand dismissively. "Stop that right now. You and Ethan are great together. Plus, I'm sure you'd find a way to make it work. Video calls, love letters—hell, I can even get you a pigeon if you want to send messages the old-fashioned way."

The thought made me giggle. "How romantic. Can't wait for the headline: 'Local Girl Sends Pigeons to New York.'"

As we played, I felt a flicker of joy surging through me. The laughter was infectious, a momentary reprieve from the storm brewing in my mind. We raced through games, competed for tickets, and even attempted to beat our high scores on Dance Dance Revolution, which turned into a hilarious spectacle of flailing limbs and off-beat music. For a while, the specter of Ethan's departure faded, replaced by the familiar comfort of friendship.

But as the night wore on, the looming reality returned, sitting heavy on my chest. I excused myself to grab a drink, trying to shake the disquieting thoughts swirling in my mind. I leaned against the bar, watching a couple laugh together, the boy leaning in to whisper something to the girl that made her blush. It struck me how easily people connected, how some relationships seemed to fit together like pieces of a puzzle while I felt like a mismatched piece, struggling to find my place.

"Penny for your thoughts?" Ryan asked, sliding up beside me, his expression warm and encouraging.

I sighed, pushing back the uncertainty. "Just thinking about how easy it seems for everyone else. Look at them—everything looks so effortless."

"Relationships take work, even when it looks effortless. You and Ethan have something real, and real things aren't easy." He leaned against the bar, his gaze steady. "But you have to decide what you want. Are you willing to fight for it?"

"I don't know," I confessed, my voice barely a whisper. "It feels so uncertain. What if I fight and lose anyway?"

"Then you lose, but at least you tried. It's better than living with the what-ifs and wishing you had done something. Take it from me, the guy who ponders every wrong turn like it's a national crisis."

I chuckled, grateful for his honesty. "You might have a point. But knowing that doesn't make it any easier."

"Maybe not, but it's a start." He grinned, his infectious energy pulling me out of my thoughts. "Let's get back to the fun! You're going to crush it tonight, and who knows, maybe I'll even get lucky and win enough tickets for that giant stuffed bear you wanted."

"Let's not get ahead of ourselves," I joked, feeling lighter. We returned to Hailey, who was still busy trying to wrangle a few tickets from the claw machine.

As we continued to laugh and play, the door to the arcade swung open, and a familiar figure walked in, silhouetted against the fluorescent lights. My heart dropped as I recognized the face—Ethan, standing there, scanning the room like a beacon of all that I was trying to push away. The cheerful atmosphere shifted, and suddenly, all the laughter faded into a distant echo.

"Is that...?" Ryan started, his voice trailing off as he followed my gaze.

I nodded, my heart racing. "What is he doing here?"

Ethan caught sight of me and broke into a smile that momentarily dispelled my apprehension. But before I could step forward, I noticed the woman at his side—a tall, striking brunette with an air of confidence. She leaned into him, her laughter ringing out like a chime, drawing him closer.

The world around me blurred as a storm of emotions swept through me—confusion, jealousy, uncertainty. I gripped the edge of the bar, feeling the chill of the moment seep into my bones.

"Should we...?" Ryan's voice was tentative, but I couldn't respond. I was frozen, caught between the joy of seeing Ethan and the twist in my gut at seeing him with someone else.

As they made their way toward us, I could feel the tension thickening in the air, a palpable shift that threatened to unravel everything we had just laughed about. Just as Ethan opened his mouth to speak, the lights flickered, plunging the arcade into momentary darkness.

In the split second of confusion, my heart pounded, and I was left with only one thought: what was about to unfold could change everything.

Chapter 21: The Parting

The sun hung low in the sky, casting a golden hue over the familiar streets of Greenhaven, but that warmth did little to thaw the chill settling deep within my bones. Each box Ethan loaded into the back of his car seemed to carry a piece of my heart with it, leaving a void that felt impossibly vast. I tried to keep the mood light, cracking jokes about our past misadventures—the time we got locked out of the Rowen mansion and had to sneak in through a window, or the day we thought we could bake cookies but ended up setting off the smoke alarm instead. Our laughter rang out, but beneath it lingered a sorrowful undertone, a muted drumbeat of goodbye that I desperately wished to silence.

"Remember, you owe me a rematch at Monopoly," I said, forcing a smile that didn't quite reach my eyes. Ethan chuckled, his dark hair falling into his eyes as he bent to tie his shoelaces.

"Only if you promise not to cheat this time," he teased, that familiar, playful glint in his eyes making my heart flutter, even as sadness settled like an unwelcome guest.

"I can't help it if you're bad at losing!" I shot back, and for a moment, the tension lifted, replaced by the comfortable banter that had defined our friendship. But as he continued to load his car, the realization that this was our last day together loomed over us like a thundercloud, threatening to burst at any moment.

Ethan took a moment to lean against the car, looking out at the street we'd walked together countless times. "You know, I was thinking about how we could make this work," he said, his voice suddenly serious. The warmth of the sun did little to chase away the sudden chill creeping up my spine.

"What do you mean?" I asked, my heart racing, a flicker of hope igniting within me.

"Long-distance relationships aren't impossible, right?" he said, scratching the back of his neck, a nervous habit of his that I had come to adore. "We could schedule video calls, plan visits. I could come back for the holidays."

My chest tightened, hope mixing with the weight of reality. "Ethan, you're going to be busy. College, new friends..." The words slipped out, tumbling over one another like a waterfall cascading down rocks, each one threatening to pull me under.

"I don't care about that. I want you to be part of my life," he insisted, his eyes earnest. They bore into mine, searching for something—reassurance, maybe, or perhaps a sign that I felt the same. "This isn't just a fling for me, Lily. You mean more to me than that."

The confession hung between us, a delicate thread of unspoken emotions ready to snap. I opened my mouth to reply, to express the whirlwind of feelings stirring within me, but just then, the sound of a distant car horn pulled me back into the reality of the moment.

"I mean it," he continued, pushing off the car and stepping closer. The closeness made my heart race, electric with unsaid words. "I want you to be in my life—however that looks. I don't want to lose you."

The pressure of his gaze made it hard to breathe. I was all too aware of the moments we had shared, the little glances and touches that had ignited something more than friendship between us. The realization that we were standing on the precipice of something beautiful and terrifying made me dizzy.

But then came the crushing weight of my own insecurities. What if he was just saying these things to ease the pain of leaving? What if the distance made us fade from each other's lives? I swallowed hard, struggling to find the words that would allow me to navigate this churning sea of emotions.

"Ethan, I..." My voice trailed off, swallowed by the impending silence.

The moment stretched, taut and fragile, like the thinnest strand of spider silk. Just then, a playful breeze whisked through the air, rustling the leaves above us, whispering secrets only the trees knew. Ethan's lips curled into a small, hopeful smile that melted away some of my hesitation.

"Promise me you'll at least think about it?" he urged, leaning closer, and suddenly, all I could think about was the warmth radiating from him, the way his fingers brushed mine.

"I promise," I said, feeling a thrill surge through me. But that promise felt heavy, laden with uncertainty.

The last box found its way into the car, and just like that, the moment slipped away. Reality crashed down like the sound of a gavel, sealing our fate. I could see it in the way his shoulders slumped slightly as he turned to face the open road, the distant horizon beckoning him.

"Guess that's it then," he murmured, running a hand through his hair, which had always looked perfect even when it was rumpled. "Time to hit the road."

The words fell flat, echoing painfully in the quiet of the moment. I felt the tears prick at the corners of my eyes, the impending goodbye washing over me like a sudden summer storm.

"Yeah, I guess so," I replied, forcing a smile that felt more like a mask than anything genuine. "You'll call, right?"

"Of course."

He opened the car door, and I wanted to reach out, to stop him, to pull him back and hold on to him for just a moment longer. But something held me back—the weight of what lay ahead, the promise of a new chapter in both our lives.

As he slid into the driver's seat, I felt the ache in my chest swell until it was almost unbearable. I could see his expression through the windshield, a mixture of determination and longing.

With a last glance, he nodded, and I stepped back, my heart thundering against my ribcage. As he started the engine, the roar filled the silence, drowning out everything else. I watched him drive away, the car shrinking into the distance, taking with it not just his presence but a piece of me that I was certain I'd never get back.

The door clicked shut behind me, and the sudden silence of my apartment felt oppressive, as if it were pressing against my chest. I paused, listening to the echoes of laughter and the soft sounds of Ethan's voice that lingered like a haunting melody in the air. The emptiness of the space loomed larger than it had moments before, a stark reminder of the absence left in Ethan's wake. With a sigh, I moved toward the kitchen, hoping to find solace in the mundane act of making a cup of tea, a ritual I had come to rely on during moments of stress.

As the kettle hummed to life, I leaned against the counter, feeling the cool granite beneath my palms. My eyes wandered around the room, taking in the photographs on the walls, memories captured in time—snapshots of late-night adventures, lazy Sunday mornings, and the countless moments that had woven Ethan and me into each other's lives. It felt cruelly ironic that the very walls I had decorated with our memories now felt like a prison, holding me captive in the isolation of my thoughts.

The kettle whistled, breaking my reverie, and I poured the steaming water over a teabag, watching the swirling tendrils of steam dance before dissipating into the air. I hoped the warm drink would somehow warm the chill settling in my bones, but the tea felt more like a hollow comfort than the embrace I longed for. As I cradled the mug in my hands, my mind drifted back to the last moments we had shared—his earnest gaze, the weight of his promises, and the undeniable connection that had sparked between us like a live wire.

Setting the mug down, I wandered into the living room, where shadows began to stretch across the floor. The late afternoon sun filtered through the curtains, casting striped patterns that looked like a painting left unfinished. I sank into the sofa, wrapping a blanket around my shoulders as if it could shield me from the heartache.

Just as I closed my eyes, hoping to drift into the comforting oblivion of sleep, my phone buzzed on the coffee table, shattering the fragile calm. I grabbed it, heart racing, hoping it might be Ethan. Instead, it was Hailey, my ever-reliable best friend.

"Hey, you! Just checking in. How are you holding up?" Her voice bubbled through the speaker, bright and sunny, a stark contrast to the gray cloud that hovered above me.

"Hey, I'm okay," I replied, forcing a smile that no one could see. "Just enjoying some quality time with my thoughts."

"Ah, the classic post-breakup activity," she quipped, her laughter infectious. "Seriously, though, do you want to hang out? I could bring over that awful rom-com you love, and we can throw popcorn at the screen."

I chuckled, the tension in my shoulders loosening a fraction. "That sounds like a plan. I might even cry into the popcorn."

"Perfect! I'll be there in twenty!" She hung up, leaving me with a warm sensation bubbling in my chest. Maybe I didn't have to weather this storm alone after all.

By the time Hailey arrived, the shadows had deepened, and my apartment felt like a cozy cocoon filled with a lingering sense of loss. She swept in like a whirlwind, arms laden with snacks and an enthusiasm that could light up the darkest of rooms.

"Okay, I brought the most ridiculous movie I could find, a metric ton of popcorn, and a box of your favorite chocolates," she announced, plopping down beside me on the couch. "We're going to eat our weight in snacks and laugh until we forget the world exists."

"Or until I start sobbing over the fact that Ethan's gone," I replied, a playful glare cast her way.

Hailey rolled her eyes but then softened, her expression shifting to one of empathy. "You'll be okay, you know. It's just a little space to figure things out. And it's not like he's moving to Mars."

"No, but it feels like it," I muttered, absentmindedly picking at the popcorn. "He's starting a new life, and I'm just...here."

Her hand found mine, giving it a reassuring squeeze. "You're not just 'here.' You're amazing, and you have a whole life ahead of you too. Besides, distance is just an obstacle—one that can be overcome with a bit of effort. If anyone can make it work, it's you two."

I appreciated her effort, but it felt like a flimsy bandage over a deep wound. The movie started, the opening credits rolling, but my mind wandered. Every laugh on the screen, every cheesy line, reminded me of Ethan, the way he'd smirk at the bad jokes and steal bites of my popcorn as if it were his right.

Halfway through, my phone buzzed again, and I shot Hailey a guilty look as I picked it up, hoping against hope that it might be Ethan. Instead, it was a message from Lucas Rowen.

Just wanted to check in. Heard about Ethan. If you need to talk, I'm here.

I hesitated, fingers hovering over the screen. Lucas had always been a good friend, someone who understood the complexities of our world better than most. Still, it felt like I was betraying Ethan somehow, reaching out to his cousin.

"Everything okay?" Hailey asked, her eyes narrowing with curiosity.

"Yeah, just Lucas checking in," I said, trying to keep my tone casual.

"Good guy. You should text him back," she encouraged. "Having a support network is crucial, especially now."

I took a deep breath and typed a quick reply. Thanks, I appreciate it. Just hanging out with Hailey.

"Who are you texting?" she pressed, elbowing me playfully. "Your secret crush?"

I laughed, the sound a little forced. "If I told you it was Lucas, would you freak out?"

Her eyes widened dramatically. "No way! You two would be adorable together! You'd have a family of gorgeous, brooding children with dark hair and sad eyes!"

I couldn't help but laugh at her wild imagination, but the thought sent a jolt of unease through me. Lucas was sweet, and he had been a steady presence, but my heart was still with Ethan.

The movie continued, but my thoughts began to swirl like autumn leaves caught in a gust. Maybe I had a second chance waiting, but did I even want it? I watched Hailey munch on popcorn, her face alight with laughter, and suddenly, I felt like I was on the outside looking in, trapped in a glass box while life carried on around me.

Just then, the doorbell rang, startling both of us. Hailey glanced at me, eyebrows raised. "I didn't order a pizza."

I shook my head, wondering who could be at the door at this hour. With a slight frown, I padded to the door, curiosity gnawing at me.

As I opened it, my breath caught in my throat. There stood Lucas, an armful of snacks and a bright smile, but what struck me most was the determined glint in his eyes.

"Thought you might need some company," he said, stepping inside without waiting for an invitation.

And in that moment, I realized that life was never quite as predictable as we imagined, and sometimes, the universe had a way of dropping surprises right in front of us when we least expected it.

The moment Lucas stepped into my apartment, the atmosphere shifted, infused with an energy that was both comforting and unsettling. His casual confidence filled the space like a familiar song, but beneath it lurked an underlying tension I couldn't quite name. I tried to shake off the heaviness that lingered since Ethan had left, forcing a smile that felt more like a mask than a reflection of my feelings.

"Nice place you've got here," he remarked, surveying the clutter of blankets, snack bowls, and the remnants of our movie marathon. He dropped his stash of snacks onto the coffee table with a theatrical flourish, sending popcorn tumbling like confetti. "Looks like you've thrown quite the soirée without me."

"Only the best for my guests," I replied, my tone playful despite the dull ache in my chest. "You know how to keep a girl entertained."

"Speaking of entertainment," Lucas began, plopping onto the couch beside me, "how are you holding up? I heard about Ethan leaving. Must be rough."

I sighed, the weight of the past few hours settling heavily around my shoulders. "It is. I mean, we were practically inseparable, and now..." I trailed off, the words feeling inadequate to express the void he had left.

Lucas nodded, his expression softening. "It's never easy to watch someone you care about move on. But you know what? You're stronger than you think. You'll get through this."

I chuckled lightly, shaking my head. "That's what they all say. And yet, here I am, a self-proclaimed emotional mess. I should probably be charging admission for this pity party."

"Don't worry. I'm here to provide snacks and witty commentary." He grinned, his infectious energy a welcome balm.

"So, what's the plan? We can cry into the popcorn, or we can put on a movie that's completely unworthy of your heartbreak. Your choice."

"Why do I feel like you're trying to distract me from my sorrow?" I asked, raising an eyebrow.

"Is it working?" he countered, tossing a piece of popcorn in the air and catching it with his mouth.

"Maybe," I admitted, unable to suppress a smile. Lucas had a way of making the worst moments feel a little less daunting. I took a deep breath and picked up a handful of popcorn, savoring the buttery goodness as the movie continued to play in the background.

The evening unfolded with laughter and lighthearted banter, our voices blending seamlessly into the warm ambiance. But as the credits rolled, I felt a shift in the air, a sudden gravity that pulled my focus away from the screen and toward Lucas. He was quiet, studying me with an intensity that made my heart race.

"What is it?" I asked, my voice barely above a whisper.

"I don't know, Lily," he said, his gaze unwavering. "I just... I want to make sure you're really okay. I can't stand the thought of you feeling alone."

The sincerity in his voice stirred something deep within me, a mix of gratitude and an uncomfortable awareness of the closeness we had cultivated. "You're a good friend, Lucas. I appreciate that," I said, trying to maintain a casual tone.

"Good friends can also be something more," he ventured, the words hanging between us like a challenge.

My breath caught in my throat. "Are you suggesting we date? Like, after everything that just happened?"

"Not suggesting. Just throwing it out there as a possibility," he replied, his eyes glinting with mischief. "I mean, we get along well, don't we? And if we're both going to be navigating this mess, why not do it together?"

"Are you serious?" I felt the heat rush to my cheeks, caught between shock and intrigue. "You think I'm ready for that?"

"Ready or not, life keeps throwing curveballs," he said, leaning back slightly, giving me space while maintaining that captivating intensity in his gaze. "I'm just offering a chance at something... different. But only if you want it."

"Lucas," I started, searching for the right words. "I just lost someone who meant the world to me. Jumping into something new feels... complicated."

"Complicated is my middle name," he replied with a grin, lightening the mood once more. "But really, I'm here to support you, no strings attached. Just think about it."

I wanted to protest, to push back against this unexpected direction, but deep down, a part of me was curious, even tempted. The idea of finding comfort in someone who understood my pain was appealing. Still, my heart was tangled in emotions I couldn't untangle.

Just then, my phone buzzed again, breaking the weight of the moment. I glanced at the screen, my stomach twisting as I saw Ethan's name flash before me.

"It's Ethan," I said, a mix of excitement and trepidation washing over me. "He's texting me."

"Open it," Lucas encouraged, his curiosity piqued.

I hesitated, the excitement quickly dampened by the weight of the last conversation we had shared. With a deep breath, I opened the message.

Hey, Lily. Can we talk?

My heart raced, a thousand thoughts crashing together. Lucas watched me closely, and I could feel his anticipation in the air.

"Should I respond?" I murmured, the uncertainty wrapping around my heart like a vice.

"Only you can decide if you want to keep the door open," Lucas replied softly, his tone understanding.

As I typed out a response, my fingers trembled. Sure, when?

Seconds felt like hours as I waited for his reply.

Can I come by tomorrow?

A thousand thoughts swirled in my mind, each battling for dominance. I felt the weight of Lucas's presence beside me, a silent reminder of the connection we'd built in such a short time. What if Ethan's visit reignited old feelings? What if I chose to lean into this budding connection with Lucas and then found myself torn?

"Whatever happens, just know I'm here," Lucas said, his voice steady and reassuring. "You can handle this."

I nodded, but doubt nagged at the edges of my mind. Ethan was back, and I was left at the crossroads, unsure which path would lead me to a brighter future. The air felt thick with tension as I sat there, heart pounding in my chest, wrestling with decisions that could change everything.

With a final, deep breath, I stood up, pacing the room. Lucas watched me, a mixture of concern and understanding etched on his face. The room felt charged, the weight of what lay ahead looming larger than ever.

And just then, as if summoned by my turmoil, the doorbell rang again. The sound pierced through the silence, and I froze, heart racing as I exchanged glances with Lucas.

"Are you expecting someone else?" he asked, his tone teasing but laced with curiosity.

"No, not at all," I replied, my voice barely above a whisper.

The doorbell rang again, insistent and demanding. I felt a rush of apprehension as I approached the door, a sense of foreboding creeping in.

"What if it's—?" I started, but Lucas interrupted, standing beside me, ready to face whatever lay on the other side.

"Let's find out together," he said, determination in his eyes.

As I reached for the doorknob, uncertainty hung in the air like a thick fog. I opened the door, heart pounding, only to find a figure standing there, cloaked in shadows. My breath caught as recognition washed over me, and the world around me seemed to still.

"Hey, Lily," Ethan said, his voice laced with a mixture of urgency and something darker, leaving me on the precipice of a decision that would unravel everything I thought I knew.

Chapter 22: A New Challenge

Life without Ethan was an unexpected struggle, a gaping hole where laughter and warmth once thrived. The mornings were the hardest. As the sunlight streamed through my window, spilling gold across the wooden floor, I felt the absence of his easy smile like a weight pressing against my chest. I poured myself into work, desperate for a distraction, channeling my energy into the revamped customer feedback system at the marketing firm. Each day became a meticulous exercise in organization and ambition, a way to stave off the emptiness gnawing at my insides.

The office buzzed with its usual rhythm: keyboards clattering, phones ringing, and the occasional burst of laughter echoing from the break room. I walked among my colleagues, my heart racing with a blend of determination and anxiety. I had made a promise to myself: I would prove my worth. The morning meetings, which had once felt daunting, now transformed into opportunities for me to shine. Each time I stood before the boardroom, armed with my carefully crafted presentations, I could almost feel Ethan's presence beside me, offering silent encouragement. I imagined him leaning back in his chair, his eyes bright with pride as I articulated my ideas.

Yet, no matter how much I threw myself into my work, the specter of Kevin always lurked nearby, like a dark cloud blotting out the sun. He thrived on creating chaos, perpetually looking for ways to undermine my confidence. His comments dripped with disdain, each word a thorn that pricked my resolve. "Are you sure you want to present that idea, Lily?" he would sneer, his voice oozing condescension. "It sounds a bit... ambitious for someone still trying to find their footing." The room often fell silent, a collective intake of breath as everyone braced for the aftermath of his jibe.

But instead of crumbling, I discovered new allies among my colleagues—those who respected my work and believed in my capabilities. They were a diverse group, each with their quirks and eccentricities, but together, they formed a vibrant tapestry of support. There was Mira, the creative genius with a penchant for neon hair and bold prints, who often dropped by my desk with coffee in hand, her infectious laughter lighting up the dimmest days. Then there was Derek, the meticulous analyst who could unravel any problem like a complex puzzle. He often leaned over my shoulder, pointing out data trends that made my presentations stronger. Their encouragement fueled my determination, reinforcing my resolve to stand firm against Kevin's tactics.

As I walked into the office each day, I began to feel a sense of camaraderie that I hadn't expected. We huddled together during breaks, brainstorming ideas and sharing laughs, and gradually, I felt the darkness that Kevin cast over me begin to lift. I found myself smiling more often, discovering new reasons to enjoy my work beyond the shadow of Ethan's absence.

On one particularly brisk Thursday, I had a breakthrough while reviewing customer feedback. A pattern emerged, something I hadn't seen before—a consistent complaint about a key feature in our product that had slipped through the cracks. My heart raced with excitement. This was my moment to shine. I dove headfirst into data analysis, crafting a compelling presentation that highlighted the issue and suggested actionable solutions. I spent the evening fine-tuning every slide, pouring my passion and determination into the project.

The following day, as I approached the boardroom, a wave of trepidation washed over me. The air was thick with anticipation, a palpable energy buzzing in the room as my colleagues gathered around the table. Kevin sauntered in last, his usual smugness radiating off him like cologne. But this time, I wasn't going to let him intimidate me. I took a deep breath and launched into my presentation, my voice steady and strong as I shared my findings.

I watched as my colleagues nodded, their expressions shifting from curiosity to interest, and finally to enthusiasm. I highlighted the potential impact of our product improvements, the way they could enhance customer satisfaction and drive sales. As I concluded, the room erupted in applause, a wave of approval washing over me. I turned to see Kevin's expression, a mixture of disbelief and resentment that made my heart swell with vindication.

"Impressive work, Lily," Mira said, her voice warm and genuine as she clapped me on the back. "You nailed it!"

"Absolutely," Derek chimed in, his eyes gleaming with admiration. "You should be proud. That was a game changer."

The exhilaration of their praise washed over me, banishing the remnants of doubt that Kevin had sown. I felt seen, appreciated, and most importantly, I felt like I belonged.

After the meeting, I lingered in the office, basking in the post-presentation glow. The laughter and chatter around me felt like music, the kind that made your heart dance. I poured myself into the feedback system, eager to implement the changes I had proposed. It was during this euphoric moment that a notification pinged on my computer—an email from Ethan. My heart skipped a beat as I opened it, the familiar flutter of excitement battling against the anxiety that had taken residence in my chest.

"Hey, Lily," it read. "I've been thinking about you a lot lately. Can we talk? I miss you."

A rush of emotions surged through me, a mix of longing and caution. I wanted nothing more than to dive into the comforting embrace of our shared moments, the laughter and deep conversations that had filled my days. But the reality of our separation loomed large, a reminder of the challenges we faced.

With a determined breath, I leaned back in my chair, feeling the rush of possibility course through me. Life had thrown me into a whirlwind, but I was ready to face whatever challenge came next.

Whether it was conquering Kevin or navigating the tangled mess of my feelings for Ethan, I felt a newfound strength rising within me, like a flame igniting in the darkness.

The email from Ethan sat in my inbox, taunting me like a half-finished puzzle. I knew I should respond, but every time I hovered over the keyboard, a wave of uncertainty washed over me. What did I want to say? I leaned back in my chair, allowing the noise of the office to envelop me. The hum of conversation, punctuated by the laughter of my colleagues, filled the air with a warmth I had almost forgotten. Yet, a chill of uncertainty crept back in. Ethan's absence had been like a thunderstorm looming on the horizon—ever-present but unpredictable.

Instead of crafting a heartfelt reply, I redirected my focus back to the task at hand. The customer feedback system was my canvas, and I was determined to paint it with bright ideas and vibrant solutions. Every piece of feedback was a brushstroke, each suggestion an opportunity to refine our approach. I dove back into the analytics, sifting through data points like a detective on the hunt. Patterns began to emerge, and I felt that familiar thrill of discovery as I identified key areas for improvement.

"Hey, data diva!" Mira popped her head over my cubicle wall, a bright smile illuminating her face. "I just heard you in the meeting. You were on fire! Kevin looked like he'd swallowed a lemon."

I couldn't help but chuckle. "I almost felt bad for him, but then I remembered that he makes a fine shadow for my bright ideas."

"Right? That guy is like a cloud that never rains, just hangs around and sucks all the fun out of the room," she said, plopping down onto the edge of my desk. "So, what's next? You're not going to let him steal your thunder, are you?"

"Not a chance," I said, my resolve hardening. "I'm digging into the feedback now. If I can fix this system, maybe I can help everyone see my value. And maybe even put Kevin in his place."

"Now that's the spirit!" she cheered. "You know, it's about time someone knocked him off his little pedestal. He acts like he owns the place, but he's just a cog in a very mediocre machine."

Her words sent a surge of energy through me, and I began to tap away at my keyboard, more inspired than ever. Mira's infectious enthusiasm was like a breath of fresh air, clearing away the cobwebs of doubt that had lingered in my mind. I started drafting new features for the feedback system that not only addressed the current complaints but also proposed enhancements that could elevate our customer service to a level that even Kevin could not ignore.

Hours melted away as I poured my heart into the project, and when the clock struck five, I leaned back, surveying my work with satisfaction. The data was crystal clear, the suggestions impactful, and I felt a rush of accomplishment. Just as I was about to save my work, my phone buzzed on the desk. A text from Ethan illuminated the screen: "Can we meet? I want to explain everything."

The air in the room shifted, as if a sudden gust of wind had swept through, stirring the mundane into the extraordinary. My heart raced as I considered his words. What did he want to explain? The past few weeks had felt like a whirlwind, and a part of me longed to dive back into that familiar warmth, to unravel the complexities of what had happened between us.

Before I could second-guess myself, I replied, "Sure. How about tomorrow at the café?" I pressed send, my pulse quickening. I was already mentally rehearsing all the things I wanted to say, all the questions swirling like leaves in an autumn breeze.

The next day arrived too quickly. I arrived at the café early, needing the time to calm my racing heart. The aroma of freshly brewed coffee filled the air, mingling with the soft chatter of patrons. I settled into a cozy corner table, my fingers wrapped around a steaming cup of chai, seeking solace in the warmth.

When Ethan walked in, he looked just as I remembered—tall, with tousled hair and those penetrating green eyes that held a world of emotions. He spotted me immediately, a flicker of relief crossing his face as he made his way to my table. The moment our eyes met, a whirlwind of memories washed over me—the laughter, the deep conversations, the moments of silence that spoke volumes.

"Hey," he said softly, sliding into the seat across from me.

"Hey," I replied, my heart doing a little flip. "You wanted to talk?"

He took a deep breath, as if steeling himself for a plunge into deep waters. "Yeah, I do. I've missed you... so much."

The sincerity in his voice struck a chord within me, and I found myself leaning forward, captivated. "I've missed you too, Ethan. Things have been... different without you."

"I know. After the last time we spoke, I needed to take a step back and really think about everything," he confessed, his gaze dropping to the table. "I was confused about how to navigate my feelings. I let fear cloud my judgment, and I didn't want to drag you into that mess."

"Fear?" I echoed, my brow furrowing. "What were you afraid of?"

He looked up, and the vulnerability in his eyes pierced through the noise of the café. "That I wouldn't be enough for you. That I would only bring you down with my own issues. I thought distancing myself would help us both."

A pang of empathy pierced through me, and I reached across the table, placing my hand on his. "Ethan, I never saw you as a burden. I saw you as someone who understood me, someone I wanted to grow with."

He squeezed my hand, a flicker of hope igniting in the depths of his gaze. "I realize that now. But when I pulled away, it only made everything harder. I thought I was protecting you, but I was only isolating myself. And you."

As he spoke, I felt the weight of unspoken words hanging in the air. My heart swelled with the possibility of reconnecting, but the shadows of our past lingered, reminding me of the distance we had traversed. "So, what now? How do we move forward?" I asked, my voice steady despite the turmoil inside.

"I want to be honest with you this time," he said, his expression earnest. "I want to figure this out together. But I need to know if you're willing to take that leap with me."

His question hung between us, a delicate promise wrapped in vulnerability, and in that moment, I realized that we stood on the edge of a precipice, both daring to leap into the unknown.

I hesitated for a heartbeat, uncertainty washing over me like a cool breeze on a sweltering day. Ethan's words lingered in the air, a tantalizing blend of hope and fear that wove through my mind. Could we really do this? The thought of stepping back into the storm of our relationship felt both exhilarating and terrifying, but the earnestness in his eyes urged me on.

"I want to leap," I said finally, my voice steadier than I felt. "But we need to be clear about what that means for us. This can't be like before, with walls built around our feelings. I want to be real, and I want you to be real with me."

Ethan nodded, his relief palpable. "Absolutely. No more walls. I'm done hiding behind them." His sincerity struck me like a spark, igniting the embers of what we had shared before.

The café buzzed around us, a cacophony of laughter and clinking cups, but at that moment, it felt like we were in our own world, a bubble suspended in time. As we discussed our feelings, each word felt like a step taken on a path we hadn't dared to walk together before. He told me about the pressure he'd faced with his family, how expectations had weighed heavily on him. "I've always been the 'golden boy,' you know? The one who's supposed to have everything figured out. But the truth is, I'm just as lost as anyone else."

"I think we all are," I admitted, feeling a kinship in our vulnerability. "It's scary to feel like everyone expects you to have the answers, and you're just trying to keep your head above water."

"Exactly," he said, his voice softening. "And being with you—being honest with you—made me realize that it's okay not to have all the answers. I want to embrace that uncertainty, and I want to do it with you."

We sat in comfortable silence for a moment, allowing the warmth of shared understanding to envelop us. The air hummed with a new energy, an unspoken promise swirling between us. Just as I was starting to feel light again, a shadow slipped across our table. I glanced up to find Kevin standing there, arms crossed, his expression a blend of smugness and irritation.

"Well, well, well, look at the two of you in a cozy little tête-à-tête," he sneered, his voice dripping with sarcasm. "I didn't realize we were running a romance novel here."

Ethan stiffened, the warmth between us dissipating like mist in the morning sun. "What do you want, Kevin?" I asked, forcing my voice to stay steady despite the sudden tension.

"Just checking on my favorite employee, of course," he replied, his eyes darting between us, searching for cracks in our facade. "You know, it's not very professional to get all chummy with your coworkers. What's next? A picnic in the park?"

Ethan stood, his chair scraping against the floor with a harsh sound. "Leave her alone, Kevin. We were just having a conversation."

Kevin's laughter rang hollow, and I felt a surge of anger bubble within me. "Oh, look at you, standing up for your girlfriend. How noble. But let's face it, you're both just playing pretend here."

"Pretend?" I shot back, unable to keep the fire out of my voice. "At least I'm not the one pretending to be someone I'm not. If you're so concerned about professionalism, maybe you should start by treating your colleagues with respect."

For a moment, surprise flickered across Kevin's face, quickly replaced by a smirk. "Touché, Lily. But remember, you're playing a dangerous game by crossing me. You wouldn't want to see how I play dirty."

As he walked away, I felt the tension in the air shift again, this time tightening around us like a noose. Ethan and I exchanged glances, and the momentary thrill of our connection dulled as reality crashed back in.

"I'm sorry about that," Ethan said, his brow furrowed. "I didn't mean to bring that energy into our talk."

"It's not your fault," I replied, frustration simmering just below the surface. "But he's right about one thing: things are going to be complicated if we pursue this."

Ethan sighed, running a hand through his hair, a gesture that sent a familiar jolt of affection coursing through me. "I know. But I think we can handle it. I believe in us."

"I want to believe in us too," I said, leaning forward, my heart racing. "But what does that look like? Can we really make this work without letting Kevin and his drama dictate our lives?"

He nodded, determination flaring in his eyes. "Let's set boundaries. No letting him get to us. If he tries to pull something, we deal with it together."

The idea of facing our challenges as a team rekindled a sense of courage in me. Just as I opened my mouth to agree, my phone buzzed again. This time it wasn't Ethan or any of my colleagues. It was a notification from work, alerting me to an urgent meeting scheduled for later that afternoon.

"What's wrong?" Ethan asked, his brow furrowing with concern.

I glanced at the screen and felt my stomach drop. "It's a meeting about the customer feedback system. They're rolling out changes... I think Kevin might be behind it."

"Why would he schedule a meeting about that?" Ethan asked, confusion lacing his voice. "Doesn't he know how hard you've worked on it?"

"Because he wants to undermine me, to make me look incompetent," I replied, dread pooling in my stomach. "If he can sway the others to doubt my work, it'll put my entire project at risk."

"Then we need to prepare," Ethan said, his expression shifting to one of fierce resolve. "What can I do to help?"

The urgency of the situation pushed me into action. "I need to gather data to support my findings, to show how valuable my changes are. If I can present strong evidence, Kevin won't be able to twist it against me."

"Let's do it," he said, standing with purpose. "Where do we start?"

We dove back into work mode, but as I gathered my notes and prepared for the meeting, a gnawing sense of unease settled in the pit of my stomach. What if Kevin had already turned everyone against me? What if the support I had built among my colleagues wasn't strong enough to withstand his influence?

As we worked side by side, the café's familiar sounds faded into the background, and I became increasingly aware of how intertwined our fates were becoming. The clock ticked down the minutes until the meeting, each tick amplifying my anxiety. Just when I thought I had it all figured out, the café door swung open, and a figure stepped inside, drawing my attention.

The world seemed to still as I recognized the person striding toward us—Ethan's mother, her expression one of concern mixed with urgency. My heart raced as she approached, her eyes flickering between Ethan and me. "Ethan, we need to talk. It's about your father."

The gravity of her words hit me like a brick, and in that moment, everything we'd been building together hung in the balance, teetering on the edge of an unseen precipice.

Chapter 23: Late-Night Messages

The sun dipped below the horizon, casting a gentle amber glow across my room, the walls painted with shades of dusk. I sank into the familiar embrace of my favorite armchair, its fabric worn from countless evenings spent lost in thought. A half-empty mug of chamomile tea sat by my side, its steam curling into the air like a delicate wisp of memory. The quiet hum of the world outside blended with the faint chirping of crickets, creating a symphony that echoed my growing solitude. This was my sanctuary, but lately, it felt more like a gilded cage, holding me captive in a world where Ethan's laughter had become an echo instead of a presence.

The clock ticked rhythmically, a reminder that nightfall was upon us once again. I glanced at my phone, heart quickening as I saw the familiar green light flicker to life. With trembling fingers, I swiped the screen to answer the call, and there he was—Ethan. The glow of his screen illuminated his features, and for a brief moment, it felt as though he were right there with me, sharing the same air.

"Hey, beautiful," he said, his voice a warm caress that wrapped around my heart like a favorite song.

"Hey yourself," I replied, fighting the grin that threatened to bloom. I couldn't help but feel a flutter in my chest as our eyes locked through the screen, that unbreakable thread connecting us across the miles.

We exchanged small talk about our day, and I reveled in the little nuances of his speech—the way he would lean back and run a hand through his tousled hair when he got animated, or how the corners of his mouth would twitch when he was trying to hide a laugh. Each glance, each shared story, was a lifeline to the world I had left behind, to the comfort of his presence that I yearned for with every fiber of my being.

But the distance loomed large. Every joke and shared memory felt like a fleeting shadow, unable to chase away the reality of our separation. "Remember that time we got lost on the way to the lake?" I asked, trying to anchor us in a moment we could both cherish.

His laughter bubbled up like a melody. "How could I forget? You were convinced we were just taking the scenic route."

"Hey, I maintain that it was a lovely detour," I shot back, smirking. "We discovered that amazing little ice cream shop."

He leaned in closer, his eyes twinkling with mischief. "Only because you bribed me with a promise of strawberry swirl."

I chuckled, the familiar warmth spreading through me. "A girl has to have her ways."

But as the laughter faded, so did the lightness of our conversation. I caught the flicker of something else in his gaze, a shadow passing over his features. "How's it really going?" he asked, the playful tone gone, replaced by something deeper and more earnest.

I hesitated, my heart twisting. "It's... okay. Just a bit lonely, you know? I miss you."

"Me too," he admitted, his voice lowering. "This is getting harder."

His confession hung between us, heavy and bittersweet. It was one thing to share laughter and memories, but it was another to acknowledge the gnawing ache of absence that clawed at both our hearts. I wanted to reach through the screen, to close the distance, to feel his heartbeat against mine.

"I wish I could just hop on a plane and be there," I murmured, frustration bubbling up. "It's not fair."

"Life rarely is," he replied, a wry smile ghosting his lips. "But hey, we can make it through this. We have our late-night calls, right? And the world is a small place."

I nodded, trying to stifle the tears that threatened to spill over. "Right. Just... it's not the same, Ethan. I want to be there. I want to hold your hand and walk under the stars, not just talk about it."

He sighed, running his hand through his hair again, an endearing habit I had grown to love. "I know. But I promise you, this is just a chapter in our story. One day, we'll look back and laugh at how we thought it was the end of the world."

I tried to believe him, to hold onto the glimmer of hope he offered. "You really think so?"

"I know so," he insisted, his confidence washing over me like a soothing balm. "You're stronger than you think. We both are."

We shared a quiet moment, allowing the silence to envelop us like a warm blanket. The shadows in my room grew deeper, but Ethan's presence brought a lightness that pushed back against the creeping darkness. I could almost hear his heartbeat echoing through the phone, a reminder that he was still with me, despite the miles that stretched between us.

As the conversation drifted back to lighter topics, I found myself wanting to capture every detail—the way his eyes crinkled at the corners when he laughed, the playful teasing that flowed like a familiar dance between us. But the longer we spoke, the more I felt a chasm forming in my chest, an aching longing that no amount of laughter could fill.

"Let's promise something," I said suddenly, the words spilling from my lips before I could second-guess them. "No matter how far apart we are, we'll keep reaching for each other, even if it's just through screens."

"Deal," he said, his smile radiating warmth that transcended the coldness of distance.

In that moment, we forged a pact, an unspoken vow that even the miles could not shatter our bond. But as the call began to wind down, I felt the familiar sting of reality creeping back in. "I should let you go," I said, my voice thick with emotion.

"Yeah," he replied softly, his gaze lingering on mine. "But I'll be here tomorrow, and the day after that. Just like always."

With a heavy heart, I nodded, knowing it was time to say goodbye. As the screen faded to black, I sat in the silence that followed, the absence of his laughter echoing through my room. The shadows seemed to close in around me, and I was left with the bittersweet taste of longing and the flickering hope that someday, soon, the distance between us would shrink, and I would feel his warmth beside me once more.

The days drifted into weeks, each sunrise marking the passage of time that felt both painfully slow and startlingly quick. Mornings greeted me with the aroma of coffee brewing, the steam curling up like the dreams I had of being with Ethan. The sound of my parents bustling about the house blended with the chirps of early birds, but it all felt muted, a background hum that didn't quite reach me. I went through the motions of school and chores, but my heart was still nestled in those late-night video calls, where the world faded away and it was just the two of us, suspended in a digital bubble.

Every day, I watched the calendar inch closer to summer, the season that promised freedom and a hint of adventure. But that promise also hung heavy with the uncertainty of what lay ahead. Would Ethan and I be able to bridge the gap when the world finally let us converge? Or would this distance, which felt manageable through a screen, become a chasm too wide to cross in reality? My thoughts spiraled, and I often found myself staring out of the window, imagining him just beyond the glass, laughing at one of my ridiculous puns.

After school one Tuesday, as I settled into my usual spot on the couch with a cozy blanket draped over my legs, I heard the familiar chime of my phone. Ethan was calling. I felt a jolt of excitement, a small spark igniting the dim atmosphere around me. As soon as I answered, his face filled my screen, and my heart leaped.

"Hey, you!" he said, a grin lighting up his features. "What's the latest? Did you finally get that teacher to stop assigning homework?"

I rolled my eyes, suppressing a laugh. "If only! Mrs. Thompson seems to think we need a lifetime supply of worksheets. You'd think we were training for a marathon, not just preparing for finals."

His laughter was like music, echoing across the distance. "Maybe she's just trying to keep us from becoming experts in procrastination."

"Too late for that," I admitted, shaking my head. "You should see my living room—it's basically a monument to unfinished projects."

"Sounds cozy," he teased, leaning closer to the camera, his expression turning conspiratorial. "Just make sure not to get lost in the chaos. We can't have you missing your big plans for the summer, right?"

"Plans?" I echoed, suddenly aware of the underlying tension in his voice. "What plans?"

He hesitated, a flicker of uncertainty crossing his face. "You know... the plans we talked about? About meeting up? I've been thinking... Maybe I should come to visit."

A rush of excitement and anxiety swelled within me. "You're serious?"

"Absolutely," he replied, his smile transforming into a confident grin. "I miss you too much. Plus, I think it's time we brought the fairy tale back to life."

I laughed, the sound light and buoyant. "You do know that fairy tales usually involve some sort of conflict, right? Like a giant or a wicked witch lurking nearby?"

"Just consider me the brave knight, ready to face whatever challenges arise—like meeting your parents for the first time," he quipped, his eyes dancing with mischief.

"Don't underestimate the power of my mom's lasagna. That's a formidable foe," I countered, a playful smirk crossing my lips.

As our banter continued, a thought bubbled up, threatening to burst the bubble of our lightheartedness. "But what about... you know, the curse?"

Ethan's expression shifted slightly, the laughter fading as reality crept back in. "It's not going to magically disappear. I know that. But maybe facing it together will make it easier."

The weight of his words settled heavily between us, a reminder of the shadows lurking just outside our dreams. But for every moment of doubt, there was an equal measure of hope. I could almost picture it: a world where we could explore together, laughter echoing through familiar spaces, our hands entwined as we navigated whatever life threw at us.

We spent the rest of the evening plotting our future adventures—imagining late-night drives with the windows down, starlit picnics, and lazy afternoons filled with laughter. Each scenario was a sweet escape from the present, a vivid tapestry woven from our shared dreams. I felt the anticipation tingling in my fingertips, and it became hard to focus on anything else.

But as the call drew to a close, an unease settled in the pit of my stomach. I could sense the unresolved tension hanging like a thick fog. "Ethan?" I ventured, my voice softer now. "Are you really ready for this?"

"Are you?" he asked, and there was a weight behind the question that pulled at my heartstrings.

"I want to be. More than anything." I hesitated, searching for the right words. "But it feels like we're stepping into uncharted territory. What if it doesn't go as we hope?"

His gaze bore into mine, earnest and unwavering. "Then we face it together, just like we always have. We're a team, right?"

"Right," I replied, swallowing back the lump forming in my throat. The truth was, our connection felt stronger than ever, but with it came the fear of falling apart. "I just don't want to lose what we have."

"Trust me," he said, his voice a low, soothing murmur. "No matter what happens, you won't lose me."

We lingered on the call a little longer, exchanging teasing remarks and soft smiles, but as the clock ticked on, reality slipped back in. I was left with the aching knowledge that no matter how tightly we clung to each other in our conversations, the world outside was still unpredictable.

After our goodbyes, the silence returned, heavy and palpable. I stared at my phone for a long moment, the screen dimming as it faded into darkness. The weight of his absence pressed down on me like a stone, and I couldn't shake the feeling that we were on the brink of something monumental.

Days passed in a haze of anticipation, each moment filled with a mix of excitement and anxiety. My thoughts danced between the possibility of seeing Ethan and the fears of what that would mean. I caught myself daydreaming in class, picturing the smile that would spread across his face when we finally stood together. Would it be just as magical as I imagined? Or would the reality feel different—colder, more daunting?

As the weekend approached, I found myself caught in a whirlwind of emotions. I thought back to our conversations, the teasing banter that made me feel light as air. I couldn't deny the thrill of his promise to visit, but uncertainty swirled in my mind like storm clouds on a summer day.

Then, as if fate were listening, I received a message that would send everything spiraling into a new direction. A simple notification flashed across my screen, a message from Ethan that read: "Hey, we need to talk." My heart dropped, and the playful banter of the past few days felt like a distant memory. What could he possibly want to discuss?

The message from Ethan lingered in the air, its abruptness striking like a sudden storm on a clear day. My heart raced, each beat drumming louder as I stared at the screen, waiting for the words to magically rearrange themselves into something less foreboding. "We need to talk" felt like a pebble tossed into a still pond, sending ripples of anxiety swirling through my mind. What could possibly require a serious discussion?

I took a deep breath, trying to quell the rising tide of apprehension. His tone in the message was casual, but I knew better than to let that fool me. Ethan was not one to resort to melodrama, yet something must have prompted him to reach out this way. As I paced my room, the familiar walls closing in on me, I imagined all the possibilities. Had something happened? Was there bad news about the curse? Or was it about us—our plans, our future?

In a moment of impulsiveness, I shot him a reply: "Okay, let's talk. When?"

As if on cue, my phone chimed, and his response lit up the screen. "Can we do a video call? I think it's better if we see each other."

I hesitated, uncertainty prickling at my skin. "Sure. Just give me a minute."

I rushed to tidy my room, tossing aside clothes and hastily straightening cushions, as if a neat environment would somehow ward off the potential chaos of the conversation to come. After a few moments that felt like an eternity, I settled back onto the couch, pulling the blanket tightly around me as a shield against the encroaching tension.

Ethan appeared on the screen, his expression a mixture of determination and apprehension. "Hey," he said, his voice steady but his eyes betraying a flicker of uncertainty.

"Hey," I replied, trying to inject some cheer into my tone. "So, what's up?"

He took a deep breath, his gaze dropping to his hands for a moment, as if the words were too heavy to bear. "You know I've been thinking about our summer plans, right?"

"Of course. You're still planning on coming to visit?" I asked, my heart racing.

He nodded, but the movement felt tentative. "Yeah, but I've been doing a lot of thinking. I know we've both been excited, but..."

"But what?" I pressed, unable to contain the anxious curiosity bubbling within me.

He met my gaze, a serious look clouding his features. "I've been looking into the curse. I feel like we should understand what we're getting ourselves into before we dive in headfirst."

I felt my stomach drop. "Ethan, we've talked about this. We can handle it together. We've always been stronger together."

"I know," he said, his voice softening. "But what if it's more complicated than we think? What if me being there puts you in danger?"

I shook my head, unwilling to accept that possibility. "You're not putting me in danger. The curse doesn't have to control our lives. I refuse to let it."

He studied me, a furrow appearing between his brows. "It's not just about us anymore. There are other things at play here, and I can't ignore them."

My heart raced, confusion and frustration swirling together. "What do you mean? Are there things you haven't told me?"

Ethan sighed, running a hand through his hair as he often did when grappling with something difficult. "There's something I've discovered that I didn't want to bring up until I had more information. I didn't want to freak you out."

I leaned forward, suddenly very serious. "Ethan, you're freaking me out right now. Just tell me what's going on."

He hesitated, the weight of whatever he was holding back heavy in the air. "The curse has a history, a deeper connection to our families than I initially realized. It's not just an inconvenience—it's tied to something far more powerful."

My mind raced, images of old tomes and forgotten legends flooding my thoughts. "What do you mean?"

"There are other families involved—those who have tried to break the curse and failed," he explained, his voice dropping to a whisper as if speaking of something forbidden. "Some of them have been watching us. Watching you."

"Watching me?" I echoed, my voice barely above a whisper. The thought sent chills down my spine. "Why?"

Ethan shifted uncomfortably, the tension in his posture amplifying. "Because they believe the key to breaking the curse lies with you, and they'll do anything to get to you."

The realization struck me like lightning, leaving me breathless. "What does that even mean? Who are they?"

"I don't know yet," he admitted, his eyes filled with a mixture of fear and determination. "But we need to be careful. This isn't just about us anymore; it's about something much larger than either of us."

I leaned back, trying to process the whirlwind of information. "So, you're saying that by coming to visit, I could be putting myself in danger?"

"Exactly," he said, the weight of the moment hanging heavy between us. "And I can't let that happen. Not to you."

The tension in the room thickened, the atmosphere charged with unspoken fears and a desperation to protect one another. "Ethan, we've faced so much together. I don't want to let this control our lives. We have to fight back."

He shook his head, frustration flickering across his face. "It's not that simple. I'm just not sure what that fight looks like yet."

A tense silence enveloped us, the uncertainty hanging thick in the air like an impending storm. I could feel the heaviness of our conversation weighing down on me, the questions swirling endlessly.

And just as I was about to voice my thoughts, a sudden noise pierced the silence, pulling my focus away. It was a loud bang, a sharp sound that echoed through the house. My heart raced as I glanced around, every instinct screaming that something was off.

"What was that?" Ethan asked, his voice taut with concern.

"I don't know," I replied, rising from the couch. The shadows seemed to deepen around me, the atmosphere shifting. "Stay on the line."

I tiptoed toward the door, the floorboards creaking beneath my feet. The noise had come from downstairs, and my stomach churned with a mix of fear and curiosity. "Hello?" I called out, my voice trembling as I strained to hear anything beyond the oppressive silence.

Ethan's face appeared on the screen, concern etched into his features. "Lily, don't go down there. It could be dangerous."

"I can't just ignore it," I whispered, feeling the weight of his gaze urging me to be cautious.

Another sound echoed from below—this time, a soft scuffling noise followed by a sharp crack. I took a hesitant step toward the stairs, gripping the banister tightly. "I'll be quick, I promise."

"No! Lily!" Ethan's voice rose in urgency, but I was already halfway down the stairs, each step amplifying the growing sense of dread.

As I reached the bottom, I paused, glancing around. The dim light from the hallway barely illuminated the space, casting eerie shadows that danced along the walls. "Is anyone there?" I called, but the only reply was the hollow echo of my own voice.

Suddenly, something shifted in the corner of my vision, and I turned to see a figure emerging from the shadows. My breath caught in my throat as I stood frozen, eyes wide with shock.

"Lily?" the figure spoke, voice familiar yet strained. "I didn't think you'd be here."

My heart raced as recognition flooded my senses. Standing before me was a face I hadn't expected to see—a face that had once been a part of my world, now an unwelcome intrusion into the fragile peace I had built with Ethan.

"What are you doing here?" I demanded, fear mingling with disbelief.

The figure stepped closer, and the air crackled with an unsettling tension. "I came to warn you."

As the words hung in the air, the weight of their implication settled over me like a dark shroud. I glanced back at the screen, Ethan's face filled with anxiety, and I realized that the storm was just beginning.

Chapter 24: Unforeseen Complications

The neon glow of the computer screens illuminated the office in a harsh blue light, casting long shadows that danced across the walls as we powered through another caffeine-laden night. Each click of the keyboard echoed in the silence, punctuated only by the occasional frustrated sigh or the rustle of takeout containers. The air was thick with tension, a palpable force that settled over us like a heavy blanket, suffocating and comforting all at once. Just days before our product launch, the weight of our collective ambitions pressed down on me, and a sense of impending doom loomed like a storm cloud on the horizon.

"Alright, team," I called out, my voice slightly hoarse from too many cups of coffee and too little sleep. "We need to fix this glitch. What are we thinking?"

My colleagues, a motley crew of tech enthusiasts and caffeine addicts, looked up from their screens, eyes bleary but determined. Sam, our sharp-witted developer with an affinity for sarcasm, raised an eyebrow. "Thinking that maybe we should have done a test run, you know, before we decided to launch the rocket?"

I shot him a glare that was half-hearted at best. "Thanks, Captain Obvious. We need solutions, not commentary."

A chuckle broke the tension, and I glanced over at Emma, our project manager. She was the glue that held us together, her calm demeanor often a stark contrast to the chaotic whirlwind of our work. "Let's break it down," she suggested, her voice steady. "What's causing the glitch?"

As we dived into the code, a whirlpool of numbers and letters blurred before my eyes. My heart raced, and the caffeine only fueled the adrenaline coursing through me. I could feel the heat rising in my cheeks as the hours dragged on. The team leaned into the problem, their focus unwavering, and for a brief moment, the anxiety that had clutched at my chest began to loosen its grip.

Just as we seemed to be making progress, a sharp ping interrupted our rhythm—a notification of another bug. The room collectively groaned, a sound that echoed the frustration we all felt.

"Of course," I muttered, running a hand through my hair, which was quickly losing its battle against my increasing stress levels. "It's like the universe is conspiring against us."

"More like our code is," Sam quipped, his fingers dancing across the keyboard with a practiced ease. "Let's blame the code for our misery. It makes for a much better villain."

As we fought against the mounting issues, I caught sight of my phone buzzing quietly on the desk. It was Ethan, his name lighting up the screen like a beacon in the darkness. My heart fluttered, but I hesitated to pick it up. Would I burden him with my chaos? Would he even want to hear about my all-nighter filled with caffeine and lines of code?

Finally, curiosity won. I glanced at the message: "Thinking of you. Let's grab dinner tomorrow?"

Just that simple invitation made my heart skip. I wanted to share everything with him—the late-night struggles, the camaraderie of my team, the sweet taste of success that felt so close yet so far. But here I was, buried under an avalanche of work and worry. I couldn't bring that heaviness to the table.

Before I could decide, Emma broke the silence. "Okay, we've found the root cause. It's a data overload issue in the back end. If we can streamline the input process, we should be able to fix this."

Relief surged through me, washing away the anxiety, if only for a moment. "Great! Let's implement those changes, and then I can run a few tests."

The hours slipped by, the glow of the monitors becoming both a comfort and a curse. We worked tirelessly, our collective energy flowing through the room like an electric current. Finally, after what felt like an eternity, we implemented the fixes and braced ourselves for the test.

"On three," I said, my voice steady. "One, two, three!"

As we ran the program, the screen blinked, and for a heartbeat, time stood still. When the system stabilized, a wave of triumph erupted in the room. We jumped up, exchanging high-fives and hugs, the adrenaline of success drowning out the fatigue that had settled into our bones.

"Pizza party!" Sam shouted, raising his hands in the air like a victory banner. "You can't celebrate success without pizza!"

We gathered in the break room, the aroma of cheesy goodness filling the air as we shared slices and laughter. The camaraderie felt refreshing, like a balm to the chaos we had just overcome. In that moment, I realized I wasn't alone in this whirlwind of stress and pressure. My colleagues, my friends, were in this with me, shoulder to shoulder, each of us battling our own demons while pushing toward the same goal.

As we laughed and joked, the weight of the impending launch began to lift. The warmth of their support reminded me of the connections that had formed, forged in the fires of deadlines and late nights. I shared a look with Emma, who nodded knowingly, her eyes sparkling with shared victory.

Suddenly, the memory of Ethan's text flooded back. "Guys, I might be late tomorrow. I have a dinner planned with someone special."

Sam's eyes widened in mock horror. "You're ditching us for a date? Sacrilege!"

I laughed, the tension in my shoulders easing. "It's not a date. It's just dinner."

"Just dinner?" Emma chimed in, her smile teasing. "You're going to need to give us the play-by-play. I want all the details."

With laughter and lightness swirling around us, I felt a spark of hope igniting deep within. Perhaps I was beginning to find my footing in this chaos after all. With my team by my side and the promise of tomorrow with Ethan ahead, I realized that even in the midst of turmoil, there was room for joy. The night stretched on, filled with the sounds of friendship and the delicious, cheesy comfort of pizza, reminding me that sometimes, even when the world feels upside down, connection is the anchor that keeps us steady.

The next day arrived with a crispness that belied the chaos of the night before. The sun filtered through the large windows of the office, casting a warm glow that danced across the haphazard piles of paperwork and empty coffee cups strewn across our desks. I could almost convince myself that everything was normal—except for the persistent hum of stress that buzzed just beneath the surface, a reminder of the looming product launch that still held us in its tight grip.

Despite the comforting ambiance, my heart raced with the knowledge that we were now in the home stretch. I could feel the weight of expectations from the higher-ups pressing down on us like a heavy fog. My phone buzzed incessantly with notifications from both Ethan and the team, a cacophony of concern and excitement that threatened to drown out my thoughts.

I glanced at my screen, where our program had crashed one too many times in the previous hours. The relief of last night's victory felt fragile, as if it could shatter at any moment. Emma, with her typical blend of calm and authority, gathered us around for a morning huddle, her voice cutting through the haze.

"Alright, team, today we finalize everything. We've made great strides, but we need to ensure all features are working seamlessly before launch day. Any bugs left to squash?"

A collective groan echoed around the table, but I couldn't help but smirk. "I think we might be out of bug spray. Who knew coding came with its own set of critters?"

"Right? I thought we were developing software, not inviting pests to a picnic," Sam chimed in, a grin plastered across his face.

"Keep the humor coming, guys. It's what's keeping me sane," Emma replied, rolling her eyes but unable to hide her smile.

As we delved back into our tasks, I found myself stealing glances at my phone, waiting for a message from Ethan. The anticipation danced like butterflies in my stomach, each ping sending a thrill through me, yet the waiting felt interminable. I tried to focus on the work at hand, the thrill of discovery nudging at my thoughts as I chased down the last few bugs in our program.

The morning melted into afternoon, and with every passing hour, the atmosphere grew tenser. Each successful fix was met with cheers, but they quickly faded into anxiety as new issues crept in like uninvited guests. It was during one of these frustrating moments that I finally received a text from Ethan.

"Hey! How's the launch prep? Want to meet up tonight?"

A flood of warmth spread through me. I typed back quickly, my fingers flying over the screen. "We're deep in the trenches here, but I'd love to see you. Need a break from all the stress!"

"Perfect. Let's go somewhere fun. You deserve it."

I felt a surge of gratitude and excitement bubbling within me. Perhaps this would be just what I needed to break the cycle of tension that had woven itself into the very fabric of our days. I glanced up from my phone, catching Emma's eye.

"Ethan's taking me out tonight," I said, a smile creeping onto my face.

"Oh? Someone's been holding out on us!" she teased, nudging me playfully.

"Just trying to maintain an air of mystery," I shot back, a playful grin returning.

But beneath the light banter, an undercurrent of anxiety thrummed in my chest. I wanted tonight to be perfect, but what if I didn't measure up? What if the chaos of my life intruded upon the delicate budding of our connection?

As the day wore on, we continued to work, and as night fell, the glow of the office lights flickered like stars against the darkening sky. Each click of the keyboard felt like a countdown, the seconds ticking away until I could finally escape into the warmth of Ethan's company.

Finally, with a burst of triumph, Emma announced, "We've done it! We're ready for the launch tomorrow!"

Cheers erupted around the office, and in that moment, it felt as though the weight of the world had been lifted from our shoulders. The high spirits lingered as we cleaned up and shared celebratory hugs.

Later, as I prepared for my evening with Ethan, I caught sight of myself in the mirror. The fatigue was evident in my eyes, but I chose to ignore it, focusing instead on the flutter of excitement deep in my chest. I dressed carefully, picking out a soft blue top that complemented my hazel eyes, letting my hair fall in gentle waves around my shoulders.

When I arrived at the restaurant, the lively ambiance enveloped me, the air filled with the aroma of grilled meats and spices. The soft glow of chandeliers cast a warm light over the polished tables, and I spotted Ethan waiting for me near the entrance, his handsome features illuminated in the dim light.

"Hey, you," he said, his smile wide and genuine.

"Hey," I replied, my heart skipping a beat as I joined him.

"Looking beautiful, as always," he said, his gaze lingering on me just long enough to send my pulse racing.

We settled at a cozy corner table, and as we talked, the worries of the day began to fade into the background. Ethan's laughter filled the air, each note pulling me deeper into the moment. The conversation flowed effortlessly between us, touching on everything from our favorite films to our most embarrassing childhood memories.

Yet, amidst the light-hearted banter, a cloud loomed in my mind. The impending launch sat heavy, a nagging reminder of the chaos that awaited us. Just as I began to feel the weight of that anxiety lifting, a familiar face from the past walked in. My ex-boyfriend, Jordan, his presence slicing through the cheerful atmosphere like a chill wind.

Ethan noticed my stiffening posture and followed my gaze. "You alright?"

I forced a smile, trying to shake off the sudden unease. "Yeah, just... an old acquaintance."

"Doesn't look like a friendly reunion," he observed, a hint of concern edging into his voice.

"No, not at all," I replied, my heart racing as I willed Jordan to leave. But he seemed oblivious to the discomfort he was causing, walking over with a swagger that made me cringe.

"Fancy seeing you here," Jordan said, his tone dripping with false charm. "I didn't know you had such refined taste."

Ethan's jaw tightened beside me, his protective instincts flaring to life. "And you are?"

I could feel the tension rising, the air thick with unsaid words. "Jordan, this is Ethan," I said, forcing the smile back onto my face.

"Nice to meet you," Ethan replied, his voice steady but laced with an edge I couldn't ignore.

"Likewise," Jordan said, his eyes glancing between us with a smirk. "I hope you know what you're getting into."

I sensed Ethan's irritation building. "We're doing just fine, thanks," he shot back, the heat of the moment crackling in the air.

As Jordan continued to prattle on, I felt the weight of my past clashing with the potential of my present, the turbulence of emotions swirling dangerously close to the surface. All I wanted was to enjoy this night with Ethan, free from the shadows that loomed over us. I took a deep breath, steeling myself against the whirlwind of feelings. The night was supposed to be about us, about the promise of something beautiful, not a ghost from my past.

With every word Jordan spoke, I felt the urge to retreat within myself, but Ethan's presence anchored me. I wasn't that person anymore, and I refused to let the shadows of my past dictate my future. The tension was palpable, but in that moment, surrounded by the laughter and clinking of glasses, I realized that I was more than capable of standing my ground. With Ethan by my side, I would face whatever came our way, knowing that our connection was worth fighting for.

The tension in the air thickened as Jordan's presence lingered at our table, a shadow creeping across the warm glow of my evening with Ethan. I could feel the unspoken questions swirling between us like leaves caught in a storm. Jordan leaned casually against the table, his demeanor relaxed, as if he hadn't just upended the atmosphere with his unwelcome arrival.

"So, Ethan," he began, his voice oozing with condescension, "how long have you been dating my ex?"

The word "ex" hung in the air, heavy and charged. I shot Ethan a glance, his jaw clenched, but he maintained a cool composure that was both impressive and frustrating. "Long enough to know she's way out of your league," he replied, the edge in his tone unmistakable.

Jordan chuckled, a sound that grated on my nerves. "Well, I always knew she had a type. Let's just say, I hope you're ready for the baggage."

The insinuation hung like a storm cloud. I could feel the heat rising in my cheeks as I struggled to maintain my composure. "Jordan, it's great to see you, but I think it's best if you—"

"Oh, come on, let's not play nice. It's been a while since I've seen you," he interrupted, his gaze flickering between us. "I mean, did you really think I'd just disappear?"

"Honestly, I hoped you'd take a hint and stay gone," I shot back, surprising myself with the fire in my voice.

Ethan turned to me, a flicker of admiration in his eyes. "Good one," he whispered, as Jordan's smirk faltered.

The tension coiled tighter, and I could sense the frustration bubbling beneath Ethan's surface. "We're here to enjoy our evening, not to rehash the past," Ethan said, his tone icy but controlled.

Jordan waved a dismissive hand. "Lighten up. I was just checking in on an old friend. But I see you're keeping busy with... what was it? Coding?" He leaned in, a glint of mockery in his eyes. "Hope that's not too boring for you."

The annoyance simmered just below the surface, and I felt the urge to push back. "You know, Jordan, some of us actually enjoy our work," I replied, biting off each word with surprising conviction. "Maybe you should try it sometime instead of standing around looking for someone to insult."

Ethan's surprise echoed in the brief silence that followed. I could see the tension in his shoulders begin to ease, a flicker of pride passing over his features.

Jordan's expression darkened, and for a split second, I feared he might retaliate. But just as quickly, his smirk returned, a mask hiding his irritation. "Fine, fine. I didn't mean to interrupt your little dinner date." He straightened up and glanced at the bustling restaurant around us. "Enjoy yourselves. I've got better things to do anyway."

He turned and walked away, the tension releasing in an unexpected rush of relief. I could feel my pulse steadying as I turned back to Ethan, who regarded me with a mixture of amusement and admiration. "You handled that like a pro," he said, a teasing smile breaking across his face.

"Thanks. I guess I'm not the same girl who just accepted the punches," I replied, feeling a surge of empowerment.

As we continued our dinner, the conversation flowed more easily, the lingering aftertaste of confrontation fading into laughter and shared stories. We delved into deeper topics—our aspirations, dreams, and fears—our words weaving a tapestry of connection that pulled us closer together.

But just as I began to relax, a chill crept in. I glanced at my phone, the screen lighting up with an alert that sent a jolt of anxiety coursing through me. An email notification from work flashed ominously across the screen, the subject line reading: "Urgent: Software Failure Detected."

I felt my heart plummet as I opened the message. "No, no, no," I whispered under my breath. My mind raced back to the earlier glitches and the fragile victory we had celebrated. The email detailed a catastrophic error in the system, one that threatened to undo all our hard work.

Ethan noticed my sudden stillness. "What is it?"

I could feel the panic creeping into my voice as I relayed the details. "We've got a major software failure. It looks like we didn't catch all the bugs last night."

His expression shifted from amusement to concern. "Do you need to go back?"

"I might have to," I replied, glancing around the restaurant, the laughter and chatter of patrons fading into a muffled background noise. "But I don't want to ruin our night."

Ethan reached across the table, his hand covering mine, grounding me in the moment. "You're not ruining anything. Your work is important, and I understand that. Just know I'm here, supporting you."

The warmth of his grip reassured me, but the weight of responsibility bore down heavily. I wanted to enjoy this evening, to revel in the blossoming connection between us, yet I could feel the urgency gnawing at my insides.

"Maybe we can just finish dinner and then I'll—"

"No 'buts.'" His gaze locked onto mine, fierce and unwavering. "You can't ignore something this big. We need to fix it before it spirals out of control."

The determination in his voice ignited a fire within me. "You're right. I just... I wanted this night to be perfect."

Ethan's thumb brushed over my knuckles, and he smiled gently. "Perfection is overrated. Let's tackle this together. We'll go back to the office, fix the issue, and then come back to this. We can finish our dinner after. Deal?"

I felt a wave of relief wash over me, mixed with gratitude. "Deal."

We settled the bill, and as we walked out of the restaurant, the vibrant nightlife pulsed around us, a reminder of the world we were stepping back into. The fresh air hit my face, and I inhaled deeply, steeling myself for the battle ahead.

As we reached the office, the fluorescent lights flickered ominously, casting an eerie glow over the empty desks. The energy shifted palpably, the buzz of excitement replaced by a grave seriousness. I logged into my workstation, the familiar sight of code filling my screen.

The emails continued to flood in, each one carrying the weight of urgency. We worked diligently, dissecting the error message and sifting through the tangled lines of code. The minutes stretched into hours, but with each breakthrough, hope flickered like a candle in the dark.

Finally, after what felt like an eternity, I spotted the error. "Ethan! I found it!" I exclaimed, adrenaline coursing through me. "The input validation logic was flawed!"

"Great catch! Let's fix it," he replied, his eyes alight with determination.

As we hurriedly implemented the changes, the atmosphere crackled with anticipation. The clock ticked down, and I could feel the weight of every second pressing against us. Just as we were about to run the tests, the door swung open with a bang, startling us both.

In stepped Emma, her face pale and eyes wide with panic. "You guys need to see this. It's bad."

The knot in my stomach tightened as she spoke. "What is it?" I asked, dread creeping into my voice.

"It's not just the software. We've got a major breach in our system. Someone's trying to sabotage the launch."

A chill raced down my spine, and I exchanged a worried glance with Ethan. The stakes had just escalated. As I processed her words, my mind raced with questions—Who could do this? Why now? And more importantly, how could we stop them?

The clock ticked ominously in the background, the launch looming just around the corner. Our night of promise and connection had morphed into a battle for survival, and as the gravity of the situation settled in, I knew we were in for a fight—one that would test not just our skills, but the very bonds we had built.

Chapter 25: The Unexpected Visitor

The morning light poured through the office windows, casting a golden hue over the polished wooden desks and the array of colorful post-it notes that were plastered like modern art across my work station. It was a beautiful day outside, the kind of day that demanded attention with its vibrant blue skies and the gentle rustle of leaves dancing in the breeze. Yet, as I settled into my chair, a familiar unease prickled at the back of my neck. Kevin's presence loomed, as palpable as the lingering scent of yesterday's coffee, bitter and burnt.

Kevin had sauntered back into our lives, returning from who-knows-where with his perfectly tousled hair and a smile that could charm the birds from the trees. He claimed to be "transitioning," as if he had merely stepped out for a quick lunch rather than abandoning us during the crunch time of our major project. My coworkers buzzed with curiosity, their whispers snaking through the office like a mischievous wind. They seemed to think this return was a cause for celebration, but I felt like a moth drawn to a flame—enticed yet deeply aware of the impending burn.

I had spent weeks crafting the presentation that would define my career. Every bullet point was meticulously crafted, every slide designed to reflect the hard work of my team, and the heart I had poured into this endeavor. But now, with Kevin back in the mix, the air felt heavy with tension. It was a palpable force, thick enough to slice through with a dull knife. As he wandered over to my desk, I braced myself for the inevitable jibe or passive-aggressive comment.

"Looks like someone has been busy while I was away," he remarked, leaning against the partition with a cocky grin that I'd once found charming. Now, it grated on my nerves. "I'm sure you've missed my invaluable input."

I arched an eyebrow, suppressing a laugh that threatened to bubble up at his audacity. "Right, because your expertise in leaving us in the lurch is exactly what I've been yearning for," I shot back, the words tumbling out before I could rein them in. My coworkers exchanged glances, and I could almost hear their collective intake of breath, a reminder that they were watching this battle unfold.

Kevin shrugged, the picture of nonchalance. "Don't worry, I'm here now to help get us back on track."

I rolled my eyes, the exasperation bubbling just beneath the surface. "Track? We were on the express train to success before you derailed us. Your return feels less like help and more like a corporate version of a horror movie."

His eyes sparkled with a mix of amusement and annoyance. "You always did have a flair for the dramatic. But don't worry; I'm here to steer the ship."

"Let's just hope you don't capsize it," I muttered under my breath, though I wasn't sure if he heard.

The meeting arrived, a gathering of minds that promised both opportunity and peril. The conference room was bright, the walls lined with inspiring quotes from industry leaders, although I found them more suffocating than uplifting as I took my seat. I was ready to present, a whirlwind of energy and ambition, but Kevin's presence stung like a wasp. The moment he sat down across the table, it was as if a thundercloud had rolled in, blotting out the sun.

As I launched into my presentation, detailing the innovative strategies my team had devised, Kevin interjected with his rehearsed charm, offering "insights" that felt more like attempts to steal my thunder. "You know, I'd suggested a similar approach last year," he interjected smoothly, a grin plastered on his face as he shifted his gaze toward our boss. "If we can just pivot slightly, we could enhance our effectiveness exponentially."

I felt the blood rush to my cheeks, irritation sparking in my chest like a lit fuse. How dare he? This was my moment, my time to shine, and he was trying to hijack it with his smarmy comments.

"Actually, Kevin," I said, my voice steady despite the storm brewing within me, "the approach we've developed has been tailored specifically for this project, and it's based on extensive research and feedback from our client. I appreciate your enthusiasm, but I think it's important to recognize the contributions of everyone involved, don't you?"

A wave of tension swept through the room, thick enough to cut. Kevin's smile faltered, and for a brief moment, I saw something raw and irritated flash in his eyes. I pressed on, fueled by the adrenaline that surged through my veins.

"Moreover," I continued, "this project is not just about numbers and strategies; it's about people and their stories. We've taken the time to understand our client's journey, and that's what makes our approach unique."

The meeting continued, but the atmosphere had shifted. My colleagues were leaning in, intrigued by my conviction. Kevin, however, was like a vulture watching a wounded animal, waiting for the right moment to swoop in. I could feel the undercurrents of competition swirling around us, thick and suffocating.

As I wrapped up, I caught Kevin's eye, a challenge sparking between us. The tension felt electric, and I knew this wouldn't be the last time he would try to undermine me. But I was ready. I would not be a mere bystander in my own career, and I was determined to reclaim my voice.

The meeting adjourned, leaving behind a room full of simmering emotions. I stepped out, the weight of the day heavy on my shoulders, but beneath it all was a flicker of defiance igniting within me. Kevin may have returned, but he wouldn't dim my light. I would shine brighter, even in his shadow, and I wouldn't let anyone, especially him, steal my spark.

The following days unfolded with the tension of a tightrope walk, every interaction with Kevin akin to a precarious balancing act.

Each morning, I arrived at the office with a sense of purpose, a shield of determination forged from the embers of my recent triumph. I had finally begun to feel at home in my role, and I was not about to let his return derail that progress. Yet, as Kevin made his rounds, pretending to be the friendly colleague, I felt my resolve fraying at the edges.

It was Thursday when he cornered me by the coffee machine, his presence so disarming that I nearly dropped my cup. "You know," he started, his voice smooth like honey but laced with a bitter aftertaste, "I really admire your enthusiasm about the project. I think we could make some improvements if we worked together more closely."

I raised an eyebrow, suppressing a laugh. "You mean, if you worked more closely with my ideas, right?" I shot back, adding a touch of playful sarcasm. His grin wavered, just a fraction, but enough for me to notice. It was moments like these that reminded me of the fine line we walked—friendship mingled with rivalry, a dance that had all the grace of a three-legged race.

"I'm just saying," he replied, feigning nonchalance, "that we could really shine if we pooled our strengths. You have a lot of passion, and I have experience." The way he said "experience" made it sound more like a curse than a blessing.

"Experience in what, exactly? Turning up when it suits you?" I quipped, pouring an extra splash of cream into my coffee, relishing the rich swirl as I watched his expression turn to a mix of annoyance and intrigue.

Before he could respond, Jess strolled into the kitchen, her bright laughter slicing through the tension like a hot knife through butter. "What's this? The world's tiniest debate club?" she teased, winking at me. "I hope you two aren't planning to bring popcorn to the next meeting."

"Just enlightening each other on the nuances of corporate synergy," Kevin replied, attempting to regain control of the conversation.

"Oh please, Kevin. You're about as synergistic as a cat in a bathtub," I said, the words escaping my lips before I could catch them. Jess burst into laughter, the sound echoing off the office walls, but Kevin's expression soured.

As the day wore on, the underlying tension began to feel like a simmering pot on the verge of boiling over. I dove back into my work, laser-focused on the project, crafting an infographic that would capture the attention of our stakeholders. Every pixel was imbued with my vision, a testament to the effort I'd poured into the project.

Just as I hit my stride, Kevin appeared at my desk once more, his gaze scanning my screen with a hawk-like intensity. "You know," he began, leaning against my cubicle with that all-too-familiar smirk, "I was thinking about our presentation. Maybe we should simplify some of the messaging. It might resonate better with the higher-ups."

I barely resisted rolling my eyes. "And here I thought clarity was my forte," I shot back, my fingers dancing across the keyboard as I resisted the urge to let frustration spill over. "I appreciate the suggestion, Kevin, but I think the current messaging really reflects our hard work and dedication."

His brows knitted together as he opened his mouth, no doubt to counter with some form of misdirection, but Jess returned, a crucial lifeline, holding up a folder filled with our project documents. "Hey, can we go over the feedback from yesterday's meeting? I'd like to finalize our strategy before the presentation," she said, her cheerful tone cutting through the air like a refreshing breeze.

"Absolutely," I replied, grateful for the distraction. Kevin retreated, but not before shooting me one last look, a mixture of frustration and determination that made my skin prickle. I knew he was plotting something, and the realization sent a ripple of unease through me.

The rest of the afternoon passed in a blur of collaboration and camaraderie with Jess. We worked side by side, bouncing ideas off one another and weaving our thoughts into a cohesive narrative. It felt electric, the synergy we shared, and I couldn't help but feel a surge of pride in what we were creating together.

But as evening approached and the office began to empty, Kevin returned with a proposition that sent my heart racing in an entirely different direction. "I was thinking," he said, leaning against my desk once more, his demeanor deceptively casual, "that maybe we should have a little get-together. Just the team. You know, a chance to unwind before the big presentation."

"Sounds like a great idea," I replied, trying to keep my tone light, though I sensed an ulterior motive behind his suggestion. "But we've got a lot to prepare for."

"Oh, come on. A little fun never hurt anyone. Plus, it could help us bond as a team. I'll handle everything; you just have to show up," he said, his smile spreading across his face like the sun peeking through storm clouds.

I hesitated. "You're not planning on turning this into your personal pep rally, are you?"

He waved his hand dismissively, the charming façade slipping back into place. "Just a casual gathering. I promise, no shenanigans—unless you count a little karaoke as shenanigans."

"Now that I could get behind," Jess chimed in, her eyes sparkling with mischief.

I chuckled despite myself. "Okay, I'll think about it. But don't get your hopes up; I have a reputation to maintain."

Kevin laughed, and I could see a flicker of triumph in his eyes as he turned to leave. The moment he stepped away, a pit formed in my stomach. I knew he was trying to win back favor, but I could not shake the feeling that he was orchestrating something more sinister beneath the surface.

As I prepared to leave for the day, my phone buzzed with a notification that made my heart skip. It was a message from Jess: "Let's talk before the gathering. I have a feeling Kevin is up to something."

The words sent a shiver down my spine. Perhaps my instincts had been correct all along. As I exited the office, I cast a wary glance over my shoulder, half-expecting to find Kevin lurking in the shadows. The evening air was brisk against my skin, a reminder that the comfort I had built was precariously balanced on a knife's edge. I would need to stay vigilant, for the storm was brewing, and I was right in its path.

The weekend came with a mix of anticipation and anxiety, the upcoming gathering weighing heavily on my mind like an overripe fruit ready to drop. Jess and I had spent Saturday morning discussing our strategies over lattes that tasted like sweetened courage. "We need to keep our eyes peeled," she had said, her brow furrowed in determination. "If Kevin tries to pull any funny business, we need to shut it down before it even starts."

I nodded, swirling my drink thoughtfully. "Right, but what if he's using this get-together to win everyone back? I can't afford to let my guard down. He's like a wolf in a sheep's clothing, and I'm the unsuspecting lamb."

Jess chuckled, leaning back in her chair, a sly smile creeping across her face. "Maybe you should bring some sheepdog energy to the party. Keep him in check."

That idea stayed with me, providing an odd sense of comfort. I spent the remainder of the day concocting a plan: to be friendly but assertive, to smile but not let my guard down. After all, it was just a gathering, right? How bad could it be?

As the evening drew near, the office transformed into a festive haven, adorned with string lights that twinkled like stars in the dusky sky. I arrived to find Kevin's touch evident everywhere—a careful blend of festive and familiar that somehow felt wrong. The scent of nachos and melted cheese wafted through the air, mingling with the sweet tang of soda. Laughter bounced off the walls like the cheerful rhythm of a lively tune, and I was determined not to let Kevin's presence dampen my spirits.

"Hey, you made it!" Jess exclaimed, her eyes bright as she wove through the crowd. She clasped my hand, her enthusiasm palpable. "Let's get you a drink before the festivities really kick off."

"Good idea," I replied, allowing her to drag me toward the snack table. As we filled our cups with something bubbly and slightly intoxicating, I caught sight of Kevin, engaged in animated conversation with a couple of colleagues. His laughter was loud and infectious, but I noticed the way his eyes flitted around the room, assessing and calculating.

"Okay, what's your game plan?" Jess asked, leaning in conspiratorially.

"Stay close to me. If he pulls any stunts, we'll confront him together," I said, scanning the room.

"Deal. Just don't let him pull you into his web of charm," she warned, and I could see the seriousness in her eyes.

Before I could respond, Kevin ambled over, his easy confidence radiating like a sunbeam. "I'm glad to see you two bonding," he said, his gaze lingering on me with a mixture of mockery and curiosity. "It's good for team morale."

I plastered on my best "professional" smile, one that I hoped would convey both friendliness and caution. "Yes, team bonding is crucial, especially with all the exciting changes on the horizon."

"Changes, indeed," he replied, his tone loaded with double meanings. "I hope you're all ready for what's coming next."

Before I could decipher the intent behind his words, he swept away to chat with another group, leaving Jess and me standing in the wake of his ambiguous warning. "What was that about?" I asked, brows knitted in confusion.

"Who knows with him? He's a master of misdirection," Jess said, a note of worry creeping into her voice. "Let's focus on having a good time. This is supposed to be fun, remember?"

The evening unfolded with laughter and light banter, the room alive with energy. I managed to engage with my coworkers, exchanging jokes and ideas, the kind of camaraderie I'd yearned for. Yet, Kevin was never far from my mind, lurking in the periphery like a shadow refusing to be shaken off.

As the night wore on, Jess nudged me playfully. "Alright, it's time for some karaoke. If we're going to go down, we might as well do it spectacularly."

I laughed, the tension easing just a bit. "Oh, you mean sing off-key in front of our bosses? Sounds like my kind of nightmare!"

"Exactly! Come on, it'll be fun!" she urged, and with a reluctant nod, I allowed her to pull me toward the makeshift stage.

As the first notes of a classic pop song filled the air, I felt the familiar flutter of anxiety settle in my stomach. We belted out the lyrics, laughter erupting around us, and for a moment, I lost myself in the joy of the moment, forgetting the simmering tension that had marked my days.

But that bubble burst when Kevin sauntered back into the limelight, stepping up beside me with a confident grin. "I think it's time for a real performance," he announced, and I could almost hear the collective gasp from the audience as he took the microphone from Jess.

"Kevin, this isn't your show," I said, trying to sound light-hearted, but the irritation crept into my voice.

He waved me off with a charming smile, his charisma wrapping around him like a cloak. "Oh, don't worry. I'll make sure everyone has a great time. Just sit back and enjoy."

He launched into an upbeat song that had the crowd clapping along, and I stood frozen, heart racing with the realization that he was, once again, commandeering the spotlight. The laughter I had enjoyed moments ago felt distant as I watched him effortlessly charm our colleagues, weaving tales and creating a spectacle that drew everyone in.

In the back of my mind, a thought lingered—he was good at this. Too good. As the audience's laughter echoed around me, I could feel the edges of my own irritation giving way to a sharper sense of determination. I would not let him take this moment from me or the project I had worked so hard on.

"Okay, this isn't happening," I muttered to Jess, who was also watching Kevin with a blend of amusement and concern. "We need to get back in control."

Just as I turned to make my way back to the snack table, a loud crash reverberated through the room, the noise pulling everyone's attention. A glass had toppled off the table, shattering on the floor, and in that split second of chaos, Kevin's expression shifted. His laughter faded, and something darker flickered in his eyes, a fleeting glimpse of frustration or perhaps something more sinister.

"Oops! My bad!" he called, shrugging in faux innocence, but the tension in the air had changed, thickening like fog rolling in over the water. I glanced at Jess, who returned my look with wide eyes, a silent understanding passing between us.

As the crowd turned to help clean up the mess, I noticed Kevin leaning in to whisper to one of our supervisors, his demeanor shifting from playful entertainer to someone far more calculating. The atmosphere hung heavy, a palpable current of uncertainty, and I felt a shiver dance down my spine.

In that moment, I knew—something was brewing beneath the surface. Kevin wasn't just trying to reclaim his place; he was playing a much deeper game, and I was right in the middle of it. As the chaos unfolded around us, I felt the ground shifting underfoot, and my instincts screamed that the night was far from over.

I just didn't know how right I was, until the lights flickered and went out, plunging us into darkness. The sudden silence was deafening, and as I fumbled for my phone to shed some light, I could feel Kevin's presence creeping back into my consciousness, a wolf waiting patiently for the right moment to strike.

Chapter 26: Standing My Ground

The air in the conference room was thick with tension, the kind that could snap like a brittle twig underfoot. The fluorescent lights overhead flickered slightly, casting a sterile glow over the long, polished table where we sat. My heart raced, a furious rhythm echoing in my ears as I locked eyes with Kevin. He was leaning back in his chair, arms crossed smugly, like a cat that had just caught a particularly feisty mouse. The condescension in his voice had grated on my nerves for the last half hour, each word laced with a confidence that belied his inability to recognize the brilliance of others.

"Look, Sarah," he said, his tone dripping with feigned sympathy. "I know you think you've done something special with that feature, but you must understand the scope of this project. It's about collaboration, not individual achievements."

Every word of his felt like a jab, and I could practically see the smirk lurking just beneath his polished exterior. It had been a long road to this moment, filled with late nights and caffeine-fueled brainstorming sessions, but I was determined to stand my ground. The chaos of my emotions, the rising tide of frustration, and the quiet embers of pride burned fiercely within me. This was my moment, and I wasn't going to let him belittle my contributions any longer.

"Actually, Kevin," I interjected, my voice steady despite the whirlwind of thoughts swirling in my mind. "I'd like to clarify that I developed that feature independently, and it's an integral part of our project." The words flowed out with a conviction that surprised even me, slicing through the silence that enveloped the room like a thick fog. My colleagues shifted in their seats, a chorus of nods and murmurs rippling through them, each one an affirmation that my voice mattered.

Kevin's expression morphed, confusion and indignation battling for dominance. The shade of red creeping into his cheeks was a sight to behold, like a ripe tomato ready to burst. "That's quite the claim, Sarah," he retorted, trying to regain his composure, but the tremor in his voice betrayed him. "I'm sure your memory is just a bit foggy."

Foggy? I had spent countless hours coding and troubleshooting, losing sleep to ensure every line of my work was flawless. I could recount each keystroke like a nostalgic song. It wasn't foggy; it was vividly clear, each moment etched in my mind like a favorite childhood memory.

"Let's not kid ourselves," I continued, leaning forward slightly, relishing the shift in power dynamics. "You may have overseen the project, but I know where my efforts lie. I presented the preliminary data, I outlined the user experience, and I executed the final prototype. Your contributions are... well, let's just say they're not as impressive as you think."

The room crackled with electricity, the energy shifting palpably as my colleagues sat up straighter, their eyes wide with a mix of surprise and admiration. I could almost hear the gears turning in their heads, contemplating the fallout of this confrontation. Kevin shifted uncomfortably in his seat, and for the first time, I saw a flicker of uncertainty pass across his features.

"Is this a joke? You think you can undermine my authority in front of the entire team?" His voice rose an octave, the bravado slipping away like sand through his fingers. The desperation was evident, and it made my heart race in a way that was both thrilling and terrifying.

"No, Kevin," I replied, my voice calm yet firm, "this isn't a joke. This is about ensuring that credit is given where it's due. I've worked hard, and I refuse to let you twist that into something it isn't." The conviction in my words hung in the air, a weighty silence enveloping the room as everyone absorbed my declaration.

I could see my colleagues exchanging glances, a silent agreement forming among them. Lucy, sitting on my left, cleared her throat, her voice cutting through the tension. "I think we all need to acknowledge Sarah's efforts. She's been instrumental in our progress, and it's time we give credit where it's due."

Kevin opened his mouth to respond, but the protest died on his lips, the steam of his indignation dissipating into a quiet realization that the tides had turned. I couldn't help but smile, a small victory blossoming in my chest. The feeling was intoxicating, a heady mix of triumph and relief as the last vestiges of doubt melted away.

The conversation shifted, my colleagues rallying around the project's milestones, highlighting each team member's contributions as though we were a tightly woven tapestry of talent and determination. I found myself riding the wave of their enthusiasm, each compliment fueling the confidence that had been stifled for too long. With every praise they offered, the shackles of Kevin's manipulation began to crumble, and I felt lighter, freer.

"Let's pivot back to the development timeline," Kevin finally suggested, attempting to redirect the meeting, but the power had shifted irreversibly. The once solid ground beneath him now felt precarious, as if the very foundation of his authority was being pulled out from under him.

The discussion evolved into a collaborative frenzy, and I thrived in the vibrant exchange of ideas. The creative energy in the room sparked and ignited like a firework display, each suggestion adding color and depth to our project. The initial tension began to fade, replaced by the palpable excitement of a team unified in purpose.

As the meeting drew to a close, I felt a sense of accomplishment wash over me, a warmth spreading through my chest. I had stood my ground, confronted my fears, and emerged victorious. My colleagues gathered their things, buzzing with renewed vigor, and as they filed out, a few lingered to offer congratulations, smiles brightening their faces.

"Nice job, Sarah," Lucy said, her eyes gleaming with pride. "I've always known you had it in you. Don't let anyone dim your light."

I grinned, a sense of camaraderie enveloping us like a warm embrace. "Thanks, Lucy. I appreciate it." I knew then that this was just the beginning, a pivotal moment in reclaiming my narrative and forging a path that was unapologetically my own. As I walked out of the conference room, the fluorescent lights flickered above me, and I felt a rush of exhilaration, a certainty that no one could take away the power of my voice again.

The meeting room was still, an electric tension crackling in the air as I took a deep breath, trying to suppress the nervous flutter in my stomach. The bright overhead lights were almost too harsh, casting sharp shadows that danced across the table, reflecting the unease that hung like a specter over us all. Kevin's expression morphed from surprise to indignation, the corners of his mouth twitching as if he couldn't quite believe I had dared to stand up to him.

"Oh, really?" he scoffed, feigning casualness while his fingers drummed impatiently on the table. "And when exactly did this miracle occur? Last Tuesday, or was it during your coffee break?"

The snickers from a couple of teammates echoed, a light ripple of amusement against the backdrop of Kevin's rising frustration. I could feel the warmth of their solidarity wrapping around me like a favorite sweater on a chilly day. Instead of retreating, I leaned in closer, maintaining eye contact. "It happened while you were too busy patting yourself on the back for your last mediocre pitch. It's fascinating how you think success can be achieved through intimidation alone."

The room erupted into a collective gasp, quickly stifled into silence, as Kevin's eyes widened. This was no longer about just me; it was about all of us. The unspoken agreement among my colleagues, a pact forged in the fires of countless late nights and shared frustrations, ignited a resolve within me. I was no longer just a cog in Kevin's grand machine; I was a crucial player in a dynamic team.

"Look," I continued, my voice rising above the silence, "if we want to succeed, it's going to require collaboration. We can't keep throwing each other under the bus just to inflate egos." My words were sharp, edged with a confidence I hadn't known I possessed, and I could see Kevin struggling to maintain his facade.

"Don't act like you're the only one working here," he retorted, but the tremor in his voice betrayed him.

"Not the only one, but certainly one of the most effective," I shot back, a playful smirk creeping onto my lips. "I mean, you haven't exactly made it hard for me to stand out."

A wave of laughter surged through the room, and for a brief moment, the atmosphere lightened. Kevin's face turned an even deeper shade of crimson, his jaw clenched tight enough that I wondered if he could crack his teeth.

"Alright, alright, let's refocus," he said, attempting to steer the meeting back to our agenda. The tension between us, however, was palpable, a living thing that seemed to vibrate through the very air we breathed.

As the discussion continued, the team rallied around my ideas. Every suggestion was met with nods of approval and enthusiastic responses, creating a warm bubble of creativity that expanded with each passing minute. I felt a sense of liberation, each idea I shared lifting me higher, each agreement solidifying my place at the table.

But just as the momentum seemed to swell, the door swung open, and in walked Jessica, our project manager. She had a keen instinct for sensing when things were off, and today was no exception. Her brows knitted together as she assessed the room, the tension thick enough to cut with a knife.

"What did I miss?" she asked, her voice a melodic counterpoint to the charged atmosphere.

"Oh, nothing much," I said, flashing a smile that I hoped conveyed my newfound confidence. "Just the usual power play between Kevin and me. You know, the dynamic duo."

Jessica's eyes narrowed slightly, a knowing look crossing her face. "I see. Well, I hope you didn't forget the real purpose of today's meeting," she said, moving to the head of the table.

With her presence, the energy shifted again, and I couldn't help but admire her poise. She had a knack for cutting through the clutter, and her no-nonsense approach kept us all grounded. "I'd like to discuss the upcoming product launch," she said, glancing pointedly at Kevin, who was now leaning back, arms crossed defensively.

"Of course," he mumbled, attempting to regain his composure.

Jessica laid out the timeline for the launch, outlining the critical steps we needed to take. "I want everyone to be on the same page," she emphasized, her gaze sweeping across the table. "If we're going to succeed, we need to be united. We can't afford any more drama."

I couldn't help but notice how she avoided making eye contact with Kevin, as if even looking at him would tarnish her commitment to teamwork.

"And I need to remind you all that we'll be presenting our progress to the higher-ups next week," Jessica continued, her tone brisk but encouraging. "I expect everyone to bring their A-game."

The pressure in the room shifted, and I could feel the collective weight of our tasks ahead pressing down on us. I exchanged glances with Lucy, who seemed just as energized by the prospect of stepping up. The lingering tension with Kevin still simmered, but now it felt manageable, almost like an annoying itch I could ignore.

"Count me in," I said, my voice steady. "I'm ready to show them what we can really do."

"Excellent," Jessica replied, a smile breaking through her earlier seriousness. "That's the spirit I like to see."

As the meeting wrapped up, I could sense a shift in the office dynamics. Kevin, though still sulking, seemed to be reevaluating his approach. Perhaps he realized that manipulation could only go so far when the rest of us were finally standing up for ourselves.

Once everyone filtered out, Lucy lingered behind, her excitement bubbling over. "You were incredible! I mean, I've never seen anyone take Kevin down a peg like that," she exclaimed, her eyes sparkling with admiration.

I shrugged, trying to downplay my victory. "Just standing my ground. If we're going to get anywhere, I figured I might as well be heard."

"Don't sell yourself short. You're not just heard; you're unforgettable," she said, a teasing lilt in her voice.

A warmth spread through me, her encouragement wrapping around me like a soft blanket on a cold night. "Thanks, Lucy. It means a lot, really."

As I gathered my things, a sense of purpose washed over me. I wasn't just a part of the project; I was an integral piece of something greater, something worth fighting for. I stepped out of the conference room, ready to tackle whatever challenges lay ahead, my confidence blossoming like the first blooms of spring after a long winter. I had found my voice, and it was powerful enough to carve out a space where I truly belonged.

With the meeting behind me, I strode through the hallways of our tech startup, the vibrant buzz of conversation around me almost like a soundtrack to my triumph. The chatter of my colleagues blended into a harmonious backdrop, laughter and excited voices carrying through the open office spaces. My heart still raced, not from the confrontation itself, but from the exhilaration of standing firm. I had faced Kevin's condescension and emerged victorious, like a knight from a long-fought battle.

Lucy caught up with me just outside the coffee station, her expression a mixture of awe and excitement. "You know, I was half-expecting you to spontaneously burst into flames the way you went after him. You were on fire!"

I laughed, the sound bubbling up with a giddy lightness. "I guess it was just a moment of clarity—or maybe caffeine finally kicked in." I filled my mug with coffee, the rich aroma wrapping around me like a warm hug. The taste was a bitter comfort, a small reminder that sometimes the best moments come with a little jolt.

As I took a sip, my gaze wandered to the large glass windows lining the office. Outside, the sun shone brilliantly, bathing the city in a golden hue that felt almost surreal. It was a stark contrast to the chaos of the meeting room, and I felt a rush of gratitude for this moment—this clarity—amid the whirlwind of corporate life.

"Seriously, though," Lucy continued, leaning against the counter, "you should ride that confidence into the next meeting with Jessica. She's going to love what you've done."

I shrugged, not wanting to get ahead of myself. "It's just one confrontation. I have to keep proving myself if I want to break through."

"Trust me, you're already breaking through," she replied, her eyes glimmering with sincerity. "Besides, you can't let Kevin have all the glory when he's sitting on his butt doing nothing."

That thought sparked a flicker of determination within me. I was tired of waiting for someone to recognize my contributions. It was time to claim my space, to let my voice resonate in a room filled with self-proclaimed experts.

"Speaking of glory," Lucy said, her tone shifting as she glanced toward the entrance of the office, "looks like someone is here to stir the pot."

I turned just in time to see a tall figure step into the room, his confident stride and sharp suit immediately capturing attention. It was Derek, our new VP of Innovation, whose reputation had preceded him like a rumor. The man had a presence that demanded attention, not just for his striking good looks but for the palpable energy that seemed to radiate from him.

"Great," I muttered under my breath, feeling the familiar twinge of anxiety creep back in. "Just what we need—a showman to remind us how insignificant we are."

"C'mon, don't be dramatic," Lucy laughed, nudging me playfully. "This could be good! Maybe he's here to shake things up a bit."

Before I could retort, Derek's voice boomed across the room, drawing all eyes toward him. "Good morning, team! I hope you're all ready to take this project to the next level!"

He exuded an infectious enthusiasm that sent ripples of anticipation through the office. I watched as he made his way through the crowd, engaging people effortlessly, his charisma weaving through the chatter like a magician's spell. He paused in front of me, a confident smile lighting up his face.

"Ah, Sarah! I've heard great things about you. Kevin seems to think you're quite the asset to the team," he said, his gaze piercing yet warm.

"Does he?" I replied, trying to mask my surprise. "I'm just trying to keep up with the pace."

"Keep up?" he echoed, a hint of mischief dancing in his eyes. "I hear you're the one setting the pace now. We could use that kind of energy on the ground floor."

The compliment caught me off guard, leaving me momentarily speechless. I had expected indifference from the upper management, not this kind of attention.

"I appreciate it," I finally managed, my heart racing as the conversation continued to unfold.

As he moved on, I exchanged glances with Lucy, who looked as though she was about to burst. "Did you see that? He was totally into you! I mean, who wouldn't be? You practically glowed when he complimented you!"

I shook my head, a little incredulous. "It was just small talk. He probably says that to everyone."

But the excitement lingered, a warm ember igniting something within me. Maybe I could channel this energy into my work, push myself to heights I'd never dared to dream of before.

The day rolled on with a newfound vibrancy, my colleagues engaging in animated discussions about the project, ideas bouncing off the walls like confetti. It felt exhilarating to be part of this collaborative wave, each suggestion and critique propelling us forward.

As afternoon approached, I retreated to my desk to refine my proposals for the upcoming presentation. The soft clattering of keyboards filled the air, punctuated by the occasional burst of laughter. I was fully immersed in my work when I heard a familiar voice drift toward me, smooth as silk.

"Hey there, superstar. Got a minute?"

It was Derek again, leaning casually against my cubicle wall, his presence commanding yet relaxed. The sight of him made my heart skip a beat, and I found it increasingly difficult to concentrate on my screen.

"Sure," I replied, my voice steadier than I felt. "What can I help you with?"

He stepped closer, lowering his voice as if sharing a secret. "I've been thinking about the project, and I want you to lead a sub-team to refine the user interface. I'm impressed with what I've seen so far, and I believe your vision could really elevate this launch."

I blinked, the weight of his words sinking in. "Lead a sub-team? Me?"

"Absolutely. You've got the creativity and the drive. Let's harness that."

Before I could respond, a commotion erupted from across the office, a frantic whispering that quickly escalated into alarmed exclamations. My stomach twisted as I turned to see several coworkers gathered around the conference room door, their expressions a mix of shock and confusion.

"What's going on?" I asked, my voice edged with concern as I caught a glimpse of Kevin's pale face through the glass.

"He just collapsed!" someone shouted, the urgency in their voice sending a chill down my spine.

My heart raced as I stood frozen for a moment, the gravity of the situation crashing over me like a tidal wave. Derek moved quickly toward the crowd, his authoritative presence cutting through the chaos, and I felt a surge of anxiety take hold.

The flurry of activity intensified, the sounds of concern mingling with whispers of panic, and I suddenly felt like a spectator in my own life, tethered to a moment spiraling out of control. I exchanged a worried glance with Lucy, who stood beside me, her face pale.

"What if he's seriously hurt?" she whispered, fear creeping into her voice.

Before I could answer, Derek reappeared, urgency etched on his features. "We need to call for medical assistance. Everyone, stay back!"

As he pushed through the crowd, I felt a jolt of uncertainty rippling through me. It was as if the ground had shifted beneath our feet, and nothing felt certain anymore.

"Stay here," Derek instructed, his eyes locking onto mine with an intensity that sent shivers down my spine.

I nodded, but the pit in my stomach only deepened. Something was wrong, and I couldn't shake the feeling that this incident was just the beginning of a series of events that would turn our lives upside down.

Just then, a scream pierced the air, shattering the tense atmosphere, leaving me paralyzed with dread.

Chapter 27: The New Normal

Life settled into an odd rhythm, a blend of routine and yearning, each day unfolding like the pages of a book I never quite wanted to read. Mornings began with the ritual of brewing coffee, the rich aroma wrapping around me like a comforting blanket as I stared out at the sun-kissed horizon. I would take my cup and stand on the balcony, breathing in the crisp morning air, letting the briskness of the day seep into my bones. This was my moment of stillness before the world unfurled its chaos, where the distant sound of traffic mingled with the cheerful chirping of birds—a melody that felt almost mocking in its simplicity.

Ethan's new job consumed him. The demanding hours stole away our weekends and turned our evenings into mere whispers of conversations. Yet, within the constraints of our schedules, we carved out moments—scheduled video chats that turned into lifelines. Each call was an exercise in connection, a bridge spanning the distance that sometimes felt insurmountable. I'd wait anxiously for his face to appear on my screen, a welcome sight that chased away the shadows lurking in my heart.

"Did I ever tell you about the time I nearly set the office on fire?" he would tease, his laughter like a balm over my worries.

"Please tell me you didn't," I'd reply, a smile breaking across my face, my heart swelling with affection for the man whose laughter I so desperately missed.

We would exchange tales of our day-to-day lives, small victories worth celebrating. I'd tell him about the project that went off without a hitch, the triumphant moment when my team nailed a presentation that had felt insurmountable. In return, Ethan would share his own trials, the hurdles he faced in his high-pressure environment, his voice brimming with determination as he recounted how he tackled each challenge head-on.

But as much as I clung to these moments, the silence in between felt deafening. There were nights when I'd lie awake, the emptiness beside me more palpable than the sheets beneath my fingers. I'd reach for my phone, a lifeline that always felt just a step away, and find myself scrolling through our conversations, cherishing every shared laugh and every tender exchange. Yet even the most heartfelt texts felt hollow compared to the warmth of his presence.

In the afternoons, when the weight of solitude pressed down like an uninvited guest, I turned to my friends—Rhea and Sam—who became my anchors amidst the emotional tide. Rhea had an uncanny knack for turning mundane moments into adventures. "What's life without a little chaos?" she often quipped, her eyes sparkling with mischief. She pulled me into spontaneous outings, whether it was exploring the hidden corners of the city or simply cozying up on her couch for a movie marathon, popcorn spilling as we laughed and cried over shared stories.

Sam, on the other hand, was the grounded force in my life. "You need to breathe, Lily," he'd remind me on days when I was too consumed by my thoughts. His calm presence provided a refuge, a place where I could let my guard down. "Just remember, he's still there, even if it feels like a million miles away."

Yet, no matter how vibrant my world became with friends, the ache for Ethan lingered. There was a gaping hole that only he could fill, an unshakeable yearning that gnawed at the edges of my happiness. In a fit of inspiration—or perhaps desperation—I began to write him letters, pouring my heart onto the pages in a way that felt more intimate than any text could convey. I would sit at my small desk, the soft light of the lamp casting a warm glow as I crafted my words, hoping he would feel the weight of my love across the miles.

Each letter became a piece of my heart, a canvas painted with my fears and hopes, my dreams woven into the fabric of our connection. I described the little things: how the leaves outside my window had begun to change, how their fiery colors mirrored the intensity of my feelings for him. I shared mundane details—like how I discovered a new café that served the best almond croissants and how I wished he were there to share them with me.

"Do you remember the last time we were here?" I wrote one evening, my pen gliding over the paper as nostalgia washed over me. "You said I had to try the caramel macchiato, and you convinced me to order a slice of that chocolate cake. We ended up fighting over the last bite, and I still think you cheated. I miss those moments more than I can say."

I sealed each letter in an envelope, writing his name on the front with an exaggerated flourish, a tangible piece of me that I longed to send off into the universe. I didn't know if he would ever receive them, but the act of writing felt like sending a piece of my soul across the distance. I imagined him unsealing each envelope, the crinkle of paper soothing like a gentle caress, as he immersed himself in my words.

As the days passed, I tucked my letters away in a small box beneath my bed, a secret collection of affection that felt both sacred and daunting. Each missive was a reminder of the love we had built and the distance that threatened to fray the edges of our connection. The world outside my window continued to spin, indifferent to my internal struggles, but within the four walls of my room, I found solace in the letters that echoed my longing—a bittersweet reminder that love, no matter how far apart, was still alive.

The days turned into weeks, each one blending into the next like colors in a sunset, beautiful but fleeting. I lost myself in the ebb and flow of work, where deadlines became my lifeline and the hum of activity around me provided a comforting backdrop. I navigated the office's rhythm with newfound confidence, surprising myself at how quickly I adapted to the whirlwind of meetings and projects. My colleagues, once strangers, transformed into allies in this corporate jungle, and the shared laughter over coffee breaks became the glue that held our team together.

"Lily, I think you might be single-handedly keeping the coffee supply in this office alive," Rhea joked one afternoon as I refilled our communal pot for the third time that day. She was leaning against the counter, her arms crossed, a playful grin lighting up her face.

"Well, someone has to! I can't have you all running on empty," I shot back, grinning as I poured a steaming cup for her. "What would you do without me? Stare blankly at your screens until your brains dribbled out your ears?"

Her laughter rang out, bright and infectious. "You might just be our office savior, Lily. I'll add that to your résumé."

Despite the banter, the emptiness in my heart remained, a persistent ache that refused to fade. It was during one of our late-night video calls that I finally confessed my struggle to Ethan. His face flickered across the screen, his features softened by the warm light of his apartment. He listened intently, his expression a mixture of concern and understanding.

"I wish I could be there with you, Lily," he said, his voice a soothing balm. "I feel like a part of me is missing, too."

"Some days feel harder than others," I admitted, my voice barely a whisper. "I keep waiting for things to feel normal again, but it's just...different. And I hate how much I miss you."

Ethan reached out, his fingers brushing against the camera lens. It was a small gesture, but it felt like a lifeline. "We'll find our way back to each other, I promise. You're not alone in this. Just hold onto those letters, and we'll get through it."

His reassurance enveloped me, yet the longing lingered, tightening its grip like a vice. I spent nights weaving my words into letters, each one a vessel for the emotions I couldn't articulate in real-time. They became my secret ritual, a way to channel my love and yearning into something tangible. The process was cathartic; the more I wrote, the lighter my heart felt.

One evening, after a particularly draining day at work, I decided to treat myself to a quiet night in. I poured a glass of wine and slipped into my favorite cozy sweater, the fabric soft against my skin. I lit a candle, its flickering flame casting shadows that danced around my living room. Settling into my favorite nook by the window, I opened my notebook, ready to pour out my soul.

As I began to write, the world outside faded away, the city's bustle reduced to a distant hum. I described the little joys—the first bloom of spring flowers in the park, the crispness of the evening air, the way the stars twinkled like diamonds scattered across a velvet sky. I wanted Ethan to feel every ounce of beauty I experienced, even from afar. But my words took a turn as my heart raced, an idea blooming unexpectedly within me.

"What if I send him a care package?" I murmured to myself, excitement bubbling up like champagne. It was a thought that felt both simple and monumental, a way to bridge the distance that felt so tangible between us. I imagined curating a box filled with my letters, little trinkets that reminded me of our shared moments, and a few of his favorite snacks to keep him fueled during those long, demanding hours.

With renewed energy, I began to brainstorm items to include. A photograph of us from our last adventure together, where we stood side by side, grinning ear to ear as we embraced the chaos of a local street fair. I'd been wearing that ridiculous hat adorned with oversized flowers he insisted looked fabulous, and he had been laughing so hard that I was convinced he would drop his funnel cake.

I chuckled at the memory, feeling the warmth of that day wrap around me like a favorite blanket. I scribbled down a list, my heart racing as I envisioned his reaction upon opening the box. I could picture him, eyes wide with surprise, perhaps even a grin breaking through his stress-ridden days. This little gesture felt like sending him a piece of home, a reminder that I was still here, cheering him on even from a distance.

As I gathered the items and carefully arranged them in the box, the anticipation grew within me. I could hardly wait to get everything ready, sealing it up with a heartfelt letter that would convey my love and support. "Let's make the miles between us a little less daunting," I whispered as I tied the twine around the package, the act itself feeling like a promise.

With a satisfied sigh, I set the box aside and prepared for bed, the thrill of the idea lingering in my mind. But as I lay there, my heart fluttered with something I hadn't anticipated—a spark of hope igniting in the quiet corners of my soul. Perhaps this was the new normal, a blend of longing and creativity, a space where love could flourish despite the miles.

Days passed as I finalized my care package, and the excitement bubbled up within me, each item lovingly chosen. Finally, the day arrived to send my little piece of joy off into the world. I headed to the post office, my heart racing as I stood in line, anticipation coursing through my veins. With each passing second, I imagined Ethan's reaction, my mind spinning stories of joy and connection.

After what felt like an eternity, I handed over the package to the postal worker. "Make sure it gets there fast," I said, my voice light with enthusiasm. The worker nodded, a bemused smile on her face as if she understood the importance of my mission.

On the walk home, the sun dipped low in the sky, casting a golden hue over the neighborhood. I felt lighter, buoyed by the simple act of sending love across the distance. The world continued to move, each person around me lost in their own lives, yet I felt like I was in a secret dance of anticipation, spinning through the evening, imagining Ethan's joy in unwrapping the surprises I had sent.

The days drifted into a comfortable routine, the kind where the morning light streamed through my window, warming my skin as I scrolled through social media while sipping coffee. I reveled in the small things—my morning ritual had become a cherished sanctuary. But even in this newfound rhythm, a part of me always remained tuned into the undercurrent of longing that hummed in my chest.

As I became more entrenched in my job, I noticed the way the dynamics within the office shifted. New projects rolled in, each one more ambitious than the last, and my role expanded beyond what I had envisioned. I tackled challenges with a determined spirit, often surprised by my own resilience. Each success added another layer of confidence, and I found myself thriving amidst the chaos. Yet, no matter how much I accomplished, Ethan's absence echoed like a soft whisper in the back of my mind.

"Lily, you're a force to be reckoned with," Rhea teased one afternoon, watching me navigate a particularly complex spreadsheet. "I'm starting to think you're a superhero in disguise."

"Right, just call me Excel Girl," I replied, my fingers flying over the keyboard. "Able to conquer spreadsheets and save the day with a mere click!"

"Don't sell yourself short! With that attitude, you might just save the entire world," she quipped, a sparkle in her eyes.

Our laughter reverberated around the break room, an intoxicating sound that made the walls feel a little less isolating. Still, after each interaction, I would retreat to my desk, where the silence closed in like a thick fog. The letters I had started writing to Ethan morphed from simple messages into elaborate narratives. Each letter encapsulated my experiences, my hopes, and the stories that unfolded in my life, creating a bridge that spanned the distance between us.

It was during one of these evenings, surrounded by the flickering glow of candlelight, that inspiration struck. I decided to turn my letters into a journal, a collection of memories and thoughts dedicated to Ethan. This way, even when we were worlds apart, he could still feel the essence of my life—my triumphs, my struggles, and the mundane little moments that made up each day.

As I delved into this project, the pages filled quickly, my pen gliding effortlessly as I poured my heart into the words. I described my encounters with quirky clients, the thrill of landing a big deal, and the way the city transformed under the golden hues of sunset.

"Dear Ethan," I began one entry. "Today, I convinced Mrs. Fletcher that her cat's portrait didn't need a bowtie. You would've laughed at the look on her face when I suggested a simple background instead. 'It's a cat, not a gentleman!' I told her, and she actually considered it! You'd be so proud."

Each entry became a testament to my love, an exploration of the vibrant life I wanted to share with him. I envisioned one day handing him this journal, watching his eyes light up as he read through the snippets of my existence during our time apart.

But as I poured myself into this new endeavor, I noticed a change in Ethan's demeanor during our video calls. His usual banter became tinged with something heavier, a flicker of unease lurking behind his smiles. He would often glance away, his brow furrowed, as if battling a silent storm.

"Hey," I said one night, my heart racing as I studied his face. "What's going on? You seem... off."

His expression shifted, the vulnerability in his eyes cutting through the digital distance that separated us. "It's nothing I can't handle," he replied, but the tightness in his voice spoke volumes.

"Ethan, I know you too well. Please, just tell me."

He took a deep breath, the silence stretching between us like an unbreakable thread. "It's just the job, you know? It's a lot of pressure, and I feel like I'm barely keeping my head above water. Sometimes, I wonder if it's worth it."

My heart sank at his words. "You've worked so hard for this opportunity. You can do it. I believe in you."

"I know you do," he said, a soft smile breaking through the storm. "But it's hard when you're not here. I miss you more than I can say."

"Then let's make this easier," I suggested, trying to lighten the mood. "I'll send you more letters. You'll feel like you're living in a romance novel."

"Just promise me you won't get carried away with the mushy stuff," he said, his eyes dancing with mischief. "We don't want my colleagues thinking I'm some sort of softie."

"Oh, you mean you're not?" I teased, laughing at the absurdity. "Just wait until you read the next letter; it'll make you swoon."

The playful banter provided a temporary reprieve, but the worry lingered in my chest. I decided to dig deeper, convinced there was more to Ethan's unease than he let on. It was during one of my late-night writing sessions that I stumbled upon a new project at work—a team collaboration that aimed to innovate our marketing strategy. It felt daunting but also invigorating.

"Rhea, I need to brainstorm ideas for this new project," I told her one morning. "Let's grab coffee and put our heads together."

"Count me in! Just promise to buy the caffeine this time," she replied, her eyes twinkling with excitement.

Over steaming cups of coffee, we poured over the details of the project, throwing around wild ideas that sparked excitement. But as we plotted, a thought crept into my mind, twisting my stomach with uncertainty.

"Do you ever feel like we're all just trying to keep up appearances?" I asked, my voice barely above a whisper. "Like we're all pretending everything is fine, when really... we're not?"

Rhea looked thoughtful for a moment, then nodded. "All the time. But it's easier, isn't it? We put on our brave faces and carry on. Who wants to admit they're struggling?"

"True," I sighed, feeling the weight of my own mask. "But what if pretending catches up to us?"

Her gaze met mine, and in that moment, I realized how deeply I felt this uncertainty, this need to uncover the truth behind the smiles.

Later that evening, as I prepared to send off the latest batch of letters to Ethan, a sudden wave of apprehension washed over me. What if the pressure at his job was becoming too much? What if I wasn't there to support him when he needed me the most?

As I sealed the envelope, I glanced at my phone, the screen lighting up with a notification. My heart raced at the sight of Ethan's name. I opened the message eagerly, only to find my pulse quickening for an entirely different reason.

"Lily, I need to talk. Something's come up, and it's important."

A chill ran through me, and before I could think, my fingers flew over the keyboard. "What's wrong? Is everything okay?"

The seconds ticked by, each moment stretching longer than the last. When my phone buzzed again, I felt a mix of hope and dread.

"Can we video chat? It's better to explain in person."

A sense of urgency gripped me, a gnawing fear I couldn't shake. I agreed to the call, but as I prepared, I couldn't shake the feeling that whatever Ethan had to share would change everything.

The screen flickered to life, his familiar face appearing, but the shadow in his eyes deepened my anxiety. "Lily," he started, his voice shaky. "I don't know how to say this..."

The air crackled with tension, the world around us fading into the background as I braced for whatever revelation lay ahead.

Chapter 28: Love in Bloom

The air was thick with the sweet, intoxicating scent of fresh blooms as I opened the door, the vibrant colors spilling into my small room like a joyous tide. Sunlight streamed through the window, illuminating the delicate petals of the flowers that Ethan had sent—a kaleidoscope of yellows, pinks, and whites, each hue bursting with life. My heart fluttered, a wild, ecstatic thing within my chest, as I sank into the moment. It felt surreal, this connection we had nurtured, a rare blossom thriving despite the distance and challenges that sought to pull us apart.

Ethan's voice echoed in my mind as I recalled the video he'd sent along with the flowers, his warm, rich tones wrapping around me like a cozy blanket on a winter's night. He read my letters aloud, each word infused with a sincerity that made the distance feel smaller. As I watched him, his earnest expression shifting between laughter and tenderness, I felt like I was right there with him, tucked away in the soft sanctuary of our shared secrets.

"Your letters are like sunlight to me," he had said, his voice dipping into that playful, husky tone I adored. "I didn't know a person could write with such... passion. It's a little intimidating, to be honest." A smirk had danced across his lips, making my stomach flip, and I could almost picture the way he ran a hand through his tousled hair, a gesture I had come to find irresistibly charming.

I chuckled at the memory, still reeling from the way he brought my words to life. My letters, once a collection of hesitant scribbles and half-formed thoughts, had transformed into something more profound, a thread woven between our hearts, binding us together in a way that felt both thrilling and terrifying.

With a sense of newfound determination, I began to pen another letter, pouring my heart onto the page. The ink flowed freely, fueled by the emotions that swelled within me like an unfurling blossom. I wrote about my day, the little things that made me smile—the way the sun glinted off the lake in the morning, casting playful sparkles on the water's surface, or the way the scent of freshly baked cookies wafted from Mrs. Henderson's kitchen next door, coaxing me into daydreams of warmth and comfort.

As I filled the pages, I realized that these moments, once mundane, had taken on a richer texture in Ethan's absence. Every detail I captured became a thread in the tapestry of our connection, creating a shared experience that transcended the miles between us. I described the flowers he'd sent, each bloom representing a piece of my heart, and how they brightened my room and spirit, just as he did.

When I finally sealed the letter, I felt a surge of excitement. There was something almost magical about this process, this exchange of words that spanned distance and time. Each letter became a treasure, a snapshot of our lives woven together by ink and intention.

That evening, as twilight draped its velvety cloak over the town, I prepared for our video call. The anticipation danced in my chest like fireflies caught in a summer breeze. I settled into my favorite chair, a cozy nook draped with soft blankets, and gazed at the flickering candle on my desk. The warm glow mirrored the warmth blossoming in my heart, and I couldn't help but wonder if Ethan could feel it too, radiating through the screen, across the miles.

When his face finally appeared, that familiar smile broke over his features, and my heart soared. His eyes sparkled with mischief and warmth, the kind of gaze that made me feel seen in a way I had never experienced before. "Hey, you," he greeted, his voice a smooth melody that sent shivers of joy through me.

"Hey!" I replied, my smile widening. "I got your flowers. They're beautiful. You always know how to make my day."

"Just doing my best," he said, leaning closer to the camera, a conspiratorial grin teasing at his lips. "But I think the real beauty is in your letters. You've got a way with words, you know."

Flushing with pride, I felt the familiar flutter in my stomach. "I'm glad you like them. I find it's easier to express myself on paper."

"Maybe you should read one to me," he suggested, his eyes twinkling with encouragement.

With a laugh, I grabbed my latest letter, feeling a mix of excitement and vulnerability. As I began to read, I could see the way he leaned in, hanging on my every word, the corners of his mouth curling upward with every shared thought and emotion. My heart raced, knowing that I was sharing a piece of my soul with him.

When I finished, his expression was a mixture of awe and admiration. "You really are something else, you know that? You make me feel like the luckiest guy alive."

I could feel the warmth creeping up my cheeks, and a giddy smile spread across my face. "Well, you've definitely got me feeling lucky too. This whole... us thing? It's pretty incredible."

There was a beat of silence, a moment where everything hung in the air, charged with unspoken words and promises. I could see it in his eyes—something deeper, a yearning that matched my own. Just as I opened my mouth to voice my thoughts, a sudden crash echoed from behind him, shattering the moment.

"Ethan? Are you okay?" I exclaimed, the worry flooding my senses.

"Just a little mishap," he replied, waving a hand dismissively, though the concern creased his brow. "Nothing to worry about. But, uh, can I call you back in a minute?"

"Sure, of course," I said, though a knot of anxiety twisted in my stomach. What could have happened? As he ended the call, I sat there, my heart pounding, wondering if this was the universe reminding us how unpredictable love could be.

But in that moment, all I could focus on was the warmth that lingered in the air, the bloom of connection that flourished between us, and the hope that even amidst the chaos, love could still find a way to thrive.

The night air felt electric, crackling with the anticipation of uncharted possibilities as I lay in bed, staring at the ceiling. Shadows danced across my room, courtesy of the flickering candle I'd lit earlier, a soft glow that contrasted sharply with the whirlwind of thoughts in my mind. I couldn't shake the image of Ethan's smile from earlier, or the way his voice laced with warmth made my heart race like it was auditioning for the Olympics. Yet, with that heady bliss came a twinge of uncertainty. The crash I'd heard just before our call ended haunted me, its echo lingering long after Ethan had disappeared from the screen.

I tossed and turned, battling the unsettling feeling that something was amiss. As sleep eluded me, I pulled out my journal, the one I'd dedicated solely to my letters to Ethan. I flipped through pages filled with my scrawled confessions and vivid descriptions, each entry a slice of my heart. I found solace in my words, the ink flowing like a river of hope and longing. Maybe pouring my thoughts onto the page would help me find clarity amidst the chaos swirling in my mind.

The morning sun spilled through my window, bathing the room in a warm, golden light. I tucked the journal under my pillow and set about my day, a routine steeped in comfort. Breakfast consisted of my favorite blueberry pancakes, their syrupy sweetness reminding me of lazy summer mornings. Yet, even as I savored each bite, my thoughts drifted back to Ethan. Would he call today? Was he okay?

As I rinsed my plate in the sink, a sudden ping startled me. My phone lit up with a notification, and my heart leapt. I snatched it up, a grin stretching across my face as I saw Ethan's name flashing on the screen. I quickly tapped the video call button, my pulse racing with anticipation. When his face appeared, my breath caught. He looked a little frazzled, his hair tousled as if he'd just rolled out of bed, and there was a smudge of dirt on his cheek that made him look irresistibly charming.

"Hey, you," he said, rubbing the back of his neck, a nervous habit I recognized all too well.

"Hey! You look like you've been through a battle. Everything okay?" I asked, trying to mask the worry that crept into my voice.

He chuckled softly, a sound that washed over me like a soothing balm. "Yeah, just a little gardening mishap. I thought I could tame the wildflowers in the backyard, but it turns out they had other plans." He leaned closer to the camera, a mock-serious expression on his face. "The flowers won, I'm afraid. They're quite vicious."

I laughed, a sound full of warmth and familiarity. "I never thought flowers could be so ruthless. You might want to consider a different career path if you're getting outsmarted by daisies."

Ethan rolled his eyes, a playful smirk dancing on his lips. "I assure you, I'm far better at dealing with metaphoric weeds than actual ones. But it's not all bad. I had a little revelation while wrestling with them." He paused, his gaze intensifying as if he were weighing his words carefully. "I realized that, like those wildflowers, our connection is resilient. No matter the distance, it's blossoming in ways I never expected."

My heart swelled at his words, warmth spreading through me like a cozy fire on a cold night. "You're right. I mean, I never thought I could pour so much of myself into letters. I feel like I'm discovering parts of me I didn't know existed."

"Exactly!" he exclaimed, his excitement palpable. "I feel the same way. It's like we're weaving this tapestry together, and every letter is a new thread."

Our conversation flowed effortlessly, laughter punctuating the moments of sincerity, weaving a tapestry of connection that made the world outside my window feel distant and unimportant. But as the call continued, a sense of urgency crept into my heart, gnawing at the edges of our lighthearted banter. I had to know what had happened during that crash the night before.

"Hey, Ethan," I said, my voice taking on a more serious tone. "You mentioned a mishap last night. What happened?"

He hesitated, a flicker of unease crossing his features. "Oh, that... It was nothing, really. Just my cat knocking over a stack of boxes. I should have put them away."

"Are you sure?" I pressed, unable to shake the feeling that there was more to the story. "You know you can tell me anything, right?"

He took a deep breath, the kind that filled the silence with weight. "It's just... there are things happening here, things I can't quite explain yet. I promise I'll tell you soon. Just... give me a little time."

The vulnerability in his voice sent a ripple of concern through me. "Ethan, if there's something wrong, I want to help. You don't have to face it alone."

"I know, and I appreciate that more than you realize," he replied, his gaze softening. "But right now, it's complicated. Just trust me, okay? I'll figure it out. I always do."

Something about the way he said that felt like a promise wrapped in uncertainty. I wanted to push, to pry open the door to whatever storm was brewing in his life, but I also understood the need for space. "Okay, I trust you," I finally said, though unease lodged itself in my throat.

Our call ended soon after, but the weight of Ethan's words lingered long after he signed off. As I prepared for bed that night, my mind raced with possibilities—what could be troubling him? Each scenario unfolded like a bad movie script, complete with dramatic tension and unanswered questions.

The next few days drifted by in a blur of anxiety and anticipation. I poured my heart into my letters, each one more expressive than the last, hoping to bridge the growing gap that Ethan's cryptic words had opened. Yet, as the days slipped into weeks, a shadow settled over my heart. The flowers he'd sent began to droop, their once vibrant petals losing color, much like my spirit. I needed to hear from him, needed to know he was okay.

Finally, after what felt like an eternity, Ethan called me again, his face filling the screen. But this time, his expression was different—clouded by a tension that sent alarm bells ringing in my chest. "Hey," he said, the usual brightness in his voice replaced by a somber note.

"Hey," I replied, concern threading through my words. "You don't look so good. What's going on?"

He hesitated, the weight of his silence heavy in the air. "I don't know how to say this..."

A lump formed in my throat as I braced myself. Whatever was coming, I sensed it would change everything.

The heaviness in Ethan's gaze settled like a lead weight in my chest, a stark contrast to the laughter and lightness we had shared just days before. My heart raced as I waited, the silence stretching thin, each passing moment laden with unspoken fears. I could see him grappling with his thoughts, and I wanted to reach through the screen, to pull him out of whatever shadow had crept into his life.

"I don't know how to say this..." he finally began, his voice steady but strained, as though each word was a delicate glass figurine at risk of shattering.

"Just say it," I urged, the impatience bubbling up within me, mingling with concern. "You know I can handle it."

He ran a hand through his tousled hair, a gesture I'd come to associate with his vulnerability. "There are... some issues at home. Family stuff. My dad—he's been acting really strange lately. It's like he's hiding something. I overheard a conversation between him and my uncle that didn't sit right with me."

My pulse quickened. "What kind of conversation? What are they hiding?"

Ethan took a deep breath, visibly wrestling with the words. "It was about money—something about debts and strange deals. I can't shake the feeling that it's something illegal, and I'm worried about how deep it goes. My dad is a good guy, but he's also stubborn and secretive. He doesn't like to talk about money, especially when it comes to the family business."

The tension in his voice sent a chill down my spine. "What if it's more than just a business problem? What if it puts you or your family in danger?"

"Exactly," he said, his frustration surfacing. "I wish I could just confront him about it, but you know how he is. I've tried before, and he shuts down completely. I can't help but think he's involved in something bad."

I leaned closer to my screen, my heart aching for him. "Have you thought about going to someone else, maybe a family friend or another relative? Someone who might know how to handle it?"

"I don't want to drag anyone else into this," Ethan replied, shaking his head. "It's already complicated enough. The last thing I need is to create more problems. I thought I could deal with it myself, but now I'm not so sure. Every time I see him, I feel this pressure building, and I don't know how to release it without blowing everything up."

The helplessness in his expression made my chest ache. "You can't carry this burden alone, Ethan. It's not fair to you. You deserve to talk about this, to have someone support you."

He looked down, the weight of my words seeming to settle in. "I know. I just... I don't want to add to your stress. You've got enough on your plate with your own life."

"But I want to be here for you! You mean a lot to me," I insisted, my voice a blend of urgency and tenderness. "We're in this together, right? Whatever happens, I'm here. You don't have to go through it alone."

He lifted his gaze, a flicker of gratitude sparking in his eyes, but the tension remained unyielding. "You make it sound so simple. But I feel like I'm standing on the edge of something dark. What if I pull you down with me? I don't want that for you."

As the words left his lips, I felt a surge of determination rise within me. "Then let me help you. I'm not afraid of the dark, Ethan. I've fought my own battles; I can fight with you. Just let me in."

He studied me, the conflict swirling in his eyes like a tempest. "You really mean that?"

"Absolutely," I said, a resolute smile breaking through my worry. "We can brainstorm ideas. Maybe together we can find a way to confront this without putting you in a position where you're compromising your safety."

A hesitant smile broke across his face, though it didn't quite reach his eyes. "Okay. I'll think about it. But I have to be careful. I can't risk exposing my family to unnecessary danger, even if it means holding back the truth."

A sudden thought struck me. "You mentioned your uncle. What does he think about your dad's situation? Is he in on this, too?"

Ethan shifted uncomfortably, running a hand through his hair once more. "That's the thing. I don't know. My uncle has always been a bit of a wild card. I can't help but feel he's not just a bystander in this. I overheard him saying something about needing to settle old debts, and I can't shake the feeling that it relates to something my dad might be involved in."

"Could it be something illegal?" I pressed, my heart racing at the implications.

He nodded slowly. "It's possible. That's what worries me the most. If it goes deeper than just money, if it's tied to something dangerous—"

Suddenly, a loud crash echoed from his end of the call, startling us both. "Ethan!" I exclaimed, my heart dropping into my stomach. "What was that?"

He jumped to his feet, his expression turning alarmed. "I don't know! I'll check it out."

As he moved off-screen, I could hear muffled voices in the background, one of them sounding eerily familiar, laced with anger and urgency. My heart raced as I strained to catch the conversation.

"—you should have handled this better! If you can't control this mess, then we'll have to take matters into our own hands," a voice growled, sharp and threatening.

I leaned closer to the screen, the reality of the situation crashing over me like a tidal wave. Something was seriously wrong. I called out to Ethan, panic creeping into my voice, "Ethan! Are you okay?"

There was no response. The conversation continued, rising in intensity, and my heart raced with dread. I felt like I was watching a scene from a suspense thriller where the protagonist was oblivious to the danger lurking just behind the corner. The seconds stretched, each heartbeat pounding louder in my ears.

"Ethan!" I yelled again, desperation spilling over as I felt the panic claw at my throat. I could sense the urgency thickening the air, the weight of something monumental about to unfold.

Then, silence.

The screen went black, leaving me staring at my own reflection, the sudden emptiness echoing the anxiety that twisted my stomach into knots. Something had gone terribly wrong, and I was left in the darkness, feeling as if I were holding my breath beneath the surface of a lake, waiting for a hand to pull me back to the light.

Chapter 29: Crossroads

Spring in San Francisco burst forth with an exuberance that mirrored the conflicting emotions swirling within me. The air was thick with the fragrance of blooming magnolias and the sound of distant laughter, a warm reminder of the city's relentless charm. However, the vibrant life outside my window felt miles away from the chaos in my heart. My team and I were hurtling toward the product launch that could propel my career into the stratosphere—a coveted promotion waiting at the finish line like a glistening prize. Yet, just as I reached out to grasp that ambition, a shadow loomed larger than ever: Ethan.

He had dropped the bombshell that he might extend his stay in New York indefinitely. His voice over the phone had been so filled with excitement about the new opportunities that awaited him, but I could only focus on the knot tightening in my stomach. With each passing day, the thought of a permanent separation between us clawed at my thoughts, refusing to let go. "What if this distance is too much for us?" I had asked him during one of our late-night calls, my voice a mere whisper, trembling under the weight of my fears.

"Distance is just a physical challenge," he had said, his tone warm and reassuring, almost playful as if he were trying to lighten the mood. "We can make this work, right? I mean, it's just a matter of time before you're in New York, anyway. Besides, you always said you love a good adventure."

Adventure? The word felt both enticing and daunting. Sure, I had always craved excitement, the thrill of stepping into the unknown, but this was different. This was my heart on the line. I could feel the walls of my small apartment closing in on me, the weight of my ambition and love colliding in an explosion of doubt.

That evening, I decided to take a walk along the Embarcadero, hoping the bay's cool breeze would clear my mind. The sun dipped below the horizon, painting the sky in hues of orange and pink, as the first stars began to twinkle into existence. I could hear the distant sounds of sea lions barking, their playful energy a stark contrast to the turmoil brewing within me. The beauty of the city felt surreal, almost mocking, while I wrestled with the dilemma of pursuing my career or my heart.

As I wandered, my thoughts drifted back to our last encounter. Ethan had visited just a few weeks prior, and I could still feel the warmth of his embrace. We had shared long conversations over takeout, the city skyline shimmering outside my window, each word weaving a tapestry of shared dreams and whispered secrets. But the more I reminisced, the more I felt the bitterness of uncertainty creeping back in. How could I allow myself to hope when everything felt so fragile?

With each step along the waterfront, I could hear snippets of laughter from couples, friends, and families. Their carefree joy felt like an alien concept to me. I envied their ease, their ability to enjoy the present without the gnawing worry that had taken residence in my chest. As I strolled past a group of children flying kites, the colorful fabric dancing against the twilight sky, I couldn't help but wonder if I was making a mistake by wanting something so different from what they had. Shouldn't love be simple? Shouldn't it feel as light as the breeze?

Just then, my phone buzzed in my pocket, jolting me from my thoughts. A message from Ethan flashed across the screen: "Thinking of you. Can't wait to see you again."

I stopped in my tracks, staring at the words, a mix of warmth and anguish flooding through me. What if I never saw him again? What if I made a choice that led me away from him, and all I was left with was the empty echo of missed chances? A few feet away, an elderly couple strolled hand in hand, their fingers intertwined as they shared whispers and soft laughter. A deep pang of longing settled in my heart, filling the cracks left by doubt.

"Get a grip," I murmured to myself, shaking my head. "You're stronger than this."

Yet, as I turned around to head back home, I couldn't escape the feeling that I was at a crossroads. I needed to make a choice, one that would set the course for my future, whether that meant staying rooted in San Francisco, chasing the career that had once filled me with ambition, or following my heart wherever it led.

Later that night, I returned to my apartment, the shadows stretching along the walls like memories I couldn't quite grasp. My laptop sat open on the table, a collection of documents scattered across the screen like thoughts waiting to be organized. I had deadlines to meet and presentations to finalize, yet I found it hard to focus. The cursor blinked at me, tauntingly, as if it too sensed the chaos in my mind.

With a sigh, I poured myself a glass of wine, hoping the rich flavor would coax out some clarity. Each sip was a reminder that life was about choices—some bold, some timid, and some that left us questioning everything. My phone buzzed again, interrupting my musings. This time, it was a video call request from Ethan.

I hesitated, staring at the screen as his name lit up. There was something undeniably comforting about seeing him, but I wasn't sure I was ready to tackle the questions that lingered unspoken between us. Still, my thumb hovered over the accept button. Perhaps I needed to hear his voice, to see the warmth in his eyes, to remind myself why I was fighting so hard to keep our connection alive.

Taking a deep breath, I accepted the call. His face appeared on the screen, the familiar smile spreading across his lips, making my heart flutter despite the storm brewing in my chest. In that moment, all the worries and tensions faded into the background, leaving just him, just us, as we navigated the uncertain waters ahead together.

Seeing Ethan's familiar smile bloom on the screen felt like a soft blanket on a chilly night, but even that warmth couldn't entirely stave off the chill of uncertainty swirling around me. His background—a cozy apartment drenched in the warm glow of a desk lamp—looked inviting, and for a moment, I was envious of the normalcy it represented. "Hey you," he greeted, his voice a low rumble that sent shivers down my spine. "Miss me yet?"

"Always," I replied, attempting to infuse my words with the casualness I used to feel. "But that's not what I'm worried about. You might be staying there forever, remember?"

"Ah, the dreaded 'forever,'" he said, feigning seriousness as he leaned closer to the camera. "You're being dramatic."

"I'm just trying to keep it real." I chuckled, even as a knot formed in my stomach. "Do you even know what 'real' looks like in New York?"

His eyes sparkled, filled with mischief. "It's mostly pizza and the occasional rat. But I hear they're friendly."

"Great. I'll send you a postcard of a rat holding a slice," I shot back, but the playful banter felt like a temporary bandage over a wound that was beginning to fester.

"Honestly, though," he said, his smile fading slightly. "I don't want to leave you behind. But if this opportunity is as good as I think it is, it could change everything for us."

His words hung in the air, heavy and electrifying. The prospect of him staying in New York was exciting but also terrifying. This was his dream, and yet my heart sank at the thought of being left behind like an old suitcase, discarded and forgotten. "What if everything changes?" I said softly, my voice barely above a whisper.

"Then we adapt," he replied, confidence threading through his tone. "We're good at that, aren't we? We'll figure it out together. I promise."

"Together," I echoed, but the word felt more like a question than a certainty. The idea of sharing a future together felt nebulous, clouded by the reality of our individual lives pulling us in different directions. "But what if it's not enough? What if I get that promotion, and you're still in New York?"

"Then I'll be the world's best cheerleader, or a really terrible one, depending on how the team does," he joked, but the humor fell flat. The specter of failure loomed over us, and the walls of my apartment suddenly felt too close, trapping me in a whirlwind of possibilities and fears.

We spent the next hour exchanging dreams and aspirations, but as the conversation dwindled, the underlying tension lingered like an unwelcome guest. I tried to focus on the words he said, but my mind kept drifting back to my own future—one that was becoming increasingly uncertain. The weight of my ambitions sat heavily on my shoulders, battling against the fear of what could happen if we lost this connection.

As I settled into bed that night, the faint sounds of the city outside—honking cars, distant laughter, and the low murmur of conversations—played a comforting lullaby. But my mind was restless, replaying every word Ethan had said, every promise he had made. Would he truly follow through? I couldn't help but wonder if we were both clinging to a dream, a fantasy of what we thought our relationship could be, instead of confronting the harsh reality that lay ahead.

Morning dawned in a golden haze, sunlight filtering through my curtains, yet the promise of a new day brought little comfort. I stood in the shower, letting the water cascade over me, desperately hoping it would wash away my doubts. Instead, the steam fogged the mirrors, mirroring my mental state—cloudy and unclear.

At the office, the buzz of excitement was palpable as my team prepared for the launch. We were all hands on deck, and the atmosphere thrummed with energy. I threw myself into the preparations, organizing tasks and finalizing presentations, trying to drown out the noise in my head. Yet, as I stood in front of the whiteboard, detailing our marketing strategy, my thoughts drifted back to Ethan.

The meeting was a whirlwind of ideas and brainstorming, but I felt detached, like I was watching from a distance as my colleagues tossed around suggestions. As we wrapped up, I noticed Mia, my boss, leaning against the doorframe, her brow furrowed in concern. "You've been a bit out of it lately," she remarked, crossing her arms. "Everything okay?"

I forced a smile, the kind that never quite reached my eyes. "Yeah, just a lot on my plate, you know?"

"Just make sure you don't drop any of those plates. You've worked too hard to let anything slip through your fingers now." She gave me a pointed look before leaving the room, her words ringing in my ears.

That night, I poured myself a glass of wine and sank into the couch, surrounded by the remnants of a whirlwind week. The television flickered in the background, but I barely registered the show playing as my mind drifted back to Ethan. I could picture him now, sitting in his cozy apartment, likely surrounded by takeout containers and empty coffee mugs, laughing at some random meme he'd come across. But would that still be enough for us?

The phone buzzed, jolting me from my thoughts. A text from Ethan lit up the screen: "Just landed. Can't wait to see you this weekend." My heart skipped a beat, a mix of excitement and trepidation flooding through me. It felt like a lifeline thrown into the tumultuous sea of my thoughts.

With a sigh, I responded: "Can't wait! Let's figure this out together."

His reply was immediate: "Together. Always."

But even as those words sparked warmth within me, doubt crept back in. What did "together" mean when the world felt like it was pulling us apart? The uncertainty loomed like a dark cloud, threatening to overshadow the light that came with seeing him. I knew the weekend would bring clarity or chaos, a turning point that would either solidify our bond or unravel everything we had built.

As I settled into bed, the weight of my thoughts enveloped me like a heavy blanket. I closed my eyes, hoping for a dream that would provide the answers I so desperately sought, but instead, my mind was a whirlwind of scenarios. Would we navigate this storm together, or would the distance drown us both? The clock ticked softly in the background, each second echoing the heartbeat of my uncertainty.

The weekend arrived, bringing with it a mixture of anticipation and dread. I found myself pacing the small confines of my apartment, the golden afternoon light spilling through the windows, casting playful shadows on the walls. I had spent the morning tidying up, organizing everything in a futile attempt to impose order on the chaos of my emotions. The air buzzed with the scent of fresh flowers I had picked up at the market—lilies and sunflowers—symbols of hope that felt oddly juxtaposed against the gnawing uncertainty in my chest.

As the clock ticked closer to Ethan's arrival, my heart raced. I couldn't help but replay our last conversation, the uncertainty between us thickening like the fog rolling in from the bay. I busied myself with setting out snacks, a mix of cheese and crackers, along with a bottle of my favorite wine, hoping that the ambiance would mask the palpable tension hanging in the air.

When the doorbell rang, I nearly jumped out of my skin. I opened the door to find Ethan standing there, his hands stuffed in his pockets, a hint of that infectious smile tugging at the corners of his lips. The sight of him, looking so effortlessly charming in his worn jeans and a soft t-shirt, sent a rush of warmth flooding through me.

Yet, as I stepped aside to let him in, a flicker of doubt gnawed at my insides.

"Hey, you," he said, pulling me into an embrace that felt both familiar and foreign, as if we were two people trying to reconnect in a world that felt off-kilter.

"Hey," I replied, pulling back slightly to catch a glimpse of his expression. He seemed to sense the heaviness between us, his brow furrowing just a bit.

"Nice place," he remarked, glancing around as if trying to take in every detail. "It feels... cozy."

"Cozy is one way to describe it," I said, a hint of sarcasm in my voice. "More like a small cage for my spiraling thoughts."

"Spiraling thoughts, huh?" he asked, feigning a serious look as he raised an eyebrow. "Care to share?"

I laughed lightly, though it didn't quite reach my eyes. "Well, it involves me questioning everything, so buckle up."

"I'm ready for the rollercoaster," he said, his tone light, but his gaze earnest.

We settled on the couch, wine poured, and snacks laid out before us, the air thick with unspoken words. I tried to steer the conversation toward lighter topics, recounting tales of the office chaos leading up to the launch, the team's wild ideas for marketing, and the colorful personalities I worked alongside. But each story felt like a temporary distraction, a flimsy veil over the truth we both knew was lurking beneath the surface.

Finally, after a particularly amusing anecdote about a colleague's ill-fated attempt to market gluten-free doughnuts, Ethan leaned in, his expression shifting. "So, what's really going on with you? I can sense the wheels turning in your head."

I hesitated, staring into the glass of wine as if it held the answers I sought. "It's just... everything feels so uncertain right now," I admitted, my voice quieter than I intended. "Your decision to stay in

New York for a while longer, and my career taking off... it's like we're at this fork in the road, and I have no idea which path to take."

"Let's not forget that forks can lead to pretty amazing destinations," he offered, his eyes sincere. "I don't want you to feel like you're losing something by chasing after your dreams."

"But what if chasing those dreams means losing you?" I shot back, my heart racing as I let the words tumble out. "What if we're just two ships passing in the night, destined to drift apart?"

"Look, I get it. It's scary," he said, his tone shifting to one of understanding. "But maybe we don't have to make all the decisions right now. We can figure this out together, step by step. There's no rush."

His reassurances should have calmed my racing heart, but instead, they only added fuel to the fire of my anxiety. "Together," I echoed, my mind spinning with possibilities and fears. "What if we decide to take that step, and it only leads to more heartache?"

"Or it could lead to something incredible," he countered, his confidence unwavering. "You know I'm all in. I don't want to go anywhere without you in my life, regardless of distance."

I wanted to believe him, to cling to that flicker of hope, but the truth of our situation loomed like an insurmountable wall. "Ethan, it's not just about wanting to be together. It's about the reality of our lives. You're in New York, I'm here. What happens if we can't make it work?"

A silence fell between us, thick and suffocating, as we both grappled with the weight of what had been left unsaid. He took a deep breath, his expression contemplative. "Then we find a way. I'm not going to pretend this isn't hard. But if it's worth fighting for, then we fight."

"Is it worth fighting for?" I whispered, the question slipping out before I could stop it.

Before he could respond, my phone buzzed insistently on the coffee table, breaking the fragile moment. I glanced down, the sight of my team's group chat flashing across the screen, and my stomach dropped. The message read: "We need to talk. Urgent. There's a problem with the launch."

"Sorry, just a second," I murmured, my heart racing as I typed back a quick response. "What's going on?"

Ethan watched me, concern etching his features as I stared at my phone, anxiety bubbling to the surface. I could feel the mood shift like a sudden gust of wind, tearing through the warmth of our earlier conversation.

"Everything okay?" he asked, leaning forward, his eyes narrowing.

"I don't know yet," I admitted, trying to remain calm. "They said there's a problem. It could be about the launch or... something worse."

Before I could process it, another message pinged through, this one sending a chill down my spine: "They found a major security flaw. We need everyone at the office ASAP."

"What? A security flaw? What does that even mean?" I exclaimed, a whirlwind of panic threatening to engulf me.

"I'll go with you," Ethan said, already reaching for his jacket.

"No! I mean, yes, but—" I faltered, my thoughts tangled in a web of urgency. "What if it's bad? What if they want to cancel the launch? This could be everything I've worked for!"

"Then we deal with it," he said firmly, his expression resolute. "Together, remember? Now, let's go."

With that, we rushed out the door, the gravity of the situation pulling me under. The streets of San Francisco blurred by in a rush of lights and colors, the promise of a bright future suddenly clouded by looming uncertainty. As we neared the office, I could feel the weight of impending decisions pressing down on me, a storm brewing just out of sight. Little did I know, the real turbulence was just beginning, waiting to unravel everything I thought I knew.

9 798227 075802